MOLLY KNOX OSTERTAG

THE HIDDEN WITCH

graphix

AN IMPRINT OF

SCHOLASTIC

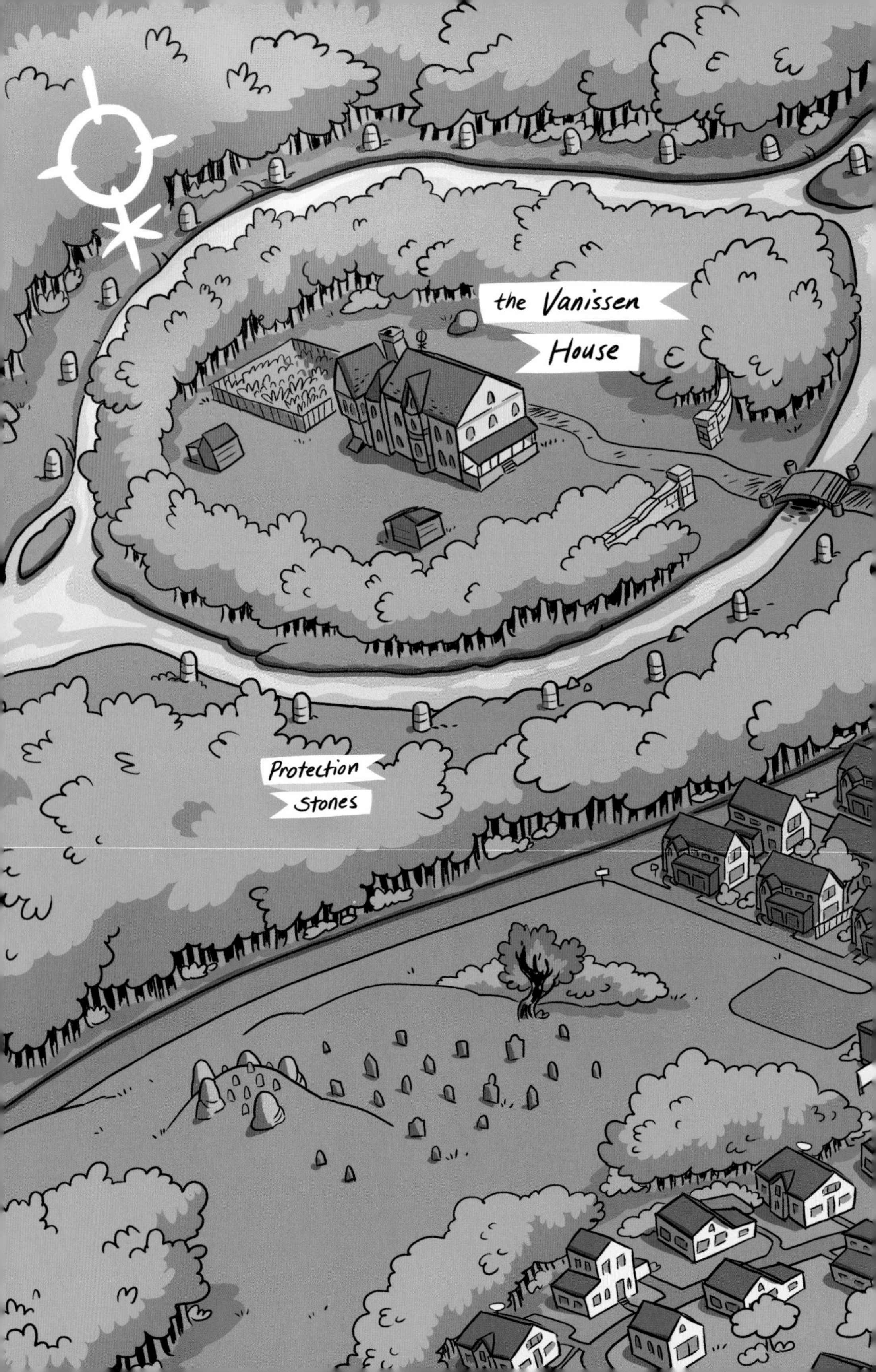
the Vanissen House
Protection Stones

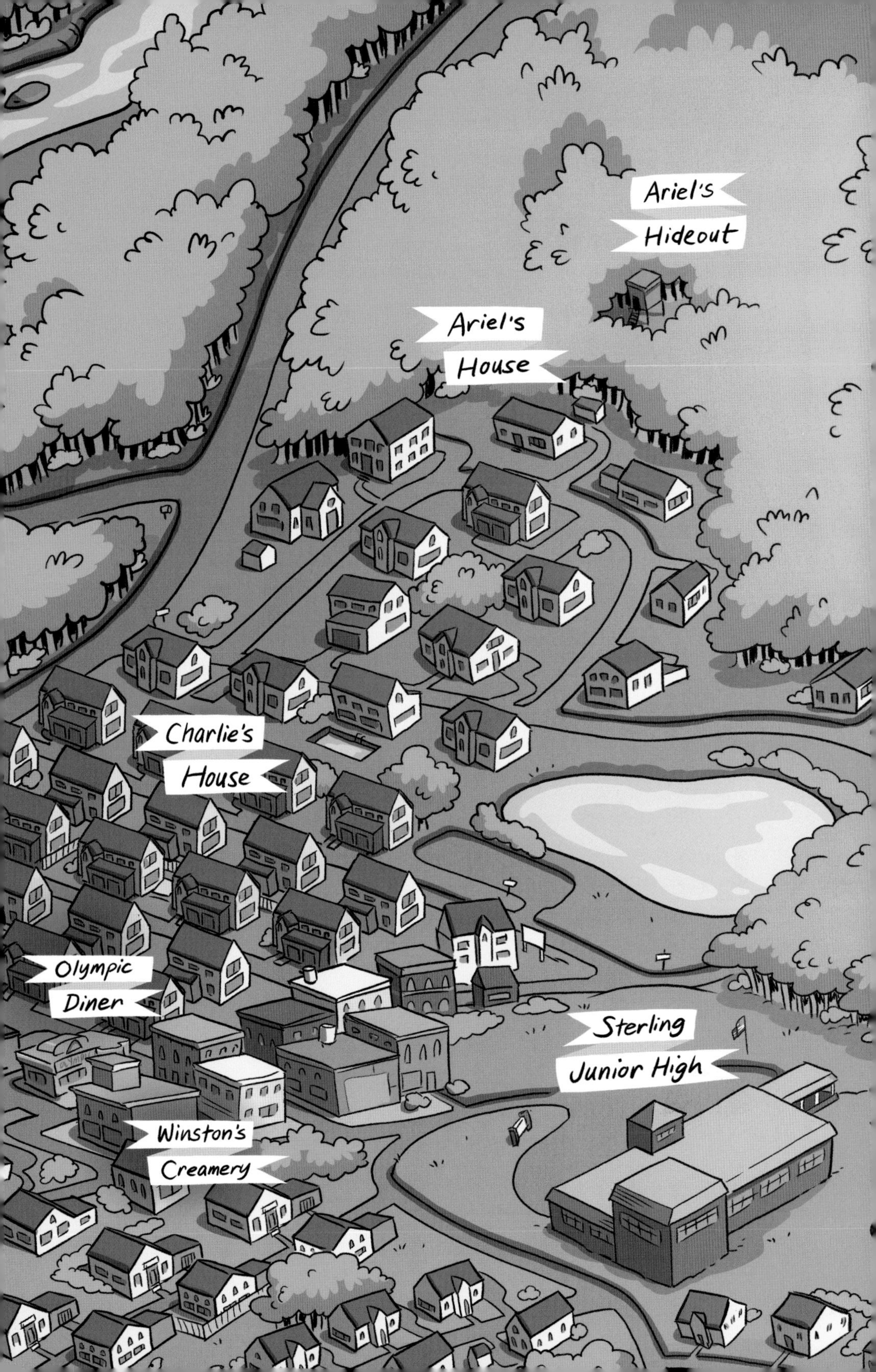
Ariel's
Hideout
Ariel's
House
Charlie's
House
Olympic
Diner
Sterling
Junior High
Winston's
Creamery

This book is dedicated to Noelle,
who is my very favorite witch.

Library of Congress Control Number Available

ISBN 978-1-338-25376-4 (hardcover)
ISBN 978-1-338-25375-7 (paperback)

10 9 8 7 6 5 4 3 2 1   18 19 20 21 22

Printed in China   38
First edition, November 2018
Edited by Amanda Maciel
Lettering and Color by Molly Knox Ostertag
Additional color by Niki Smith
Author photo © Leslie Ranne
Book design by Molly Knox Ostertag and Phil Falco
Creative Director: David Saylor

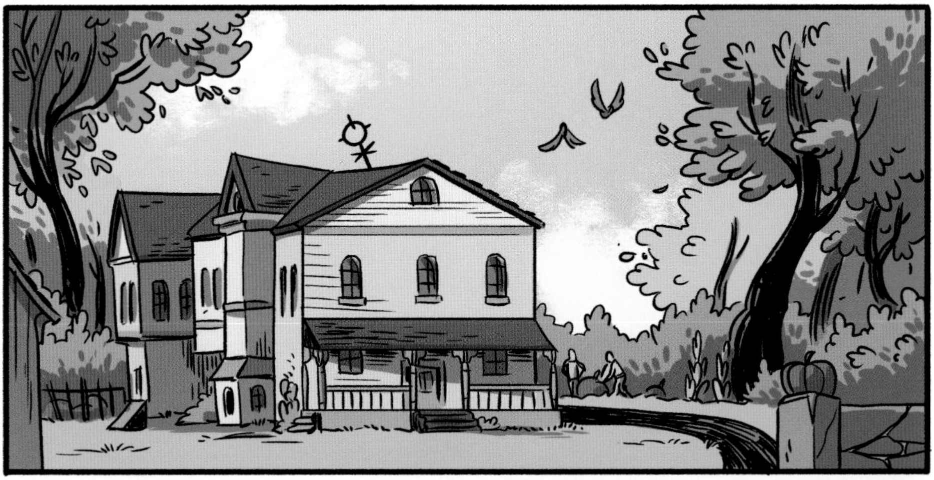

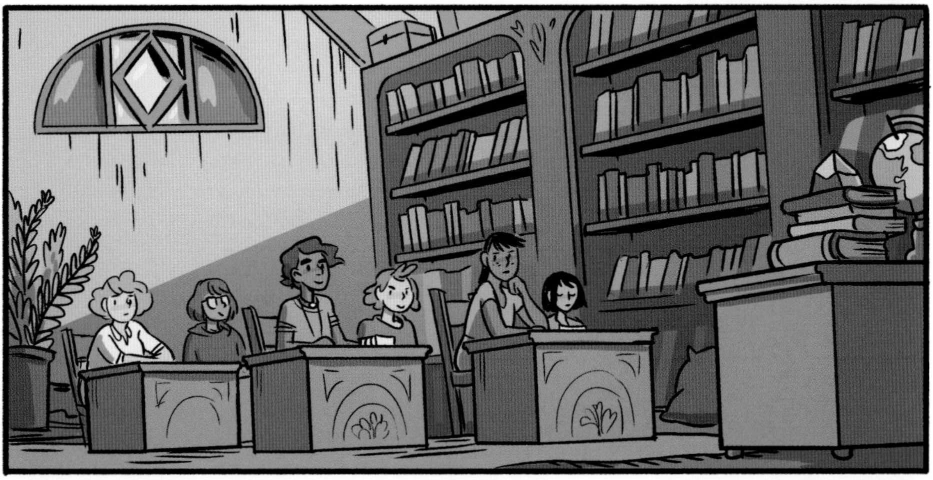

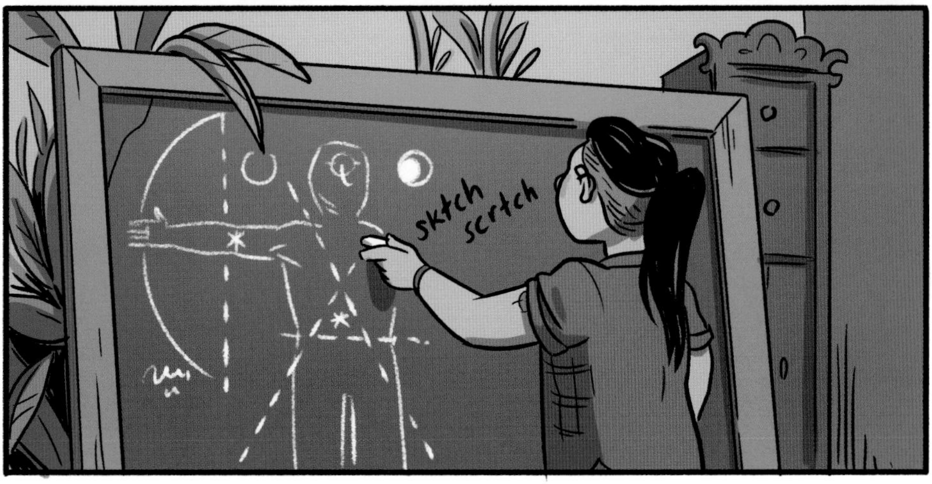
sktch scrtch

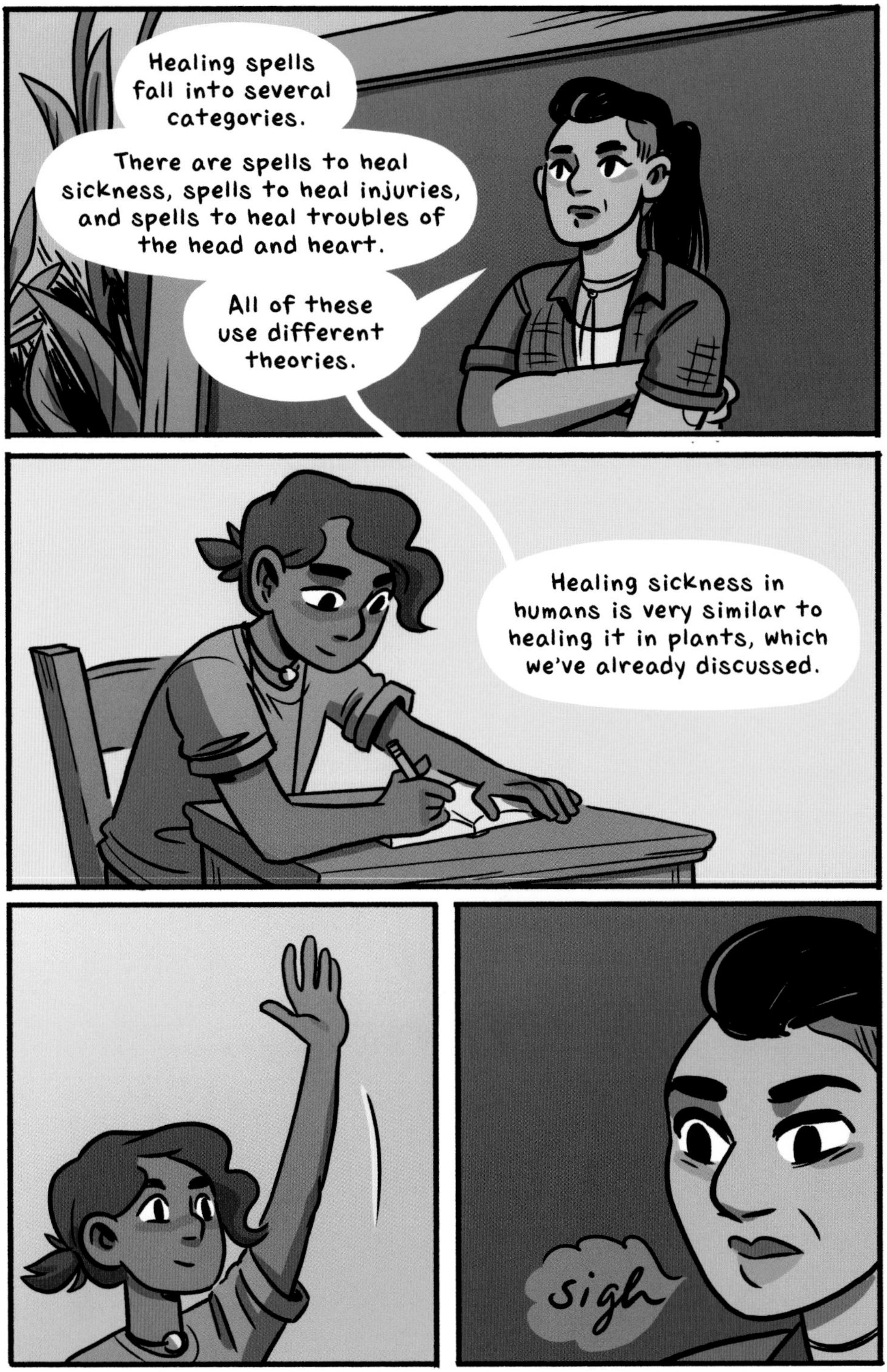
Healing spells fall into several categories.
There are spells to heal sickness, spells to heal injuries, and spells to heal troubles of the head and heart.
All of these use different theories.
Healing sickness in humans is very similar to healing it in plants, which we've already discussed.
sigh

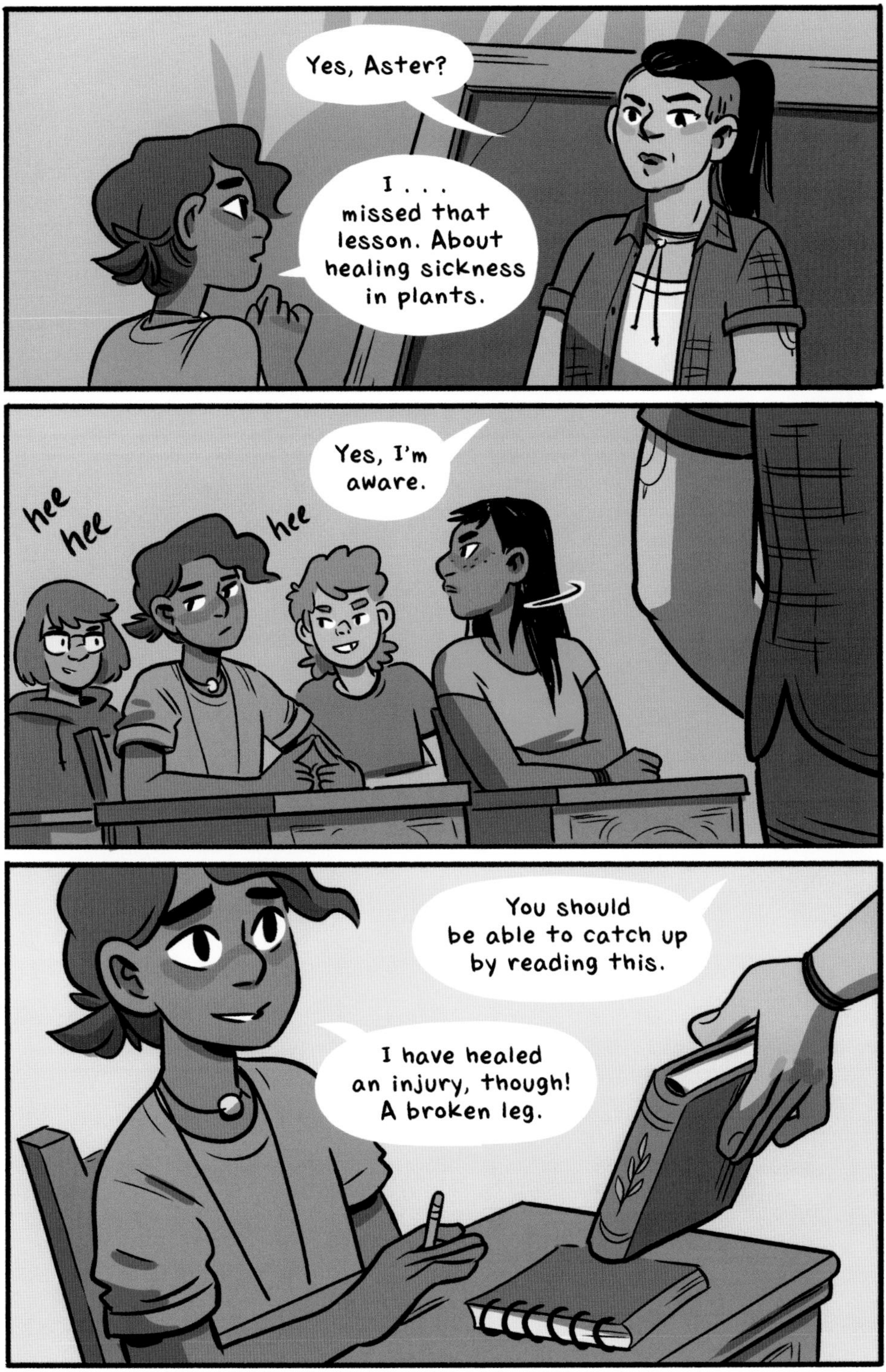
Yes, Aster?
I . . . missed that lesson. About healing sickness in plants.
Yes, I'm aware.
hee hee
hee
You should be able to catch up by reading this.
I have healed an injury, though! A broken leg.

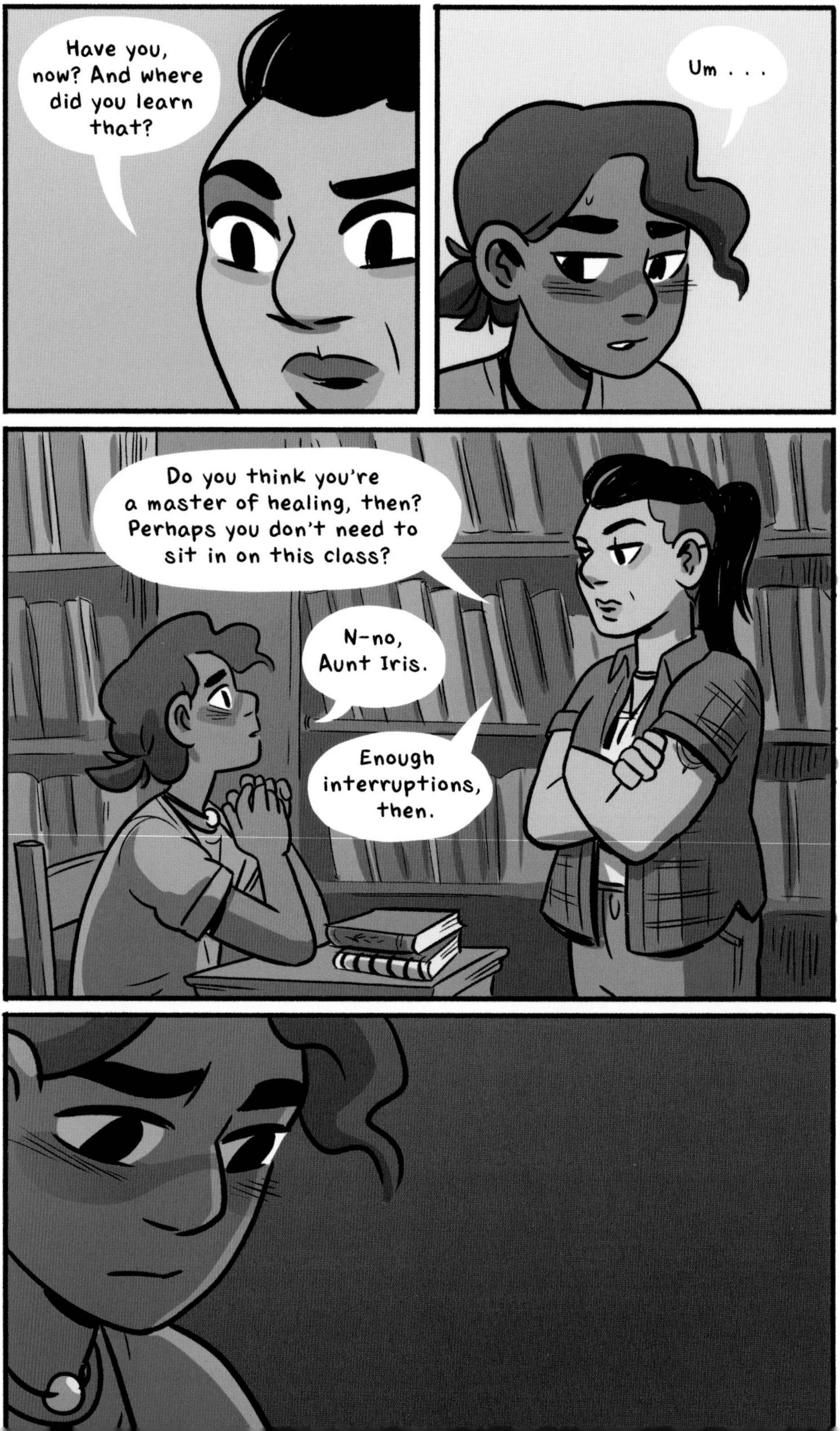
Have you, now? And where did you learn that?
Um . . .
Do you think you're a master of healing, then? Perhaps you don't need to sit in on this class?
N-no, Aunt Iris.
Enough interruptions, then.

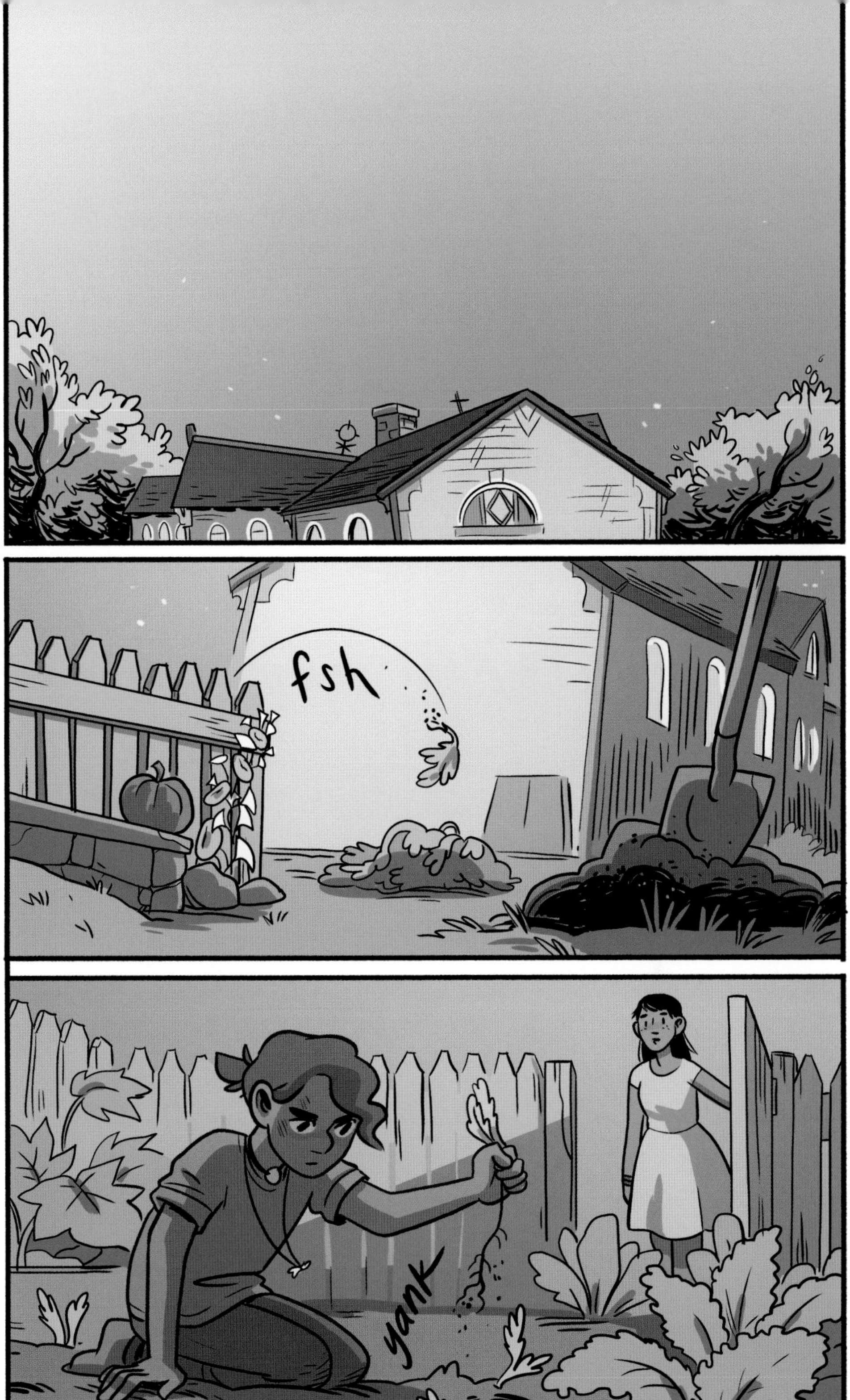
fsh
yank

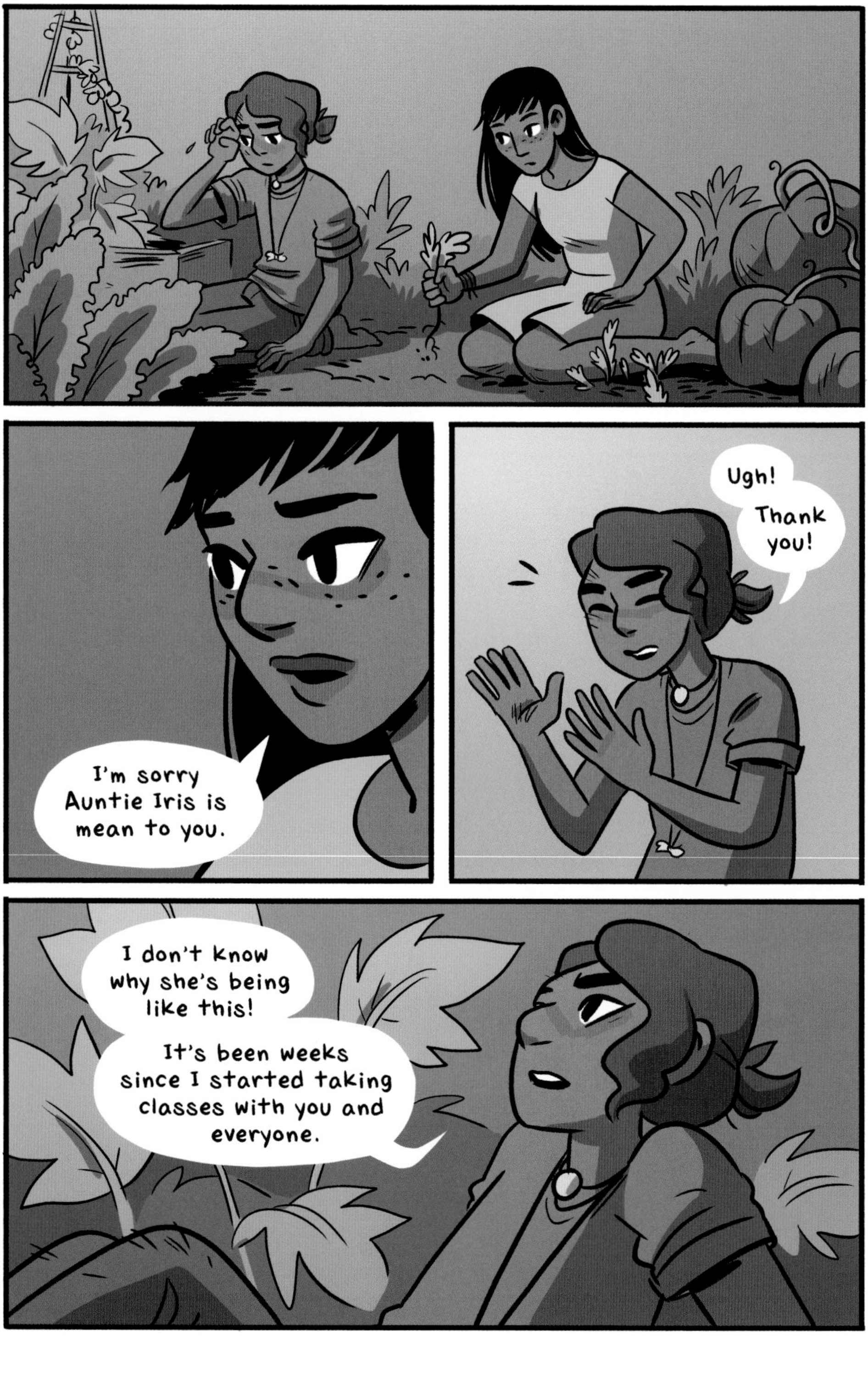
I'm sorry Auntie Iris is mean to you.
Ugh!
Thank you!
I don't know why she's being like this!
It's been weeks since I started taking classes with you and everyone.

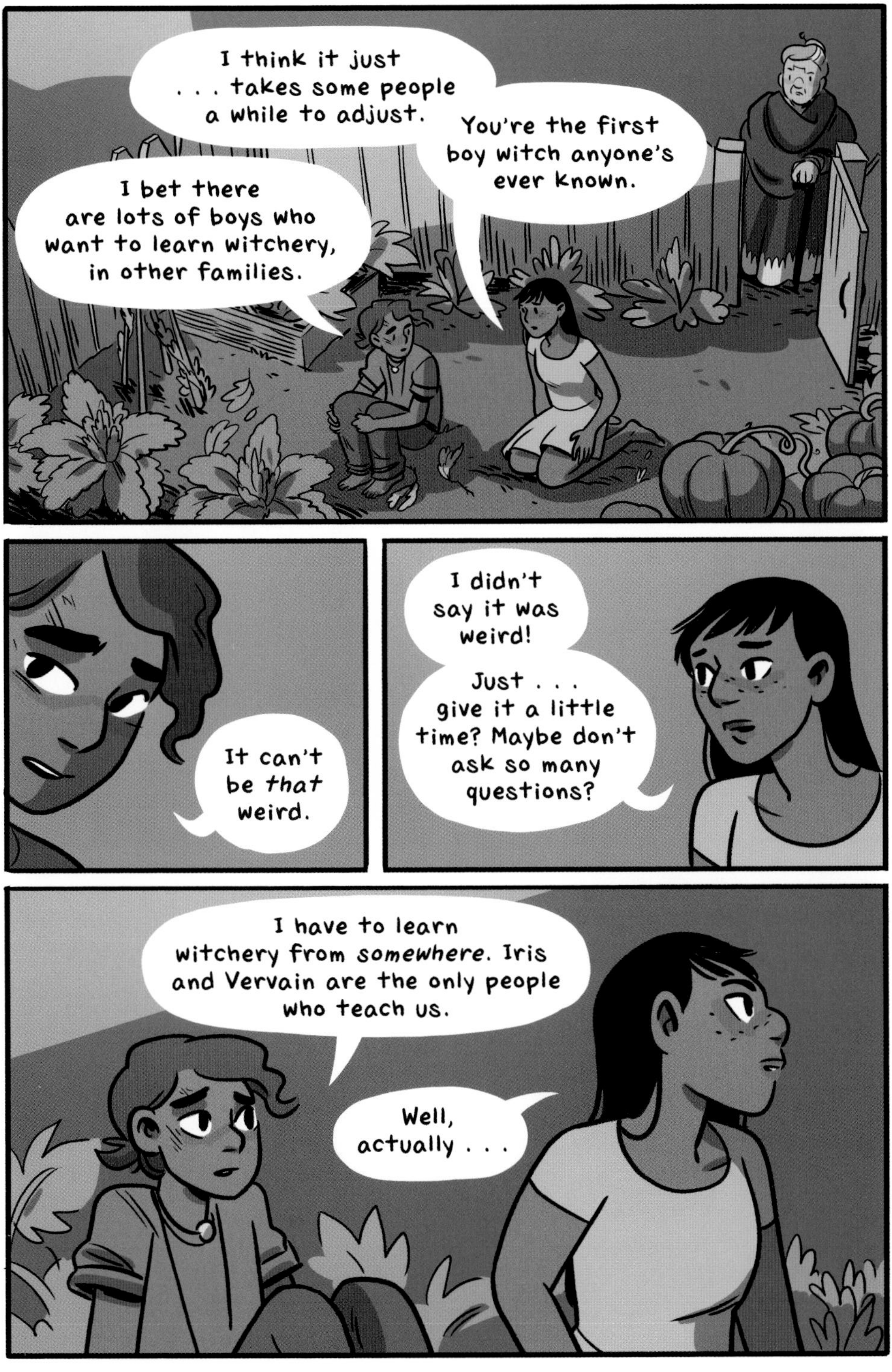
I think it just . . . takes some people a while to adjust.
You're the first boy witch anyone's ever known.
I bet there are lots of boys who want to learn witchery, in other families.
It can't be *that* weird.
I didn't say it was weird!
Just . . . give it a little time? Maybe don't ask so many questions?
I have to learn witchery from *somewhere*. Iris and Vervain are the only people who teach us.
Well, actually . . .

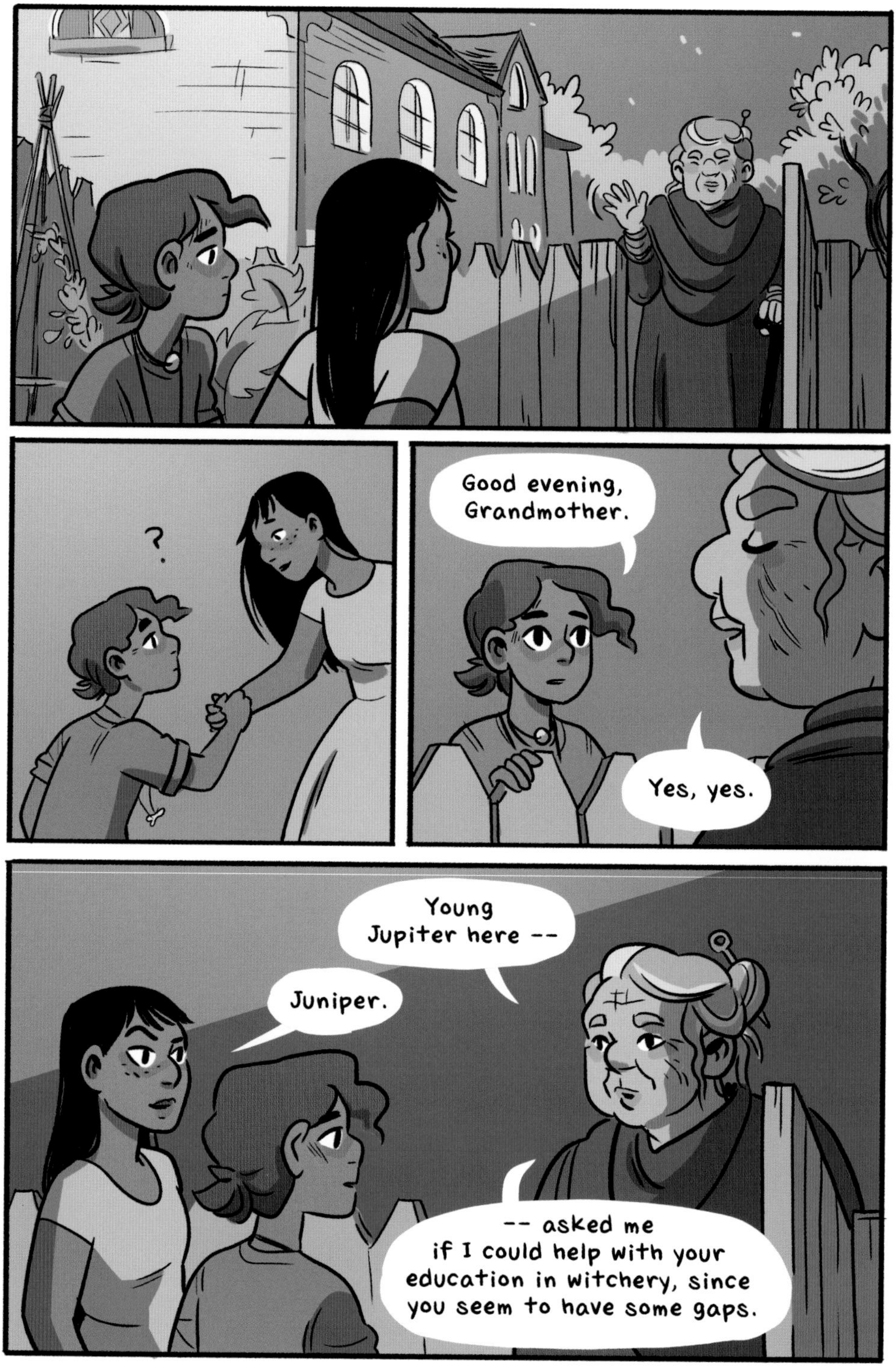
?
Good evening, Grandmother.
Yes, yes.
Young Jupiter here --
Juniper.
-- asked me if I could help with your education in witchery, since you seem to have some gaps.

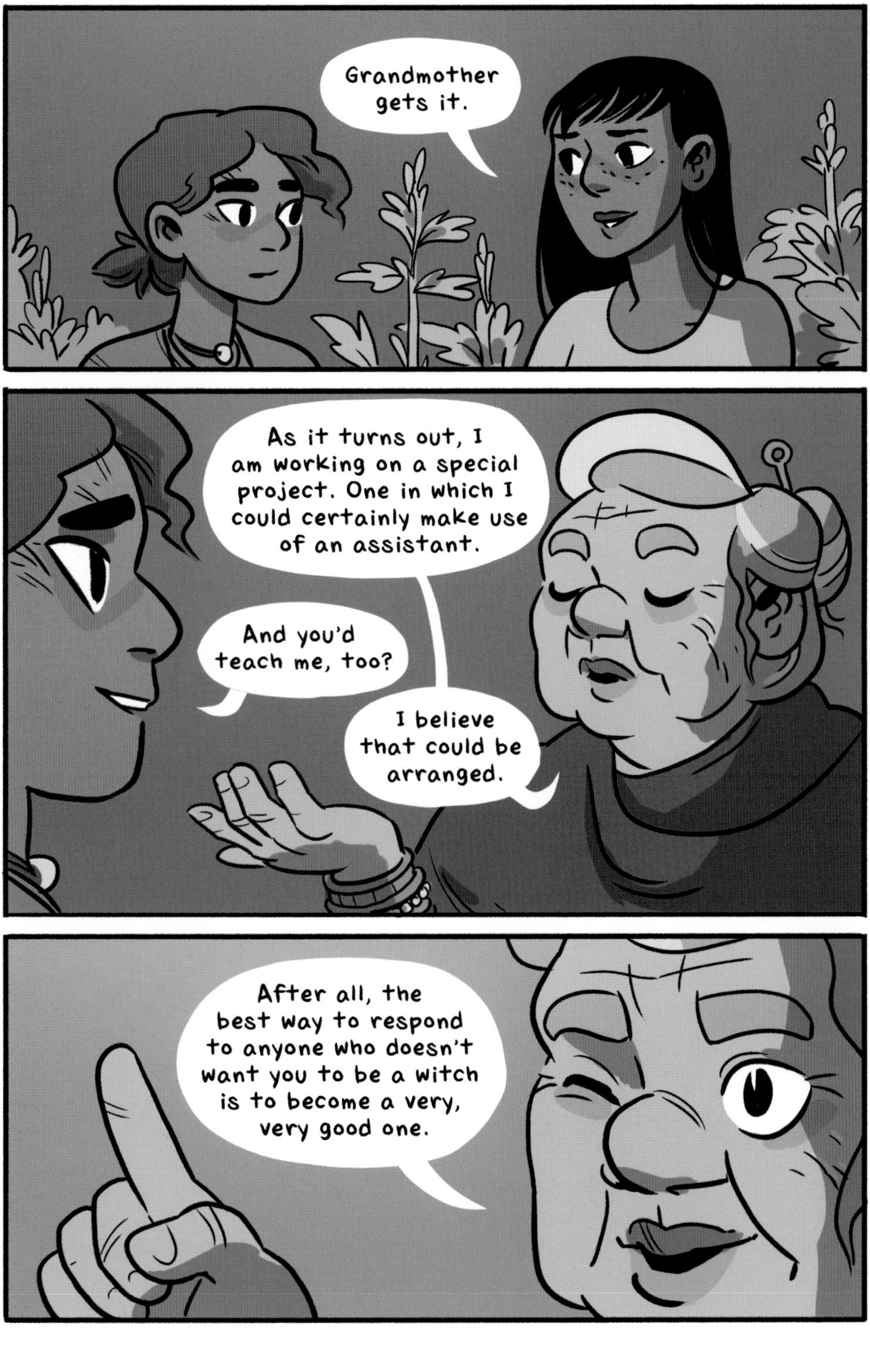
Grandmother gets it.
As it turns out, I am working on a special project. One in which I could certainly make use of an assistant.
And you'd teach me, too?
I believe that could be arranged.
After all, the best way to respond to anyone who doesn't want you to be a witch is to become a very, very good one.

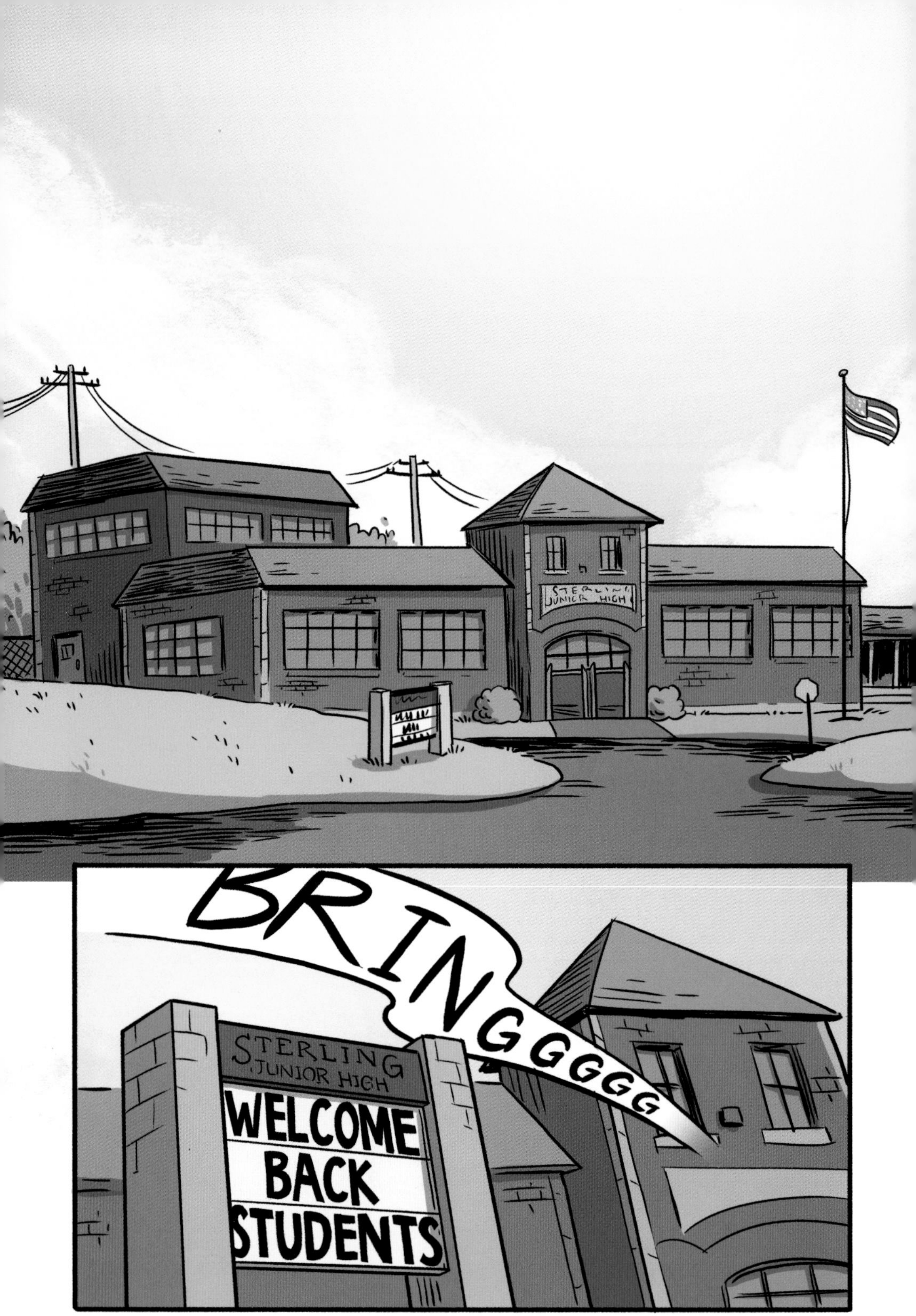
STERLING JUNIOR HIGH
BRINGGGGGG
STERLING JUNIOR HIGH
WELCOME BACK STUDENTS

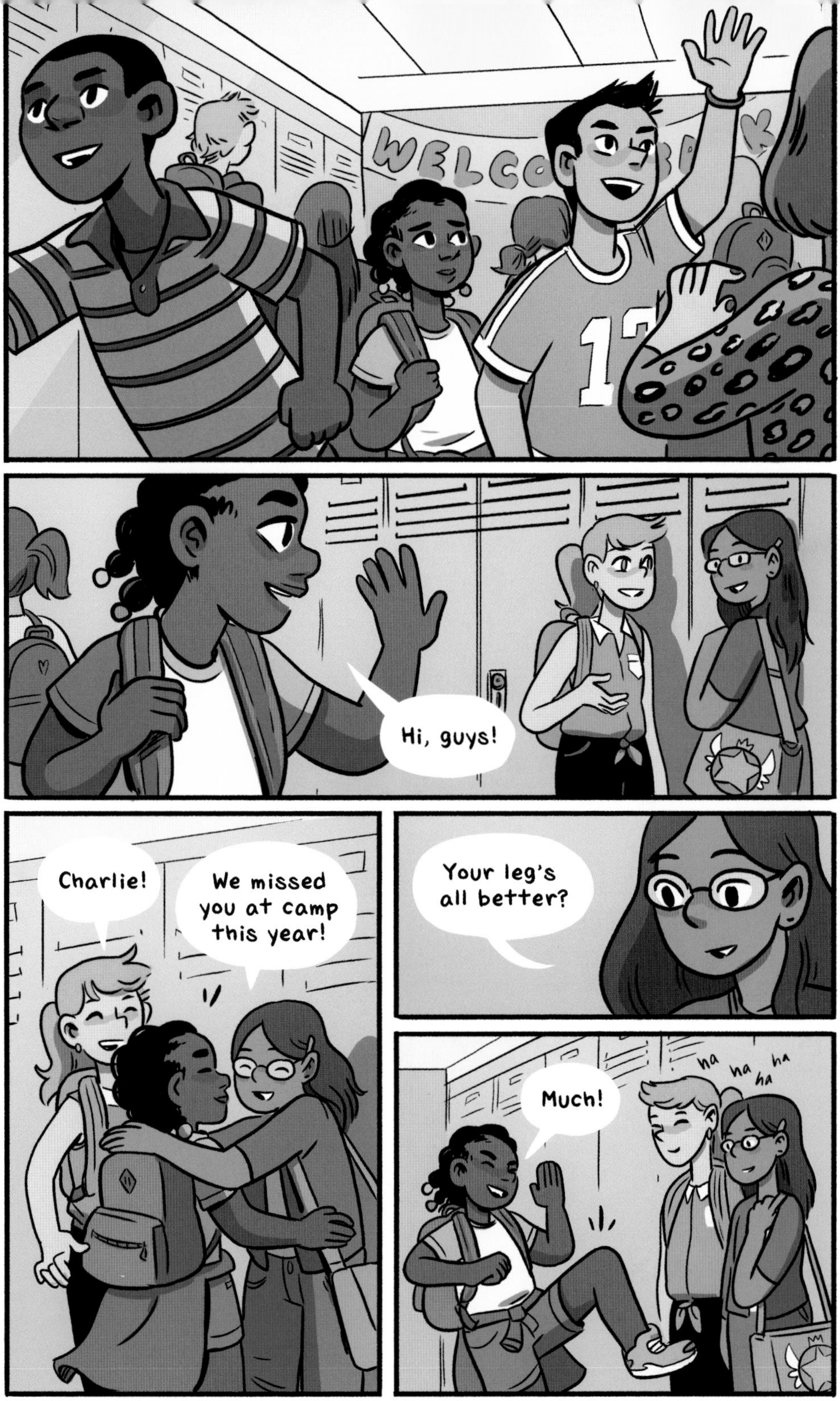
WELCO B K
Hi, guys!
Charlie!
We missed you at camp this year!
Your leg's all better?
Much!
ha ha ha ha

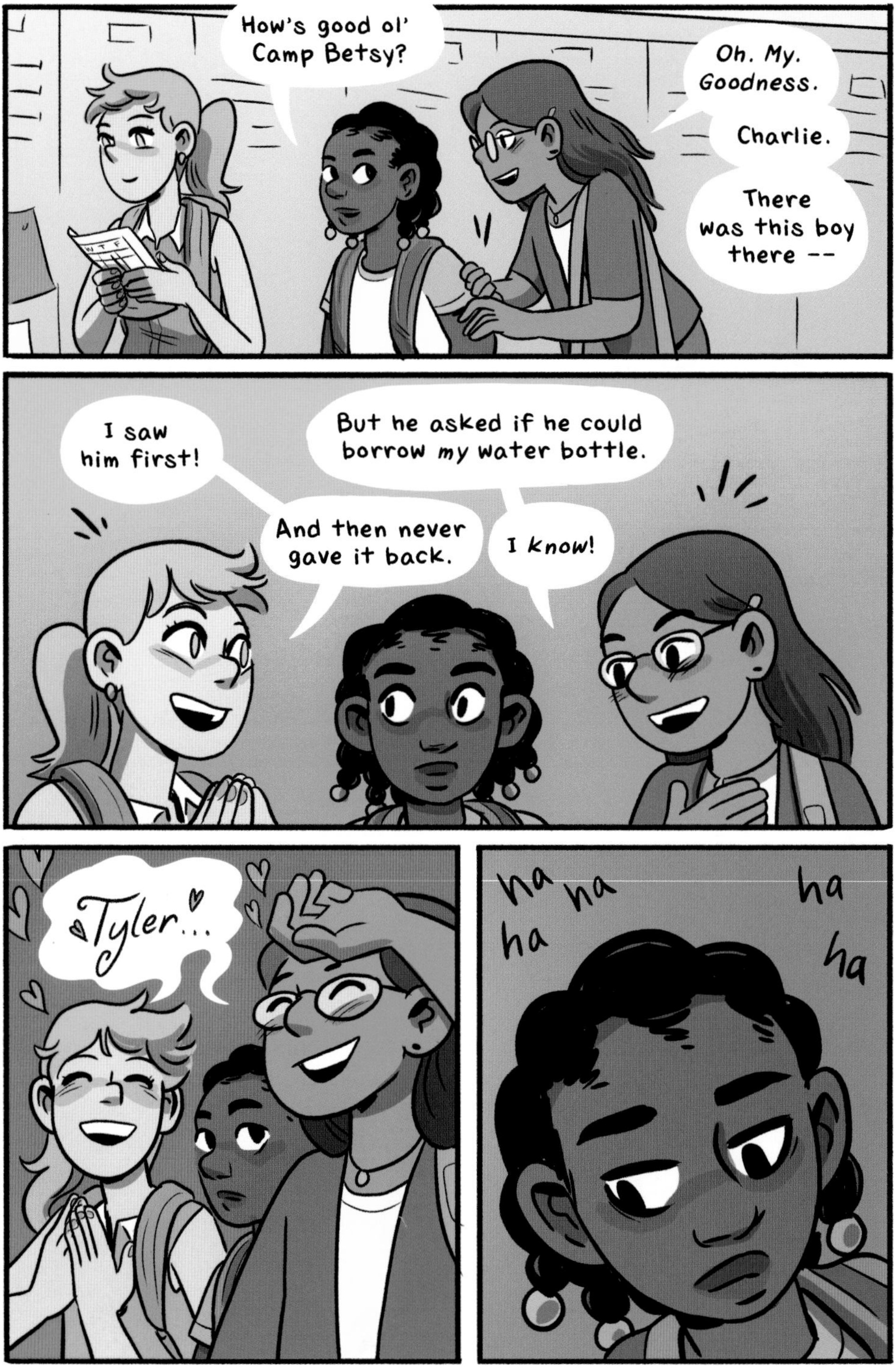
How's good ol' Camp Betsy?
Oh. My. Goodness.
Charlie.
There was this boy there --
I saw him first!
But he asked if he could borrow *my* water bottle.
And then never gave it back.
I know!
Tyler...
ha ha ha ha ha

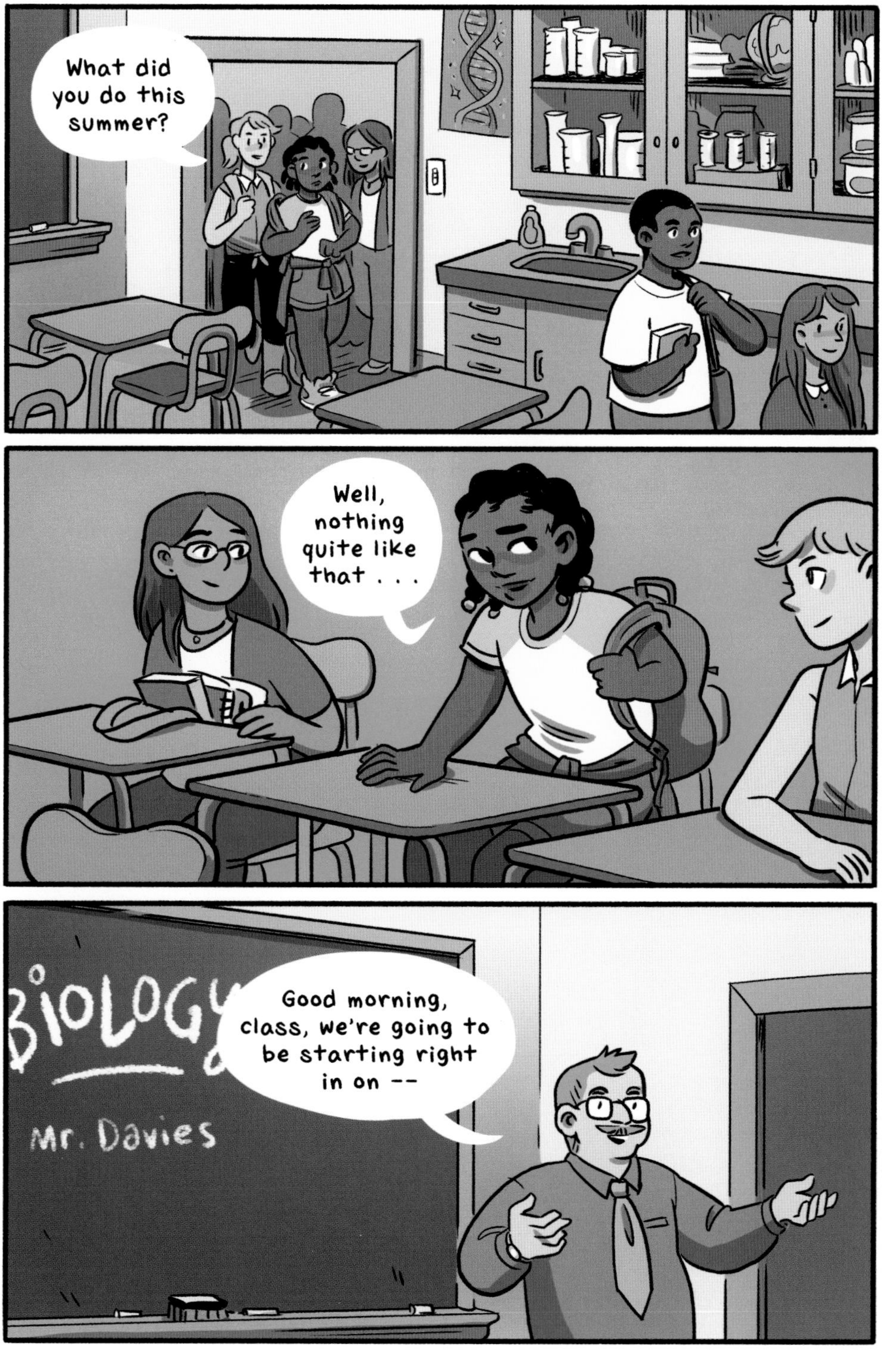
What did you do this summer?
Well, nothing quite like that . . .
BIOLOGY
Mr. Davies
Good morning, class, we're going to be starting right in on --

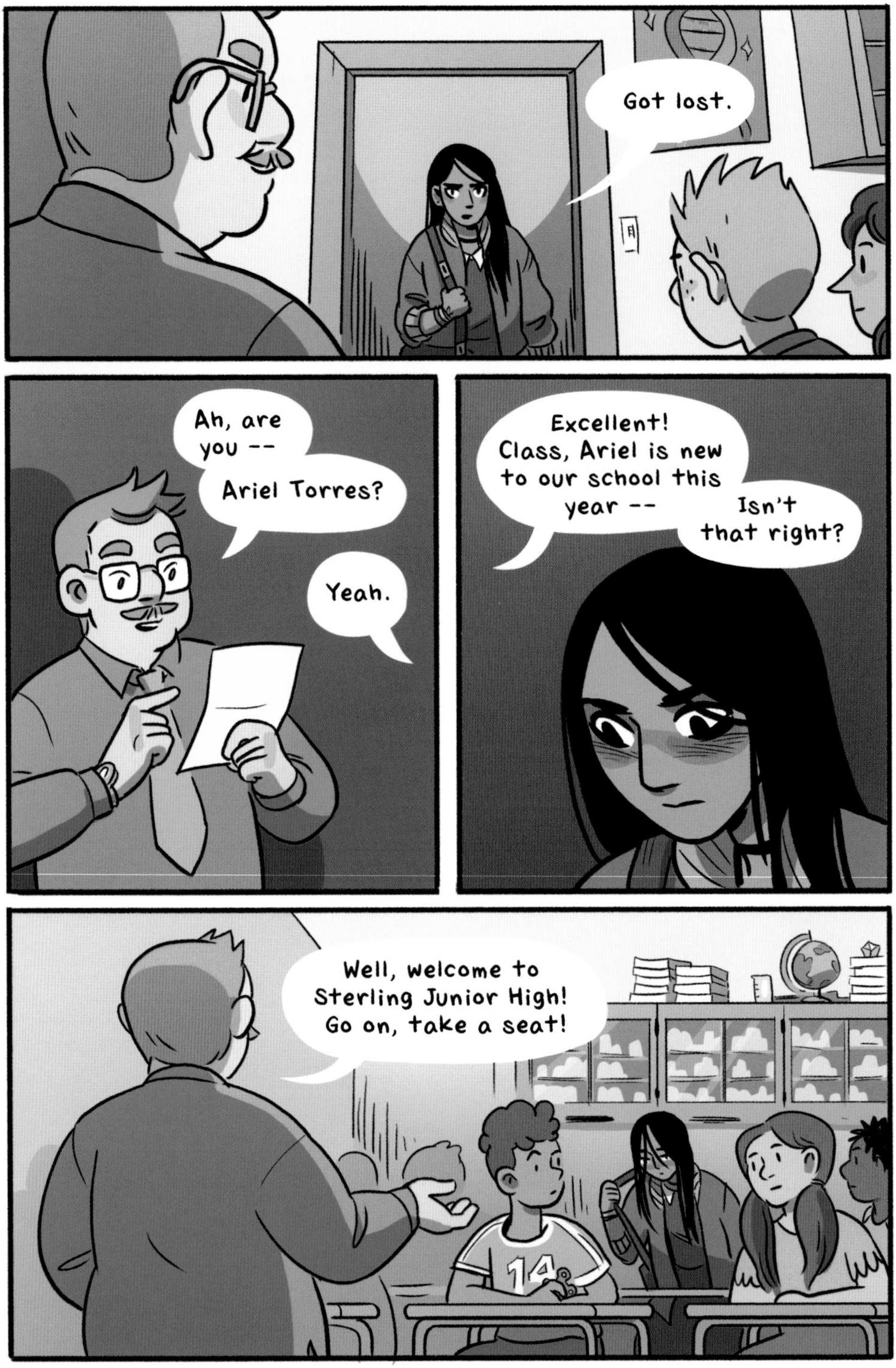
Got lost.
Ah, are you --
Ariel Torres?
Yeah.
Excellent! Class, Ariel is new to our school this year --
Isn't that right?
Well, welcome to Sterling Junior High! Go on, take a seat!

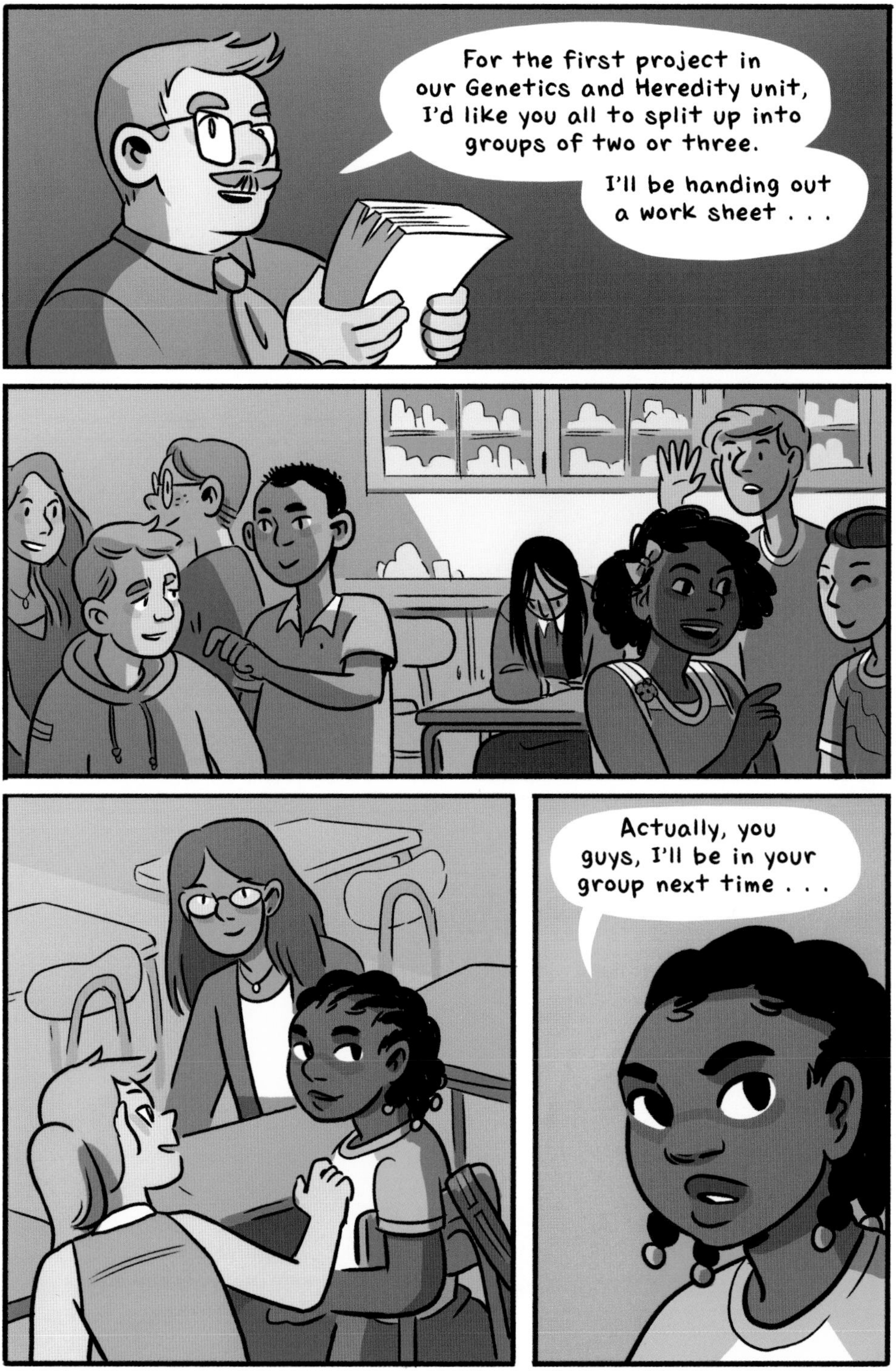
For the first project in our Genetics and Heredity unit, I'd like you all to split up into groups of two or three.
I'll be handing out a work sheet . . .
Actually, you guys, I'll be in your group next time . . .

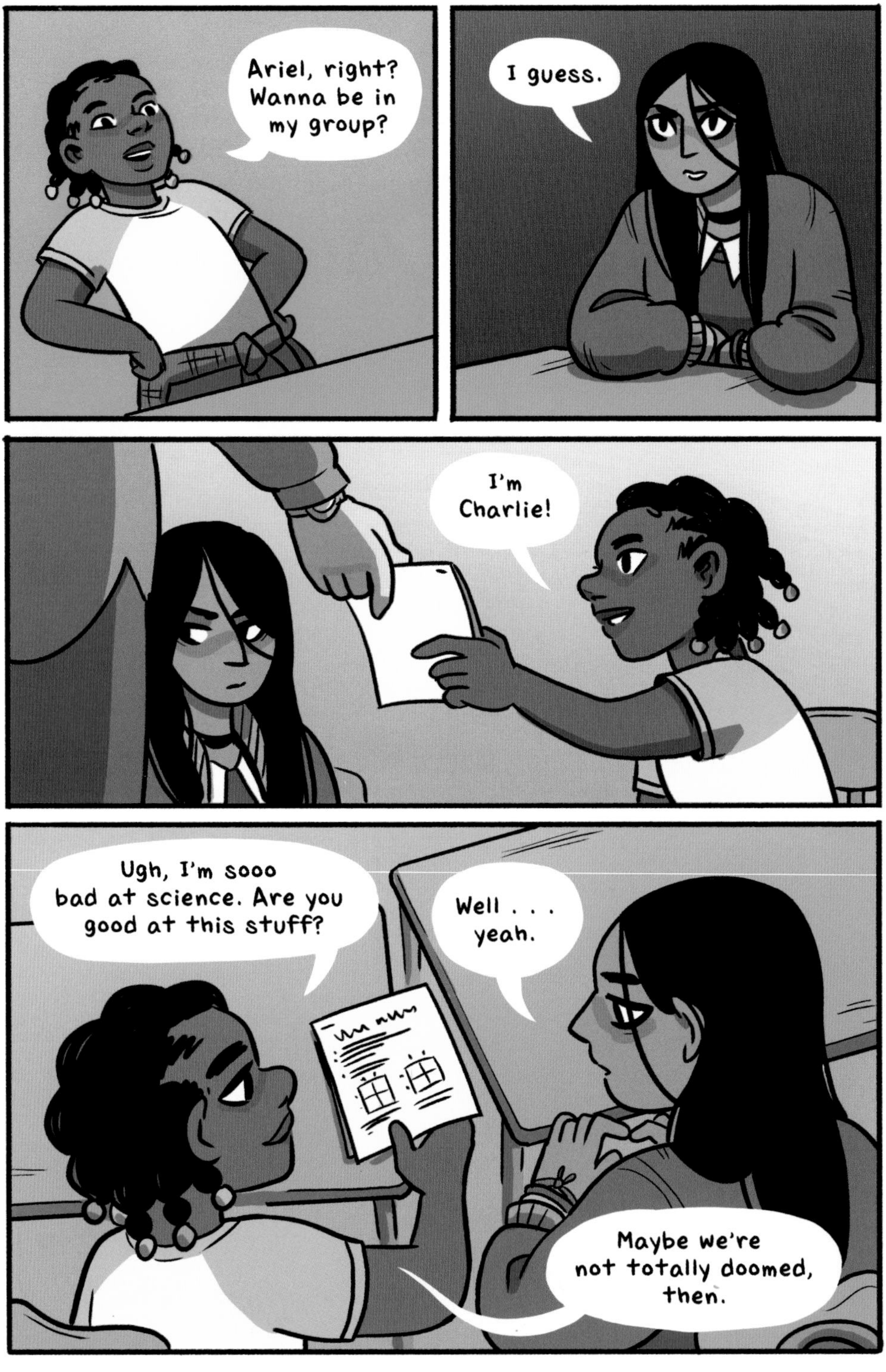
Ariel, right? Wanna be in my group?
I guess.
I'm Charlie!
Ugh, I'm sooo bad at science. Are you good at this stuff?
Well . . . yeah.
Maybe we're not totally doomed, then.

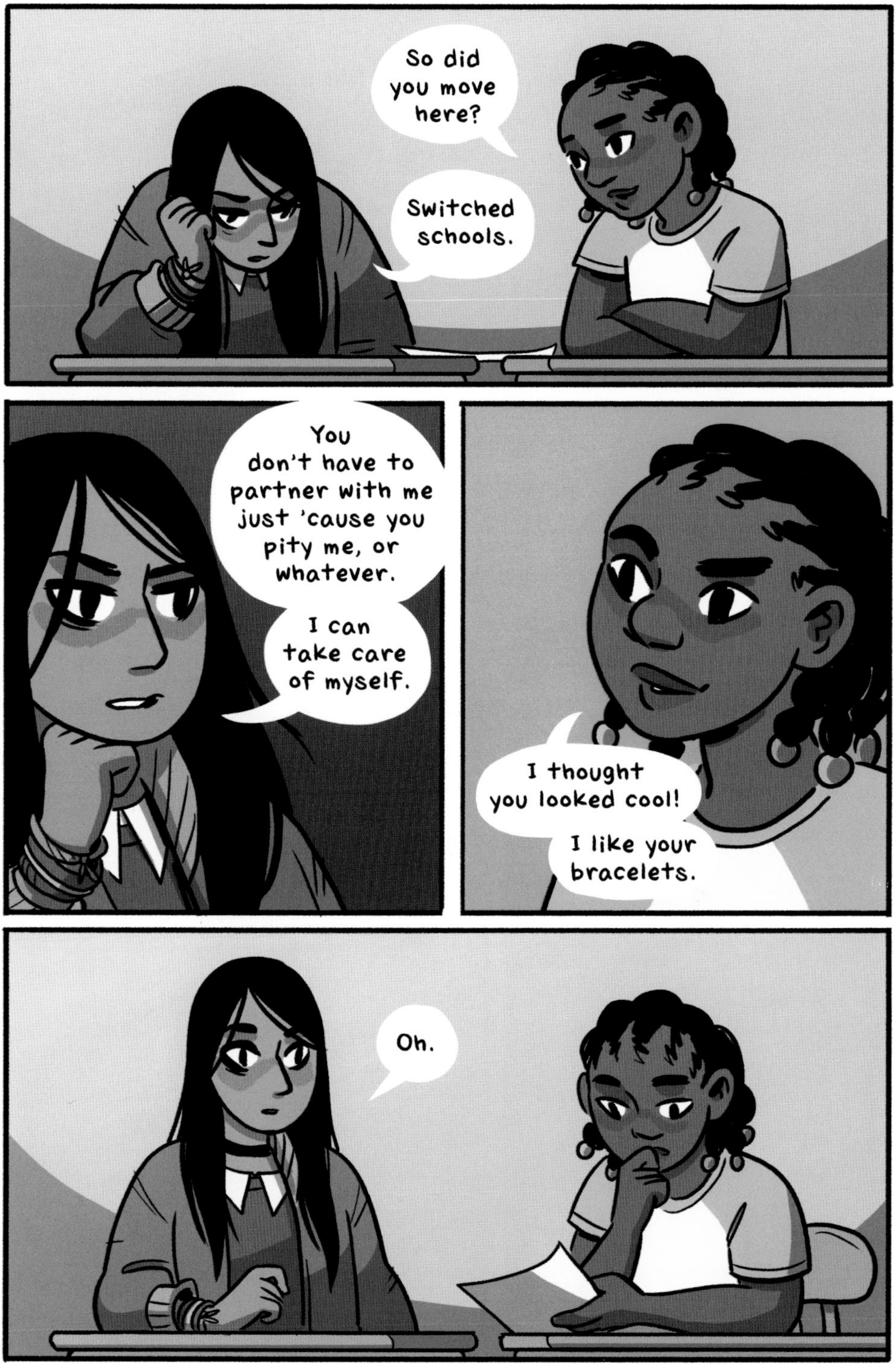
So did you move here?
Switched schools.
You don't have to partner with me just 'cause you pity me, or whatever.
I can take care of myself.
I thought you looked cool!
I like your bracelets.
Oh.

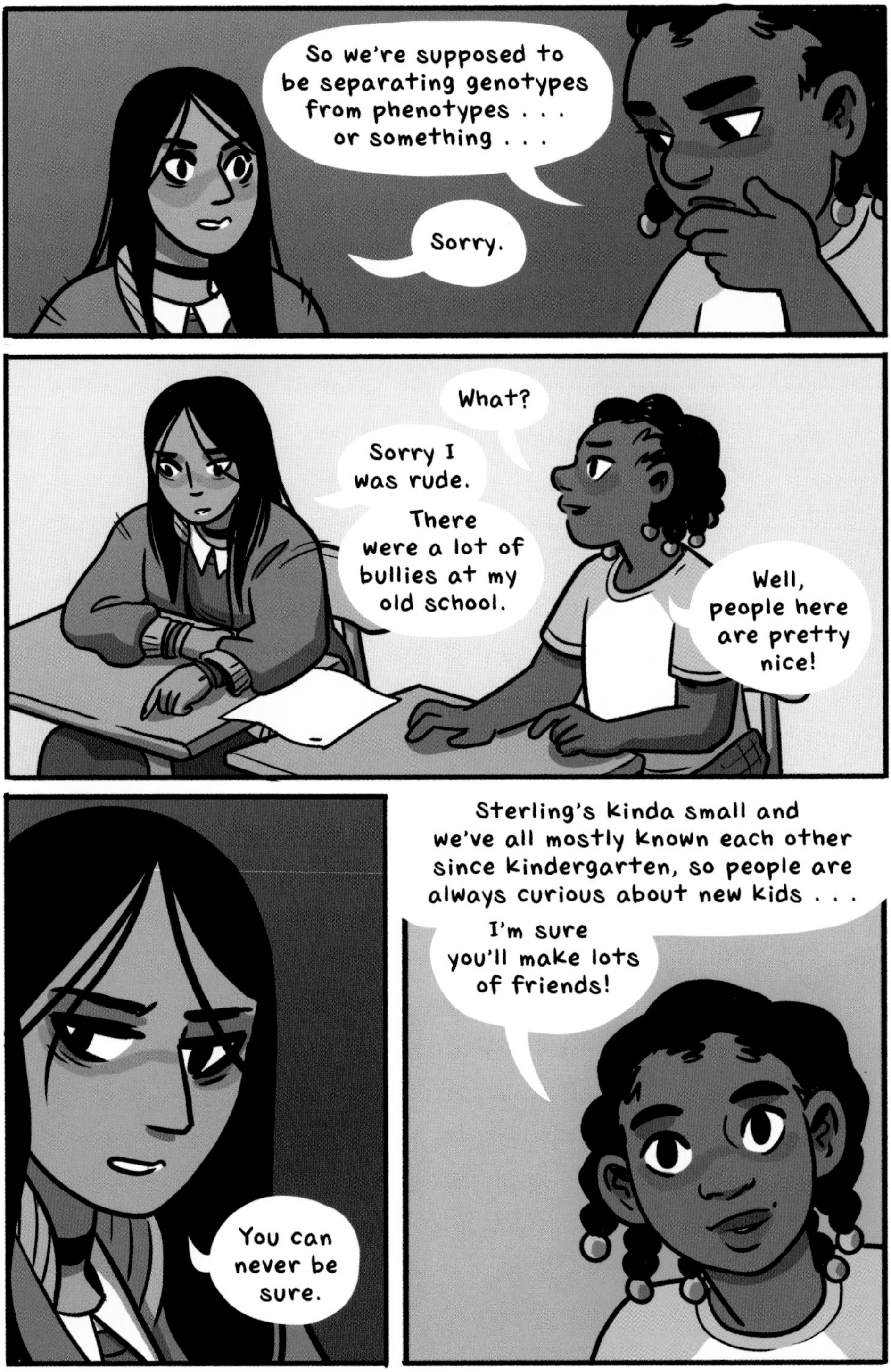
So we're supposed to be separating genotypes from phenotypes . . . or something . . .
Sorry.
What?
Sorry I was rude.
There were a lot of bullies at my old school.
Well, people here are pretty nice!
Sterling's kinda small and we've all mostly known each other since kindergarten, so people are always curious about new kids . . .
I'm sure you'll make lots of friends!
You can never be sure.

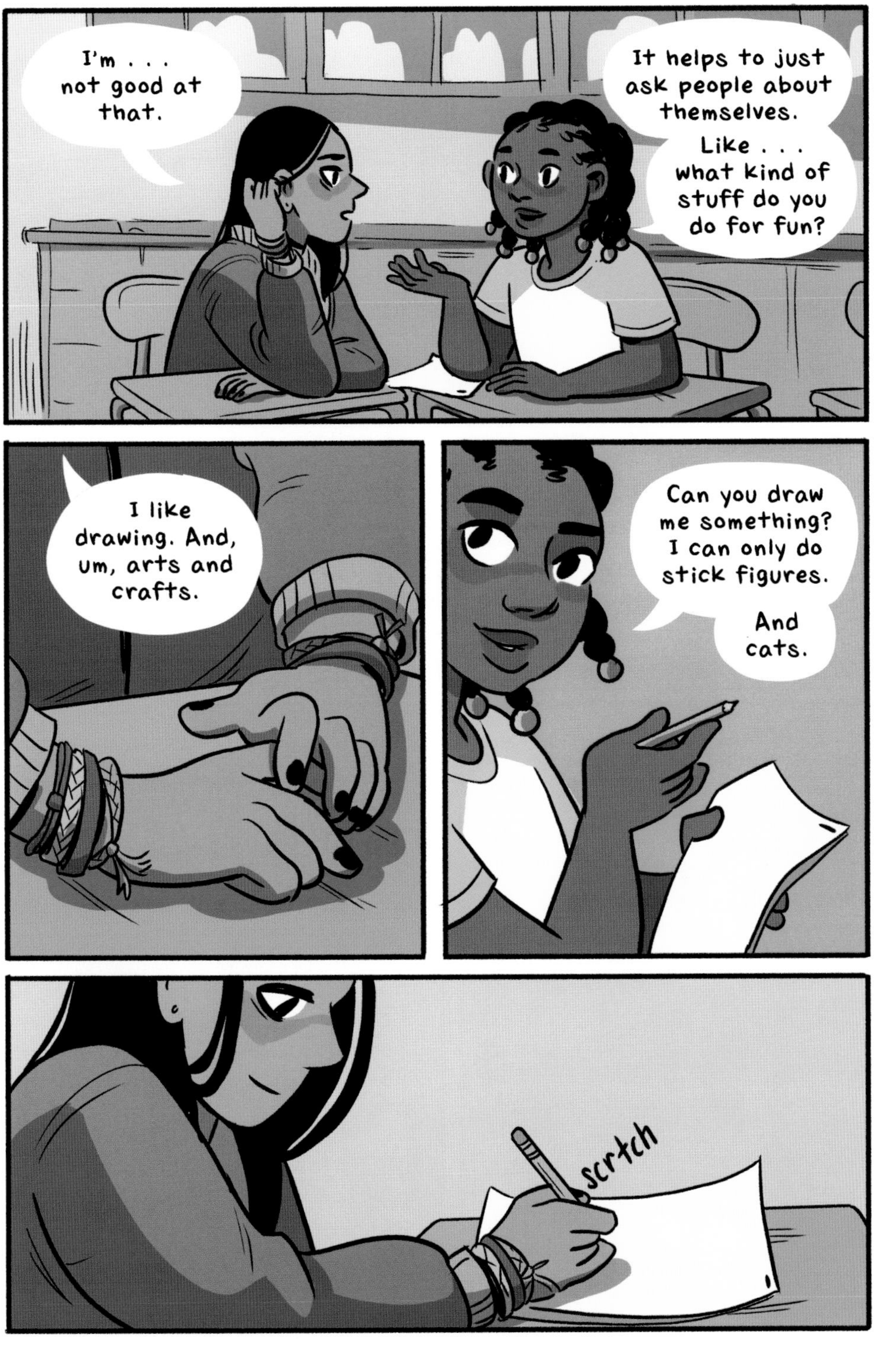
I'm . . . not good at that.
It helps to just ask people about themselves.
Like . . . what kind of stuff do you do for fun?
I like drawing. And, um, arts and crafts.
Can you draw me something? I can only do stick figures.
And cats.
scrtch

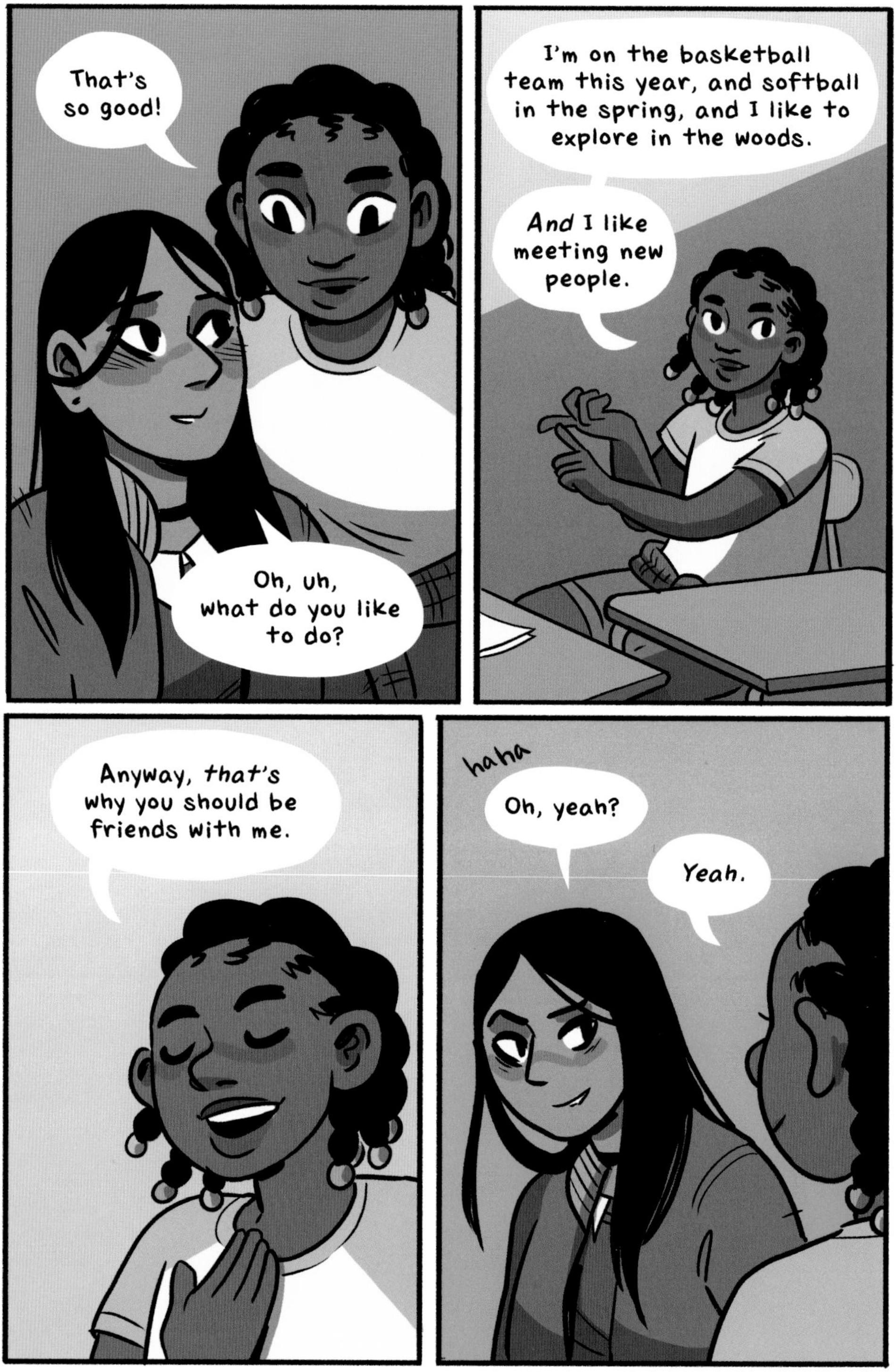
That's so good!
Oh, uh, what do you like to do?
I'm on the basketball team this year, and softball in the spring, and I like to explore in the woods.
And I like meeting new people.
Anyway, that's why you should be friends with me.
haha
Oh, yeah?
Yeah.

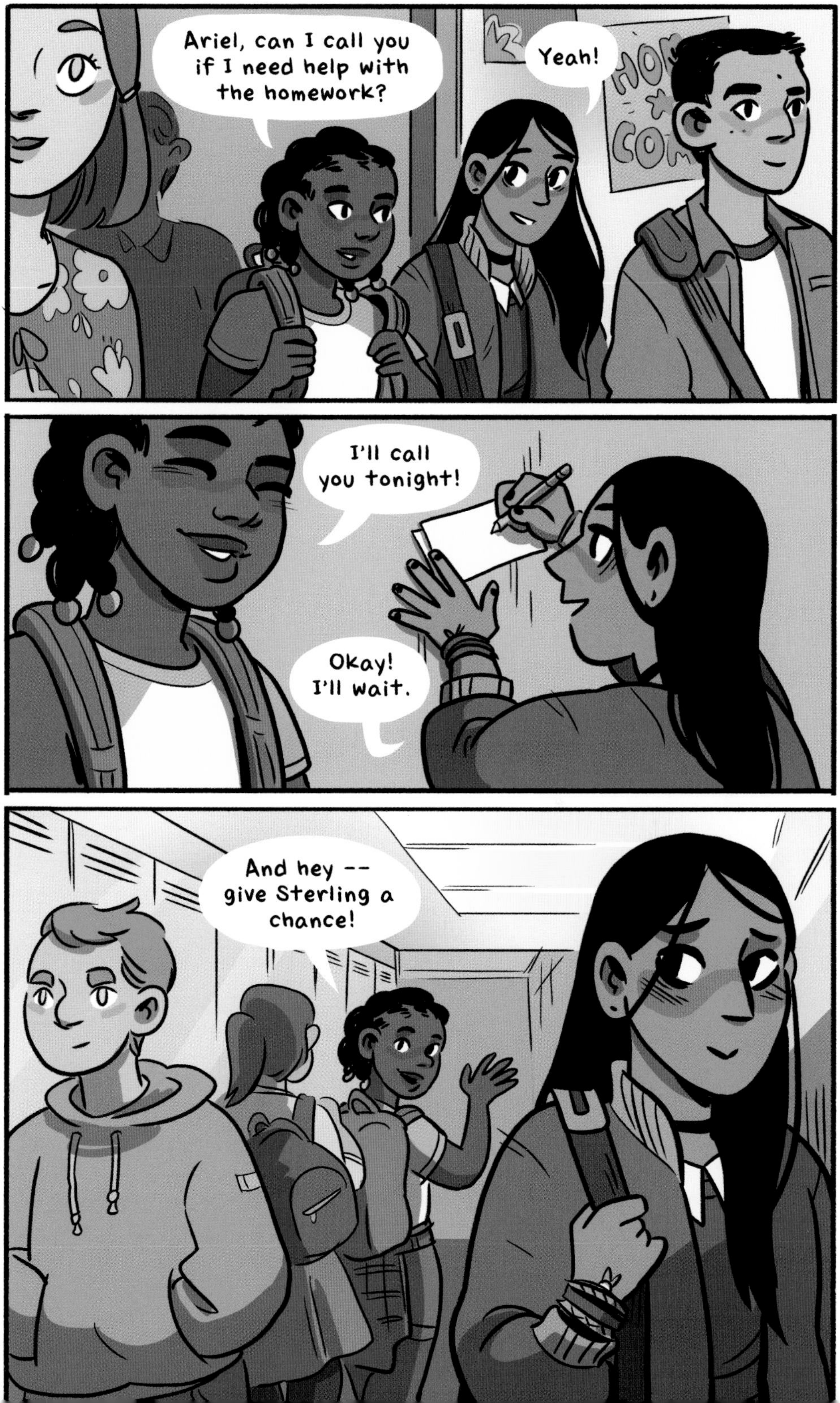
Ariel, can I call you if I need help with the homework?
Yeah!
HOM
CO
I'll call you tonight!
Okay! I'll wait.
And hey -- give Sterling a chance!

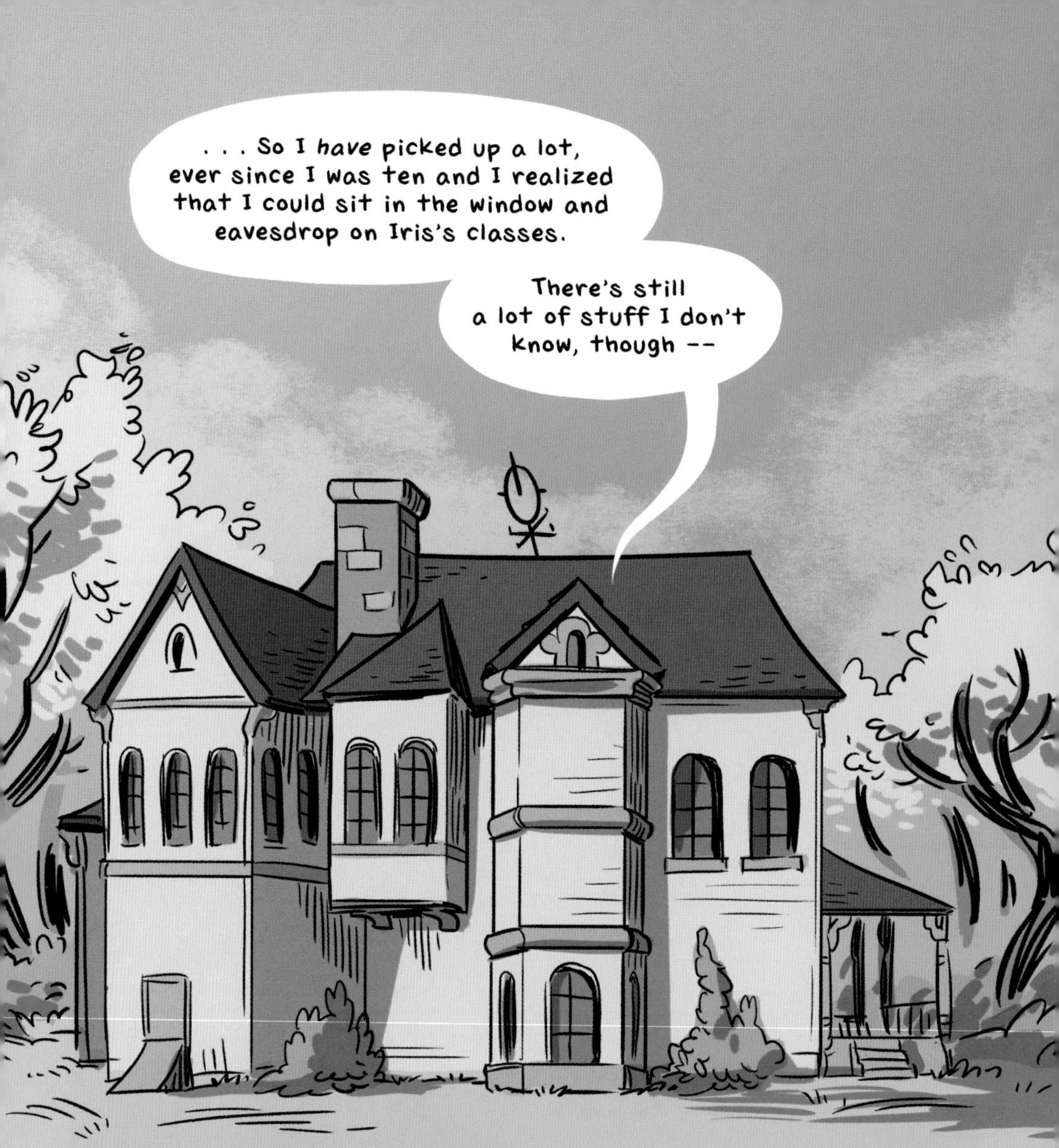
. . . So I *have* picked up a lot, ever since I was ten and I realized that I could sit in the window and eavesdrop on Iris's classes.
There's still a lot of stuff I don't know, though --

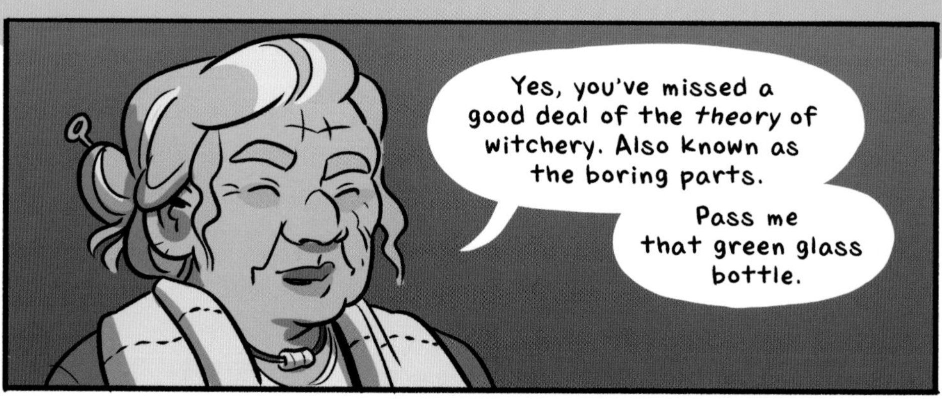
Yes, you've missed a good deal of the *theory* of witchery. Also known as the boring parts.
Pass me that green glass bottle.

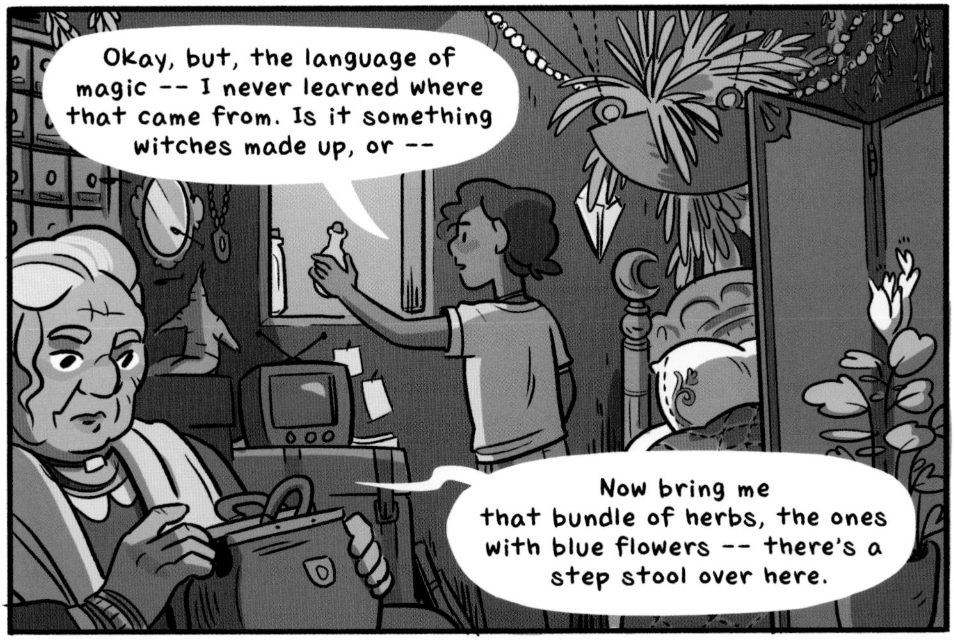
Okay, but, the language of magic -- I never learned where that came from. Is it something witches made up, or --
Now bring me that bundle of herbs, the ones with blue flowers -- there's a step stool over here.

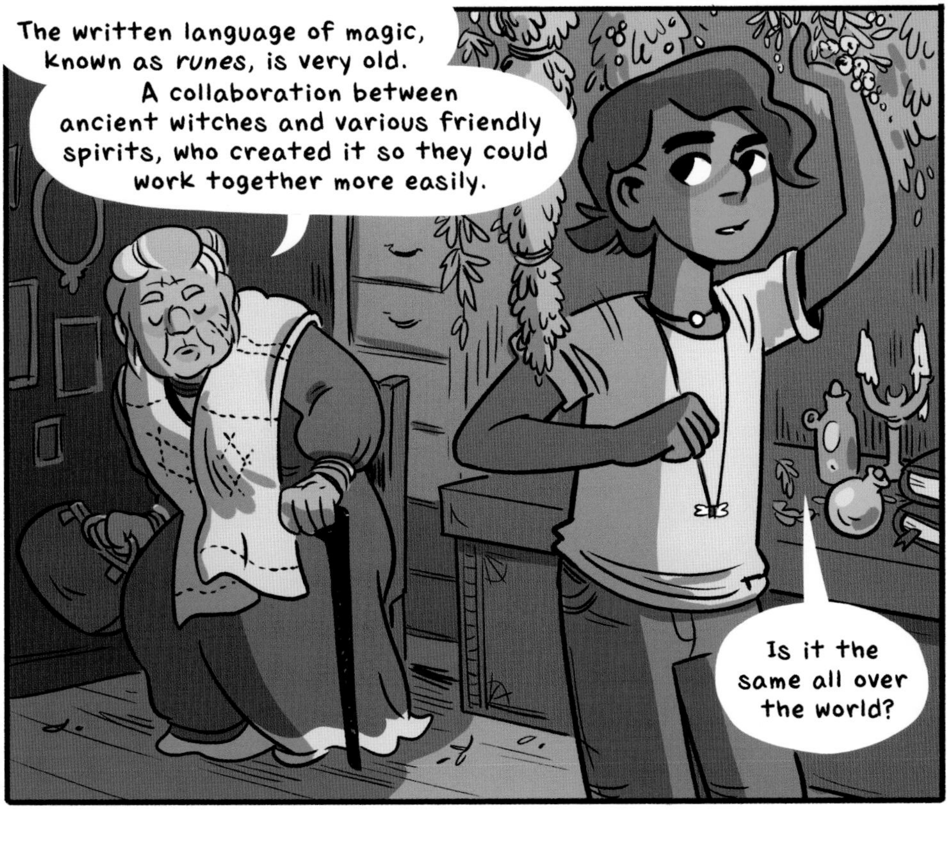
The written language of magic, known as *runes*, is very old.
A collaboration between ancient witches and various friendly spirits, who created it so they could work together more easily.
Is it the same all over the world?

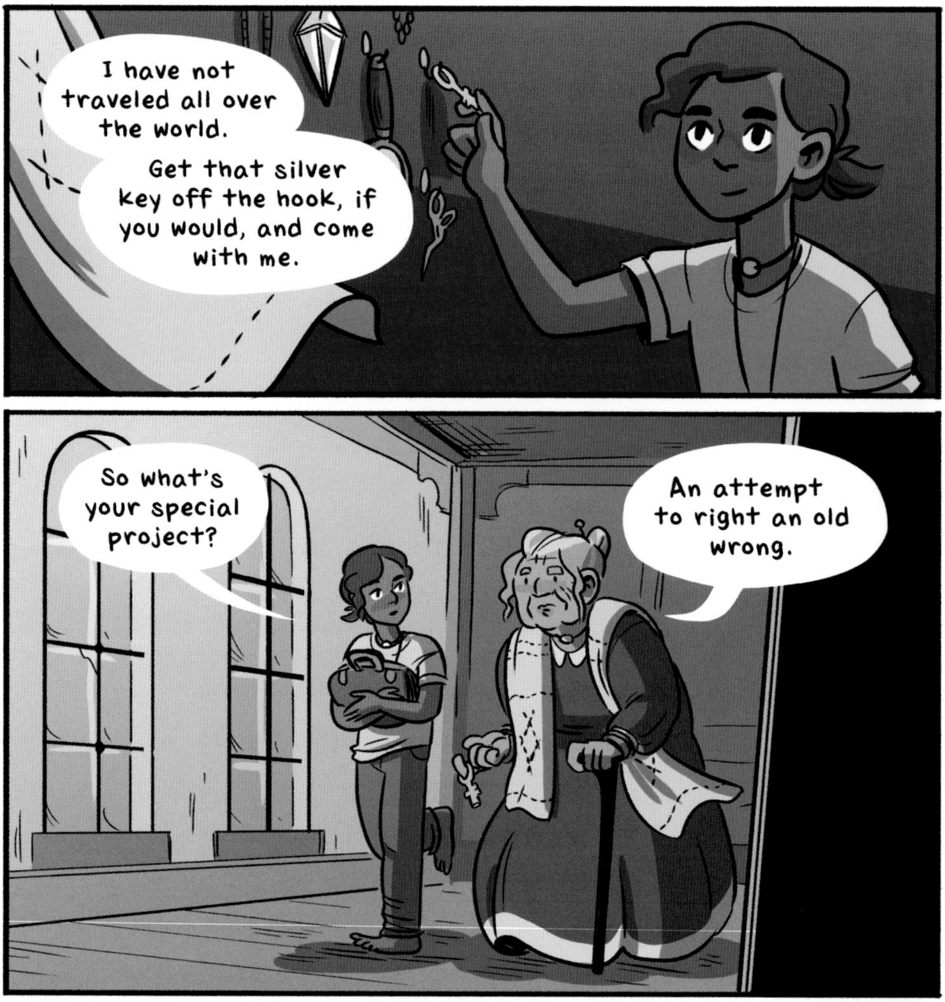
I have not traveled all over the world.
Get that silver key off the hook, if you would, and come with me.
So what's your special project?
An attempt to right an old wrong.
Oh no . . .
MIKASI

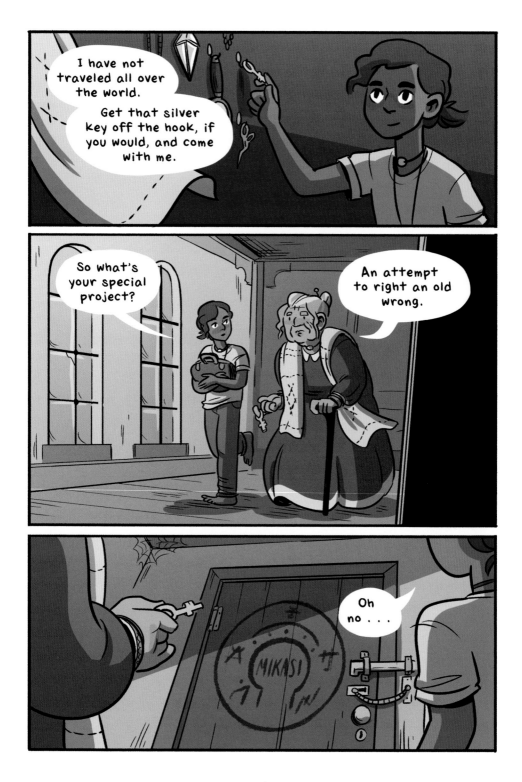

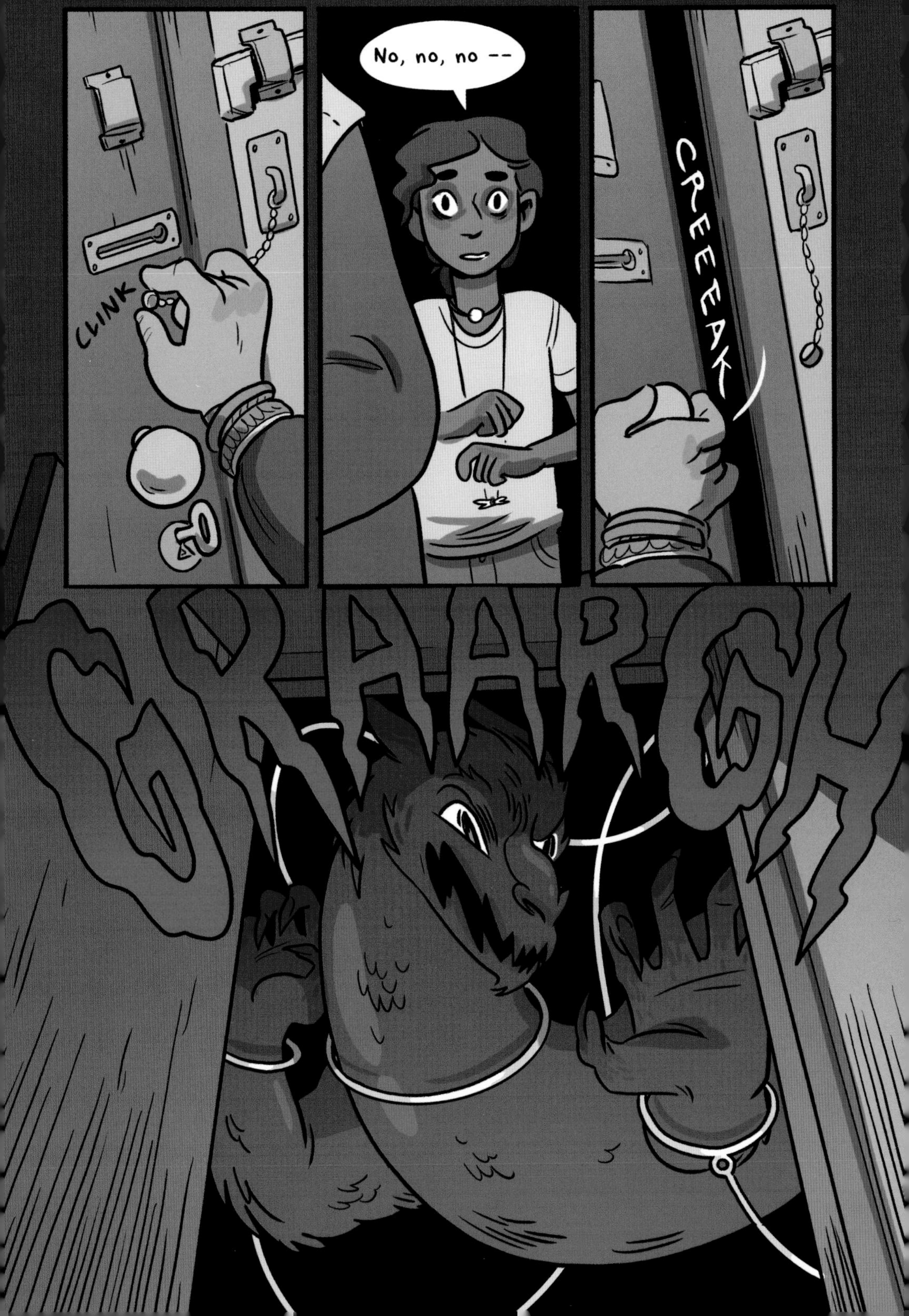
CLINK
No, no, no --
CREEEAK
GRAARGK

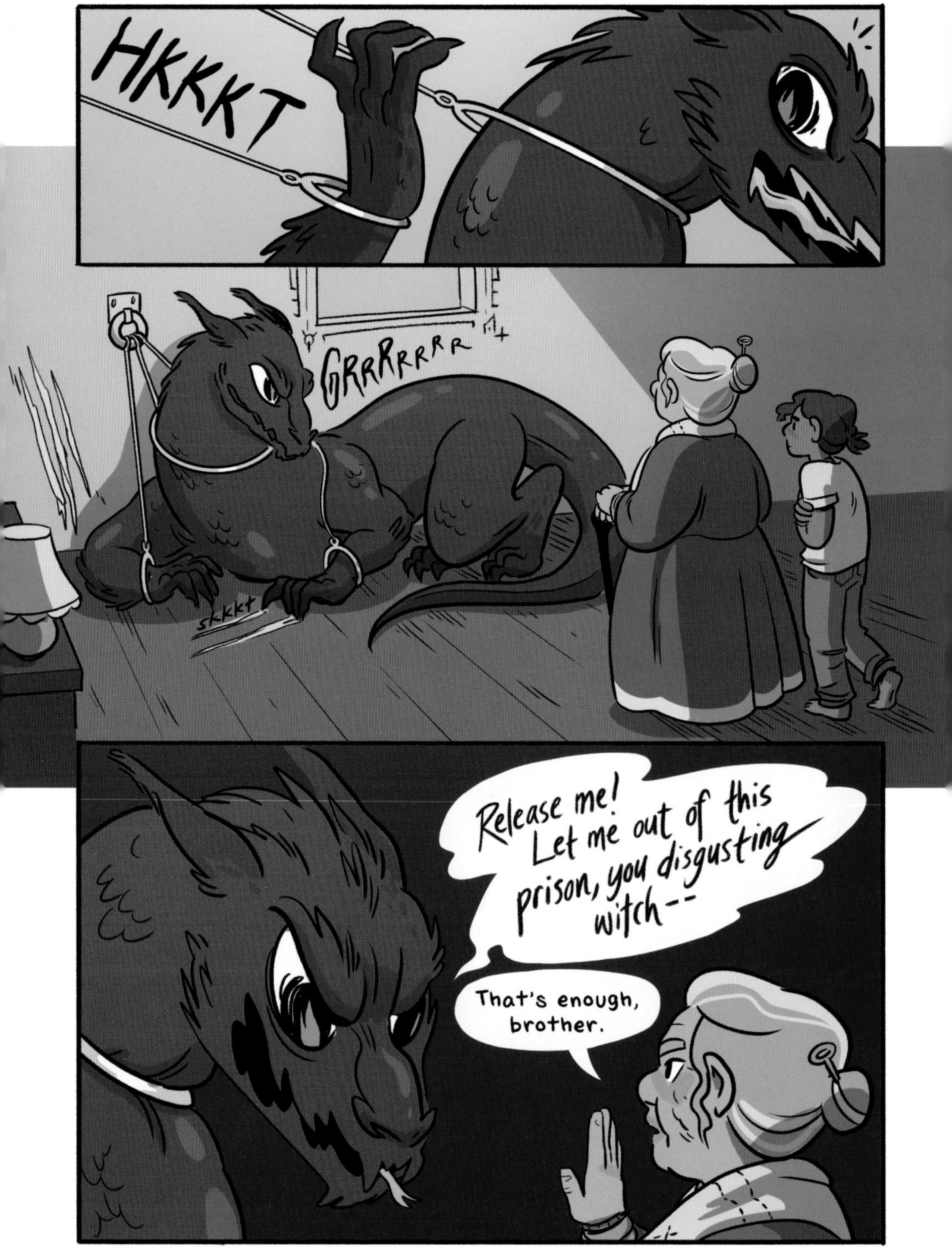
HKKKT
GRRRrrrr
skkkt
Release me! Let me out of this prison, you disgusting witch--
That's enough, brother.

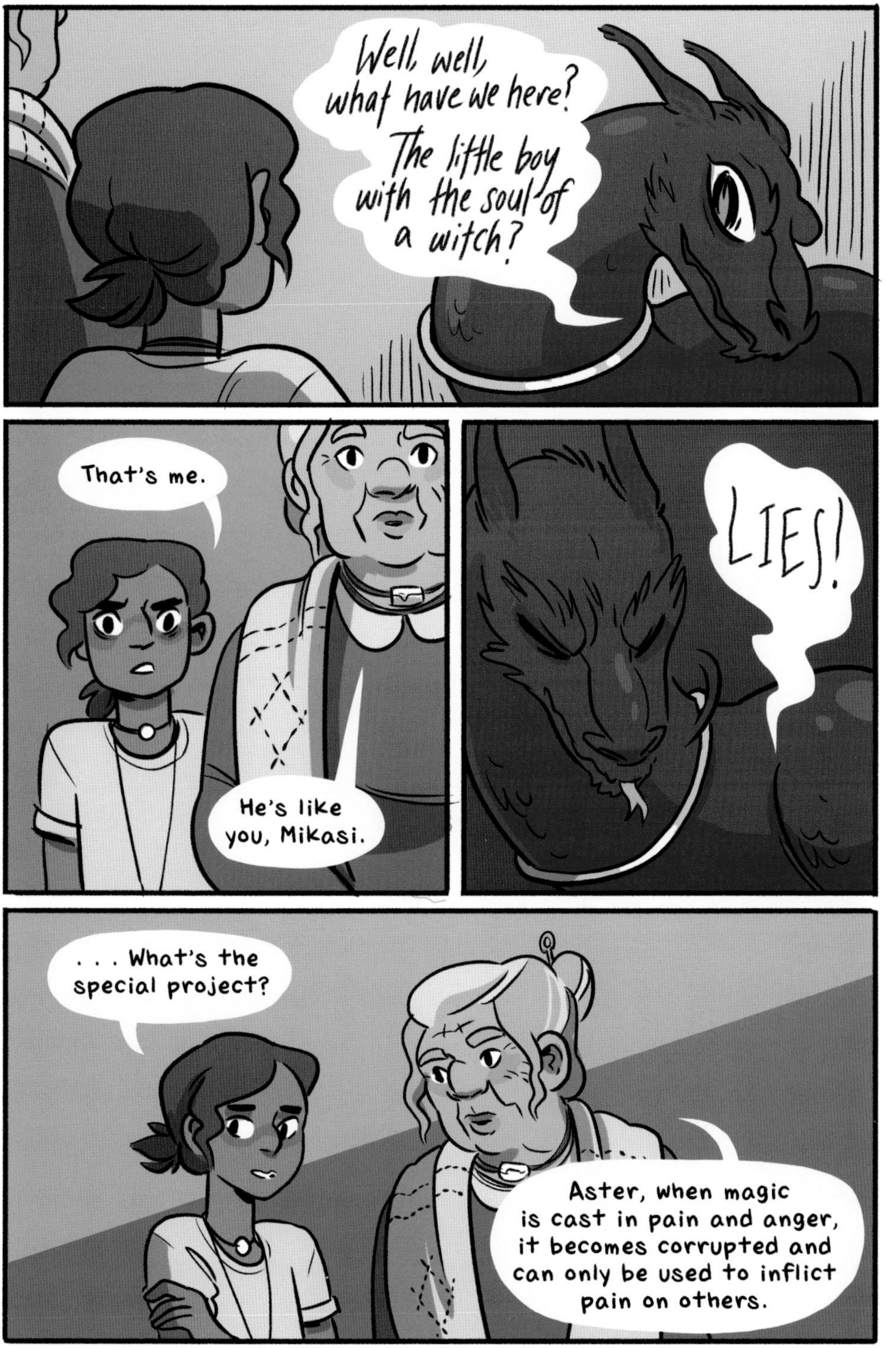
Well, well, what have we here?
The little boy with the soul of a witch?
That's me.
He's like you, Mikasi.
LIES!
. . . What's the special project?
Aster, when magic is cast in pain and anger, it becomes corrupted and can only be used to inflict pain on others.

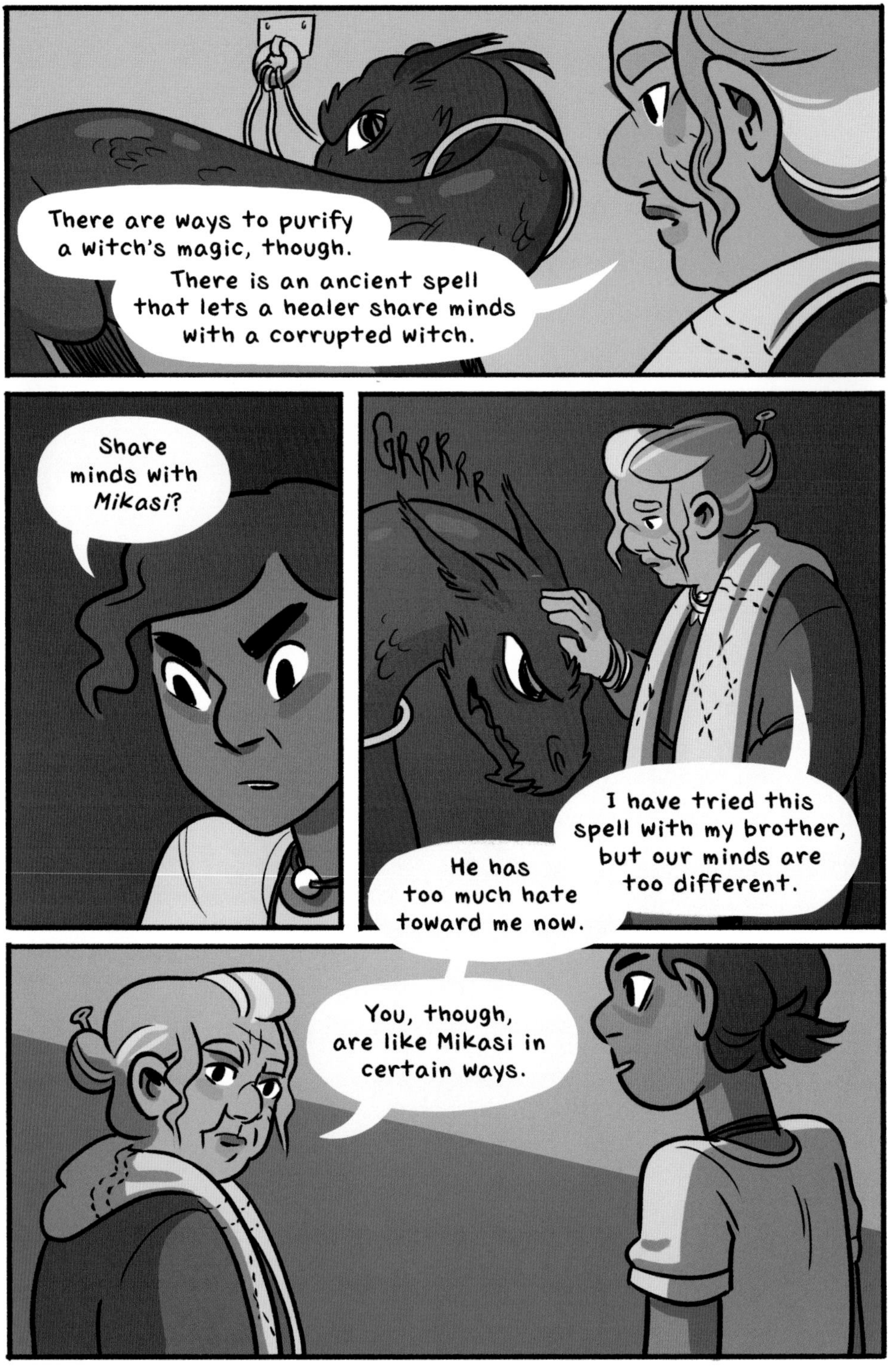
There are ways to purify a witch's magic, though.
There is an ancient spell that lets a healer share minds with a corrupted witch.
Share minds with *Mikasi*?
GRRRRR
I have tried this spell with my brother, but our minds are too different.
He has too much hate toward me now.
You, though, are like Mikasi in certain ways.

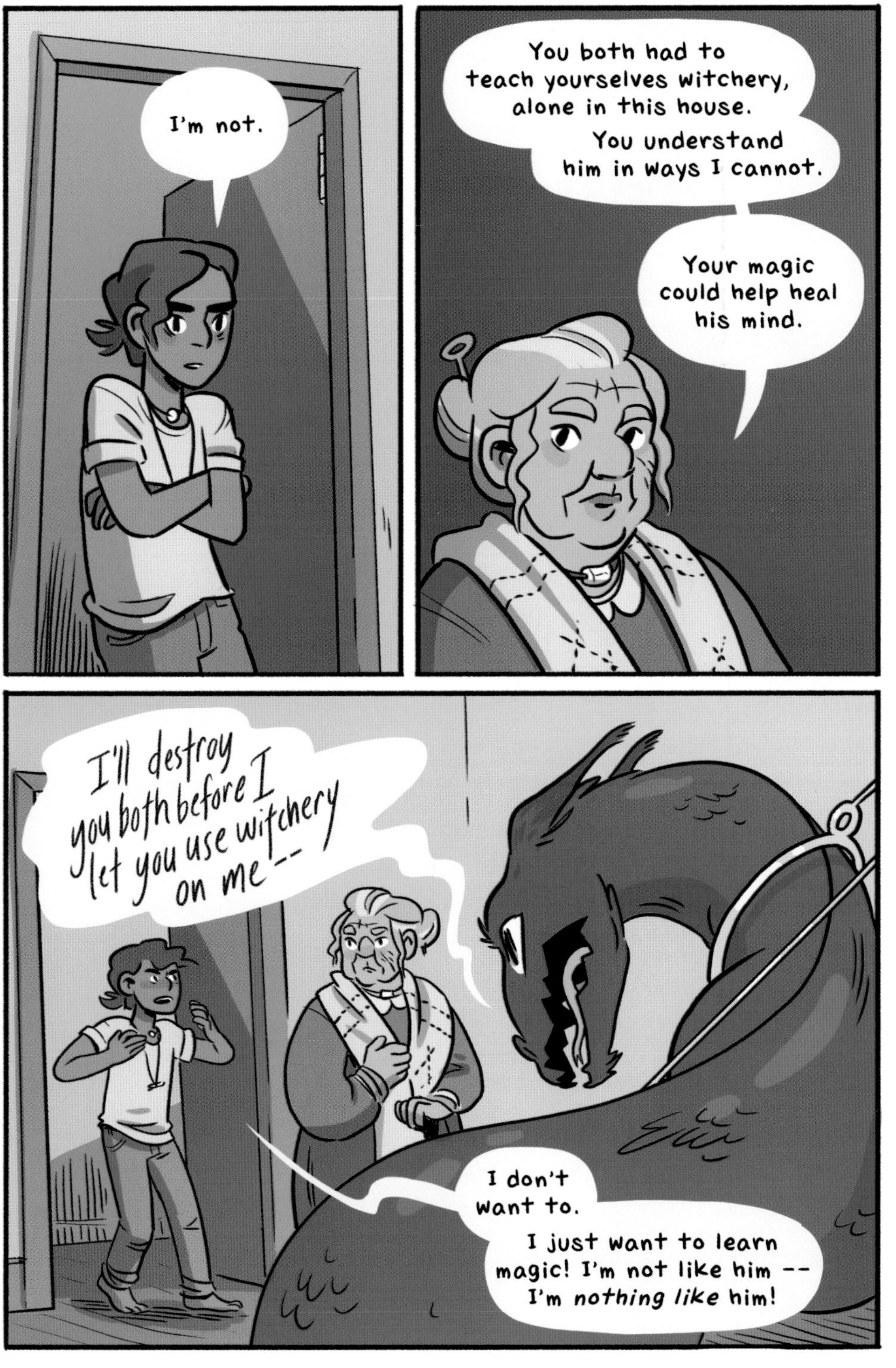
I'm not.
You both had to teach yourselves witchery, alone in this house.
You understand him in ways I cannot.
Your magic could help heal his mind.
I'll destroy you both before I let you use witchery on me--
I don't want to.
I just want to learn magic! I'm not like him -- I'm *nothing like* him!

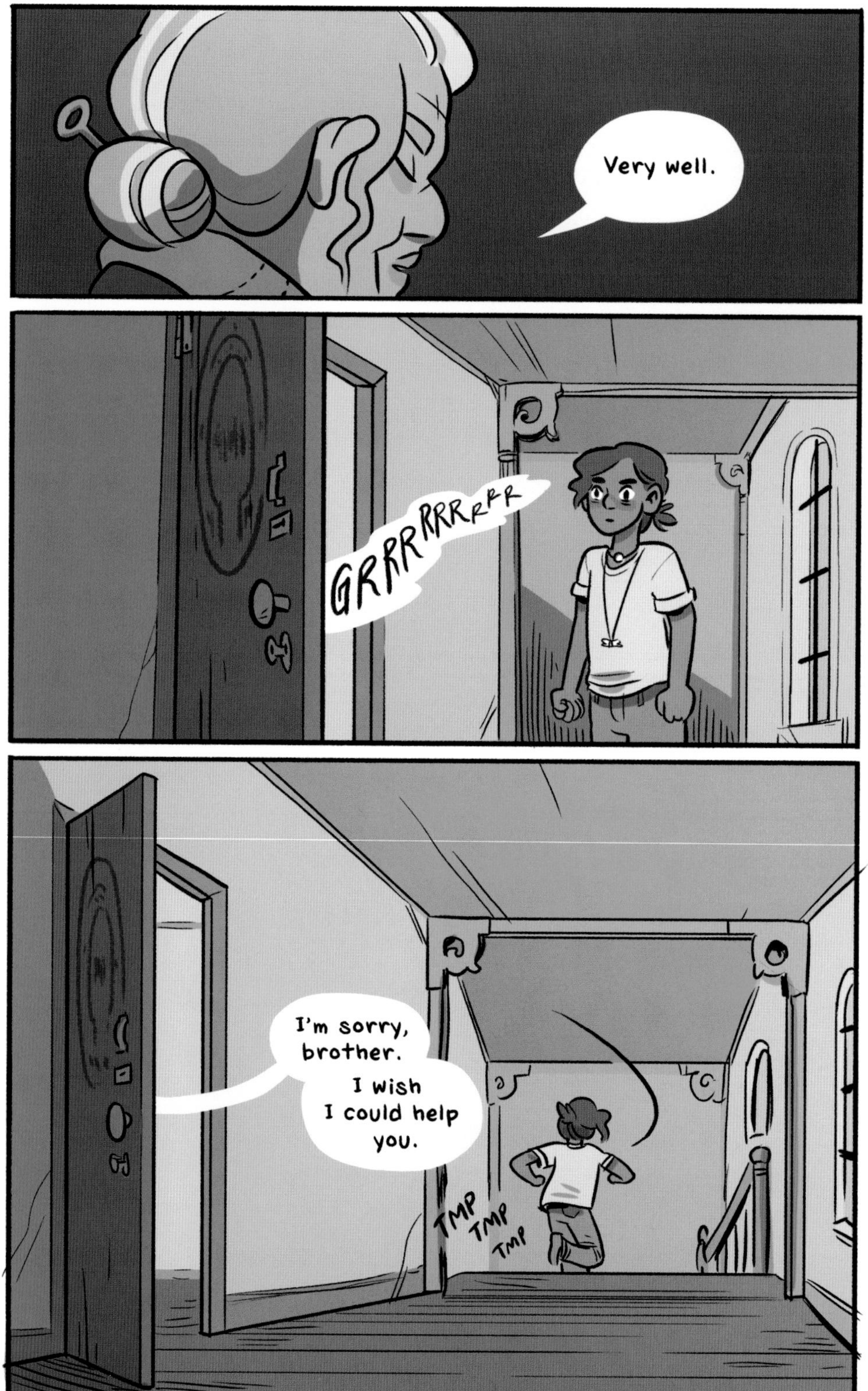
Very well.
GRRRRRRRRR
I'm sorry, brother.
I wish I could help you.
TMP TMP TMP

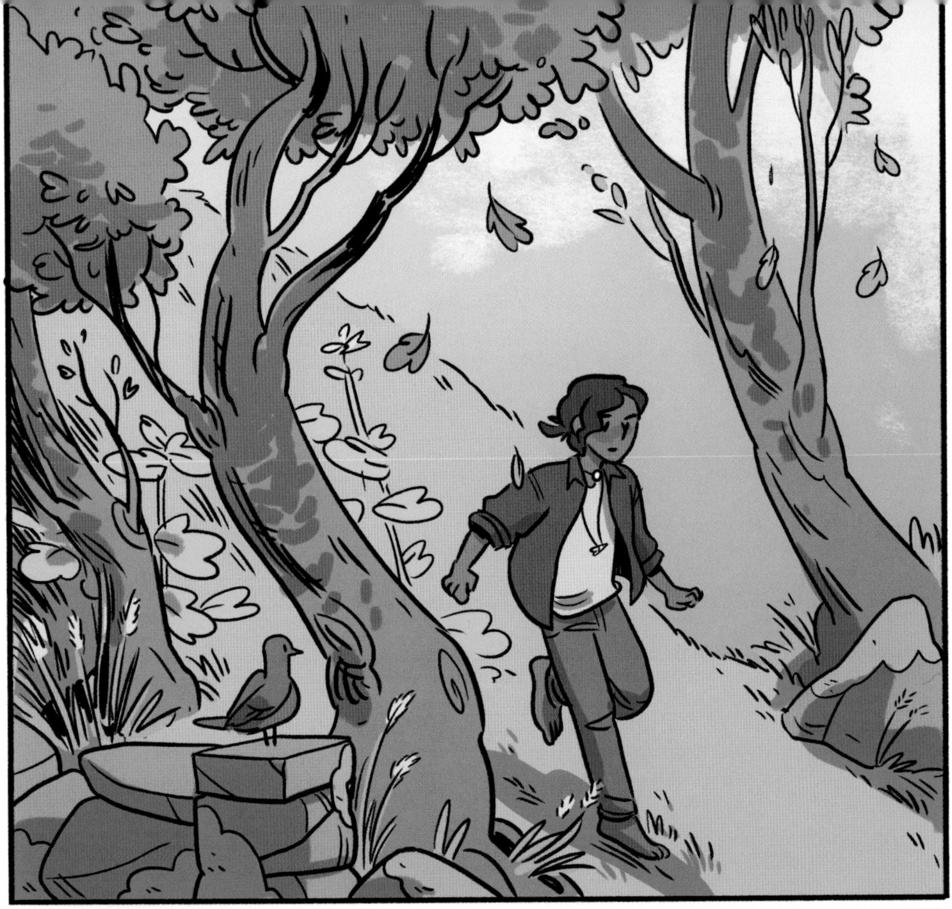

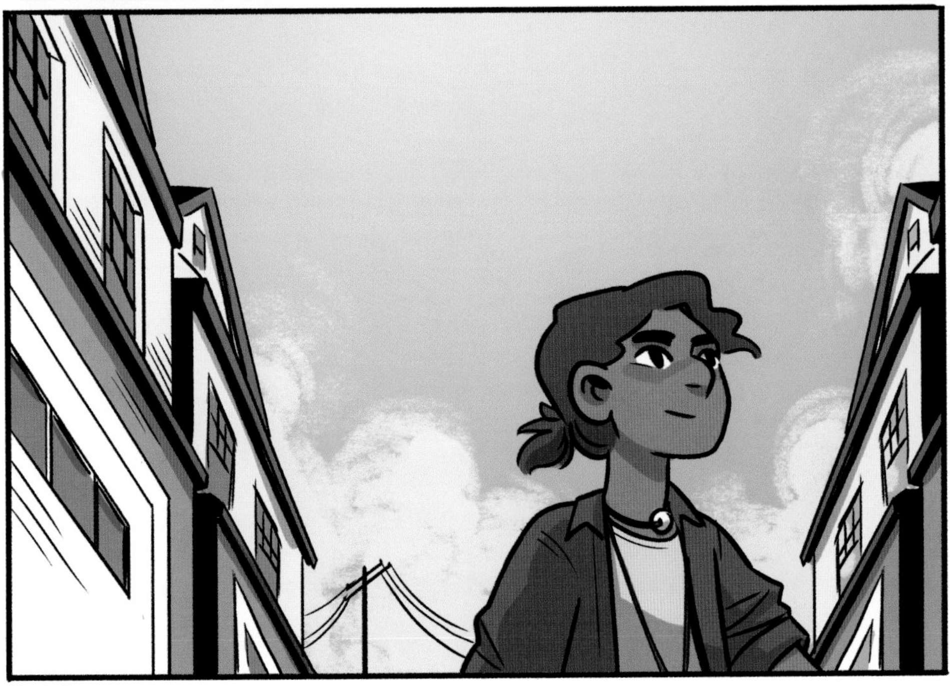

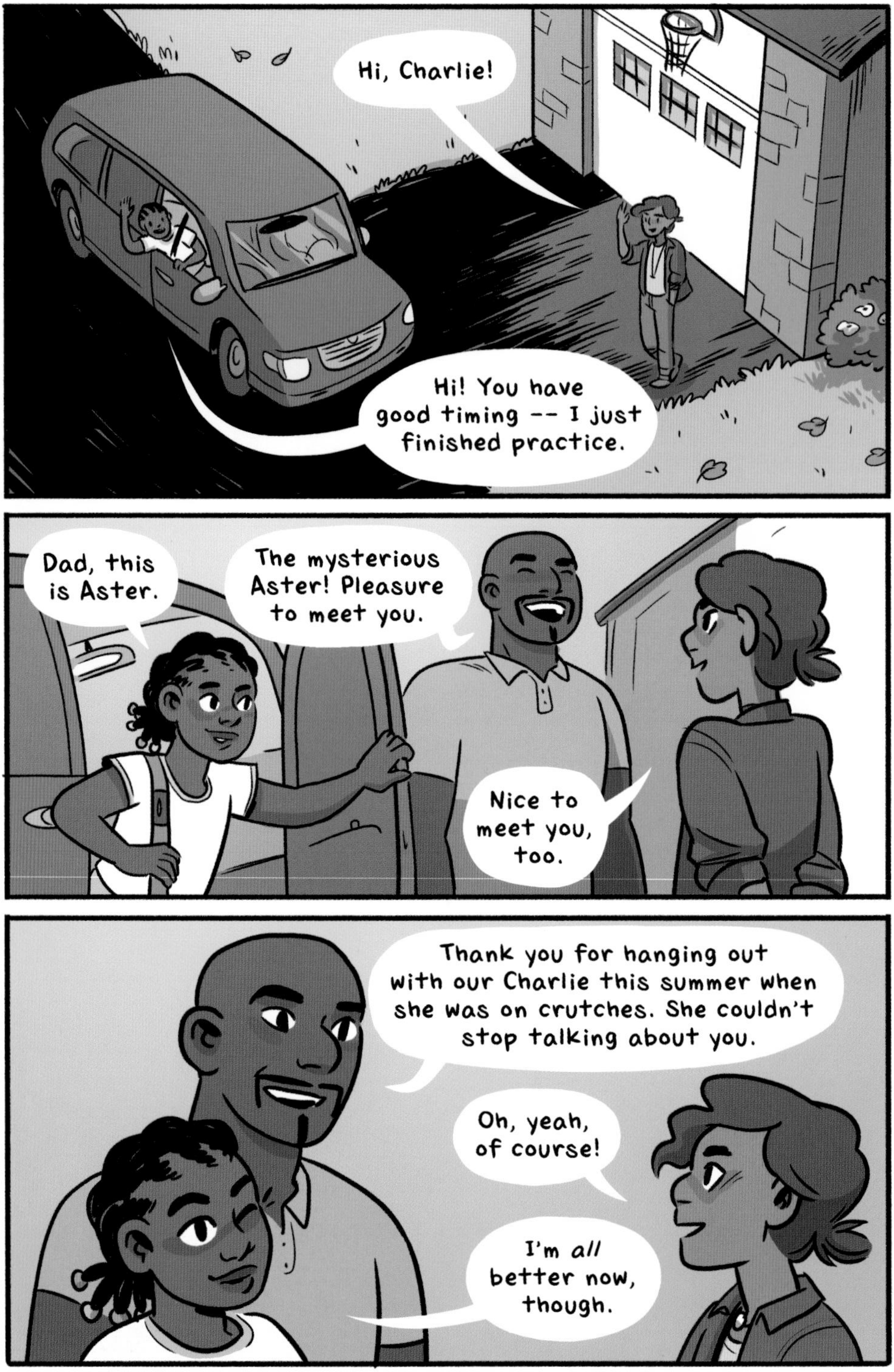
Hi, Charlie!
Hi! You have good timing -- I just finished practice.
Dad, this is Aster.
The mysterious Aster! Pleasure to meet you.
Nice to meet you, too.
Thank you for hanging out with our Charlie this summer when she was on crutches. She couldn't stop talking about you.
Oh, yeah, of course!
I'm *all* better now, though.

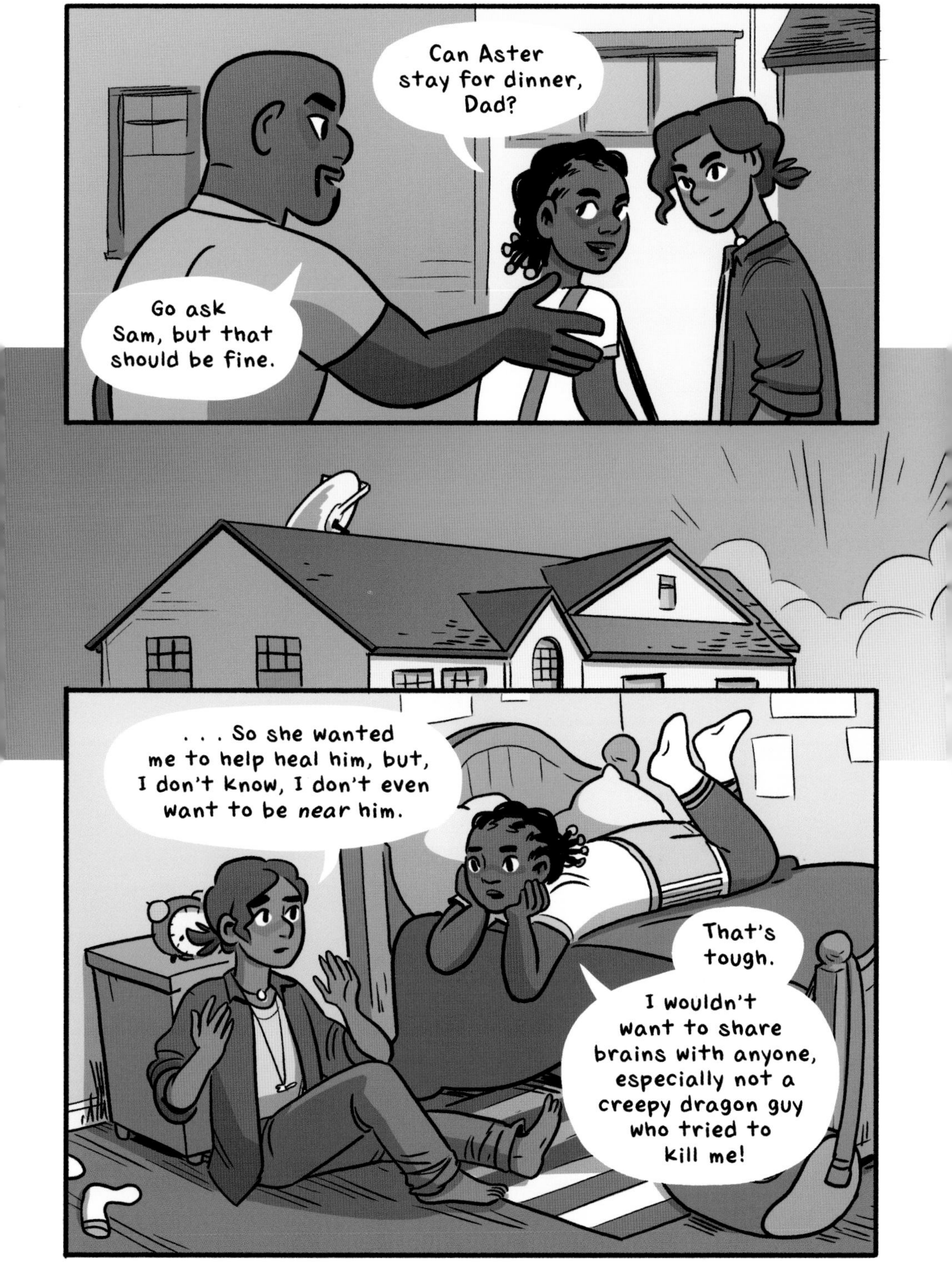
Can Aster stay for dinner, Dad?
Go ask Sam, but that should be fine.
. . . So she wanted me to help heal him, but, I don't know, I don't even want to be *near* him.
That's tough.
I wouldn't want to share brains with anyone, especially not a creepy dragon guy who tried to kill me!

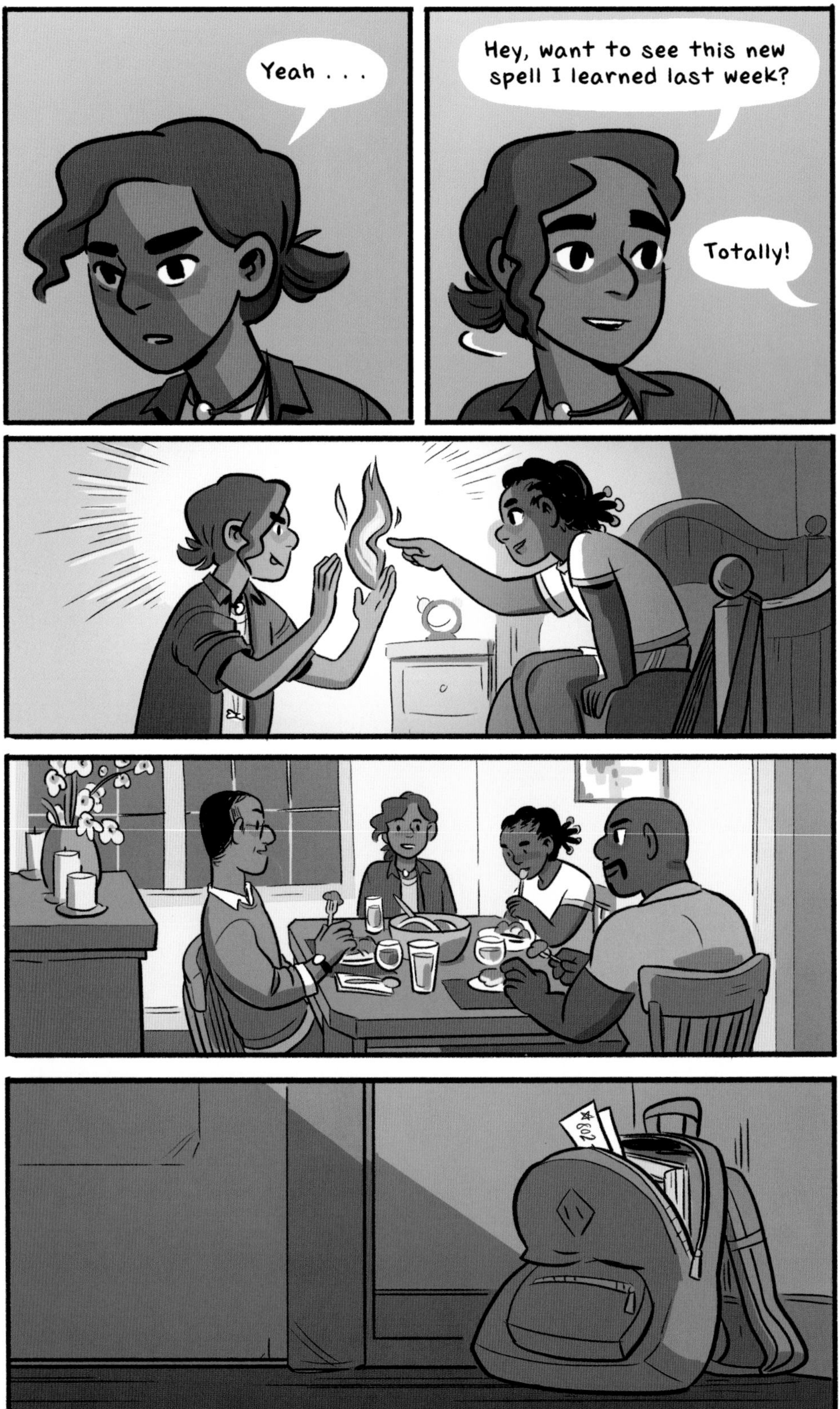
Yeah . . .
Hey, want to see this new spell I learned last week?
Totally!

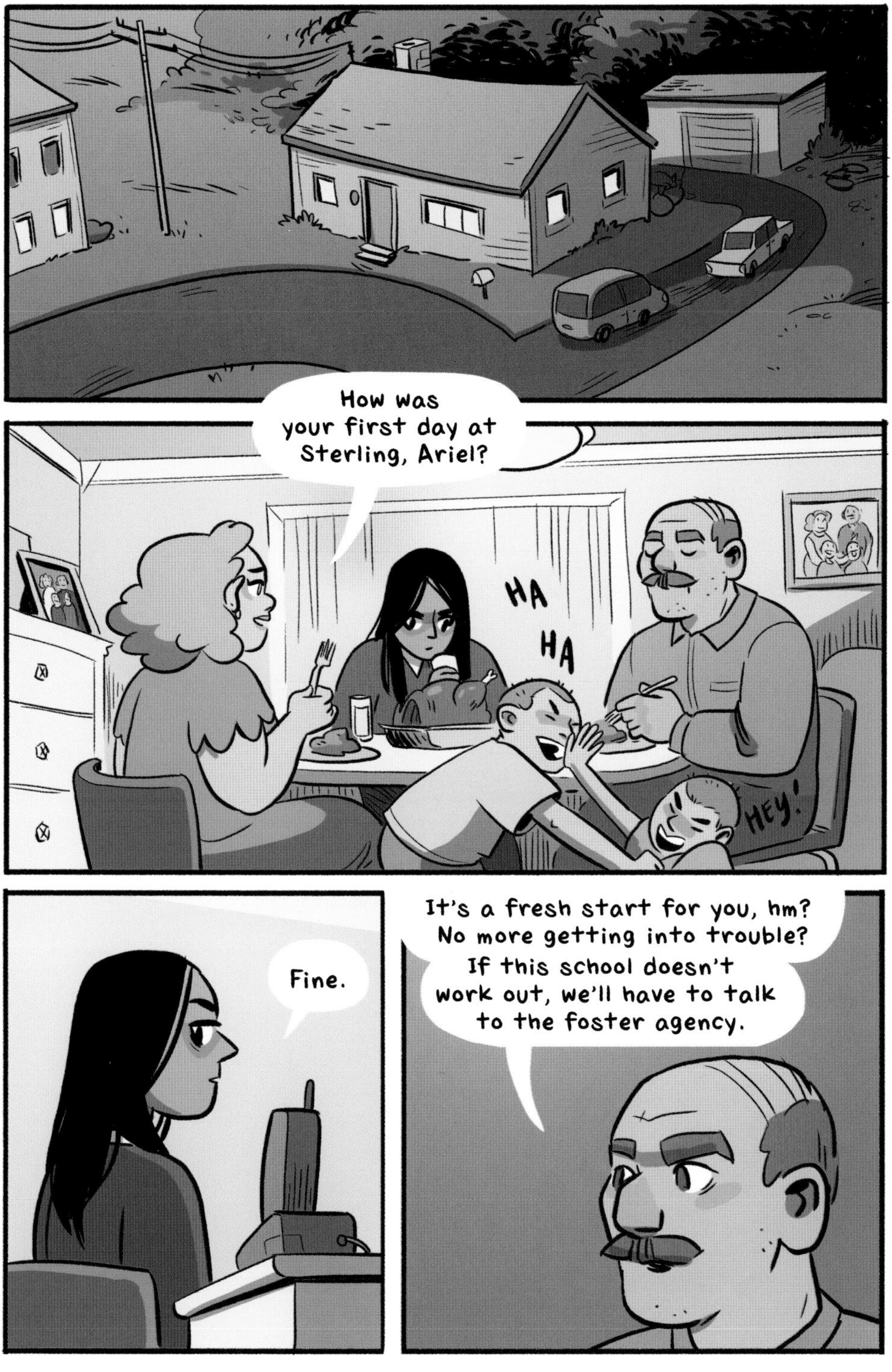
How was your first day at Sterling, Ariel?
HA HA
HEY!
Fine.
It's a fresh start for you, hm? No more getting into trouble? If this school doesn't work out, we'll have to talk to the foster agency.

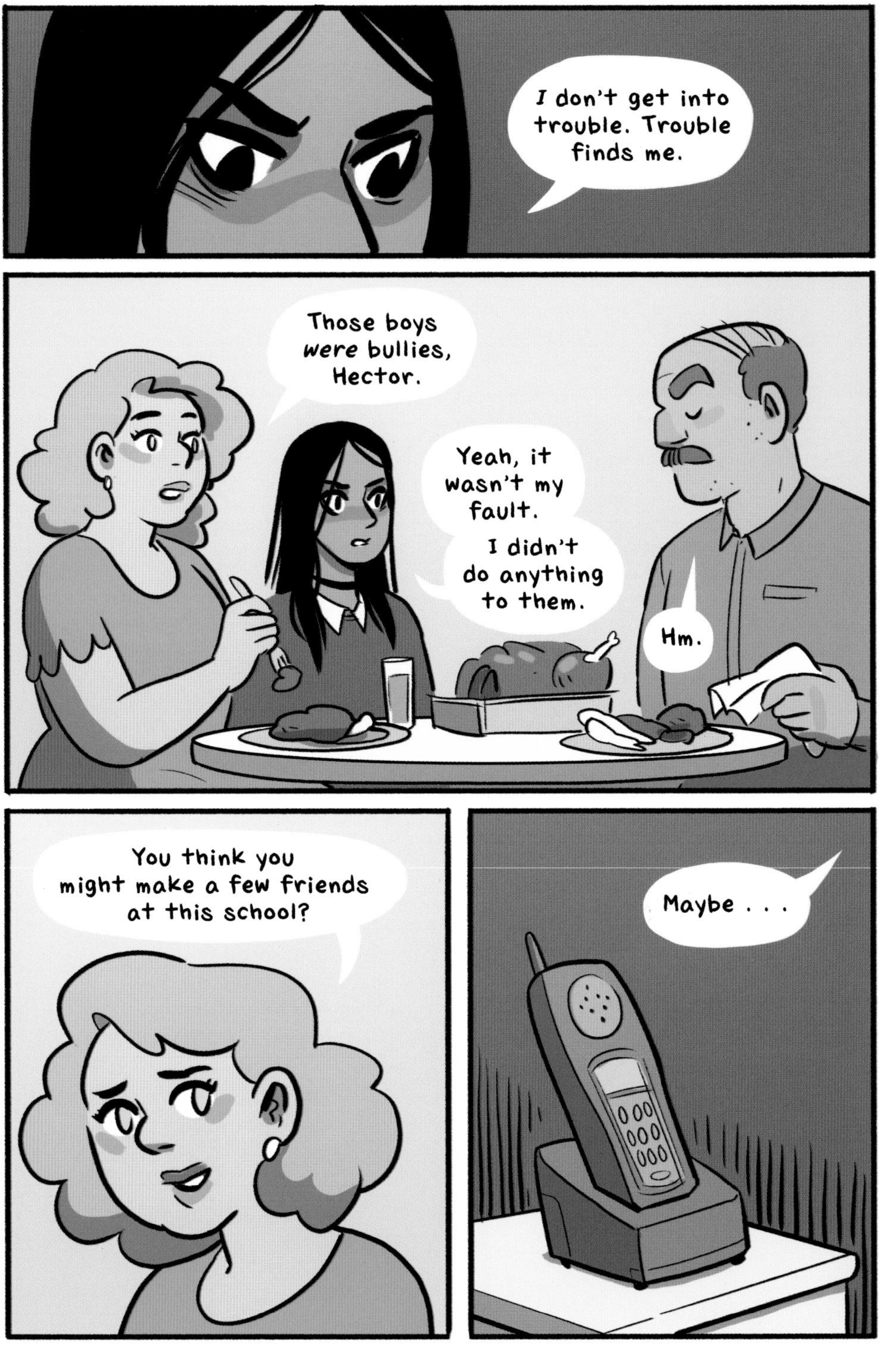
I don't get into trouble. Trouble finds me.
Those boys were bullies, Hector.
Yeah, it wasn't my fault.
I didn't do anything to them.
Hm.
You think you might make a few friends at this school?
Maybe . . .

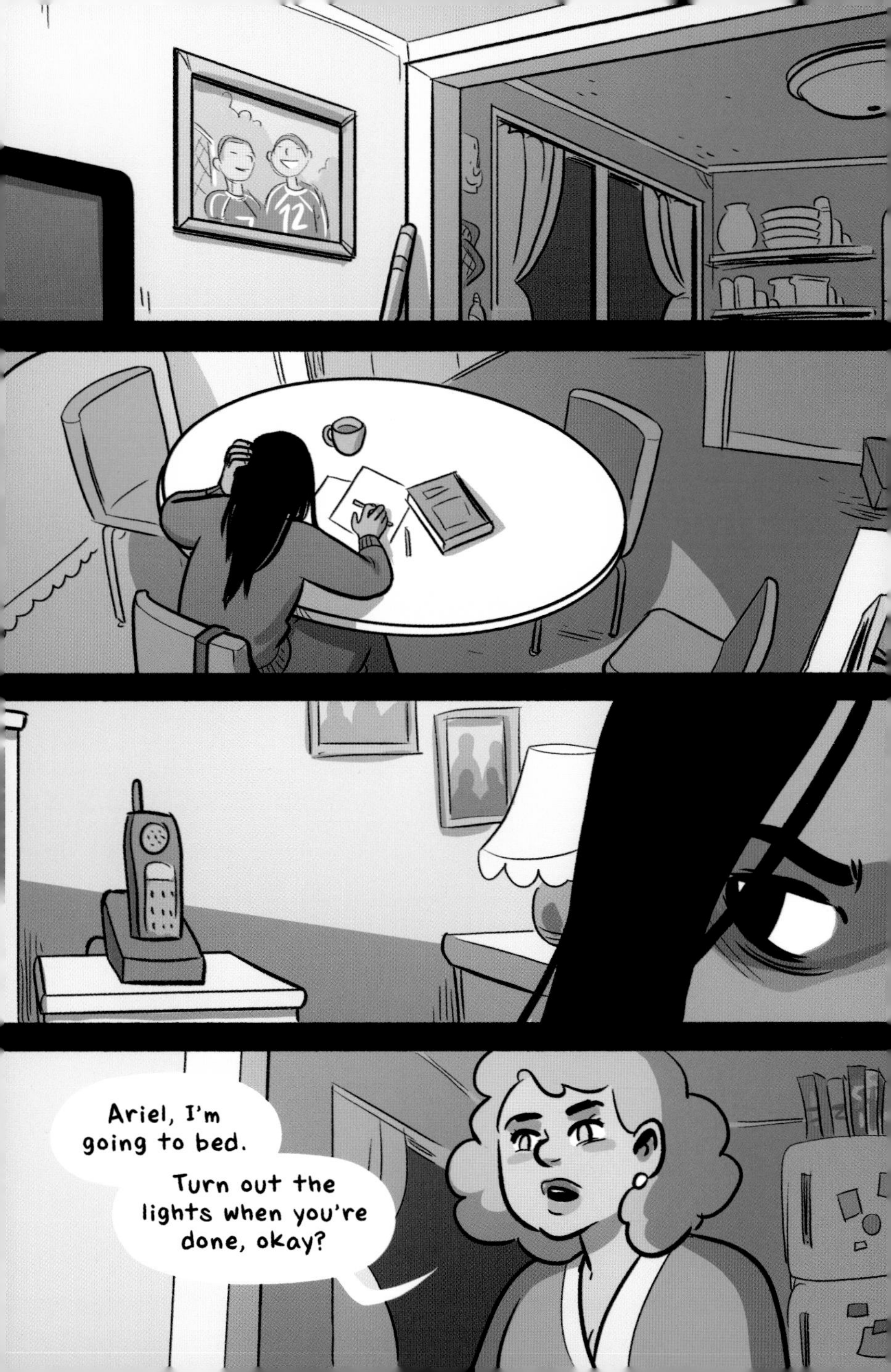
Ariel, I'm going to bed.
Turn out the lights when you're done, okay?

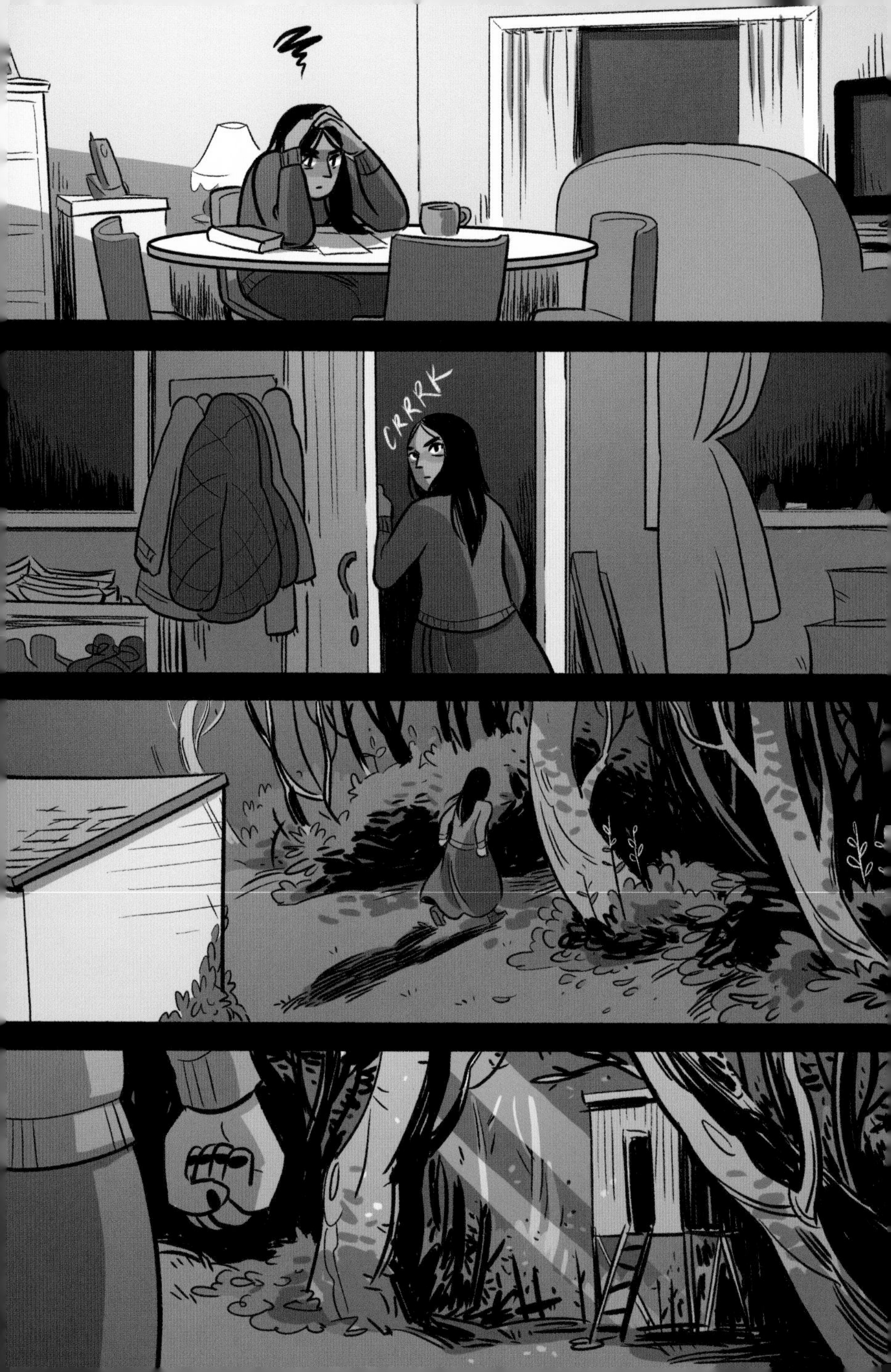
CRRRK

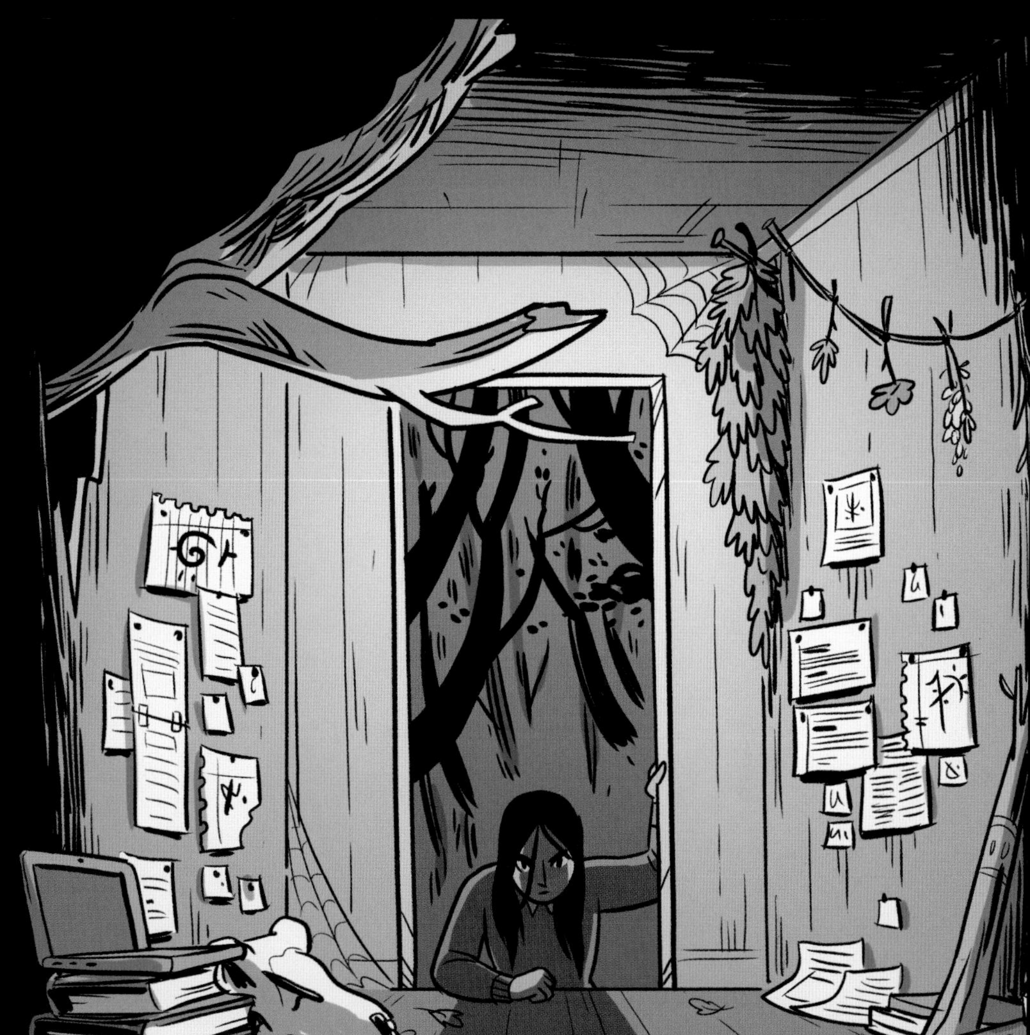

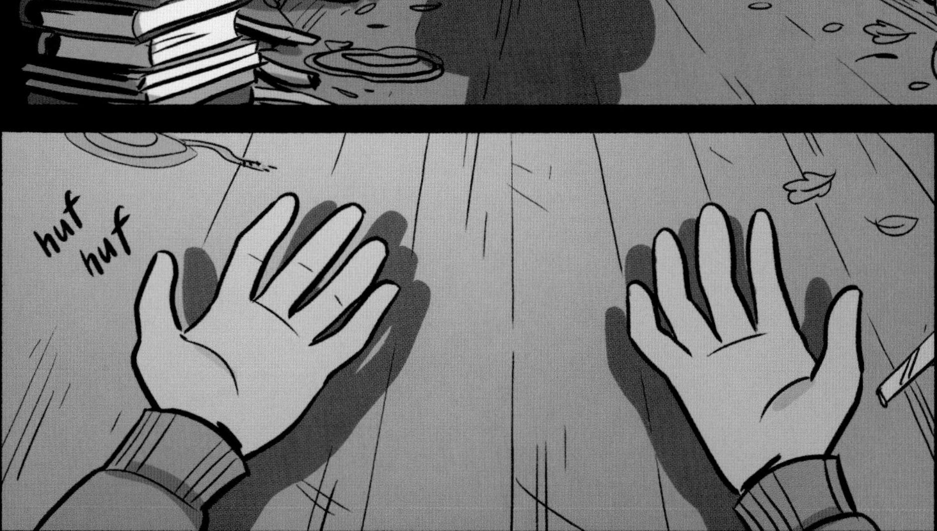
huf
huf

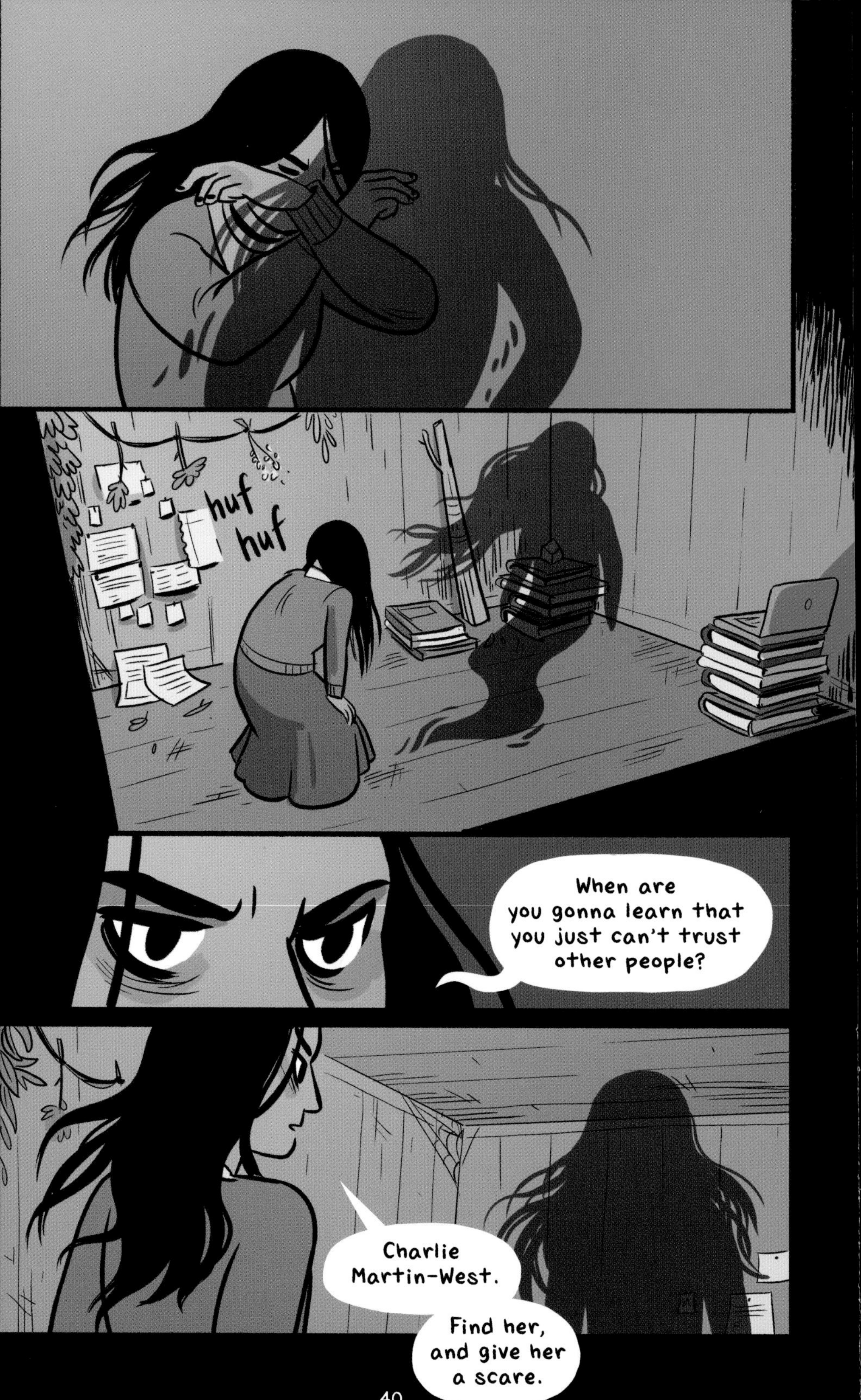
huf huf
When are you gonna learn that you just can't trust other people?
Charlie Martin-West.
Find her, and give her a scare.

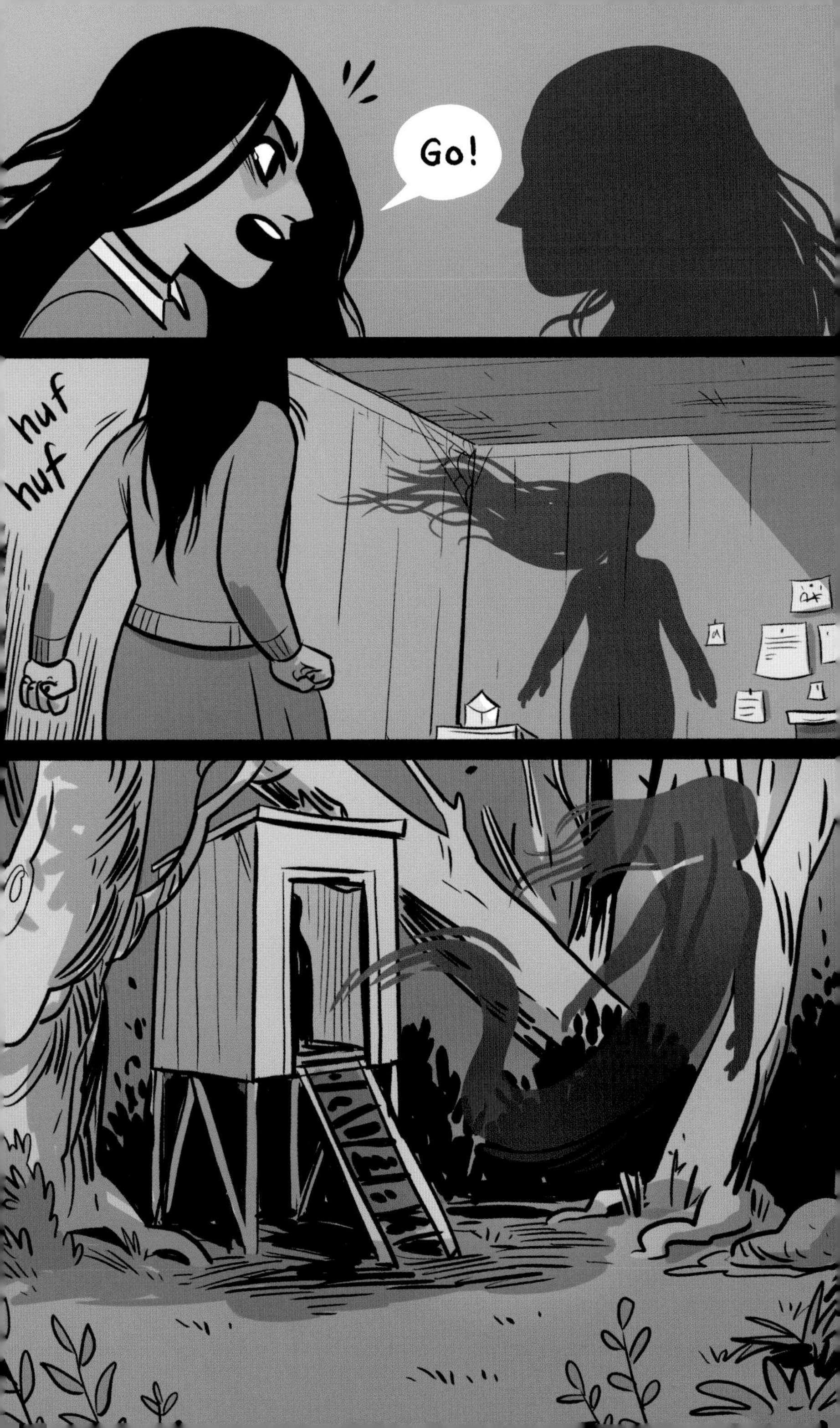
Go!
huf
huf

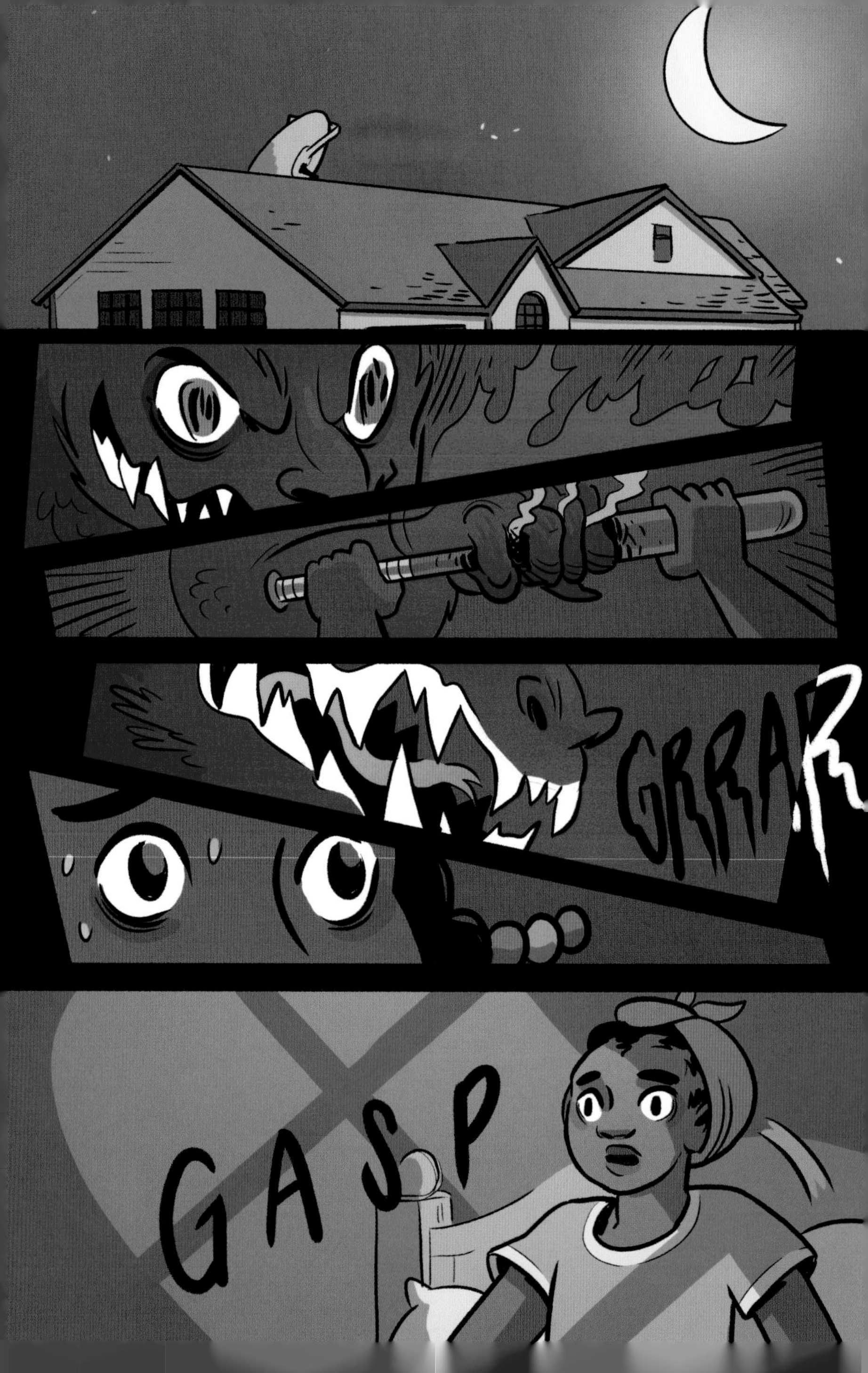
GRRAR
GASP

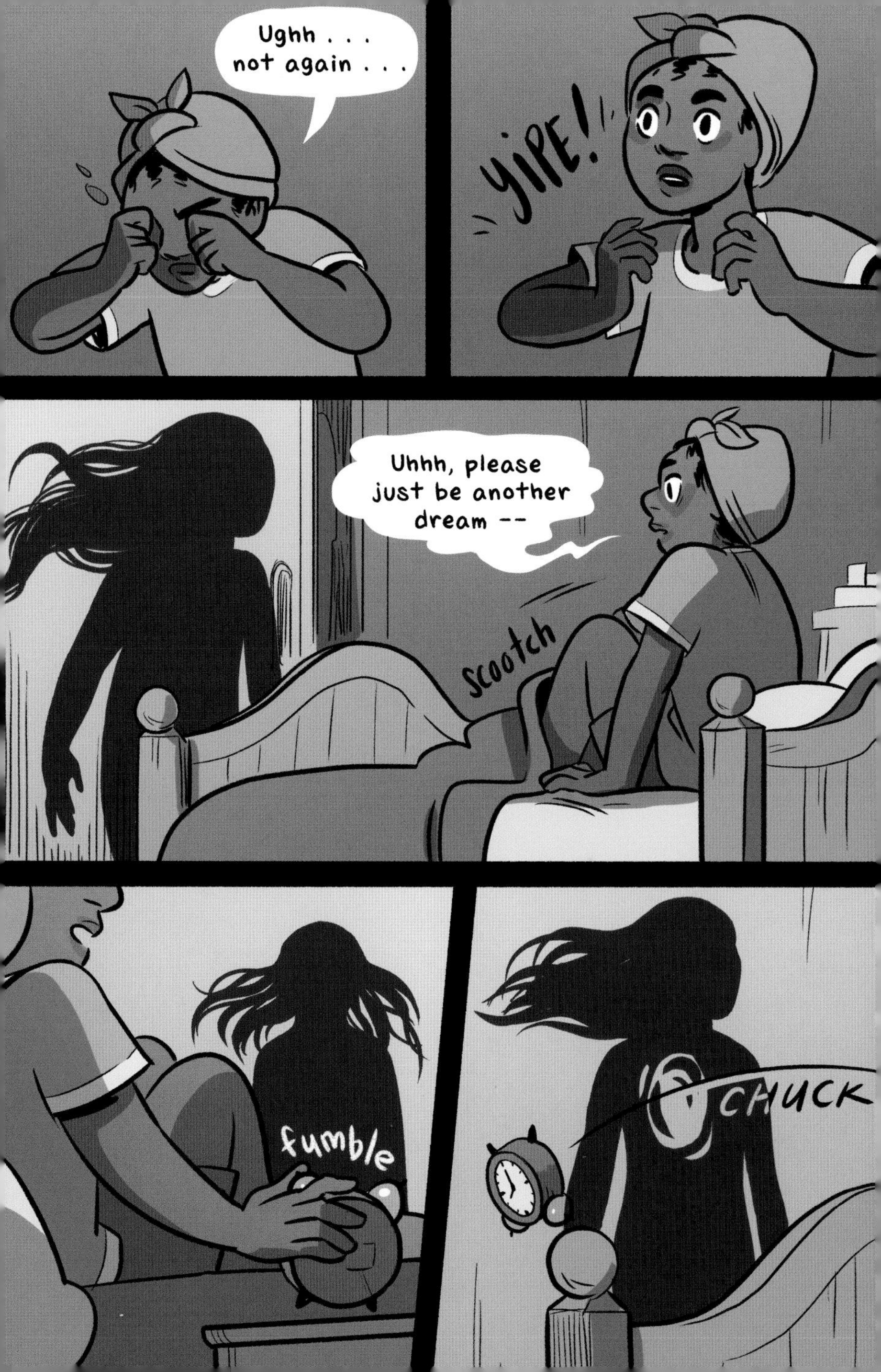
Ughh . . . not again . . .
YIPE!
Uhhh, please just be another dream --
scootch
fumble
CHUCK

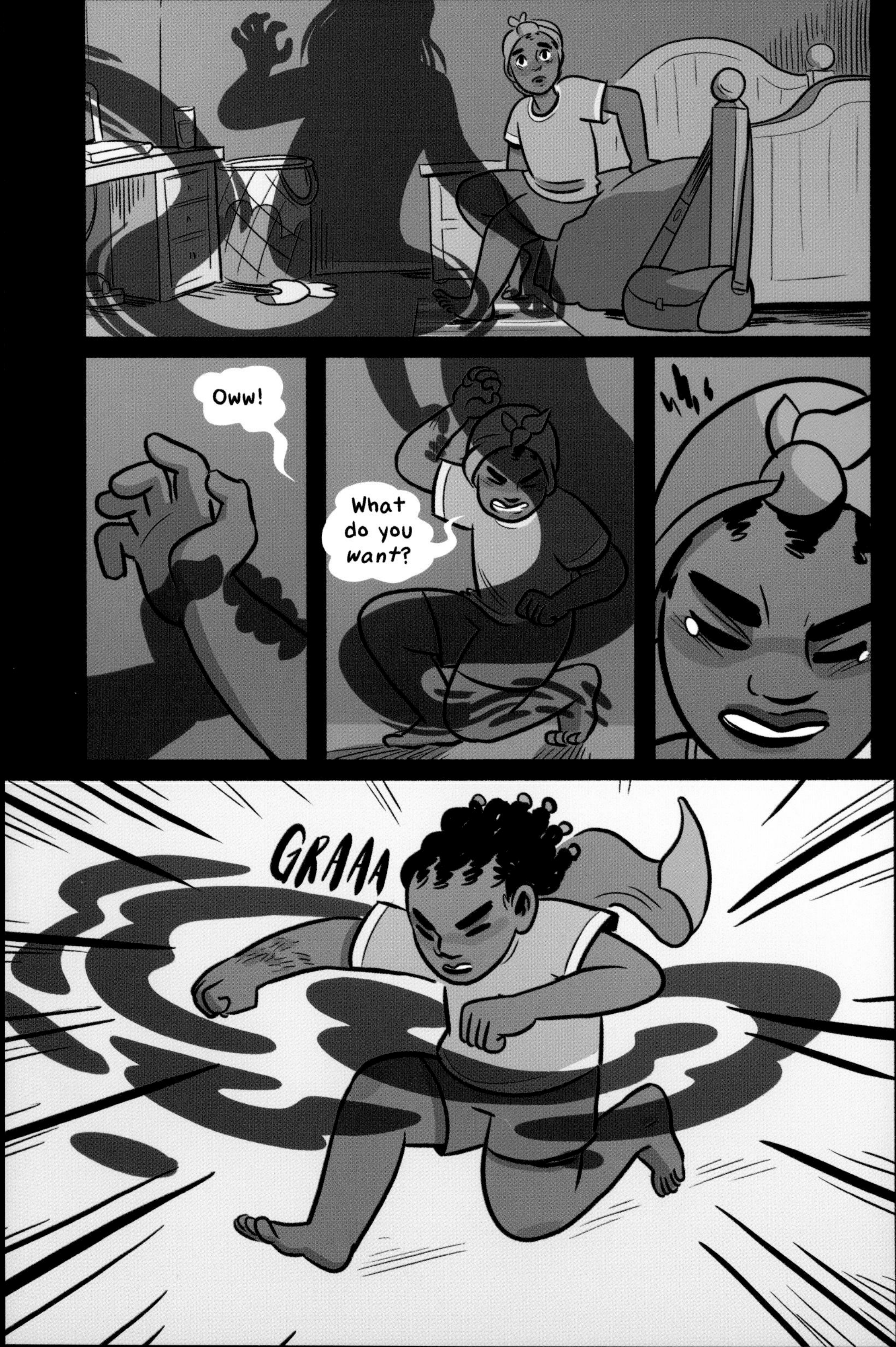
Oww!
What do you want?
GRAAA

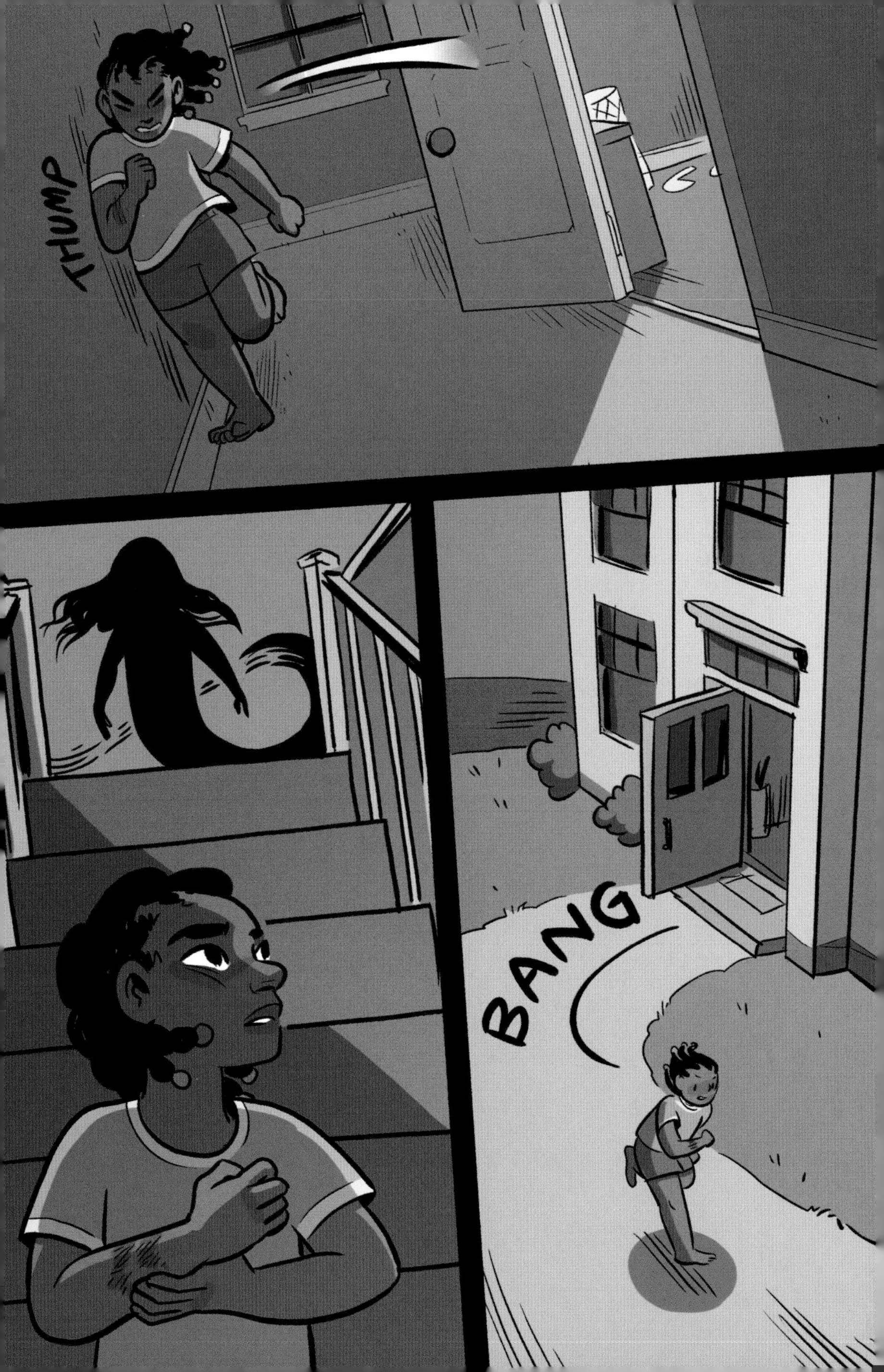
THUMP
BANG

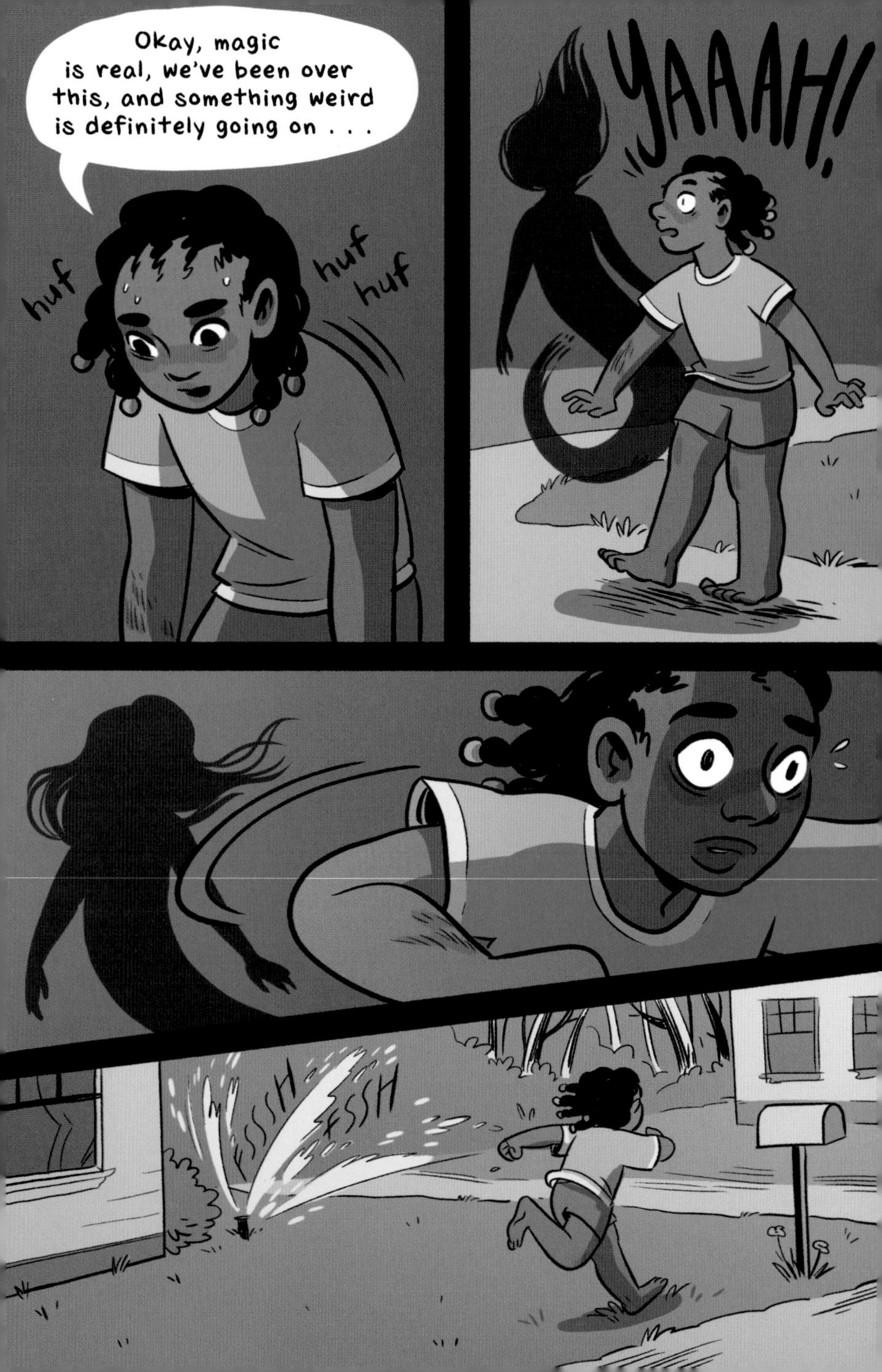
Okay, magic is real, we've been over this, and something weird is definitely going on . . .
huf
huf
huf
YAAAH!
FSSSH
FSSH

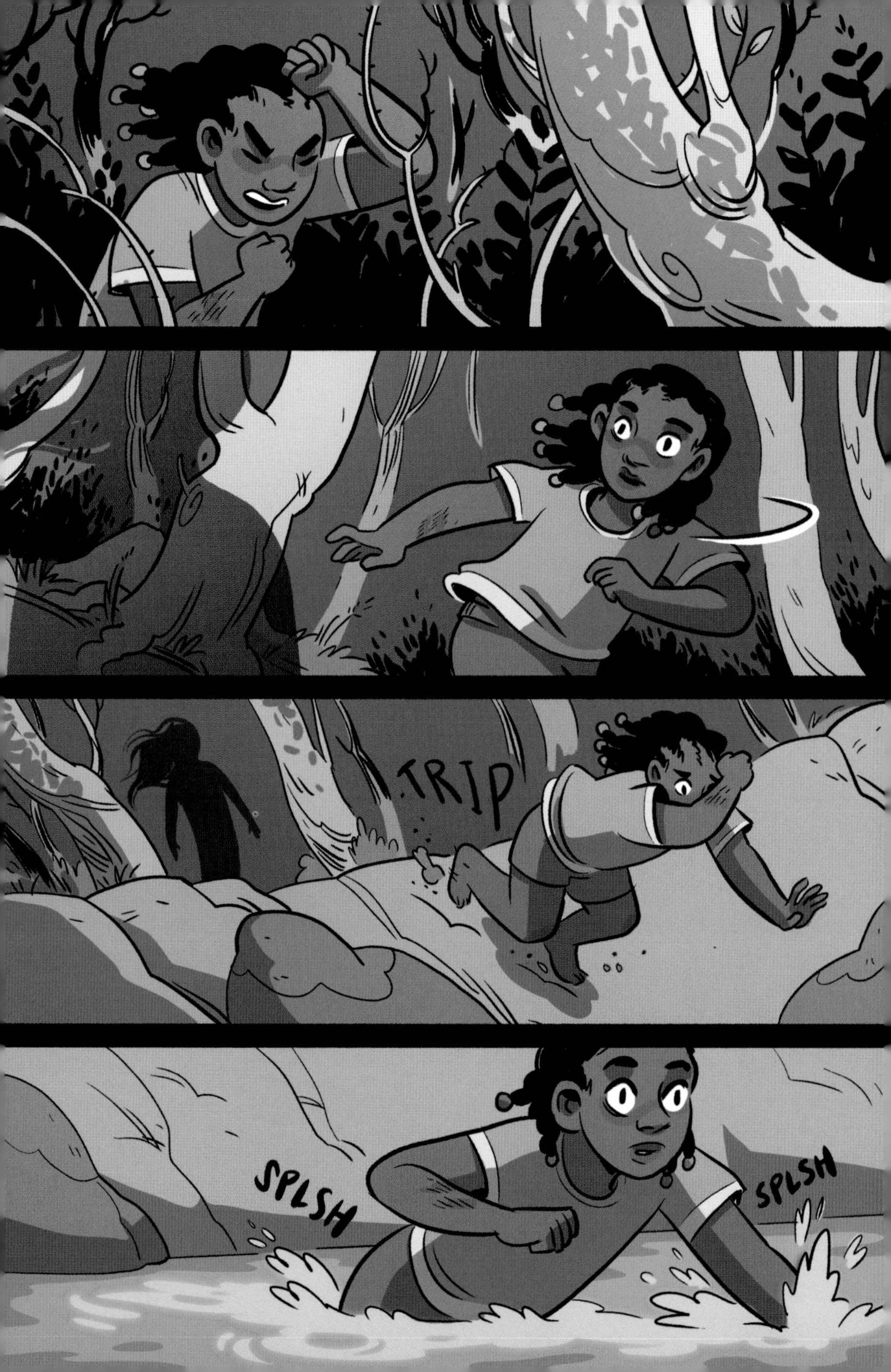
TRIP
SPLSH
SPLSH

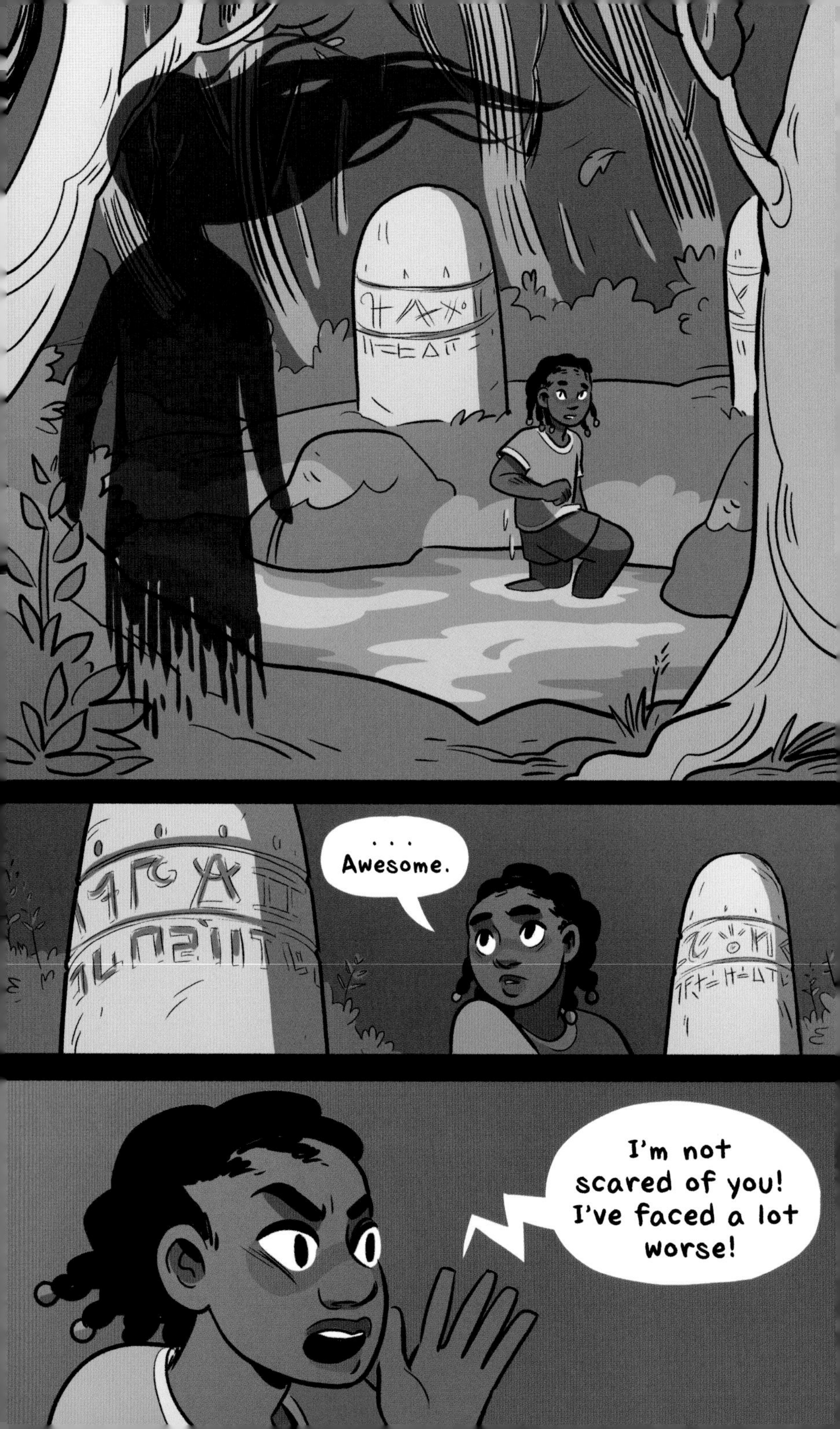
. . .
Awesome.
I'm not scared of you! I've faced a lot worse!

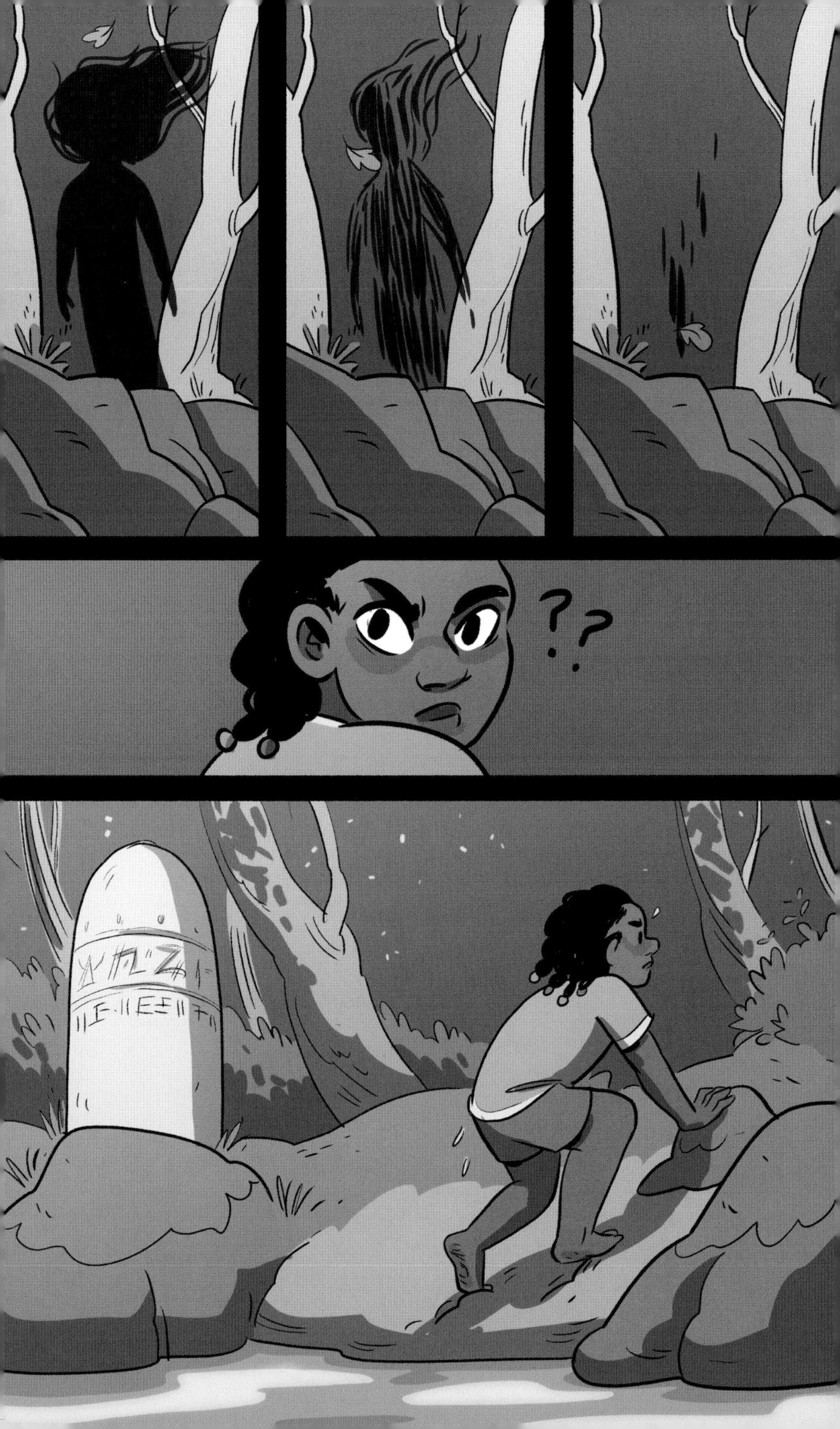
??

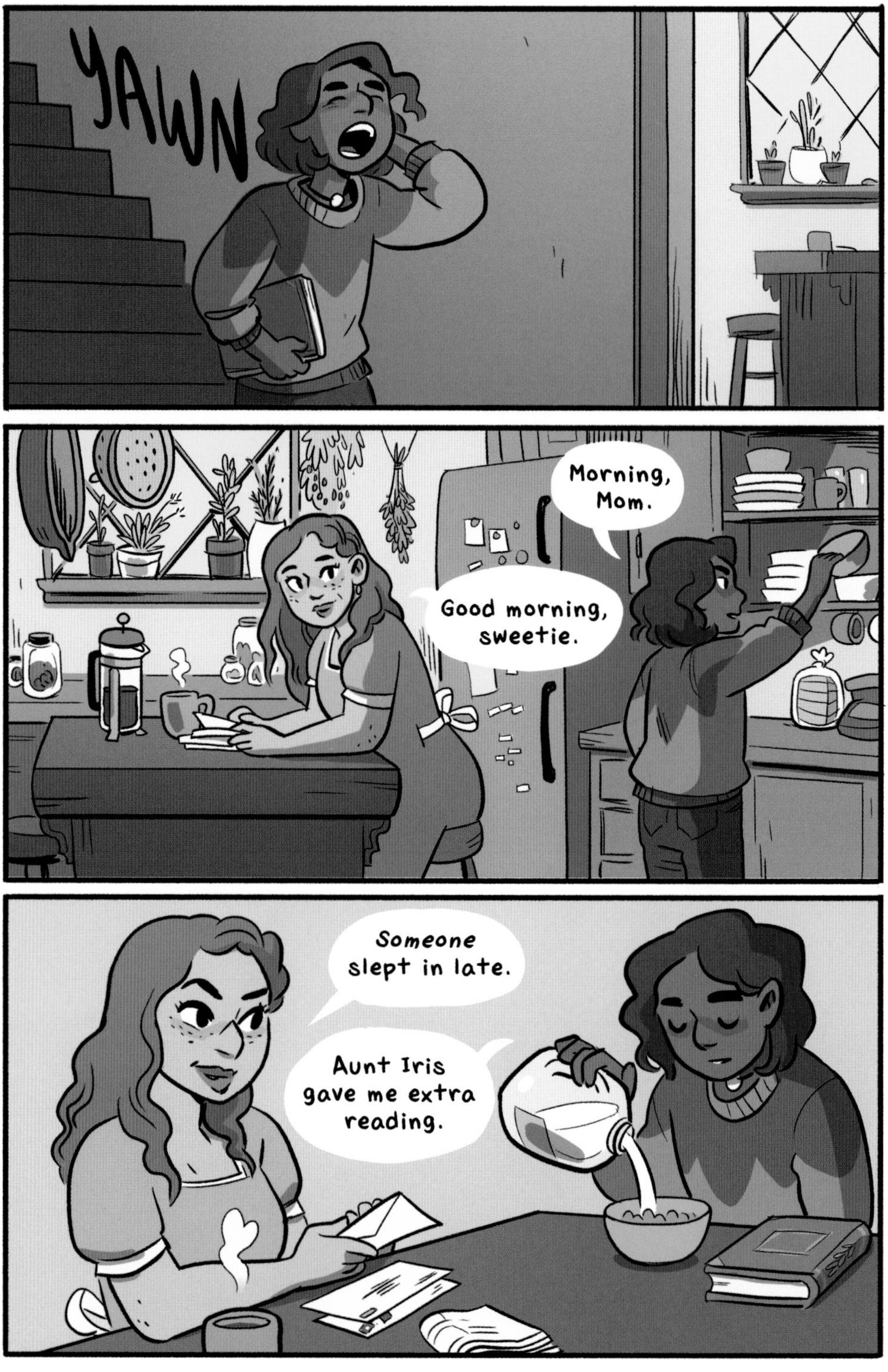
YAWN
Morning, Mom.
Good morning, sweetie.
Someone slept in late.
Aunt Iris gave me extra reading.

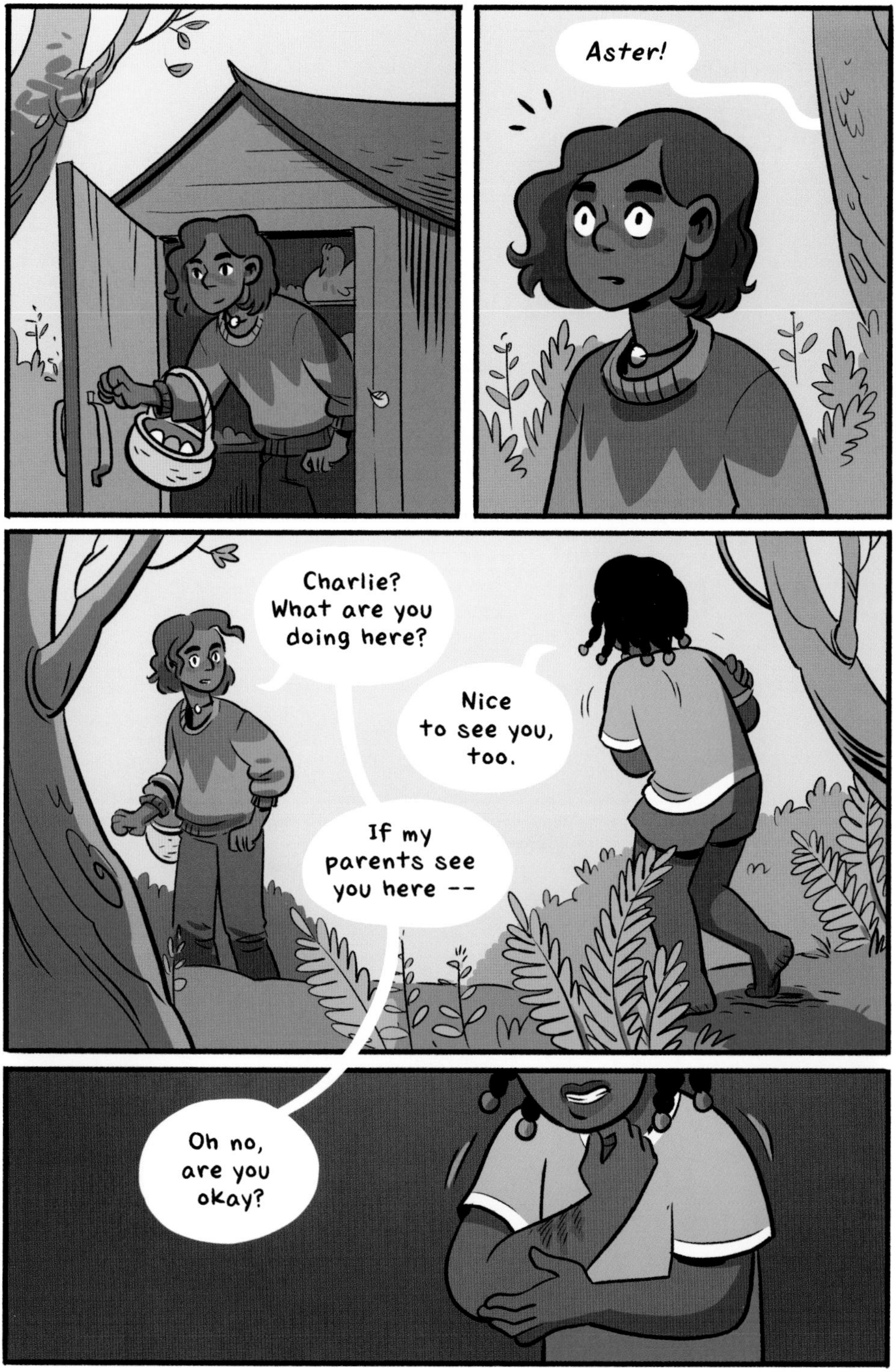
Aster!
Charlie? What are you doing here?
Nice to see you, too.
If my parents see you here --
Oh no, are you okay?

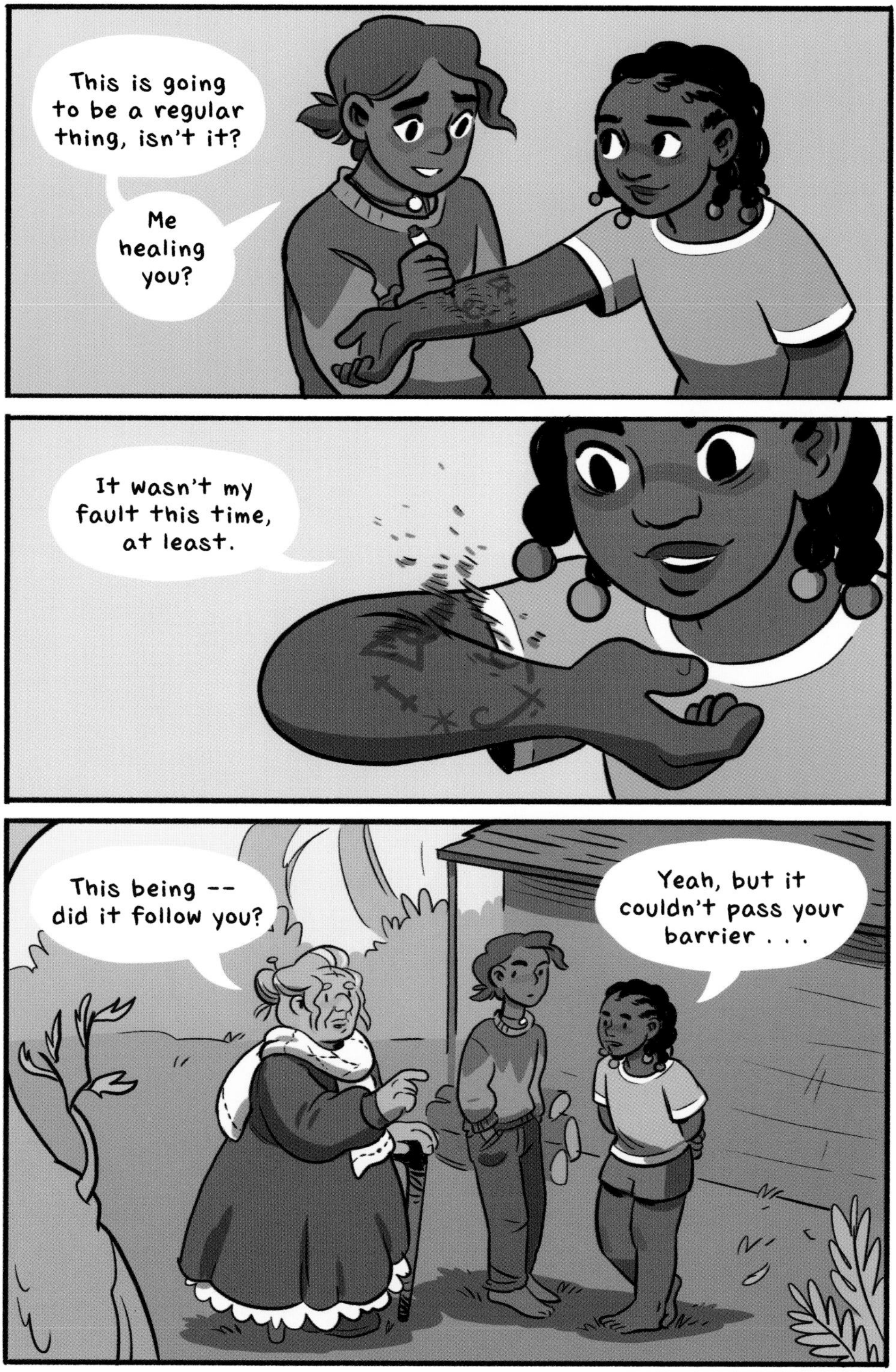
This is going to be a regular thing, isn't it?
Me healing you?
It wasn't my fault this time, at least.
This being -- did it follow you?
Yeah, but it couldn't pass your barrier . . .

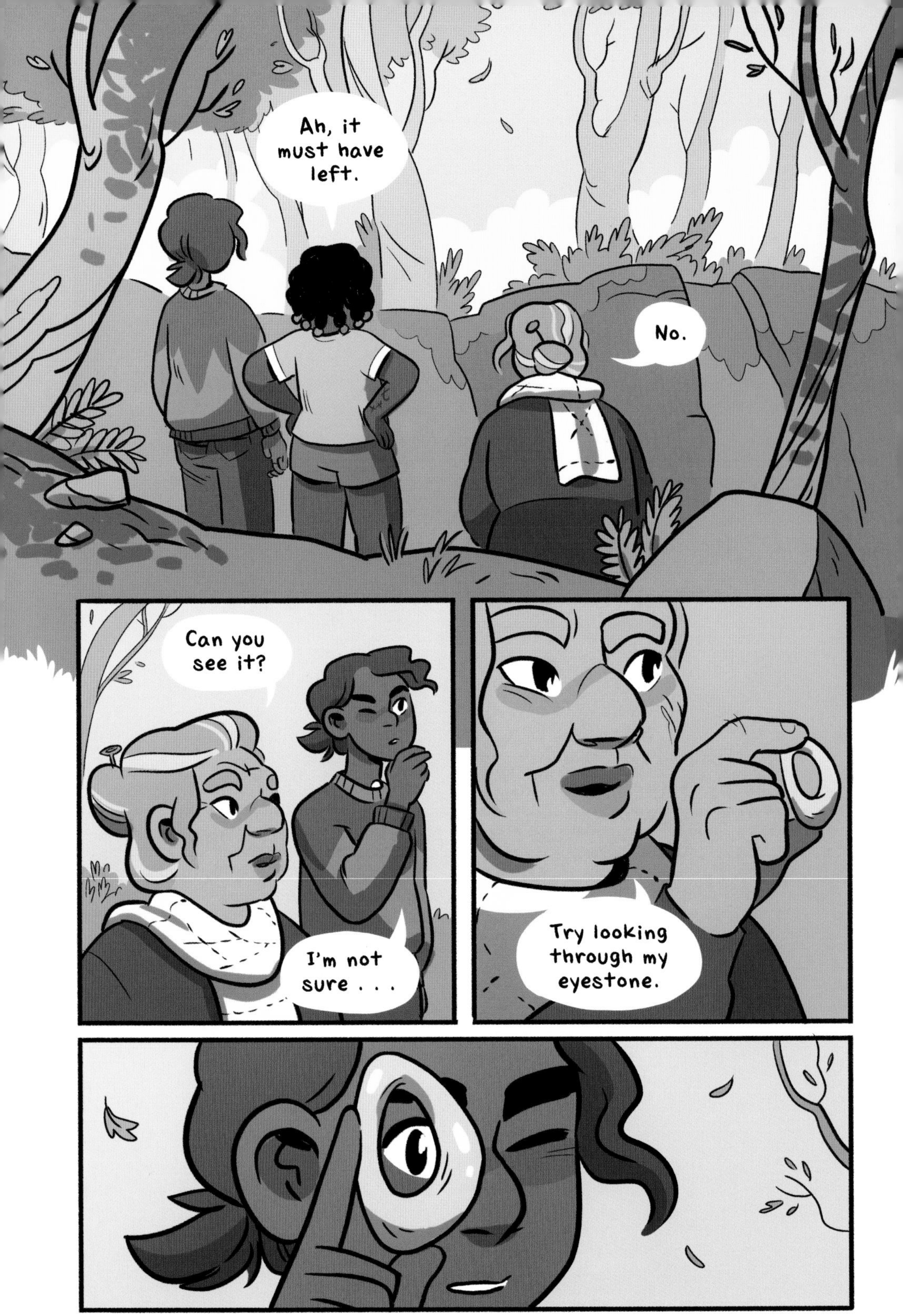
Ah, it must have left.
No.
Can you see it?
I'm not sure . . .
Try looking through my eyestone.

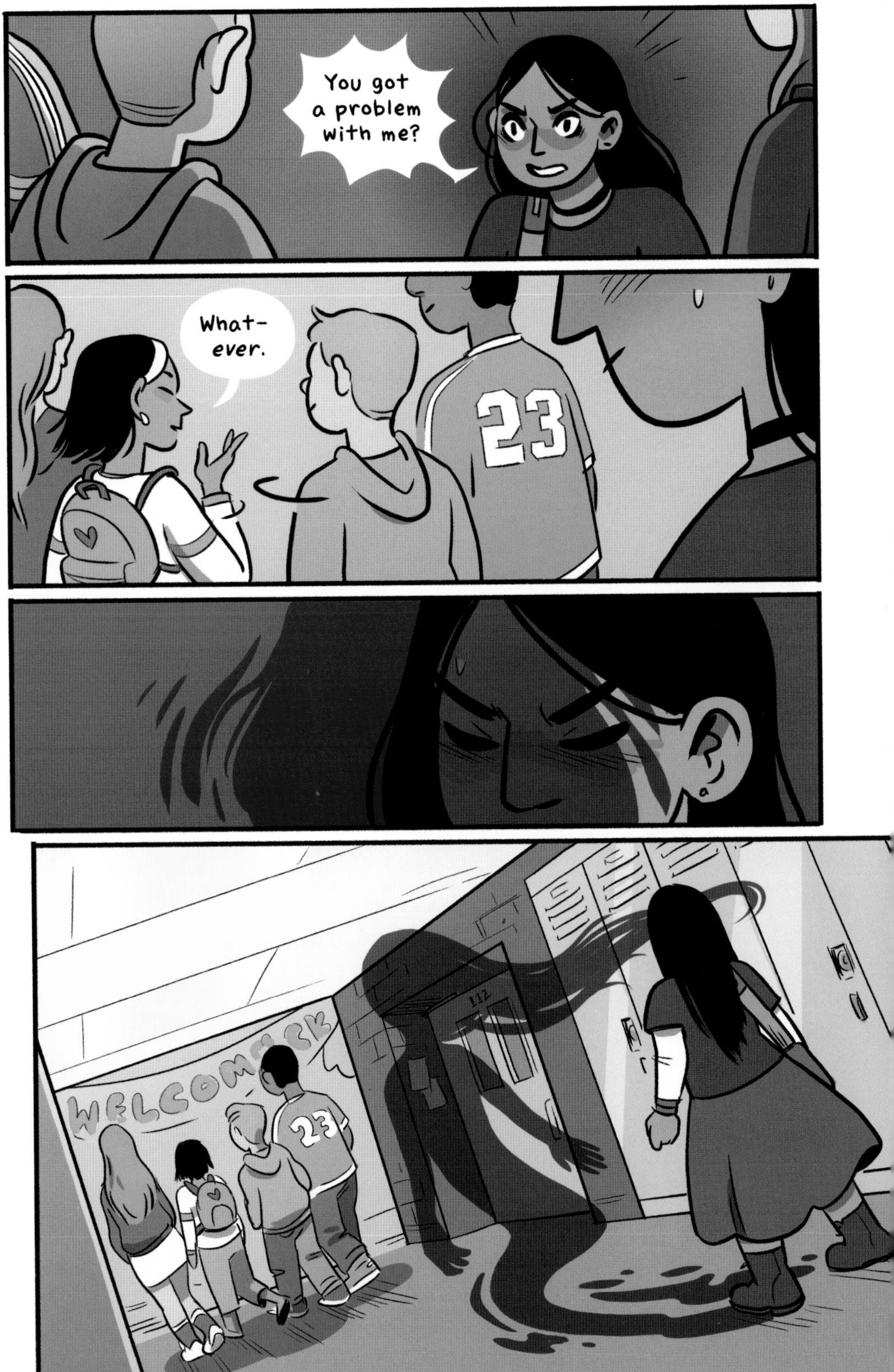
You got a problem with me?
What-ever.
23
23

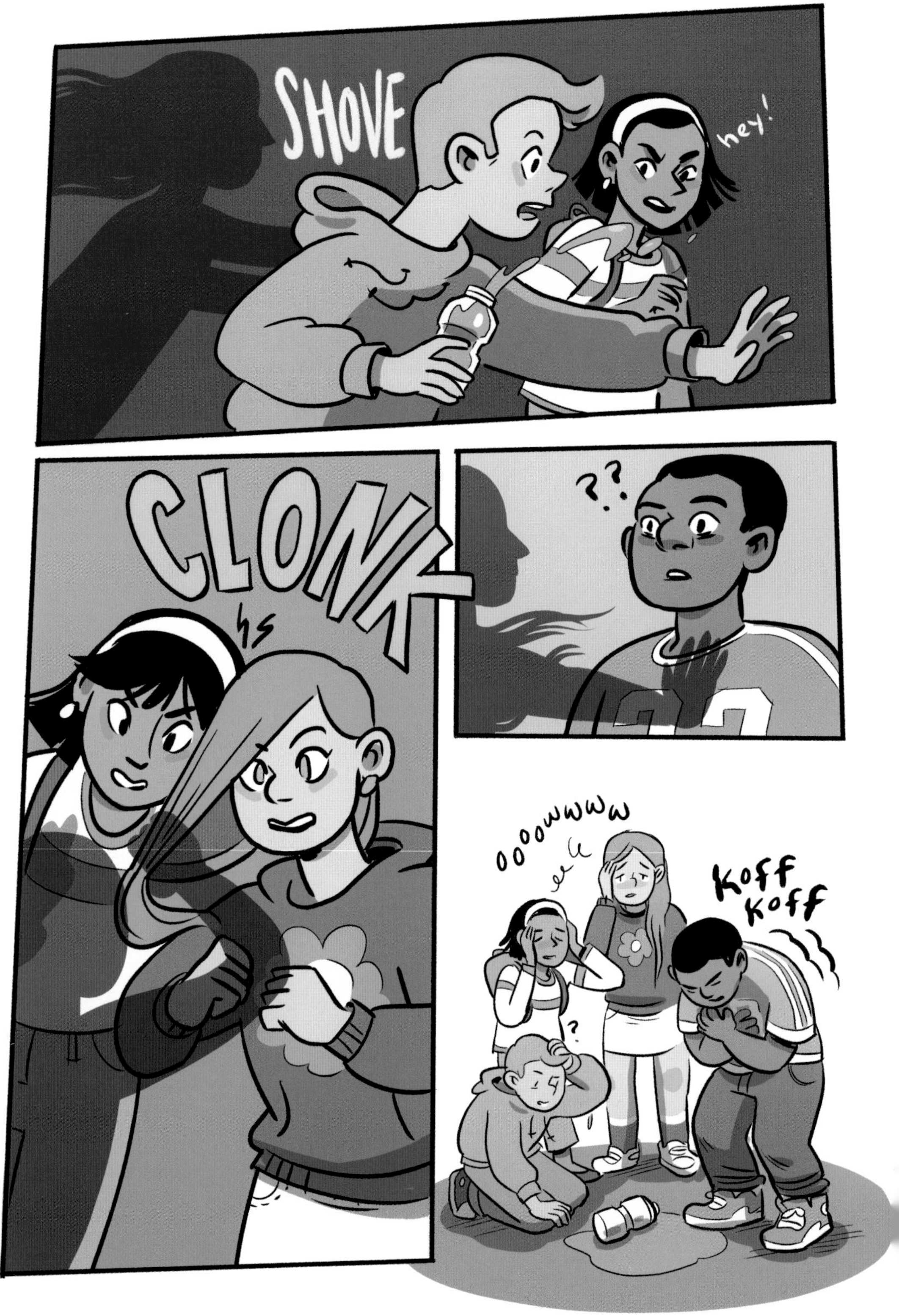
SHOVE
hey!
CLONK
??
oooowwww
KOFF
KOFF
?

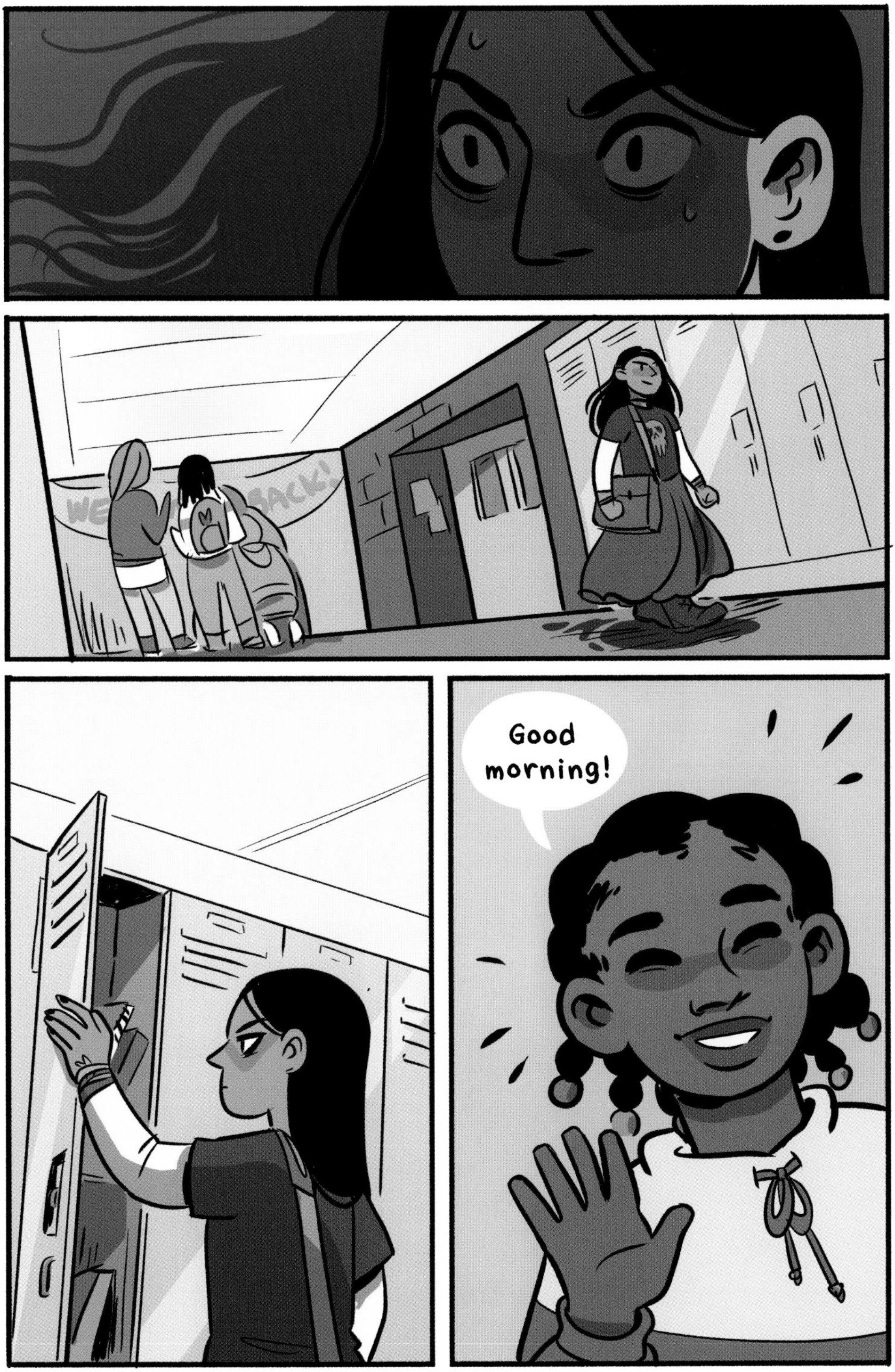
Good morning!

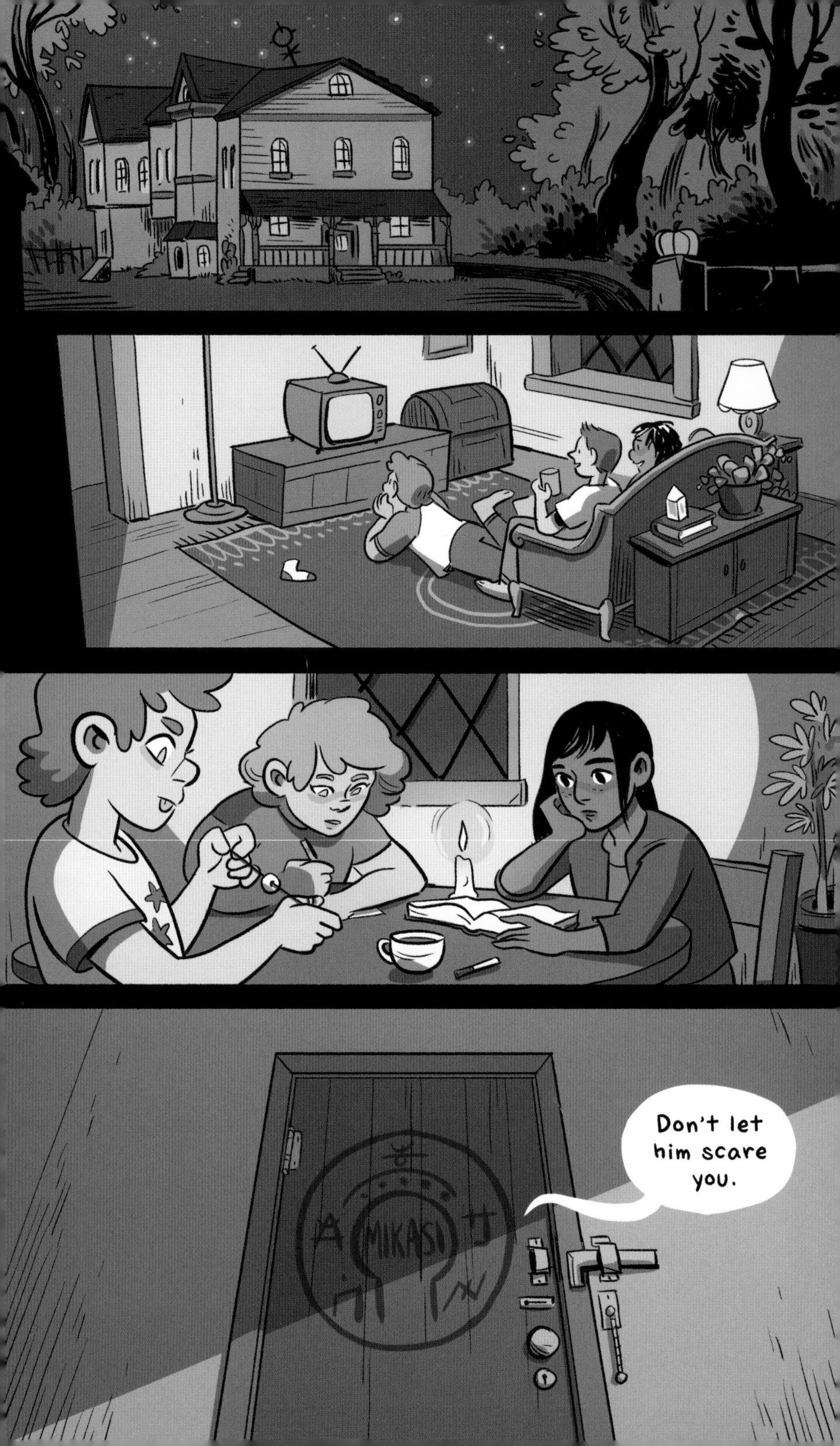
MIKASI
Don't let him scare you.

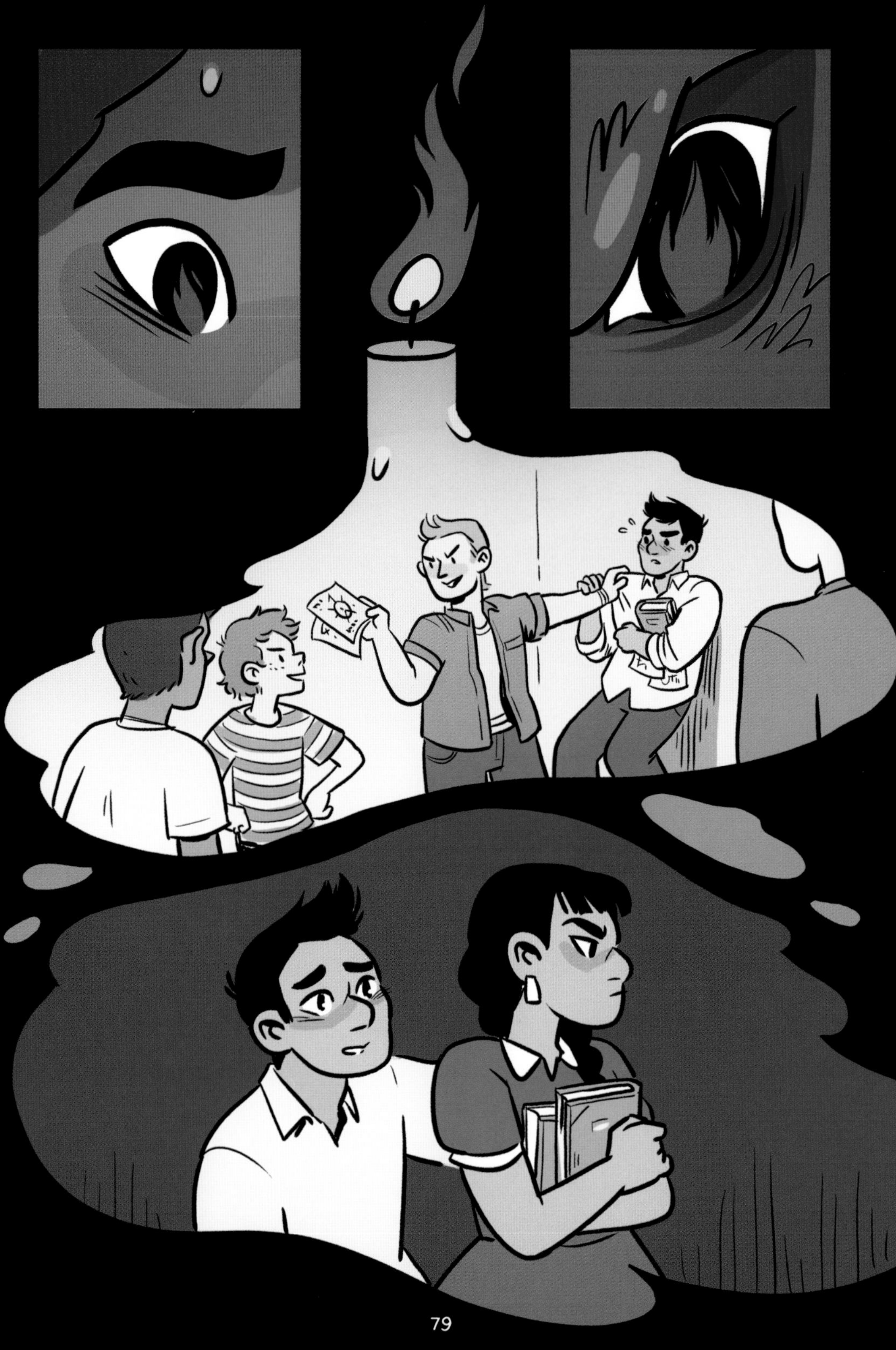

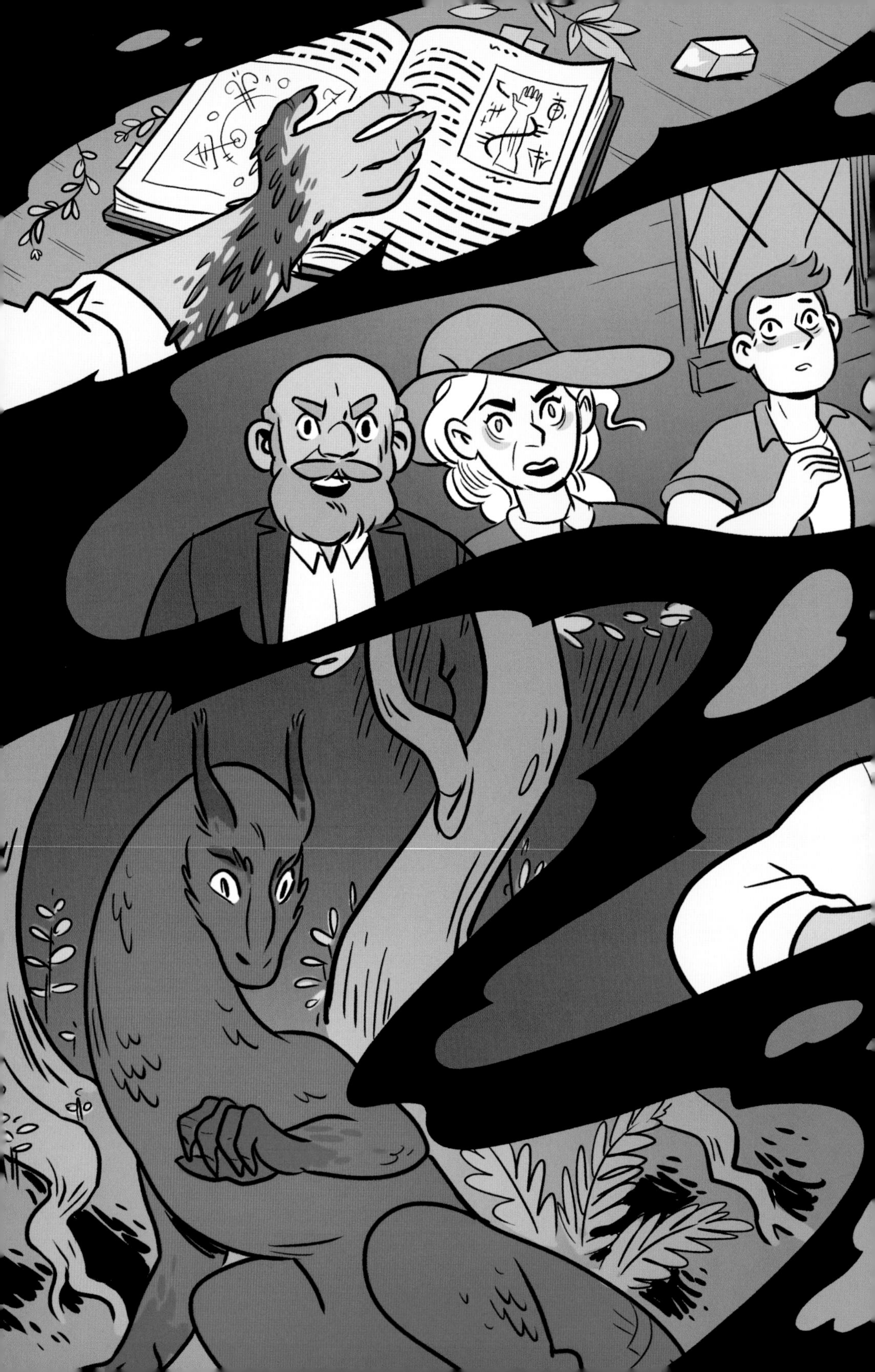

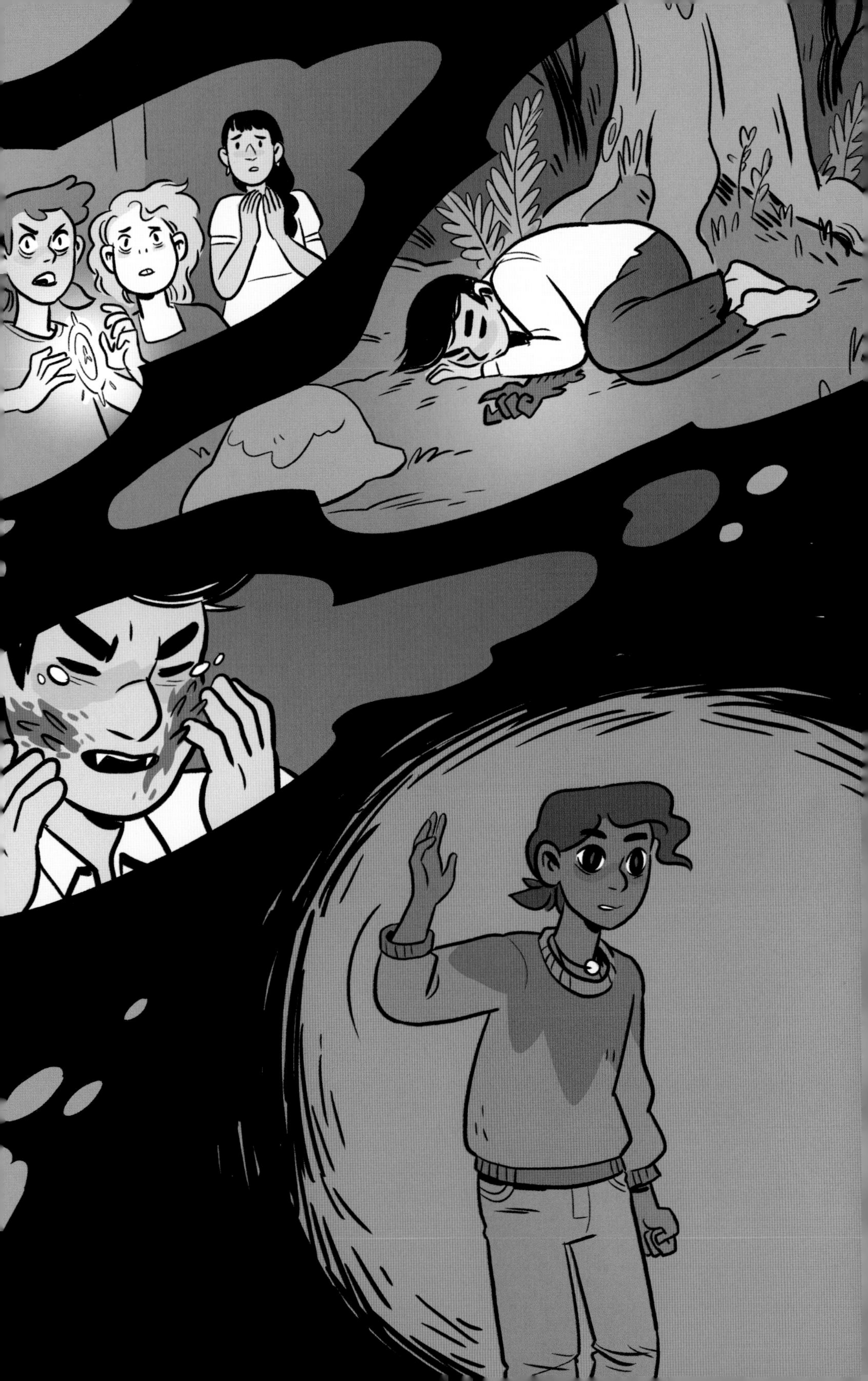

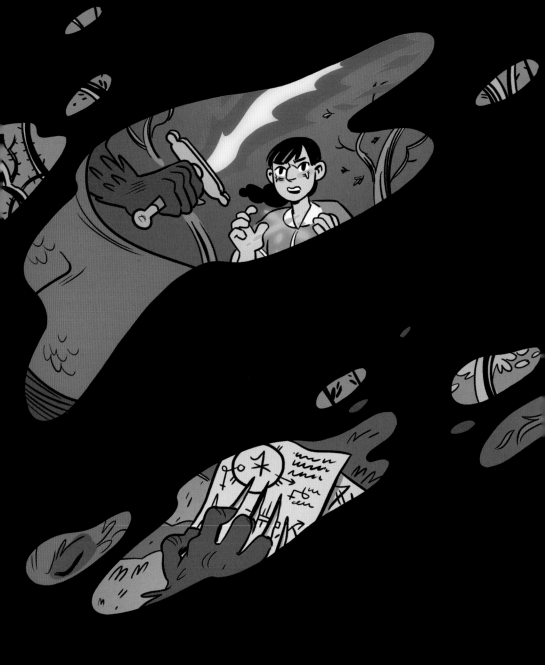

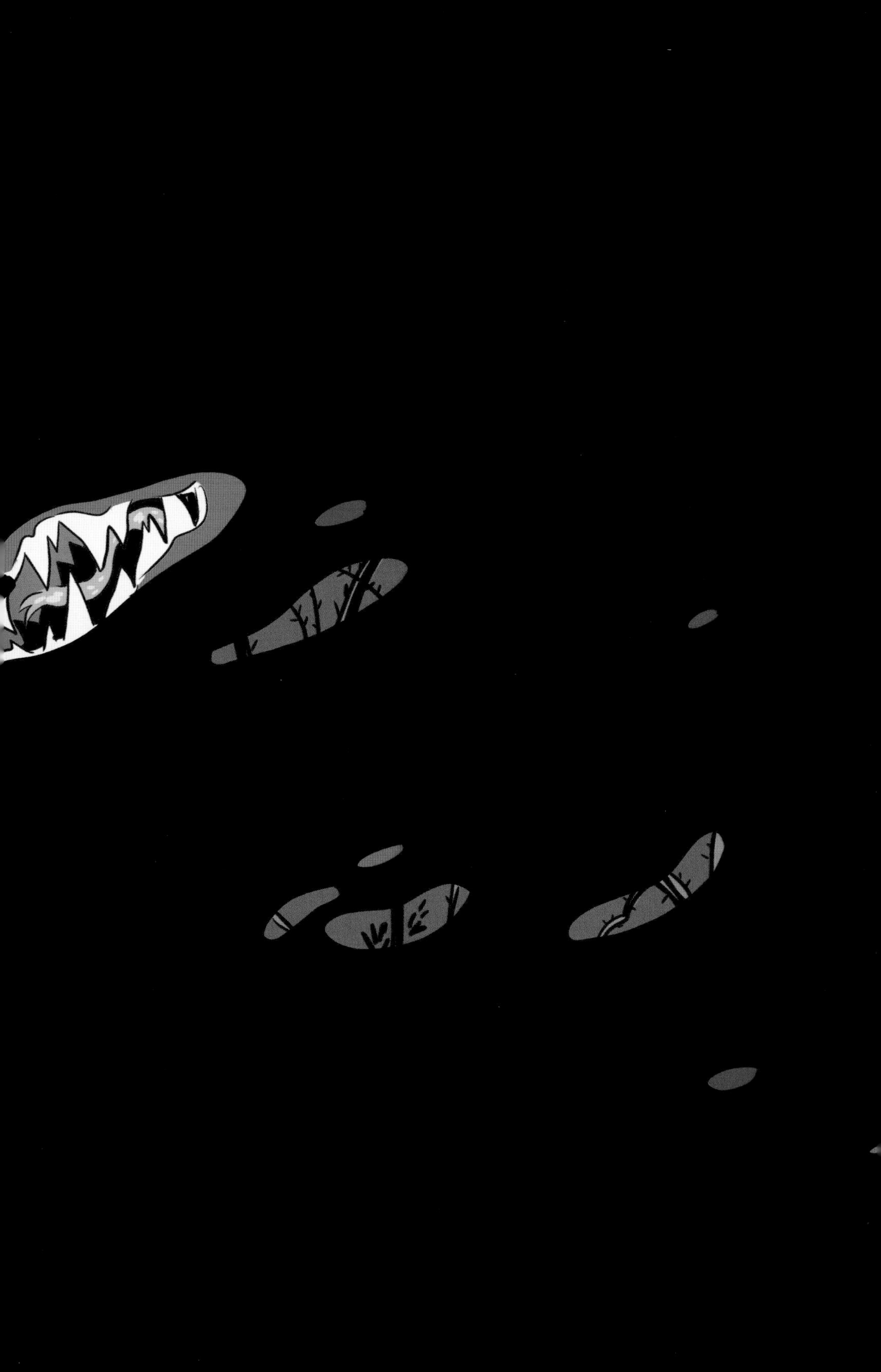

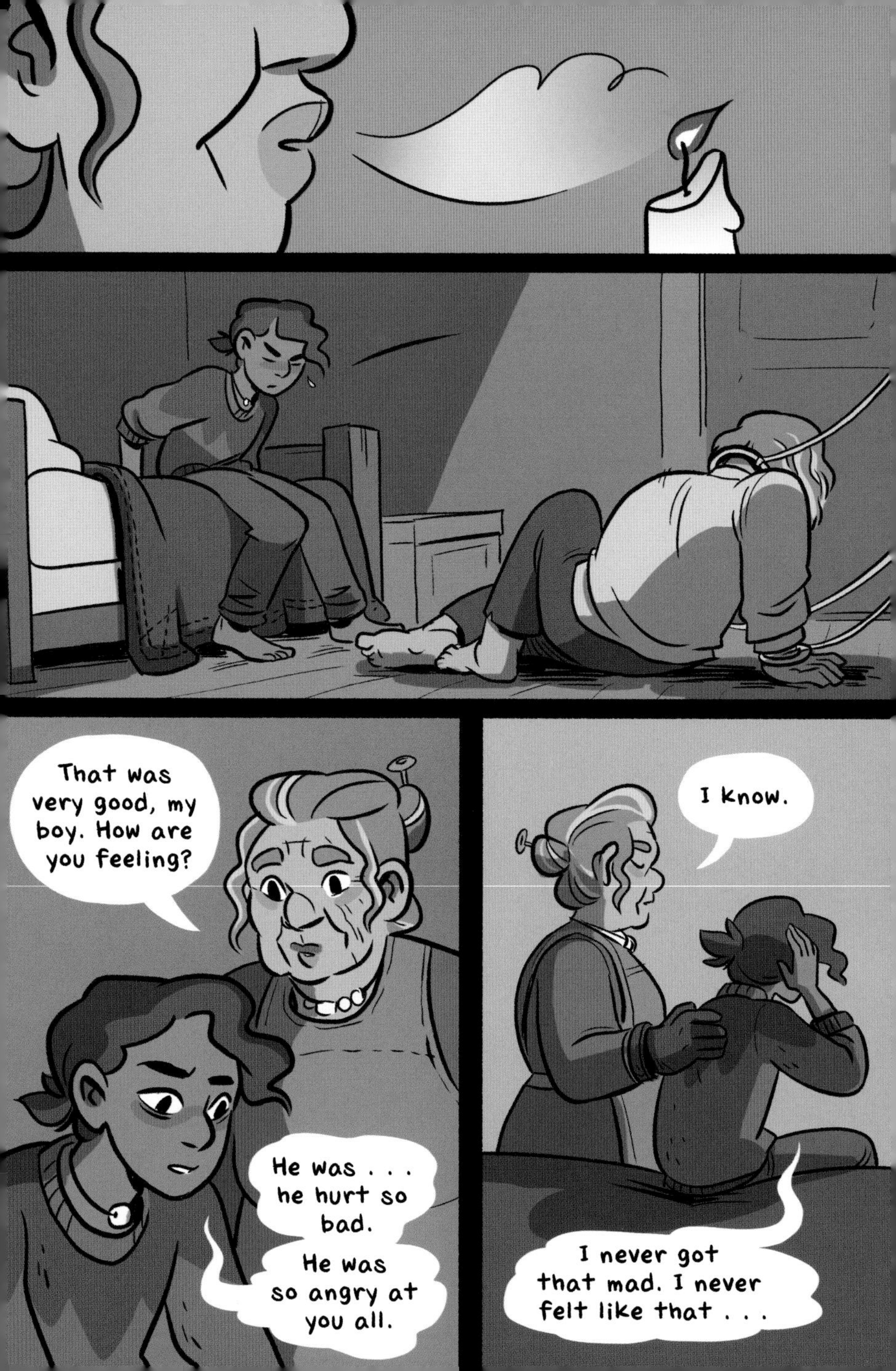
That was very good, my boy. How are you feeling?
He was . . . he hurt so bad.
He was so angry at you all.
I know.
I never got that mad. I never felt like that . . .

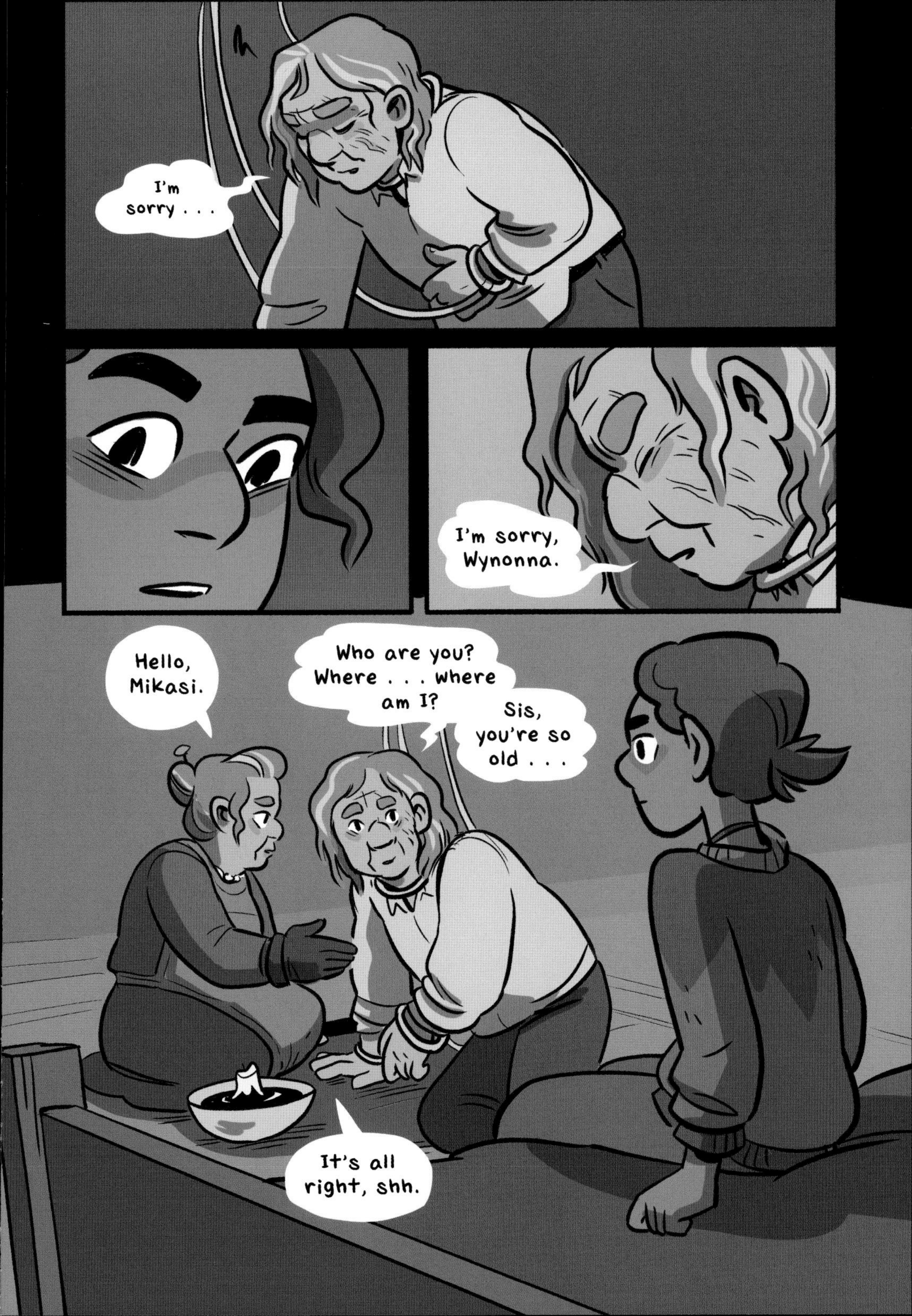
I'm sorry . . .
I'm sorry, Wynonna.
Hello, Mikasi.
Who are you? Where . . . where am I?
Sis, you're so old . . .
It's all right, shh.

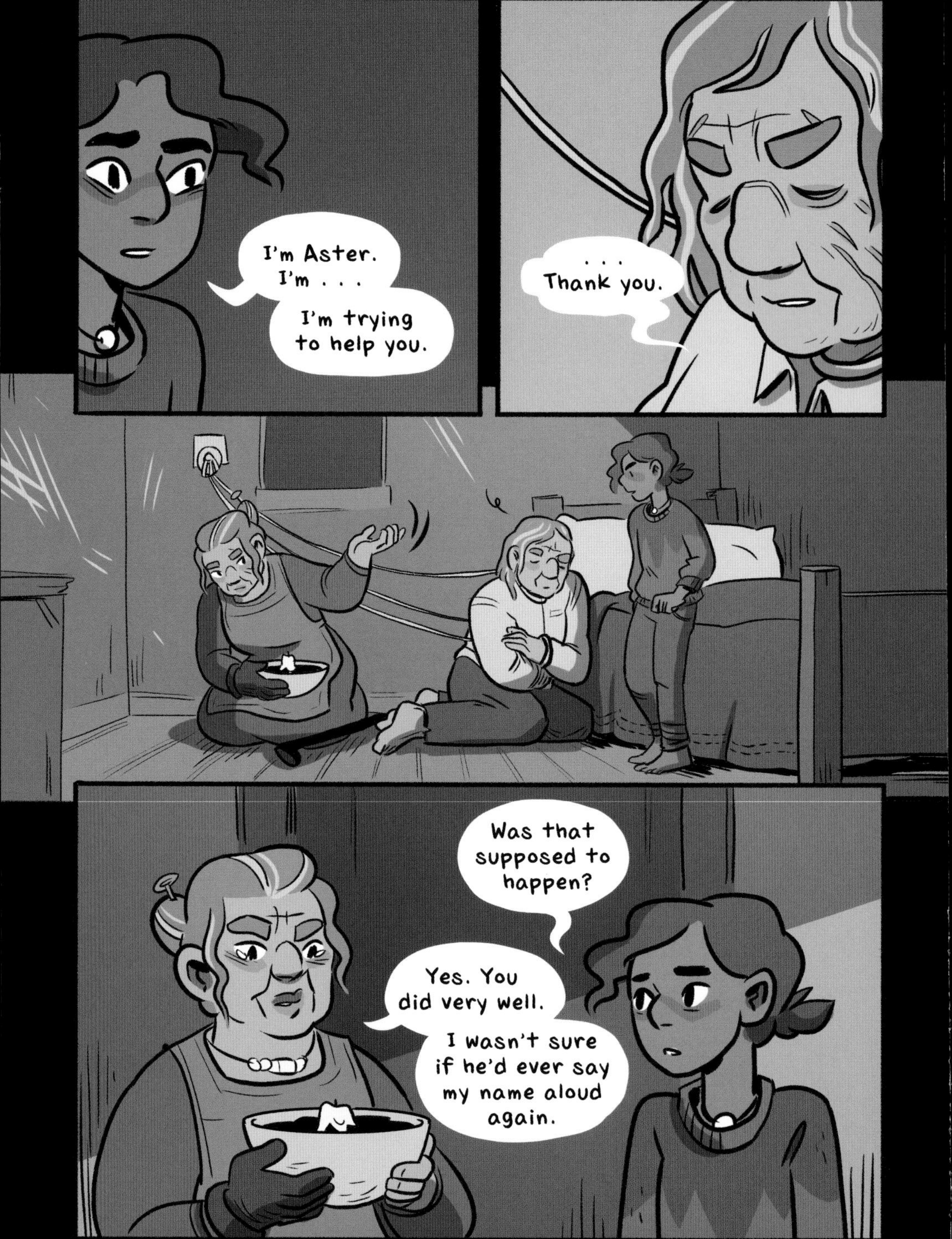
I'm Aster. I'm . . .
I'm trying to help you.
. . . Thank you.
Was that supposed to happen?
Yes. You did very well.
I wasn't sure if he'd ever say my name aloud again.

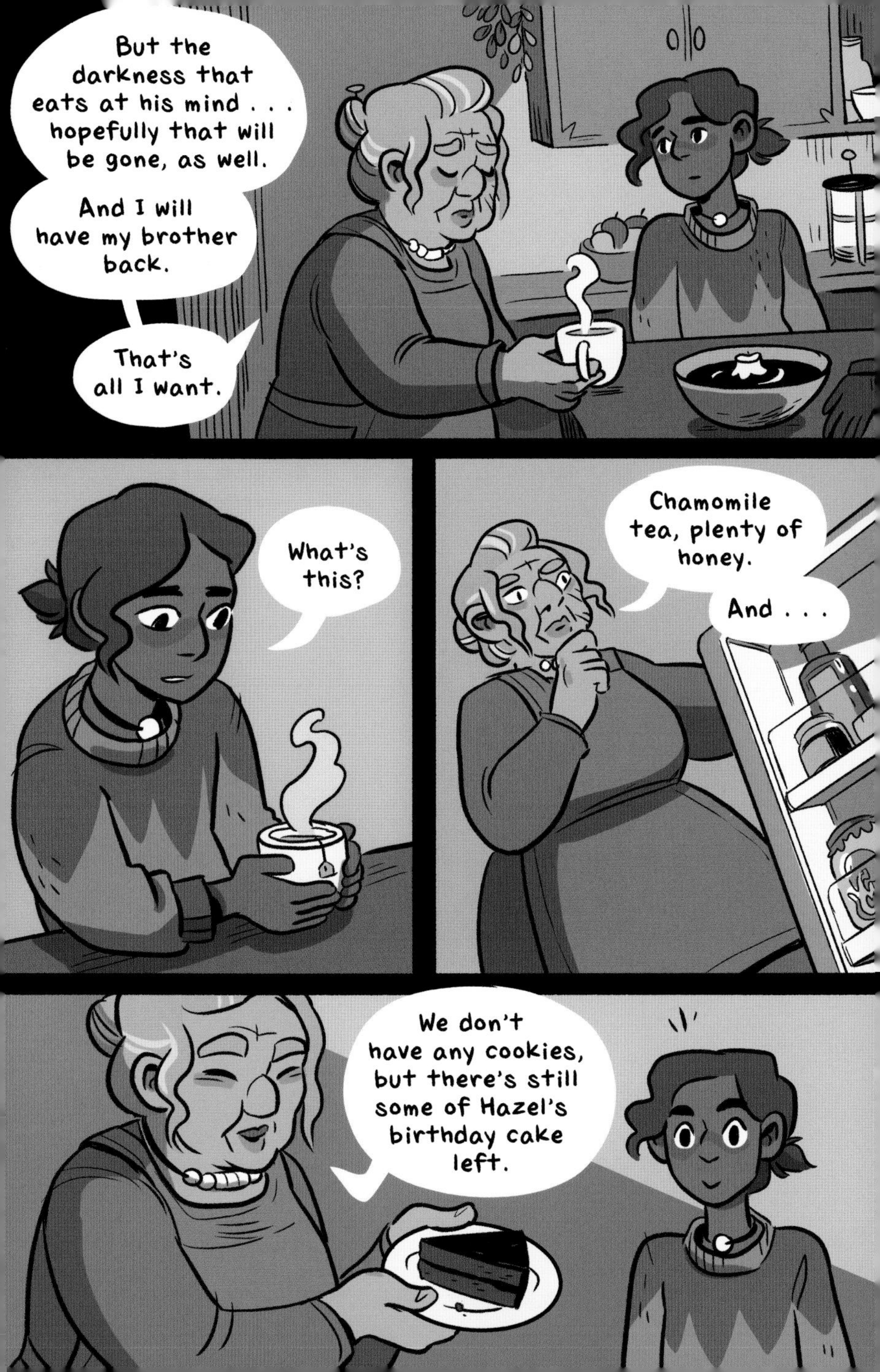
But the darkness that eats at his mind . . . hopefully that will be gone, as well.
And I will have my brother back.
That's all I want.
What's this?
Chamomile tea, plenty of honey.
And . . .
We don't have any cookies, but there's still some of Hazel's birthday cake left.

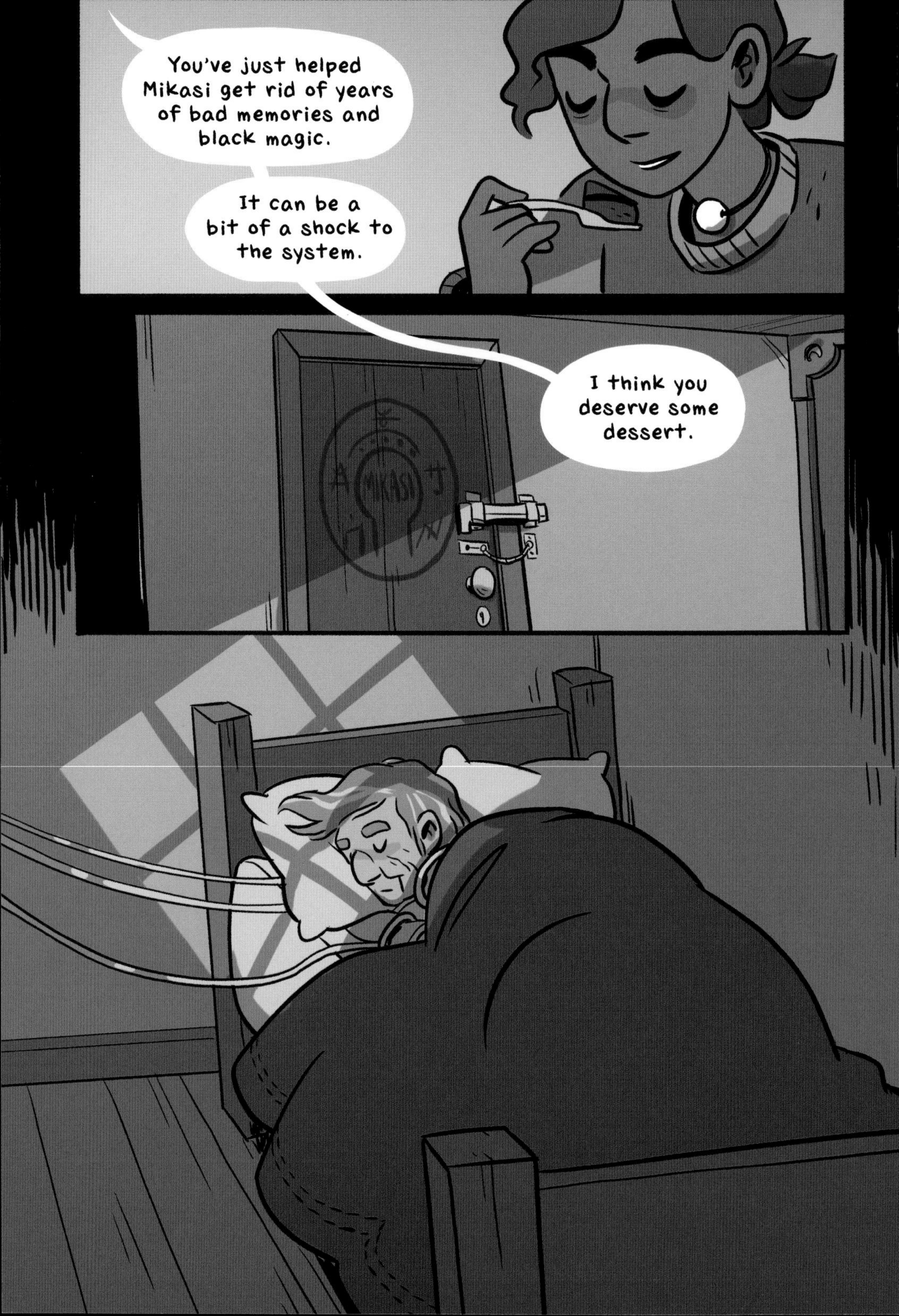
You've just helped Mikasi get rid of years of bad memories and black magic.
It can be a bit of a shock to the system.
I think you deserve some dessert.
MIKASI

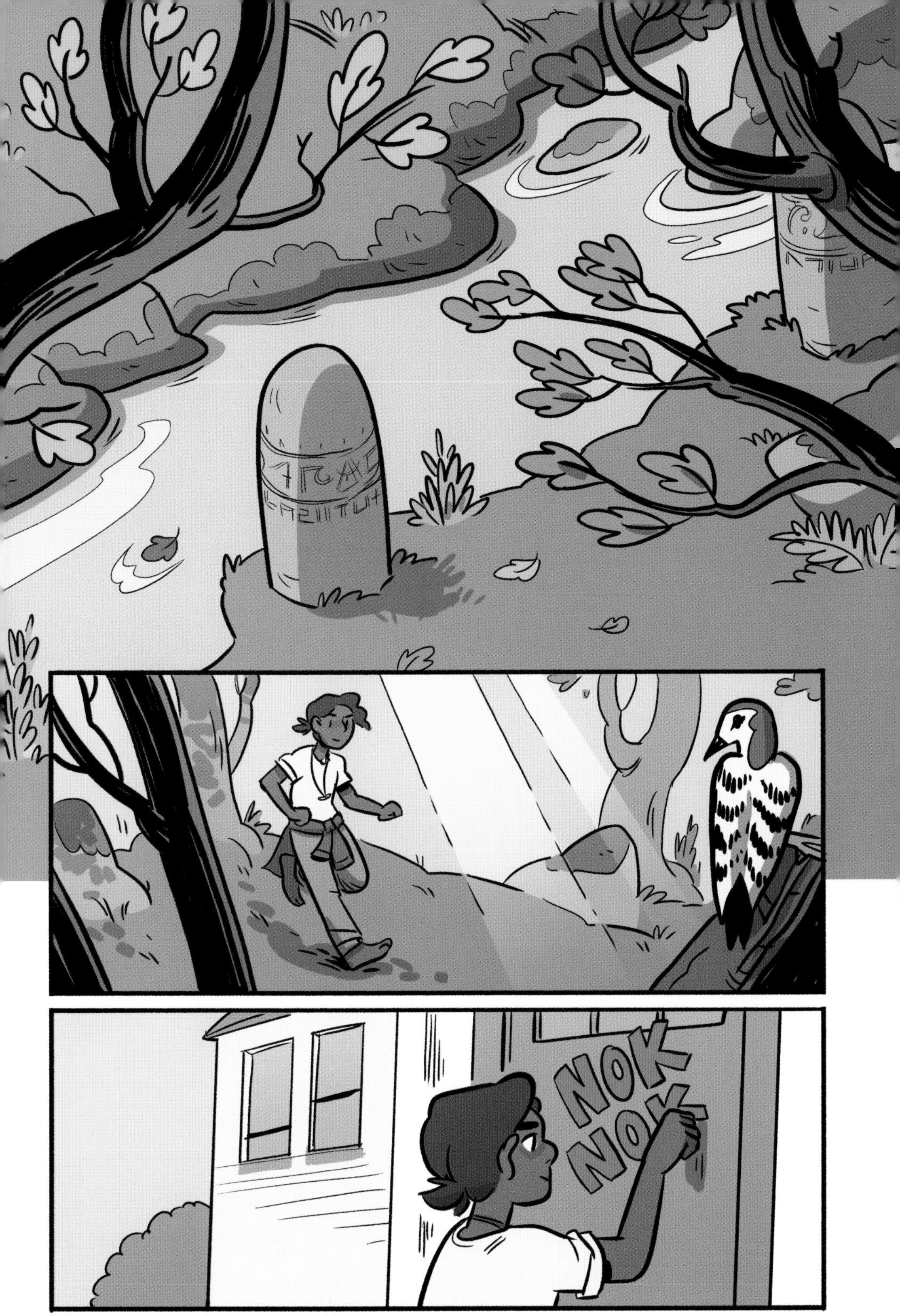
NOK NOK

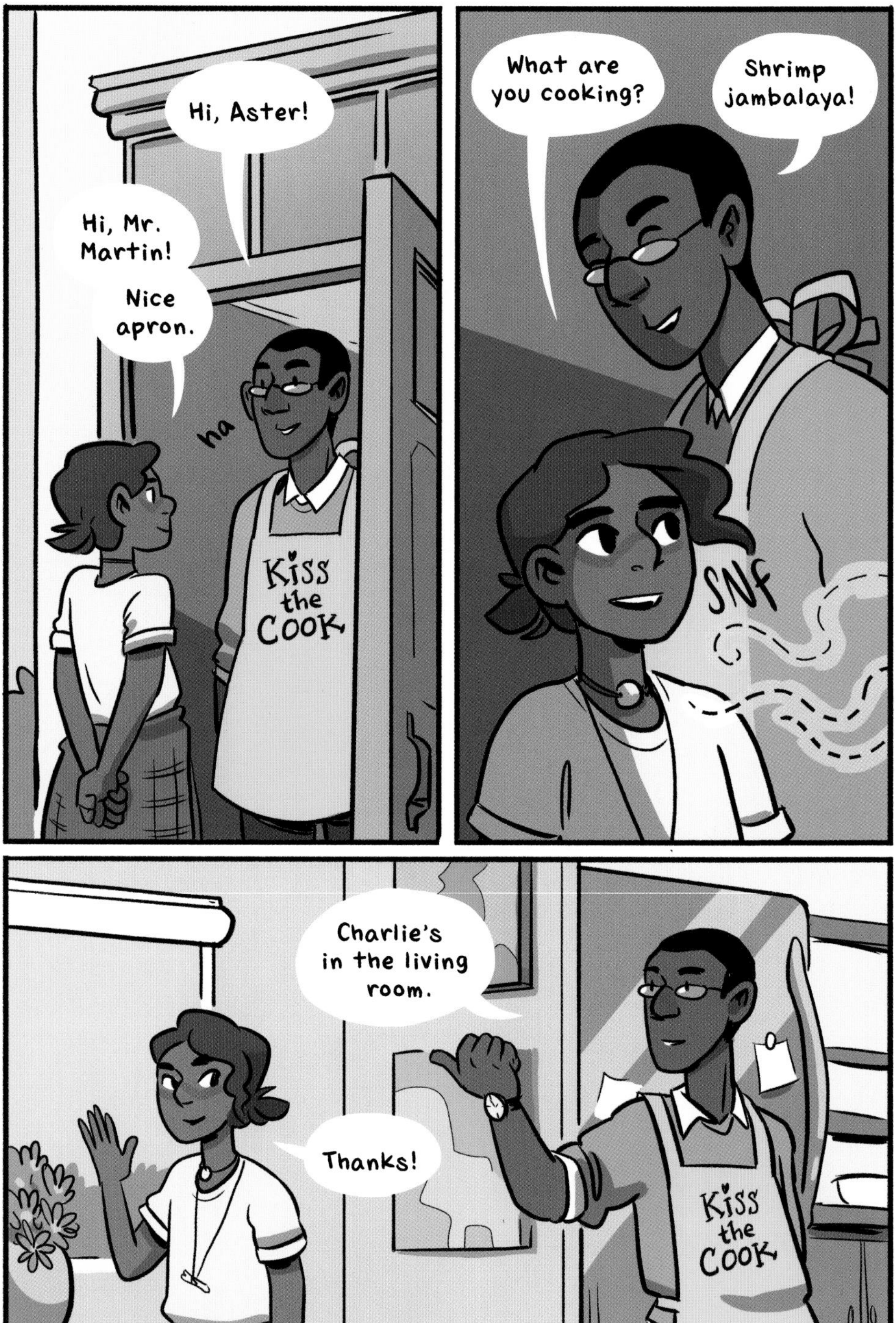
Hi, Aster!
Hi, Mr. Martin!
Nice apron.
ha
KISS the COOK
What are you cooking?
Shrimp jambalaya!
SNF
Charlie's in the living room.
Thanks!
KISS the COOK

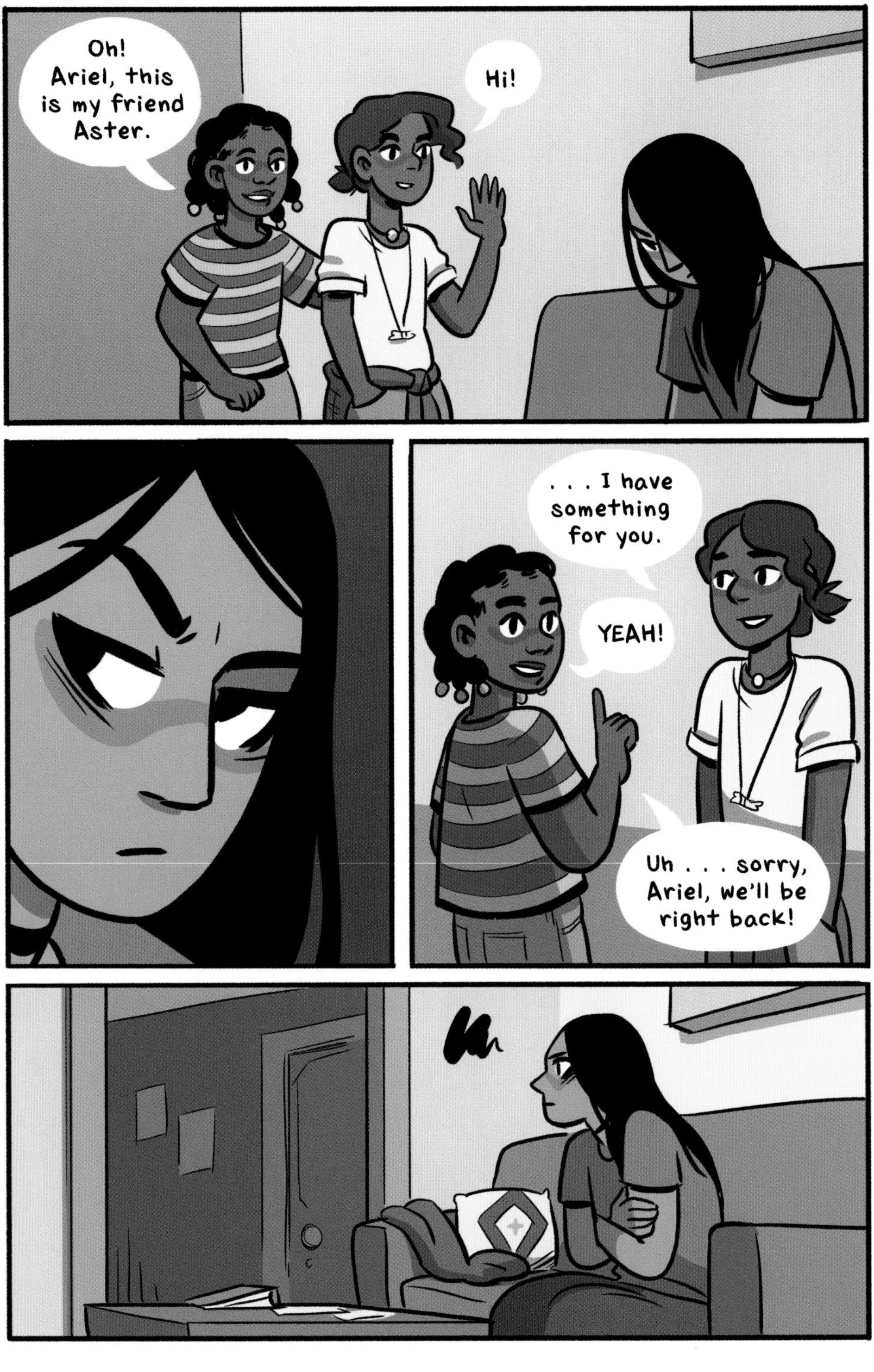
Oh! Ariel, this is my friend Aster.
Hi!
. . . I have something for you.
YEAH!
Uh . . . sorry, Ariel, we'll be right back!

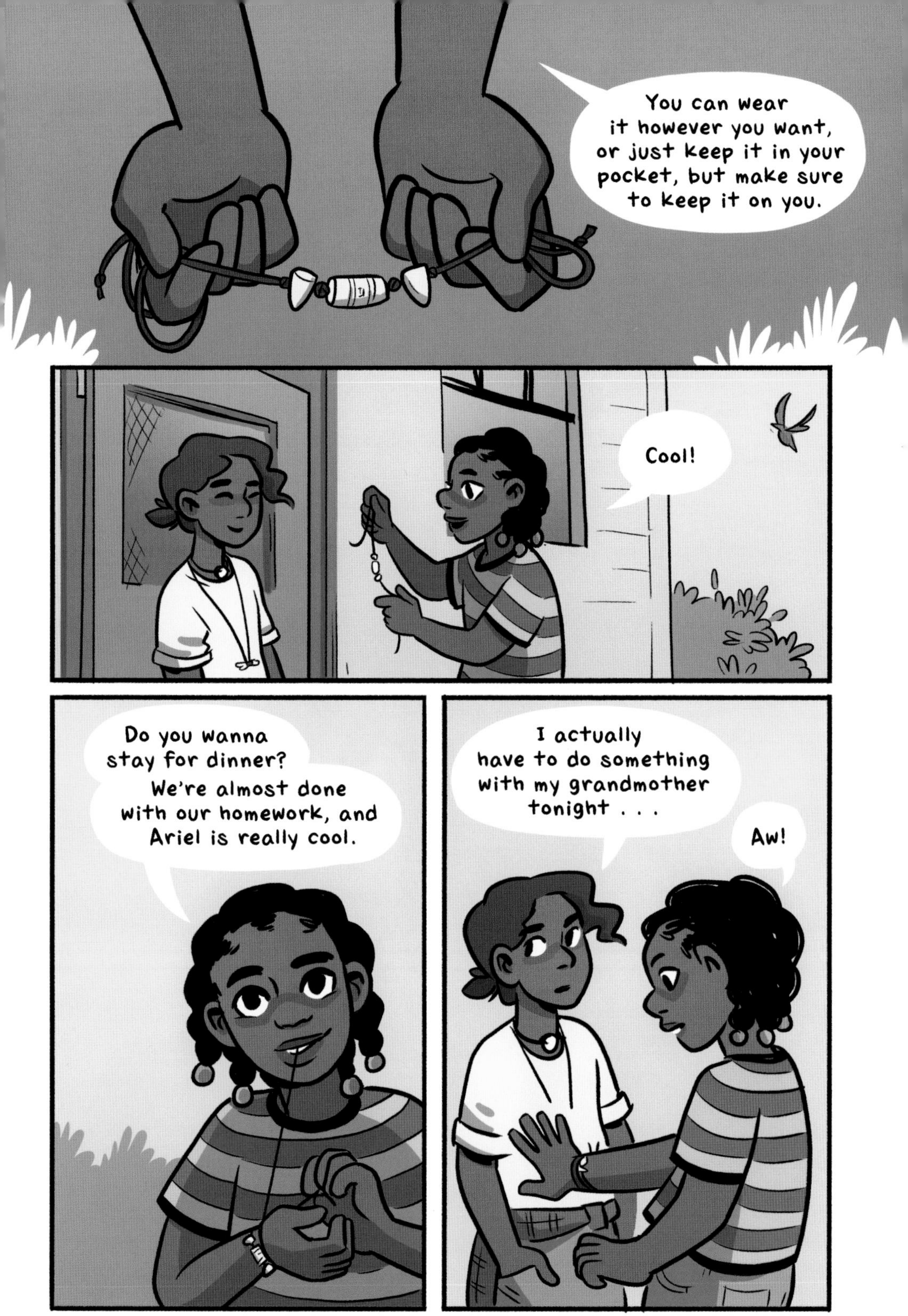
You can wear it however you want, or just keep it in your pocket, but make sure to keep it on you.
Cool!
Do you wanna stay for dinner?
We're almost done with our homework, and Ariel is really cool.
I actually have to do something with my grandmother tonight . . .
Aw!

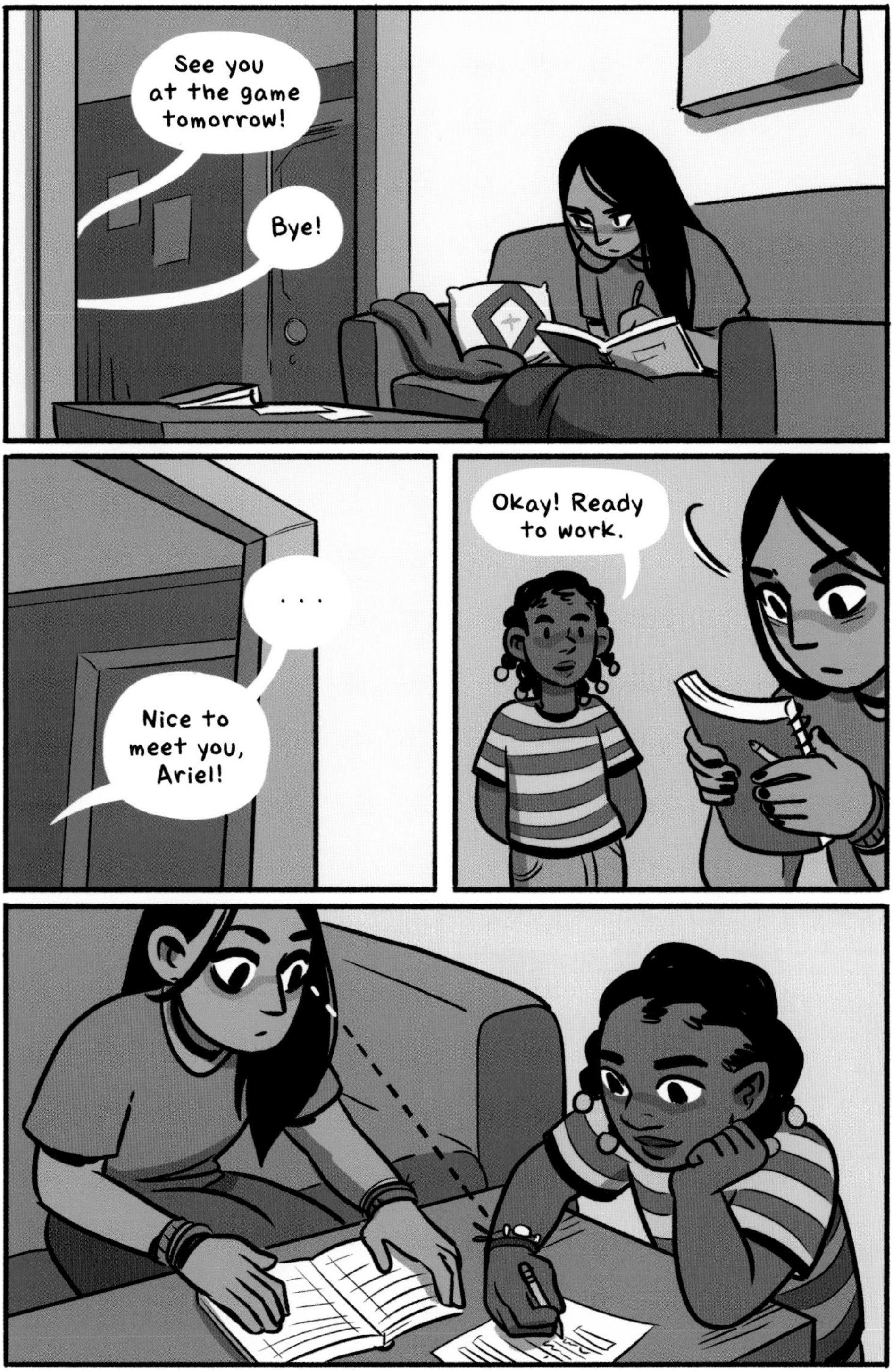
See you at the game tomorrow!
Bye!
. . .
Nice to meet you, Ariel!
Okay! Ready to work.

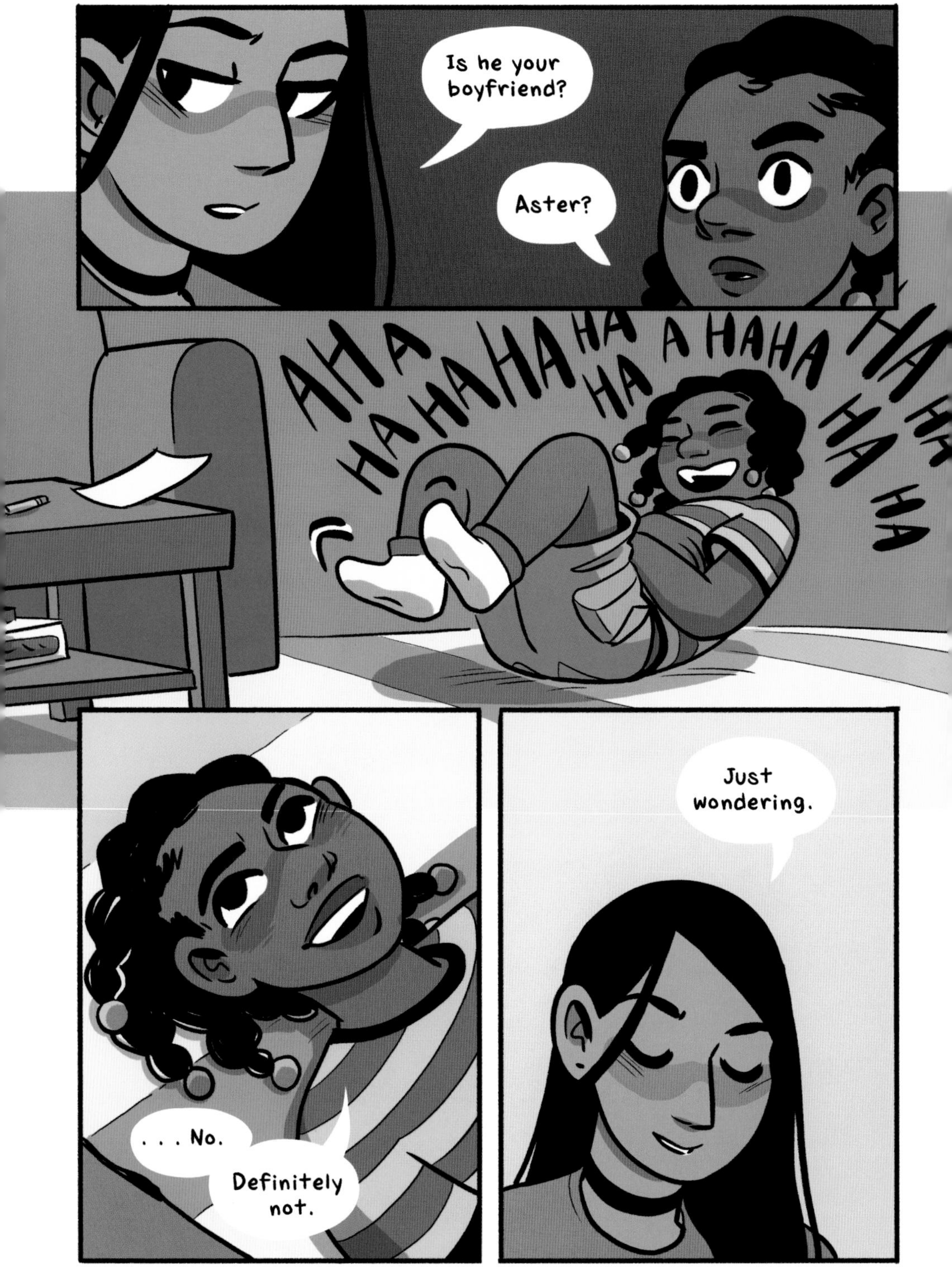
Is he your boyfriend?
Aster?
AHA HAHAHA HA HA A HAHA HA HA HA HA HA HA
Just wondering.
. . . No.
Definitely not.

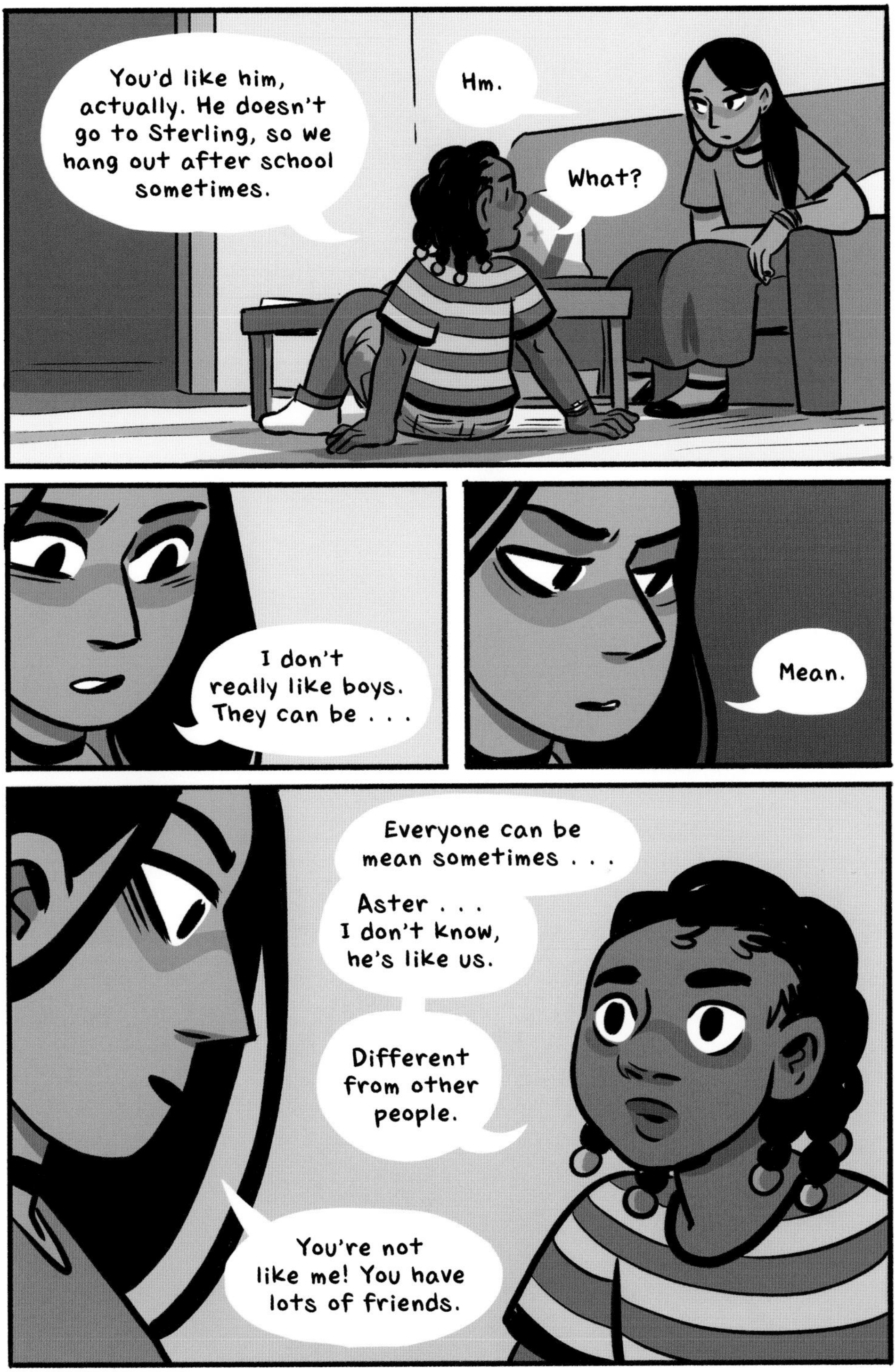
You'd like him, actually. He doesn't go to Sterling, so we hang out after school sometimes.
Hm.
What?
I don't really like boys. They can be . . .
Mean.
Everyone can be mean sometimes . . .
Aster . . . I don't know, he's like us.
Different from other people.
You're not like me! You have lots of friends.

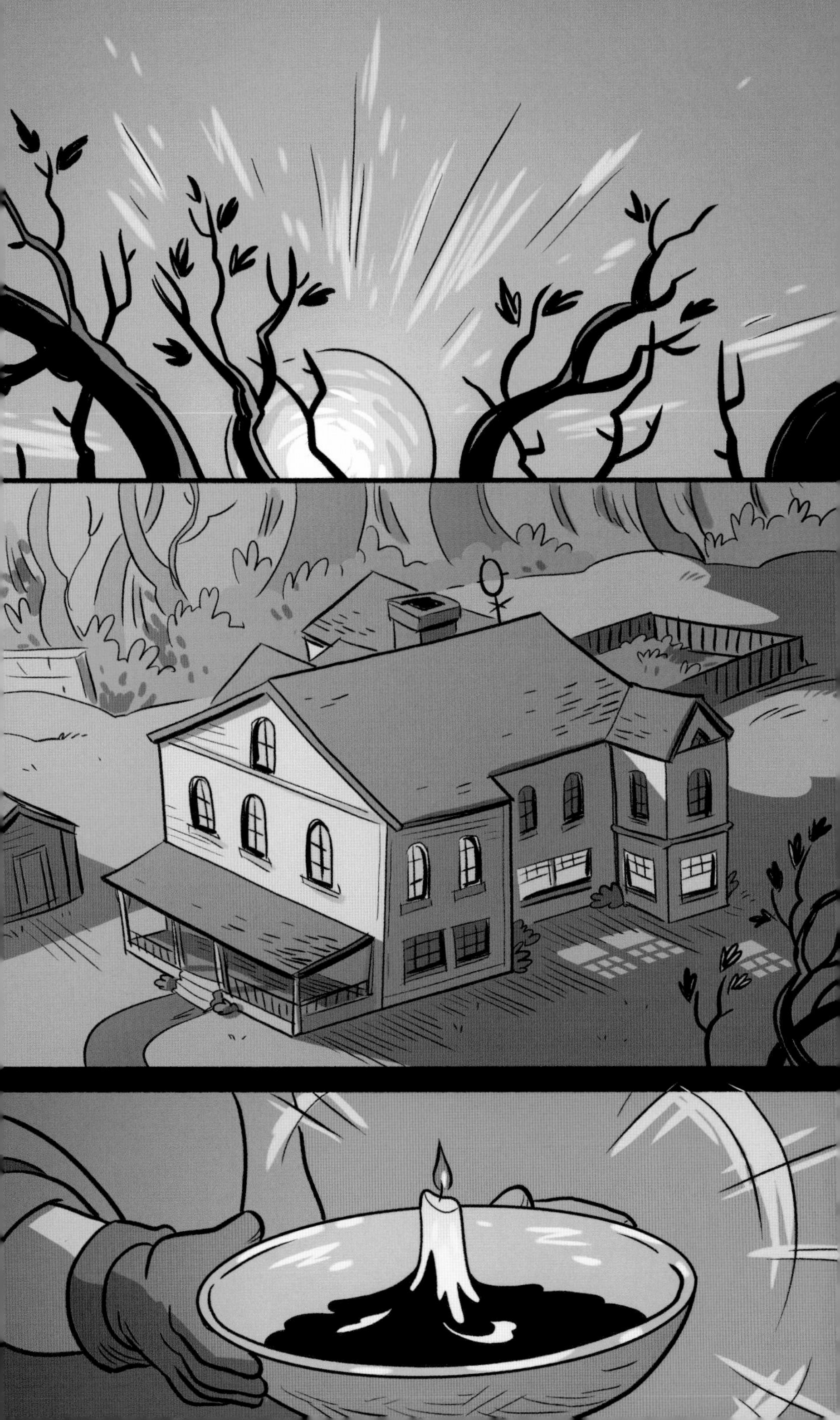

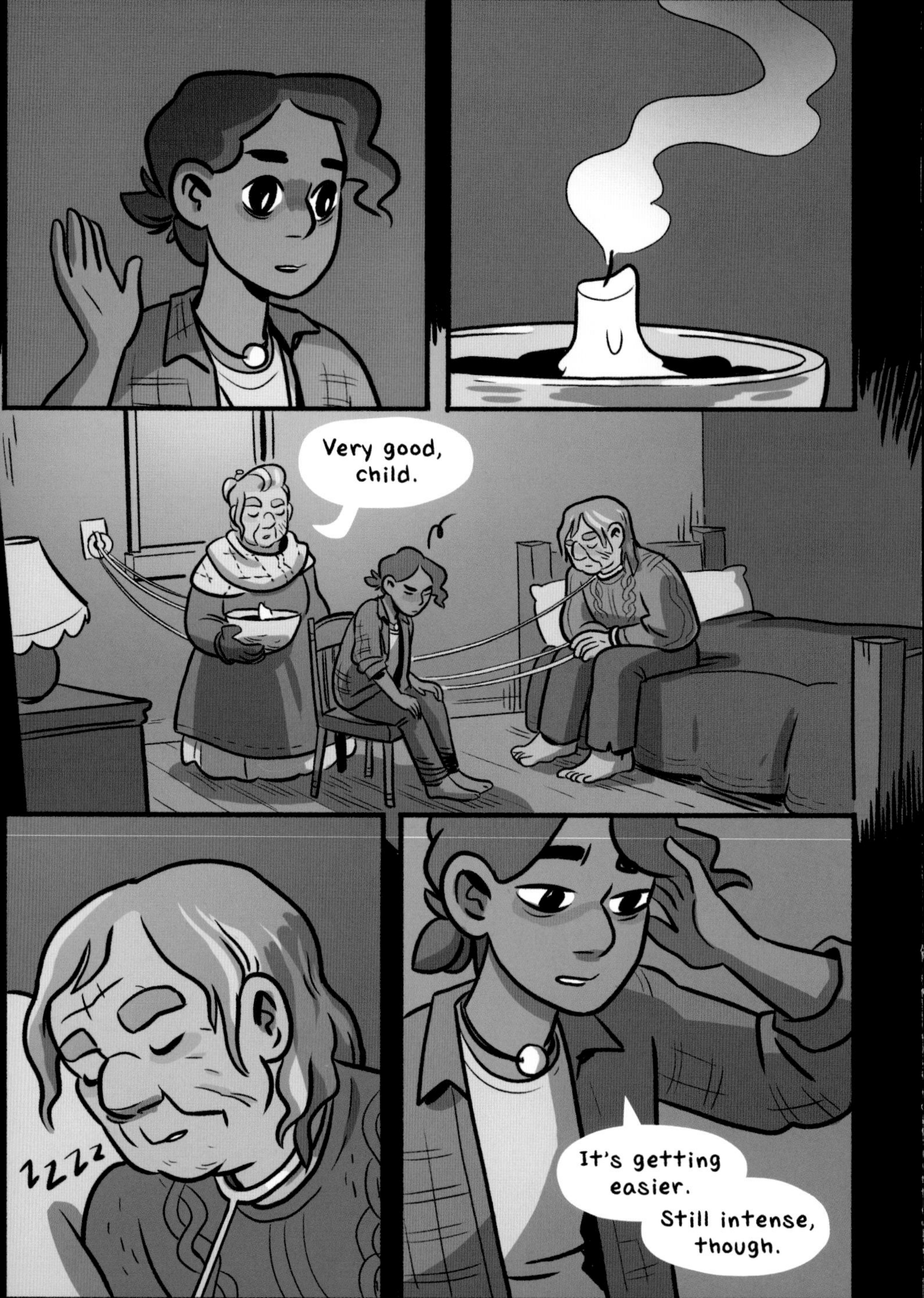
Very good, child.
ZZZZ
It's getting easier.
Still intense, though.

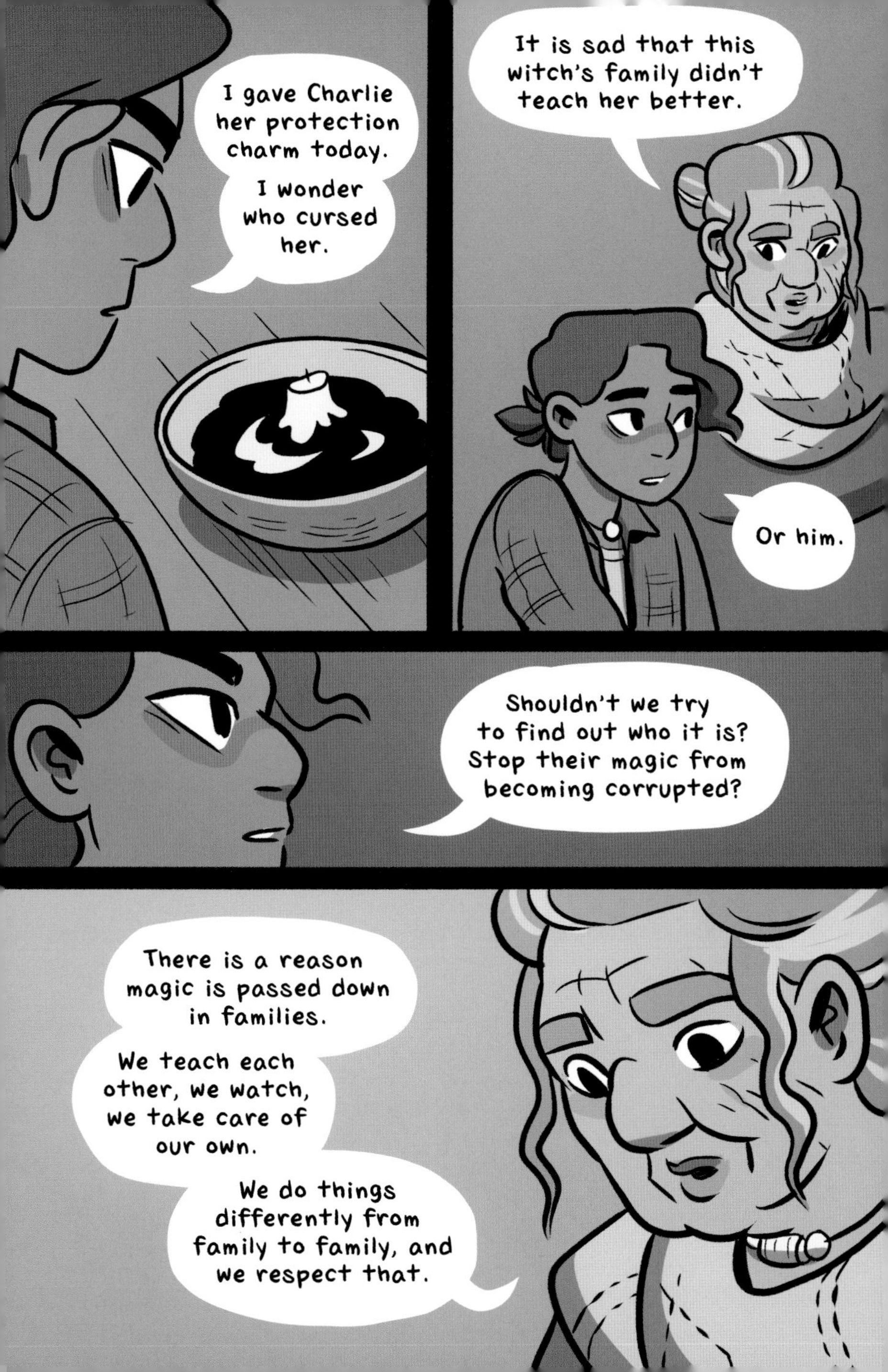
I gave Charlie her protection charm today.
I wonder who cursed her.
It is sad that this witch's family didn't teach her better.
Or him.
Shouldn't we try to find out who it is? Stop their magic from becoming corrupted?
There is a reason magic is passed down in families.
We teach each other, we watch, we take care of our own.
We do things differently from family to family, and we respect that.

Magical families used to go to war against each other, but long ago we signed a treaty for peace.
Now we help each other where we can, and stay out of each other's way when we can't.
sigh
To spiral into hate . . . at first it feels good and right. You have been hurt, and so you hurt others.
Rest, brother.
The darkness coils inside you and you cannot stop it, and one day you realize that there is no difference between you and the darkness.

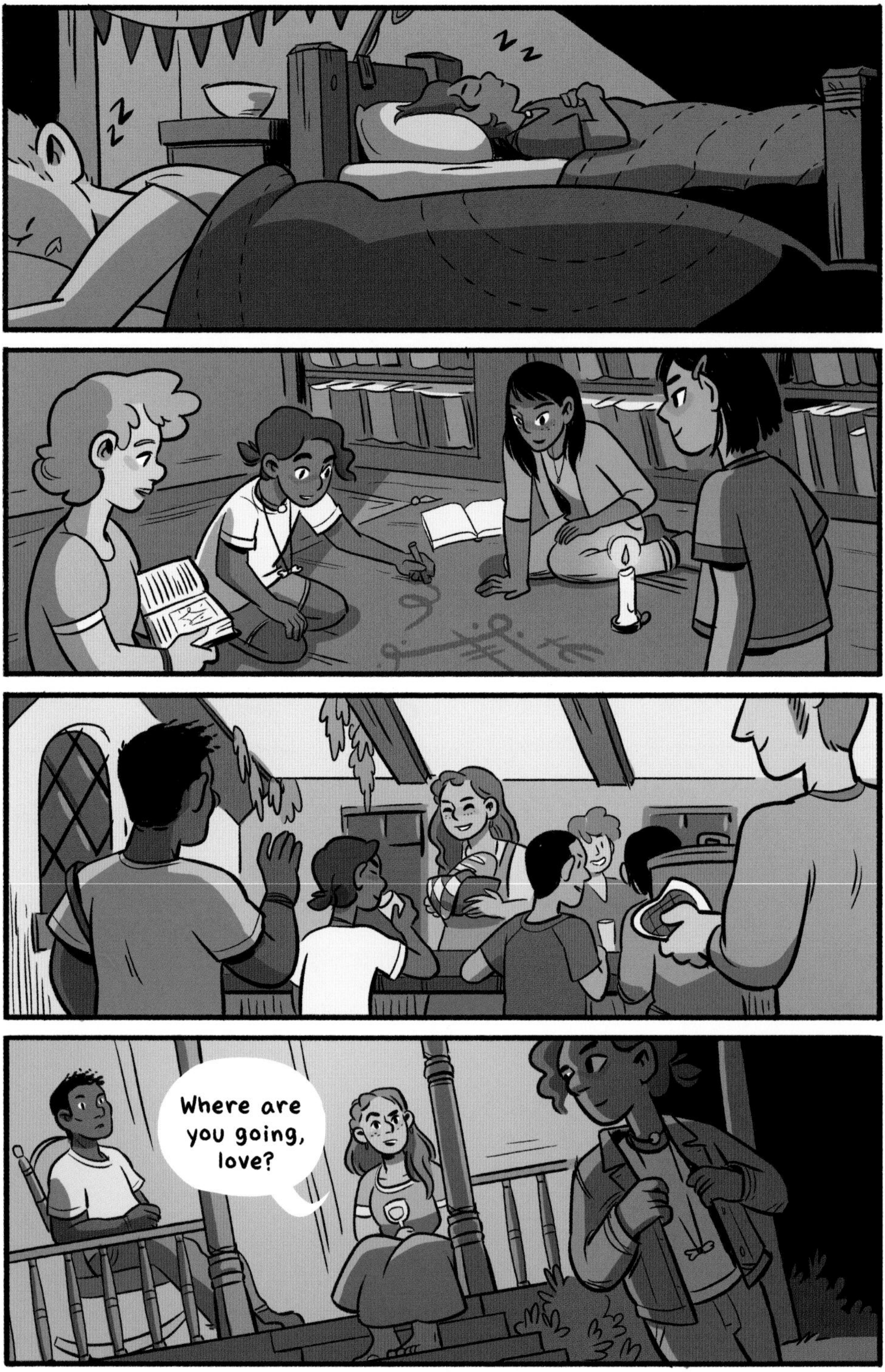
Z Z
Z Z
Where are you going, love?

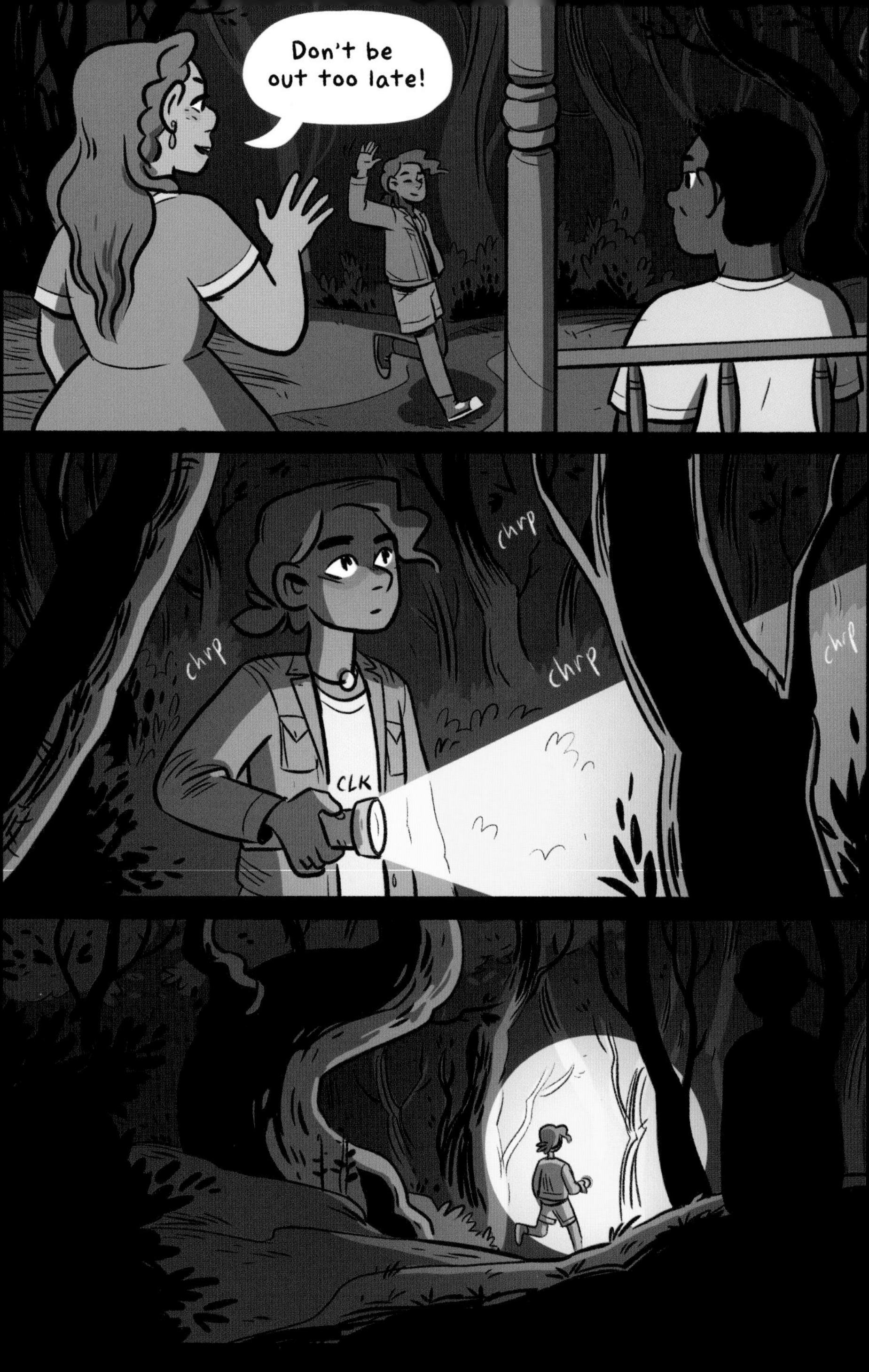

Don't be out too late!
chrp
chrp
chrp
chrp
CLK

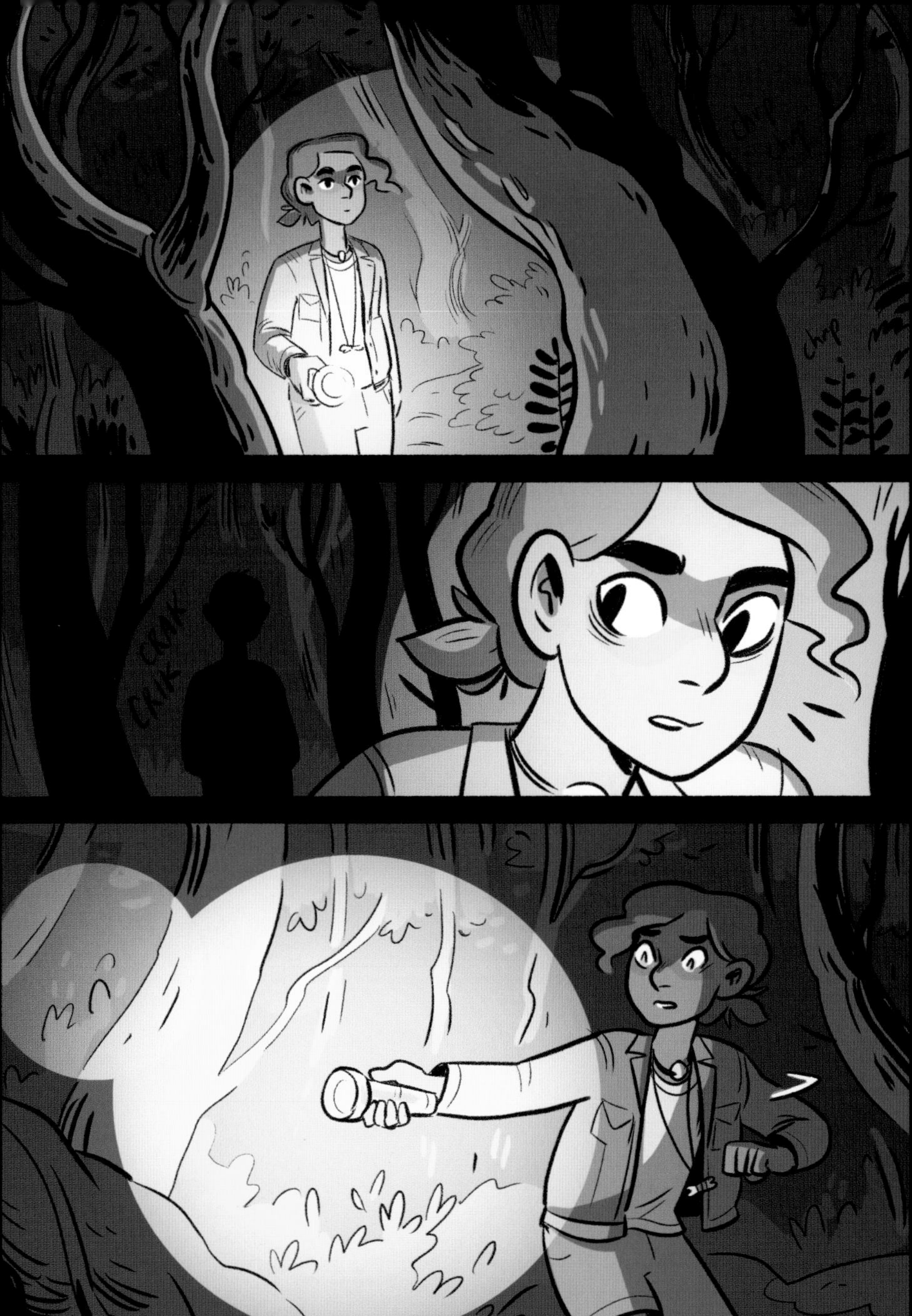
chrp
CRIK
CRAK

Ever since this summer . . .
Ever since Mikasi . . .
It scares me to shift. I used to be so excited to learn how, and now . . .
That sounds really tough.
Every time I've shifted since, I feel like . . . I might lose control. I don't want to become a monster again.
That makes sense.
pat

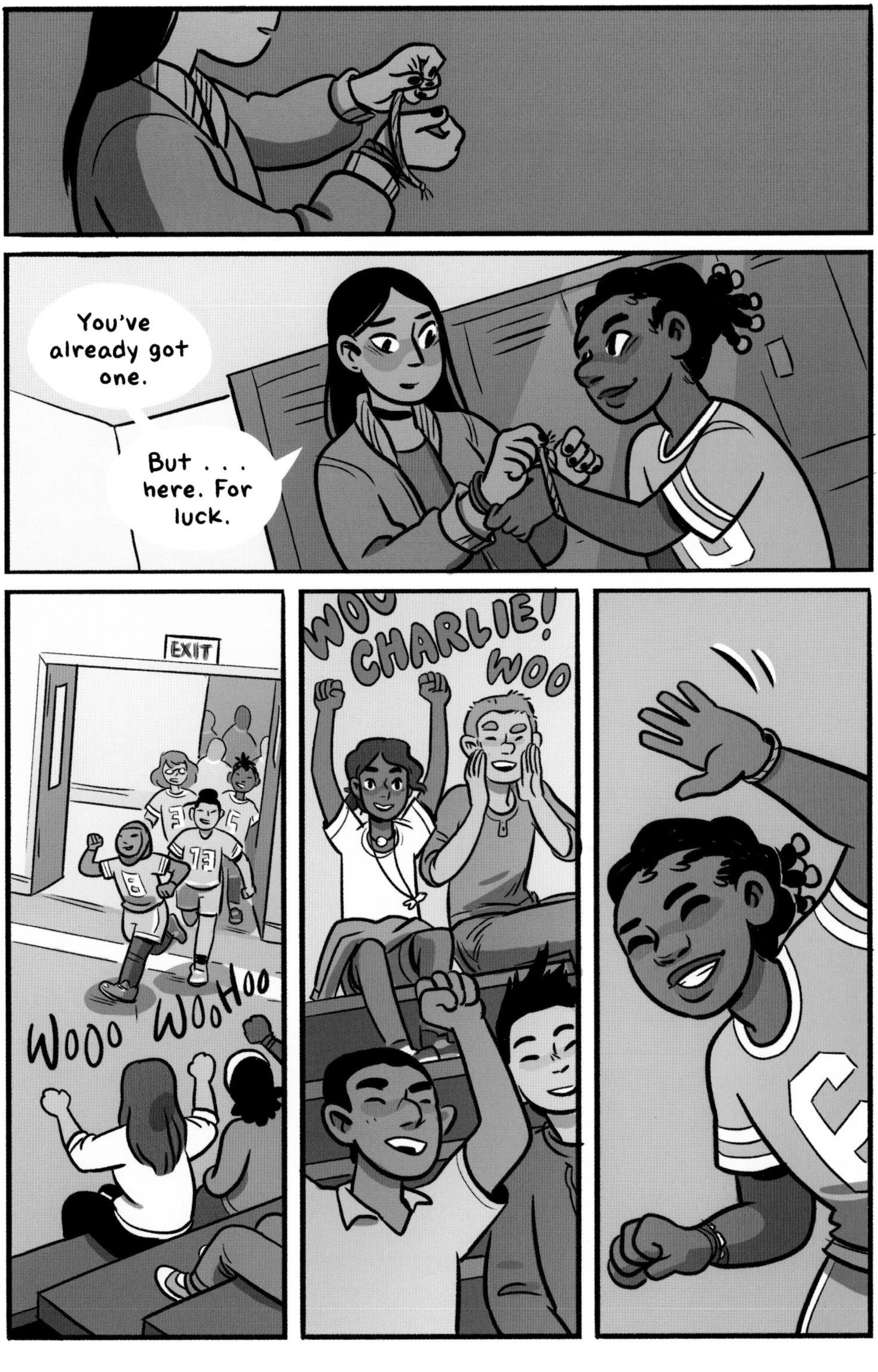
You've already got one.
But . . . here. For luck.
EXIT
WOOO WOOHOO
WOO CHARLIE! WOO

twueeeee

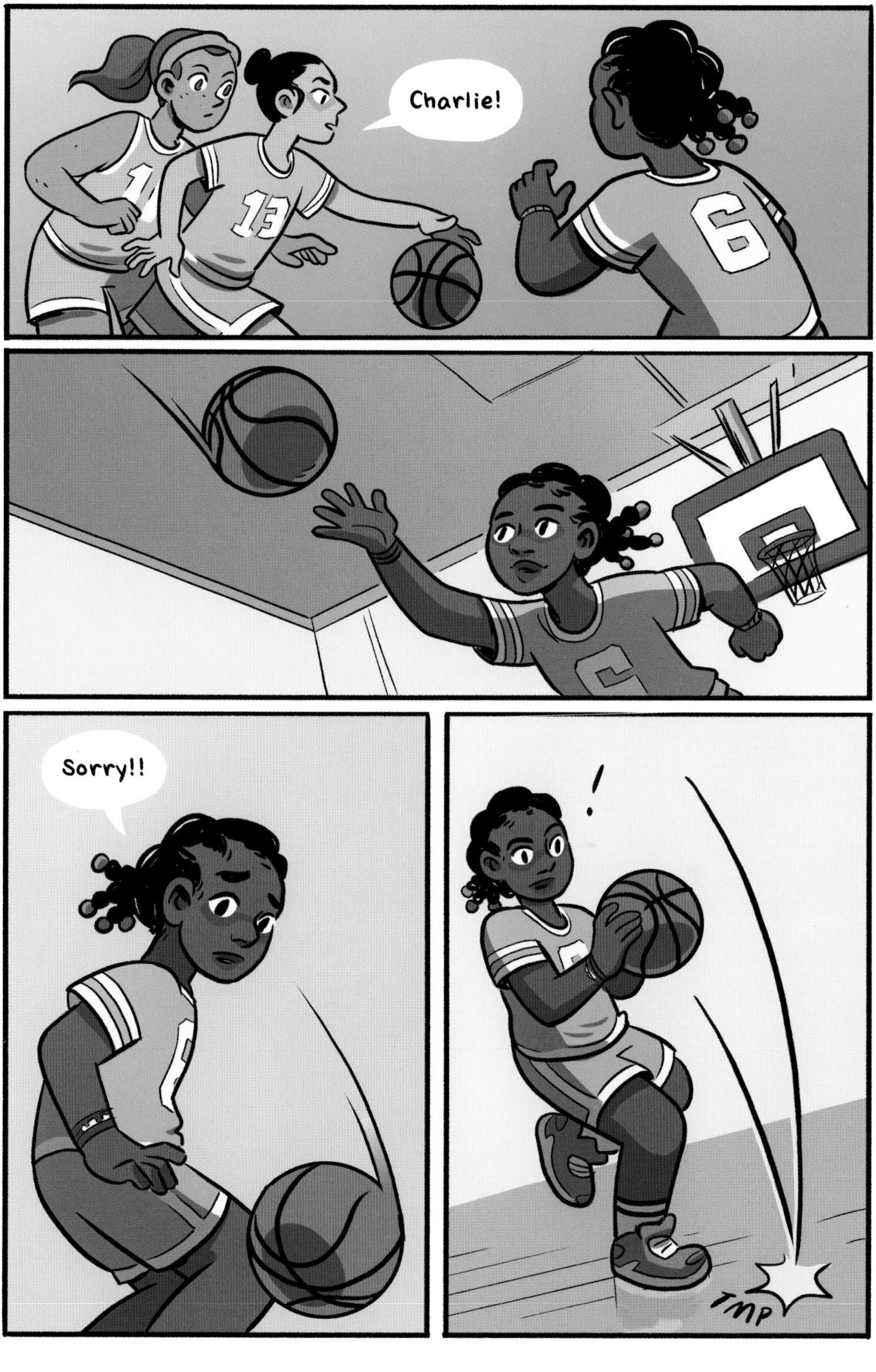
Charlie!
Sorry!!
!
TMP

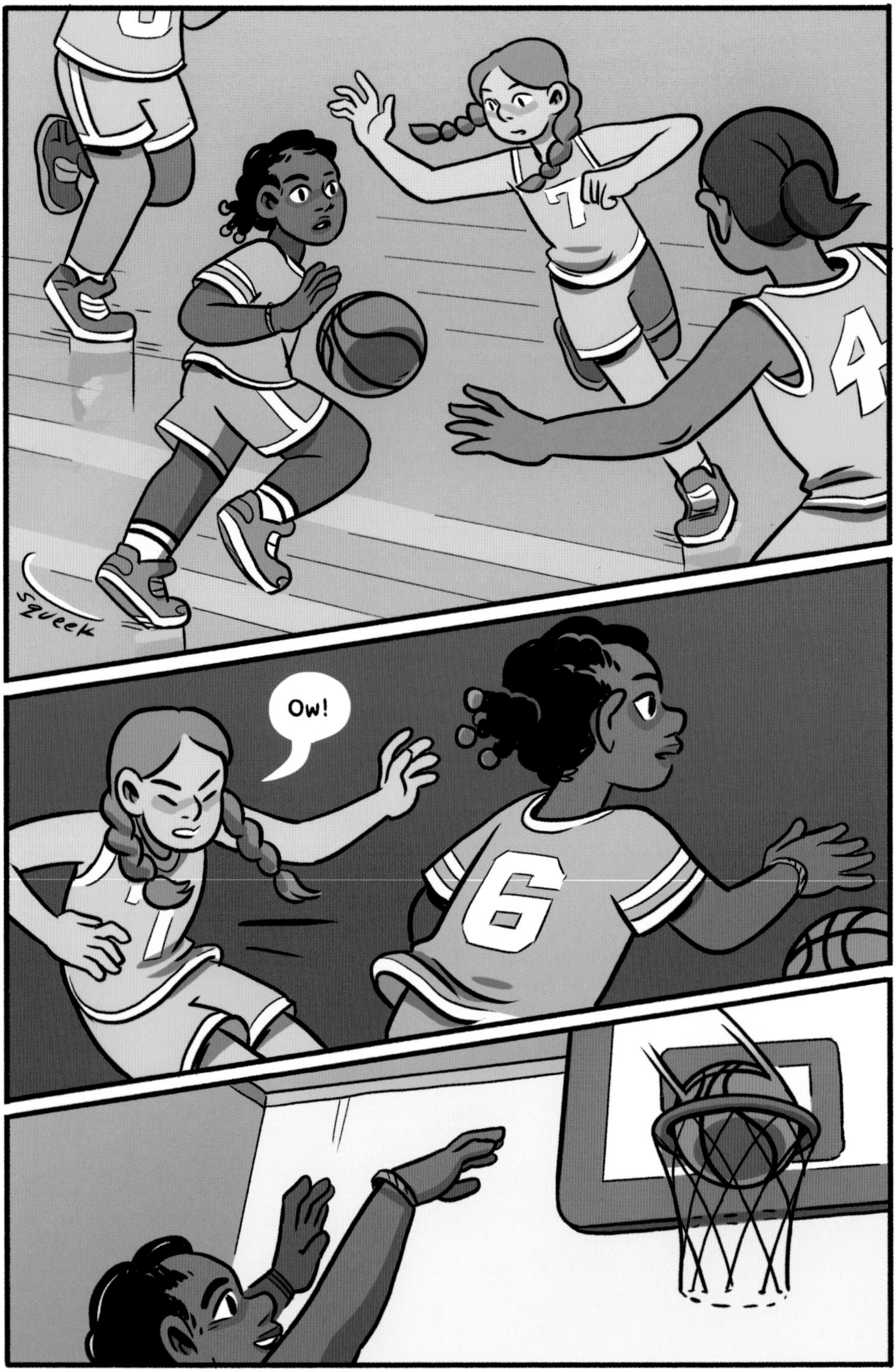
squeek
Ow!

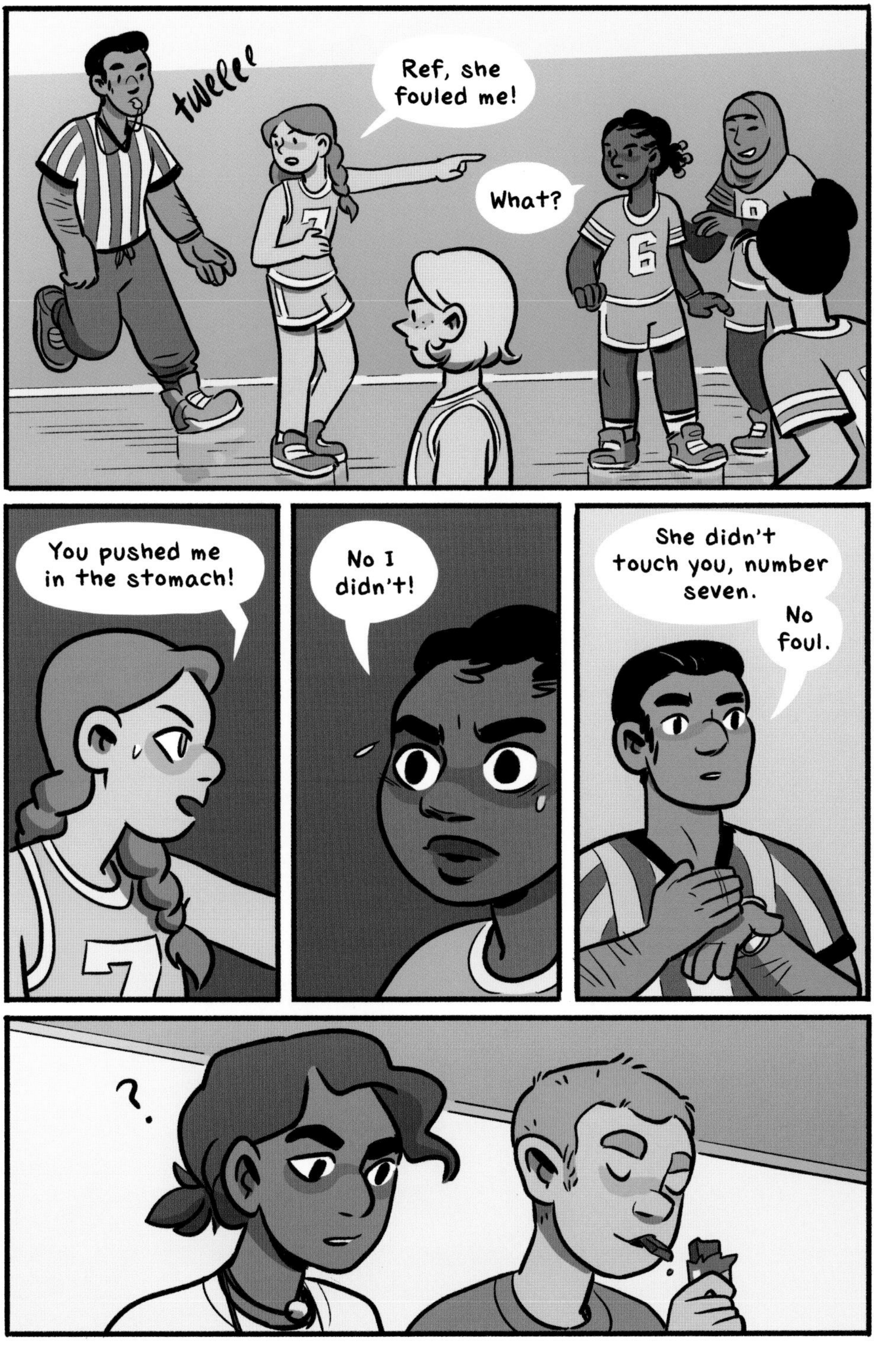
tweeee
Ref, she fouled me!
What?
You pushed me in the stomach!
No I didn't!
She didn't touch you, number seven.
No foul.
?

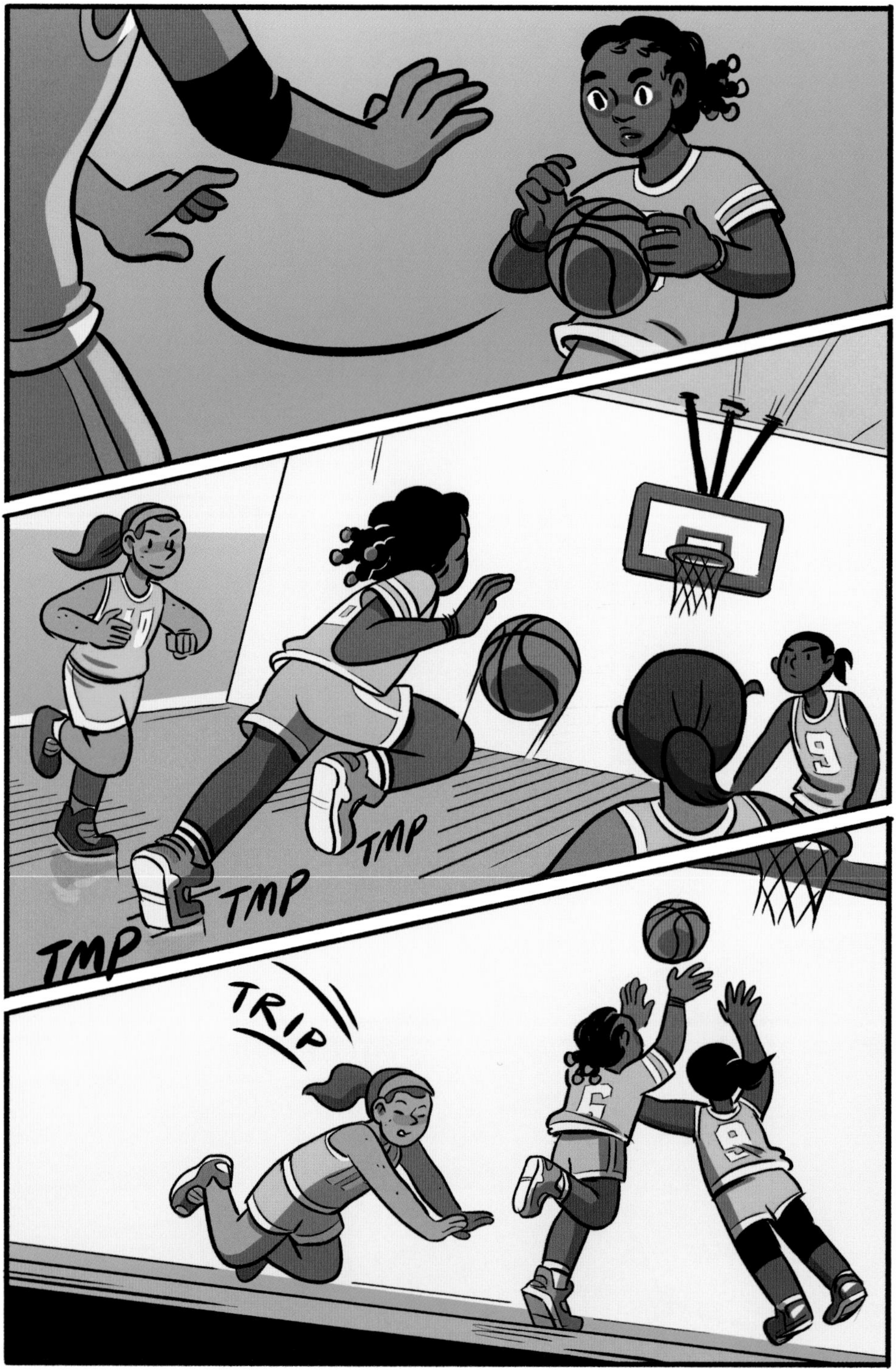
TMP
TMP
TMP
TRIP

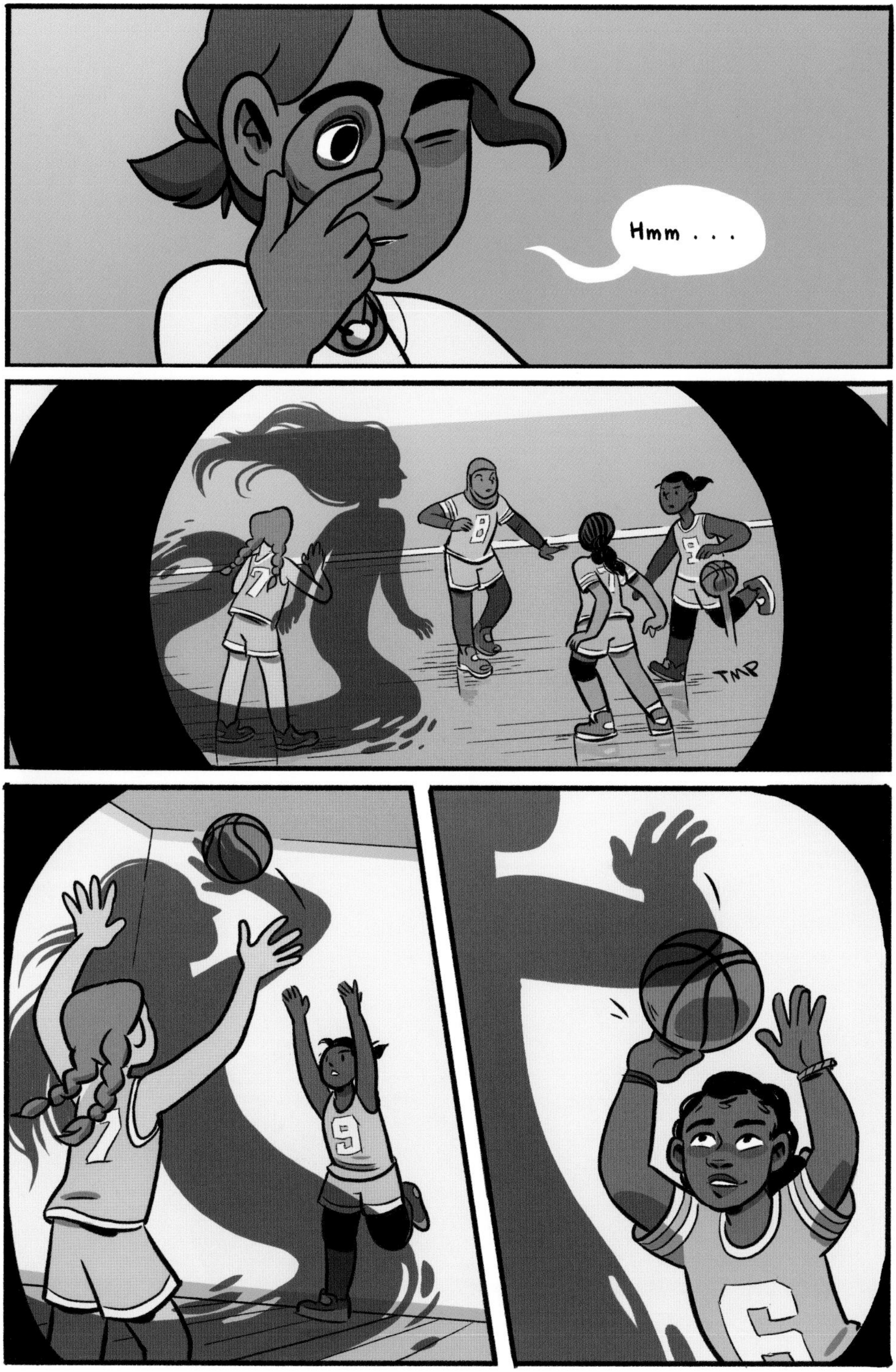
Hmm . . .
TMP

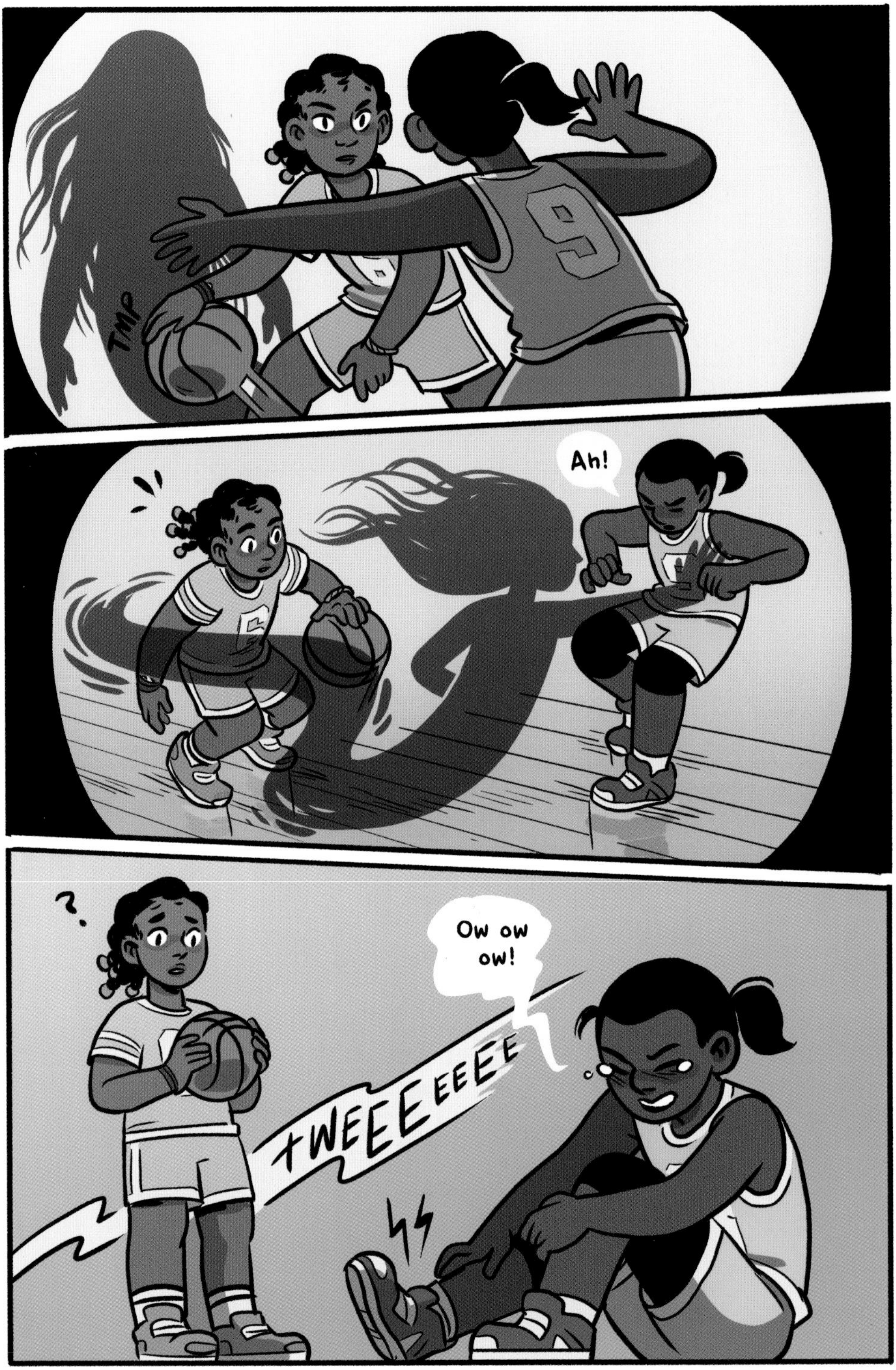
TMP
Ah!
Ow ow ow!
TWEEEeeeee

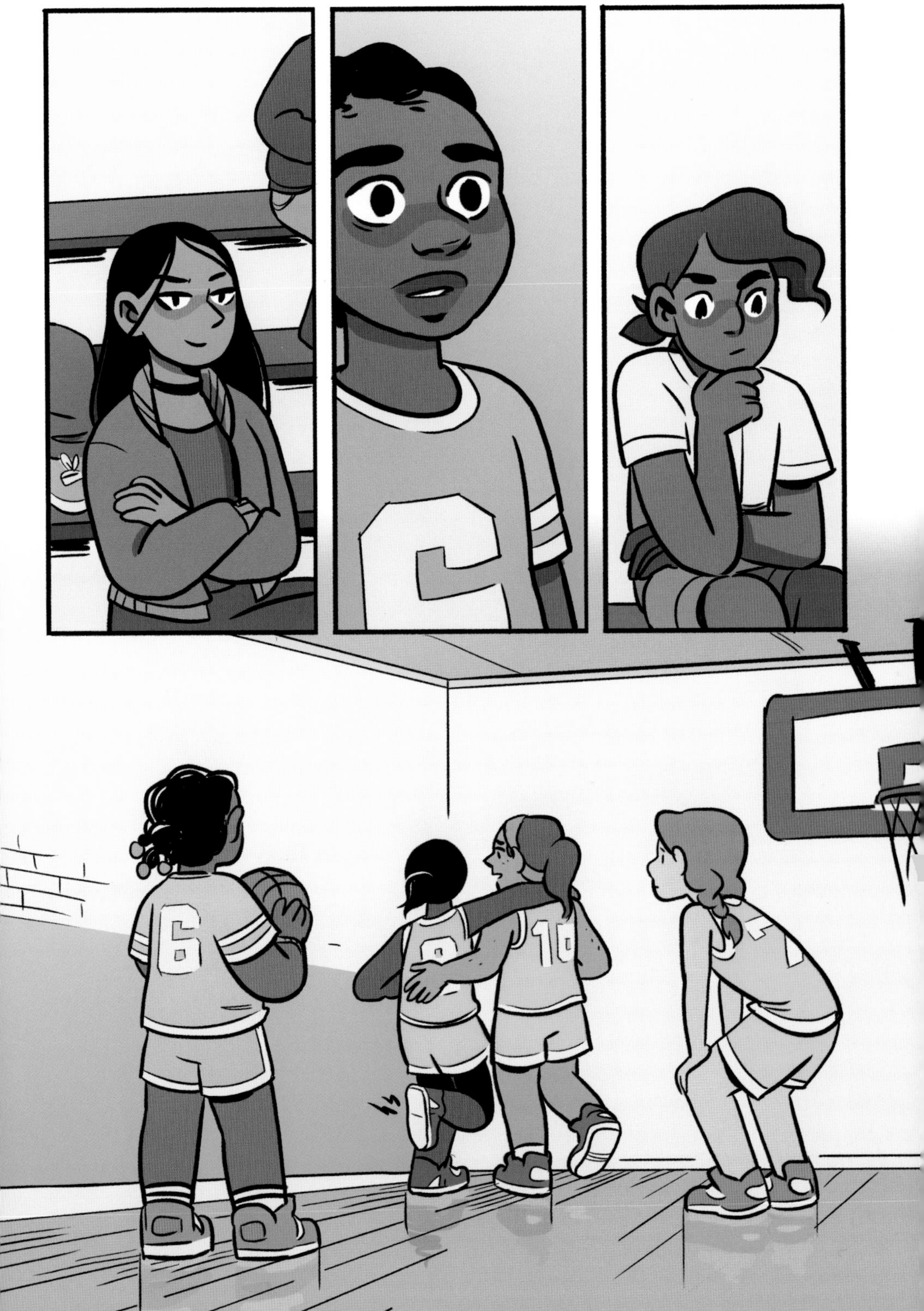

I can't believe you scored so much in your first game, hon!
I hope that girl is okay, the one who twisted her ankle . . .
You guys have fun?
Yeah!
You kids want to get ice cream to celebrate?
I think we can fit you all in the minivan.

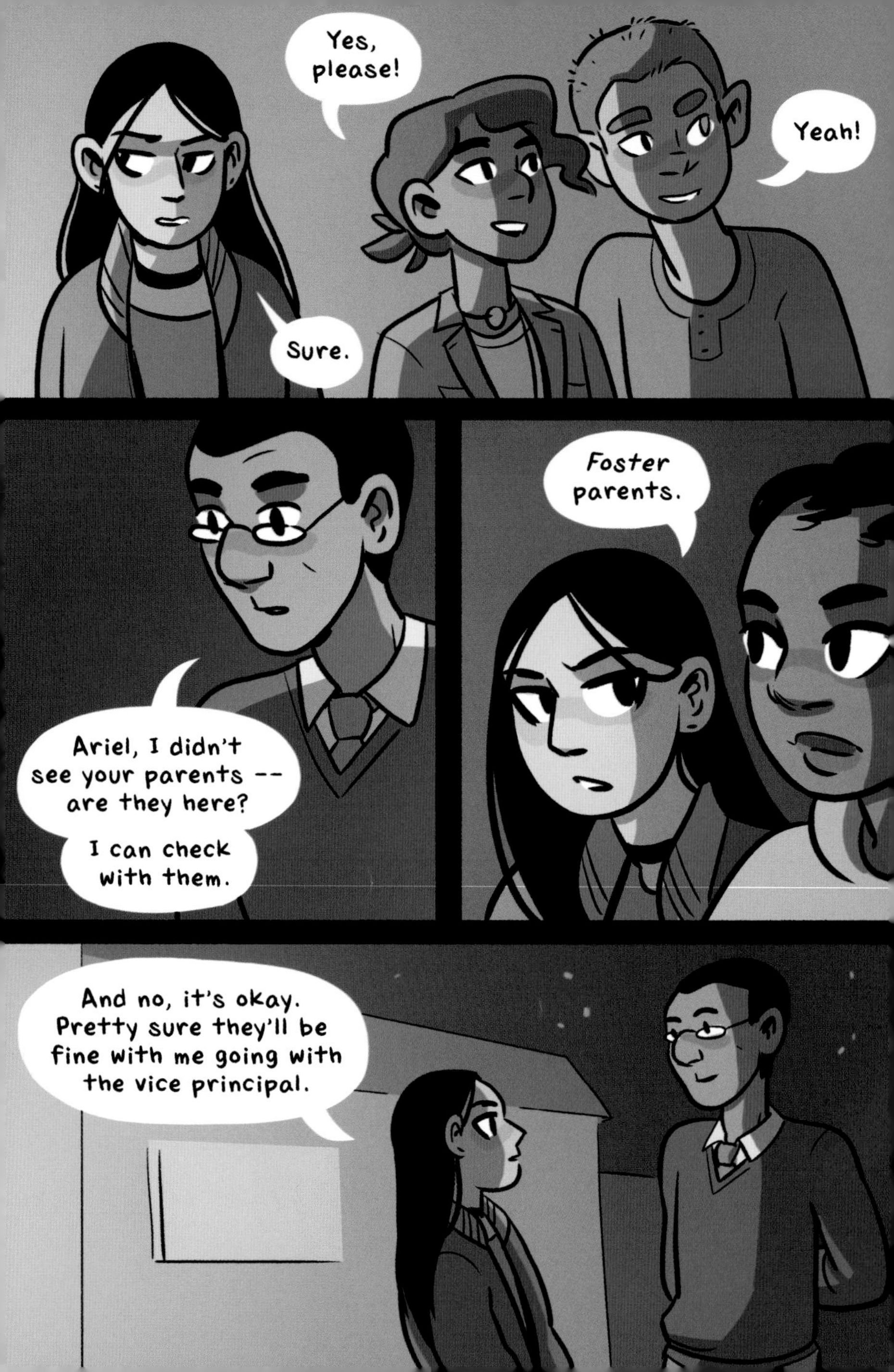
Yes, please!
Yeah!
Sure.
Ariel, I didn't see your parents -- are they here?
I can check with them.
Foster parents.
And no, it's okay. Pretty sure they'll be fine with me going with the vice principal.

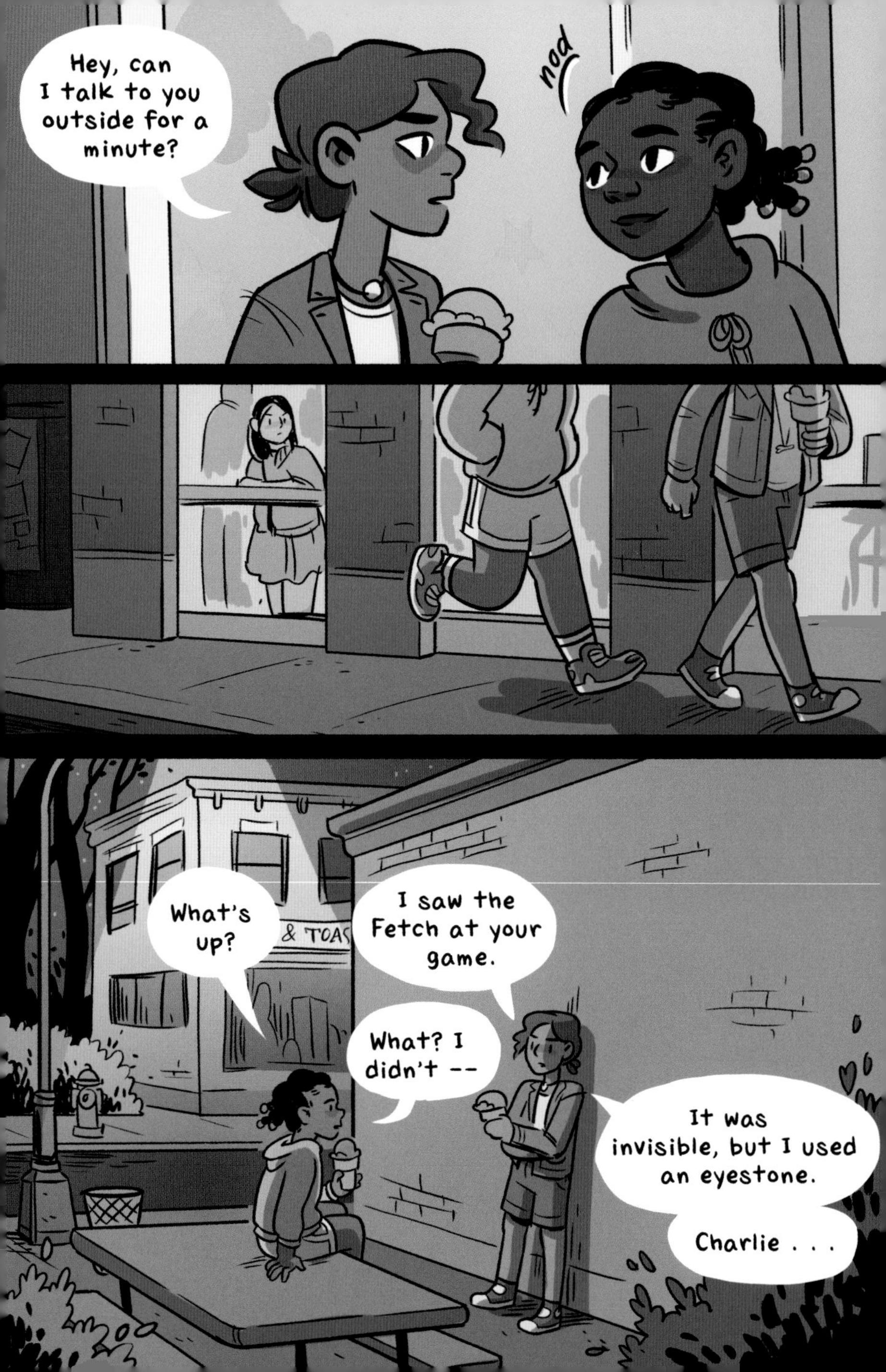
Hey, can I talk to you outside for a minute?
nod
What's up?
& TOAS
I saw the Fetch at your game.
What? I didn't --
It was invisible, but I used an eyestone.
Charlie . . .

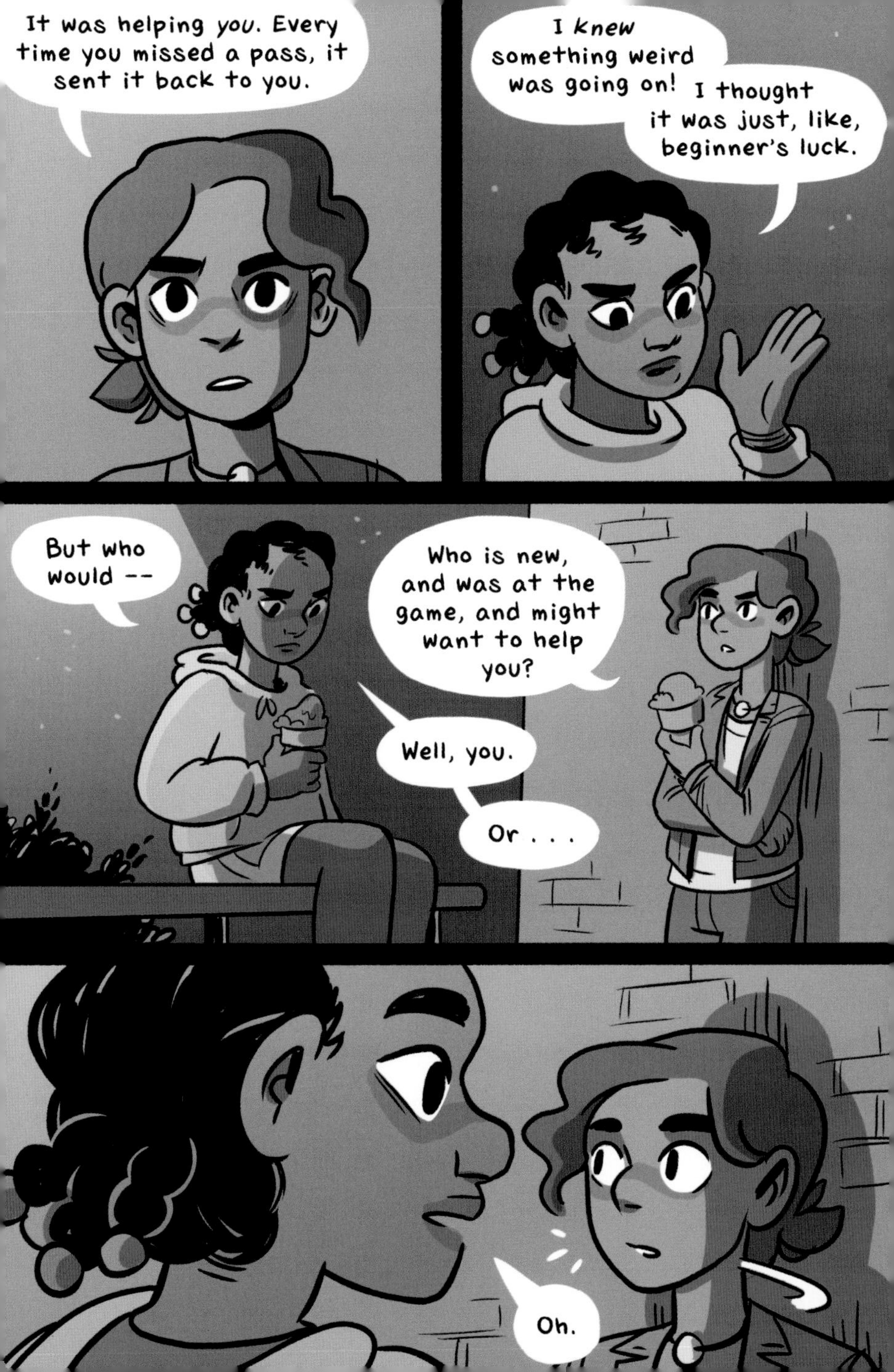

It was helping *you*. Every time you missed a pass, it sent it back to you.
I *knew* something weird was going on!
I thought it was just, like, beginner's luck.
But who would --
Who is new, and was at the game, and might want to help you?
Well, you.
Or . . .
Oh.

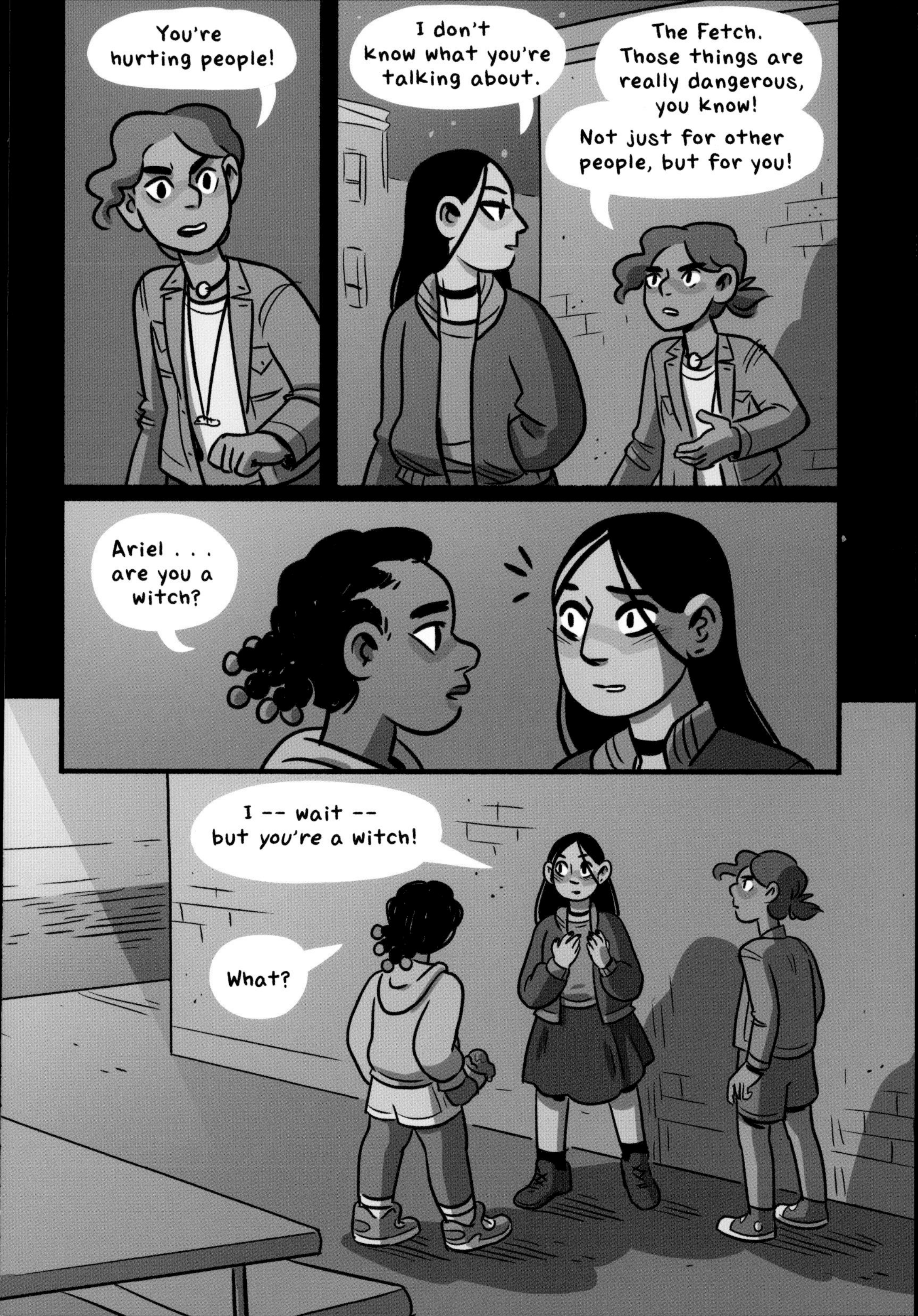
You're hurting people!
I don't know what you're talking about.
The Fetch. Those things are really dangerous, you know!
Not just for other people, but for you!
Ariel . . . are you a witch?
I -- wait -- but *you're* a witch!
What?

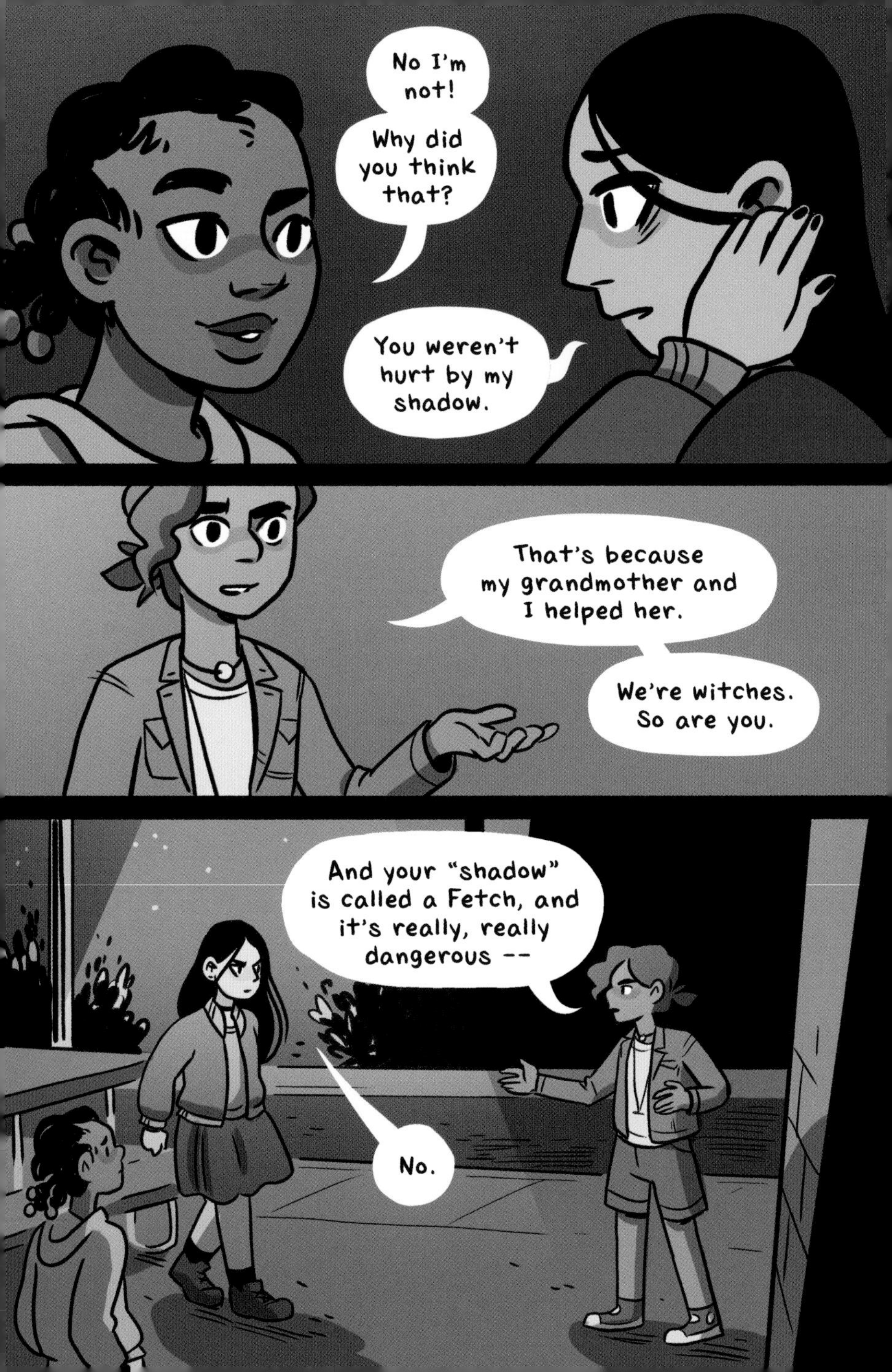
No I'm not!
Why did you think that?
You weren't hurt by my shadow.
That's because my grandmother and I helped her.
We're witches. So are you.
And your "shadow" is called a Fetch, and it's really, really dangerous --
No.

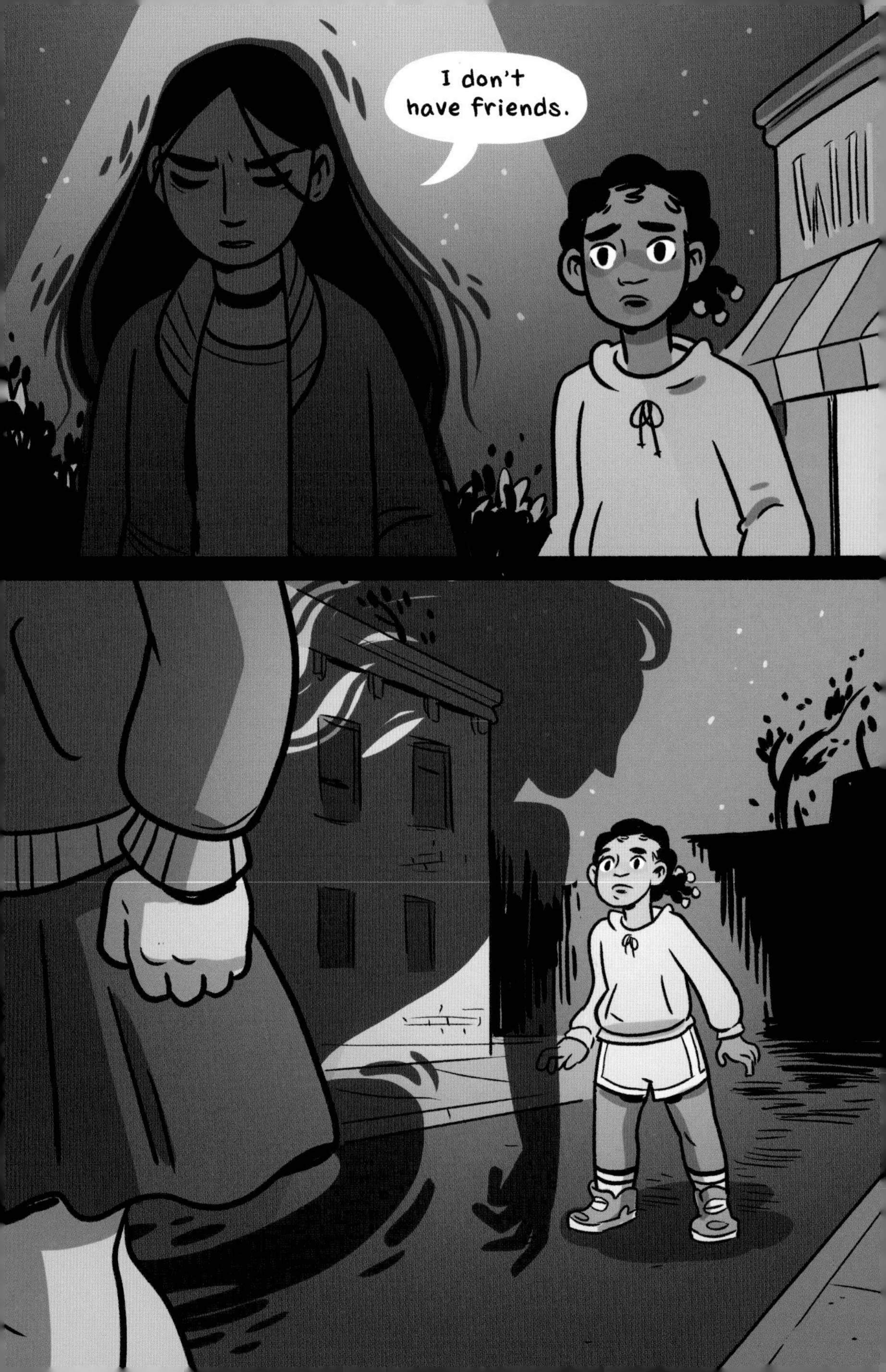
I don't
have friends.

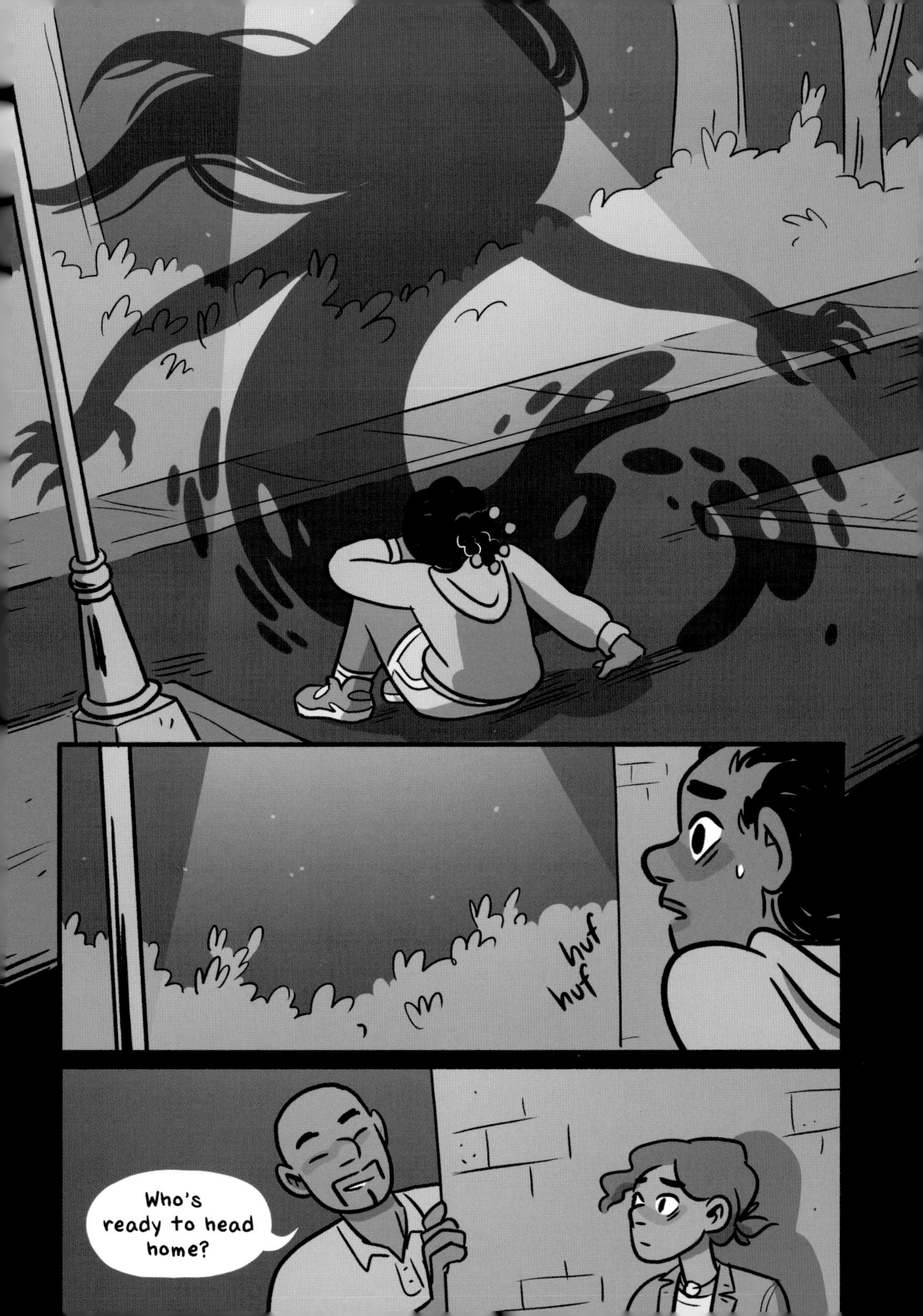
huf
huf
Who's ready to head home?

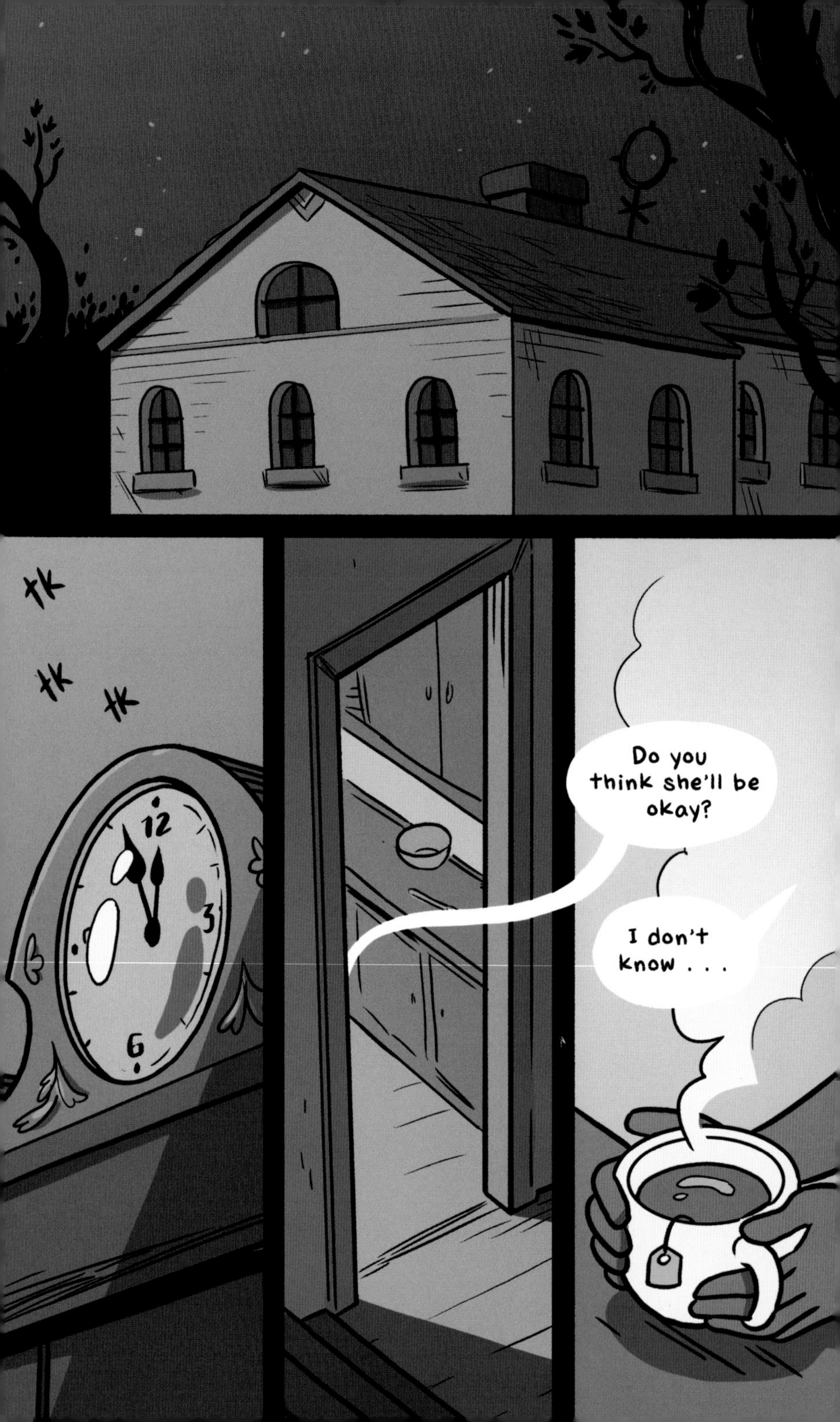
tk
tk
tk
12
3
6
Do you think she'll be okay?
I don't know . . .

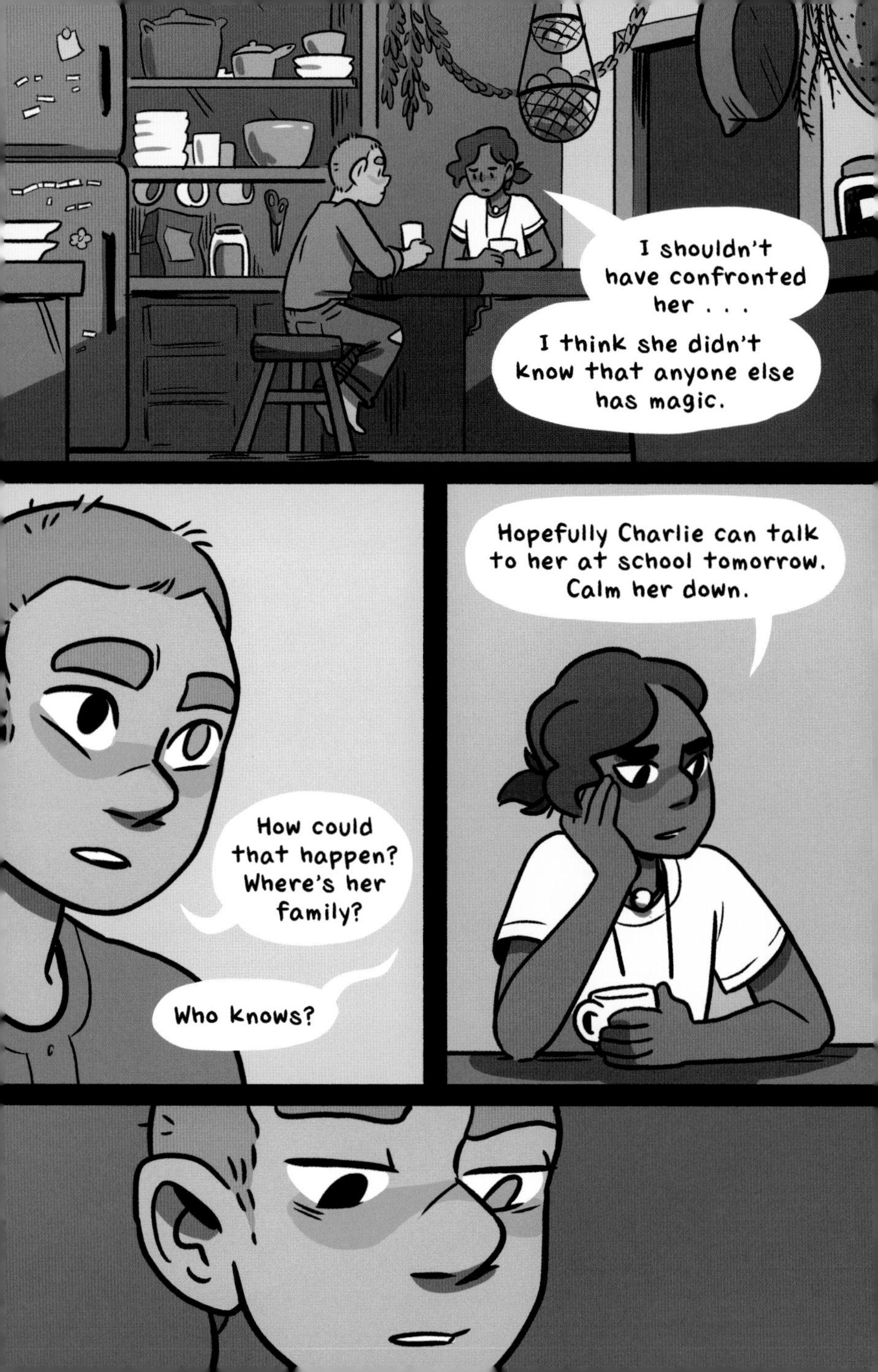
I shouldn't have confronted her . . .
I think she didn't know that anyone else has magic.
Hopefully Charlie can talk to her at school tomorrow. Calm her down.
How could that happen? Where's her family?
Who knows?

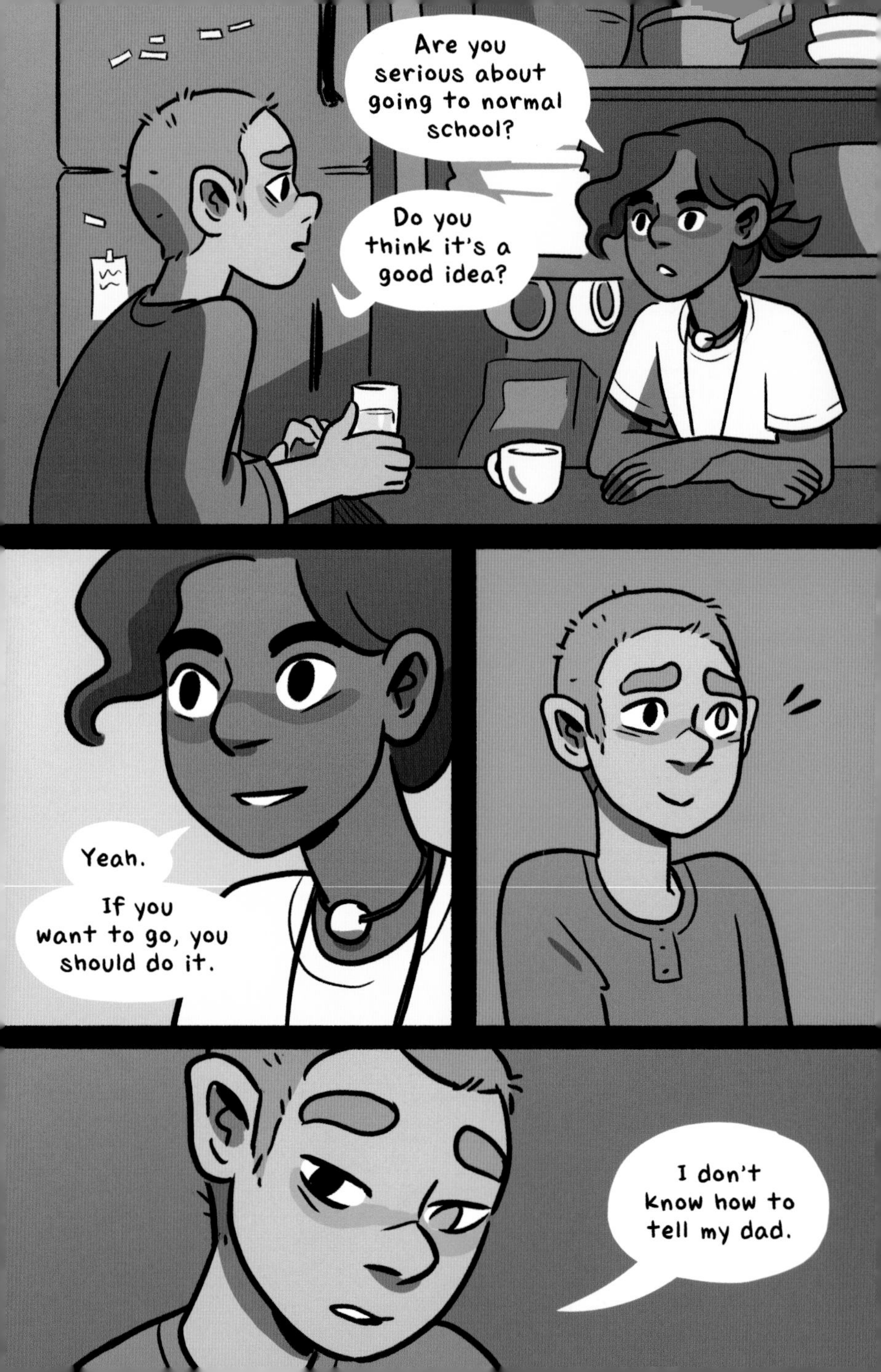
Are you serious about going to normal school?
Do you think it's a good idea?
Yeah.
If you want to go, you should do it.
I don't know how to tell my dad.

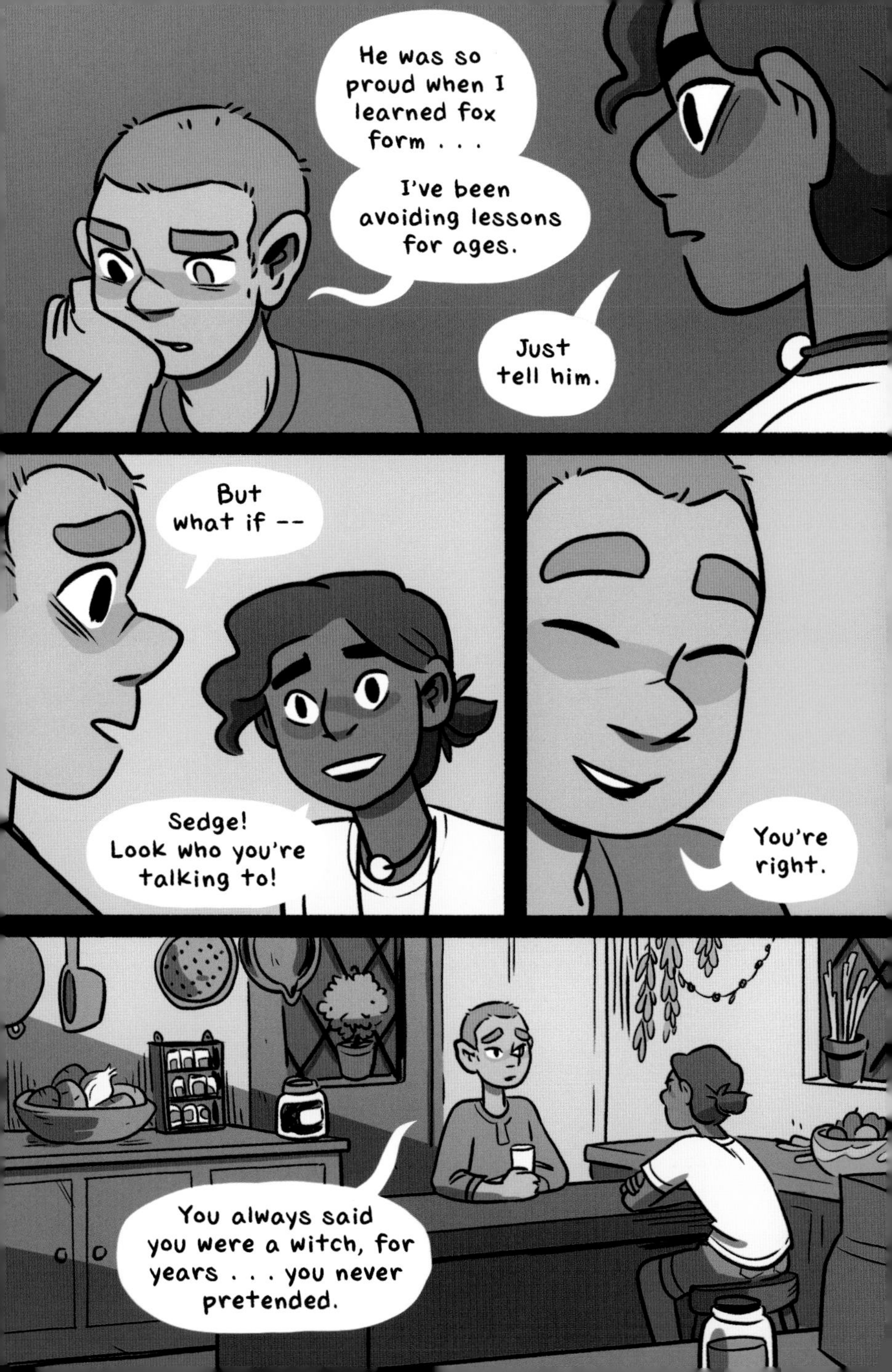
He was so proud when I learned fox form . . .
I've been avoiding lessons for ages.
Just tell him.
But what if --
Sedge! Look who you're talking to!
You're right.
You always said you were a witch, for years . . . you never pretended.

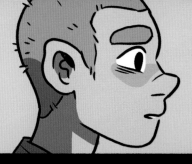

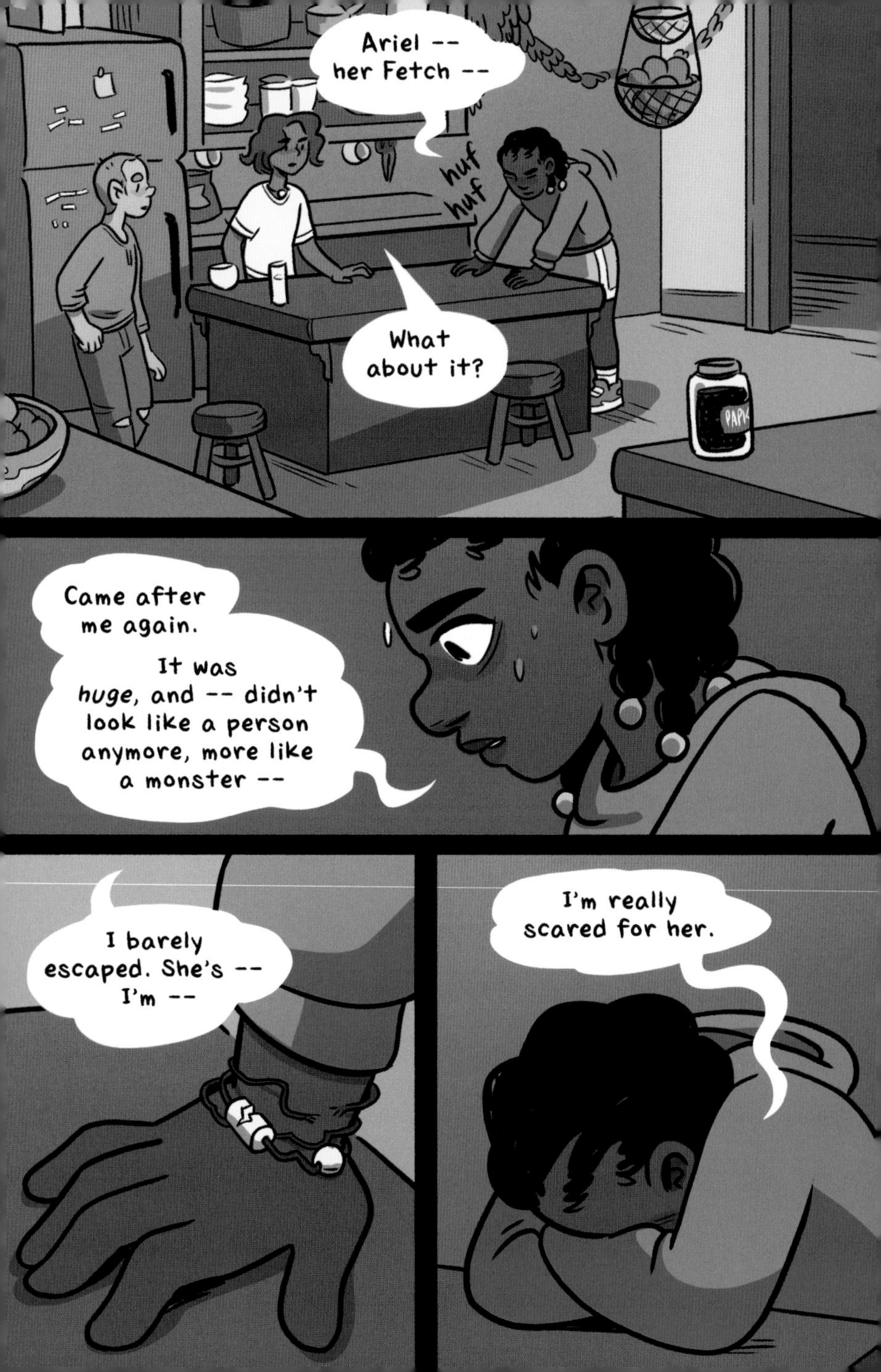
Ariel -- her Fetch --
huf huf
What about it?
PAPK
Came after me again.
It was *huge*, and -- didn't look like a person anymore, more like a monster --
I barely escaped. She's -- I'm --
I'm really scared for her.

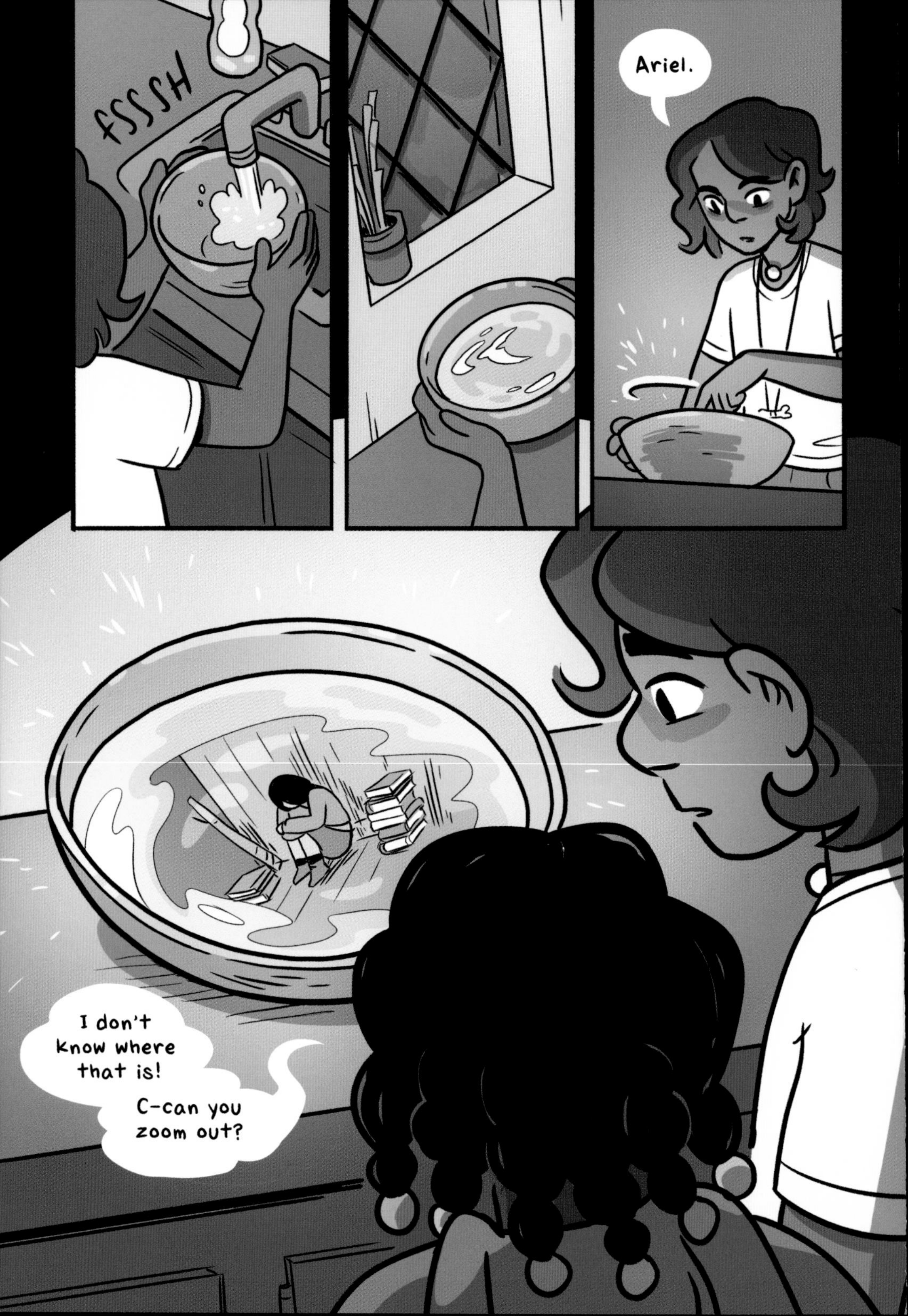
FSSSH
Ariel.
I don't know where that is!
C-can you zoom out?

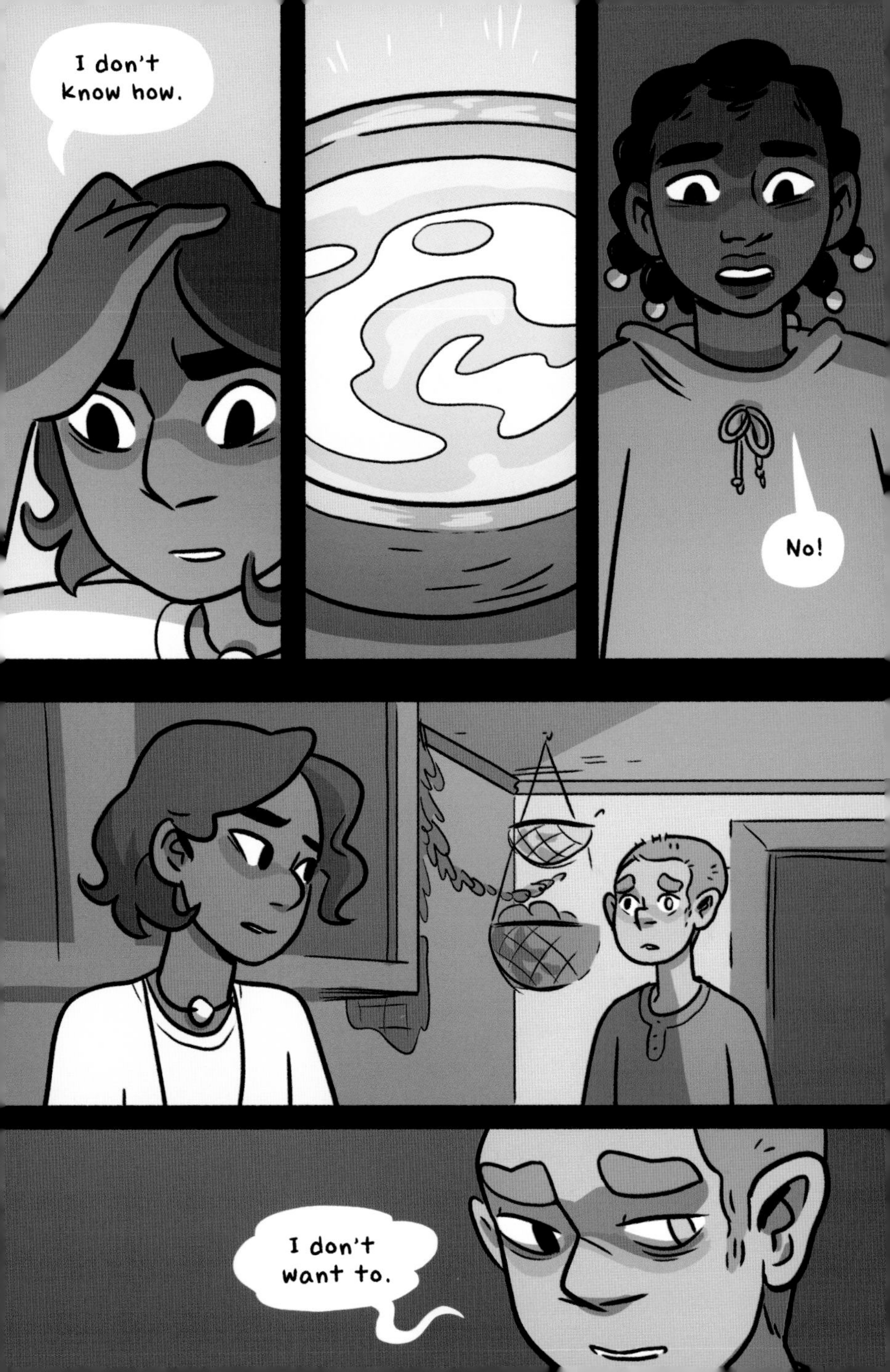
I don't
know how.
No!
I don't
want to.

I know. I'm not gonna ask.
What are you guys talking about?
I could shift into a fox and track her.
But ever since I was turned into a monster, I've been afraid that I'll lose control and won't be able to go back. I haven't shifted for weeks.

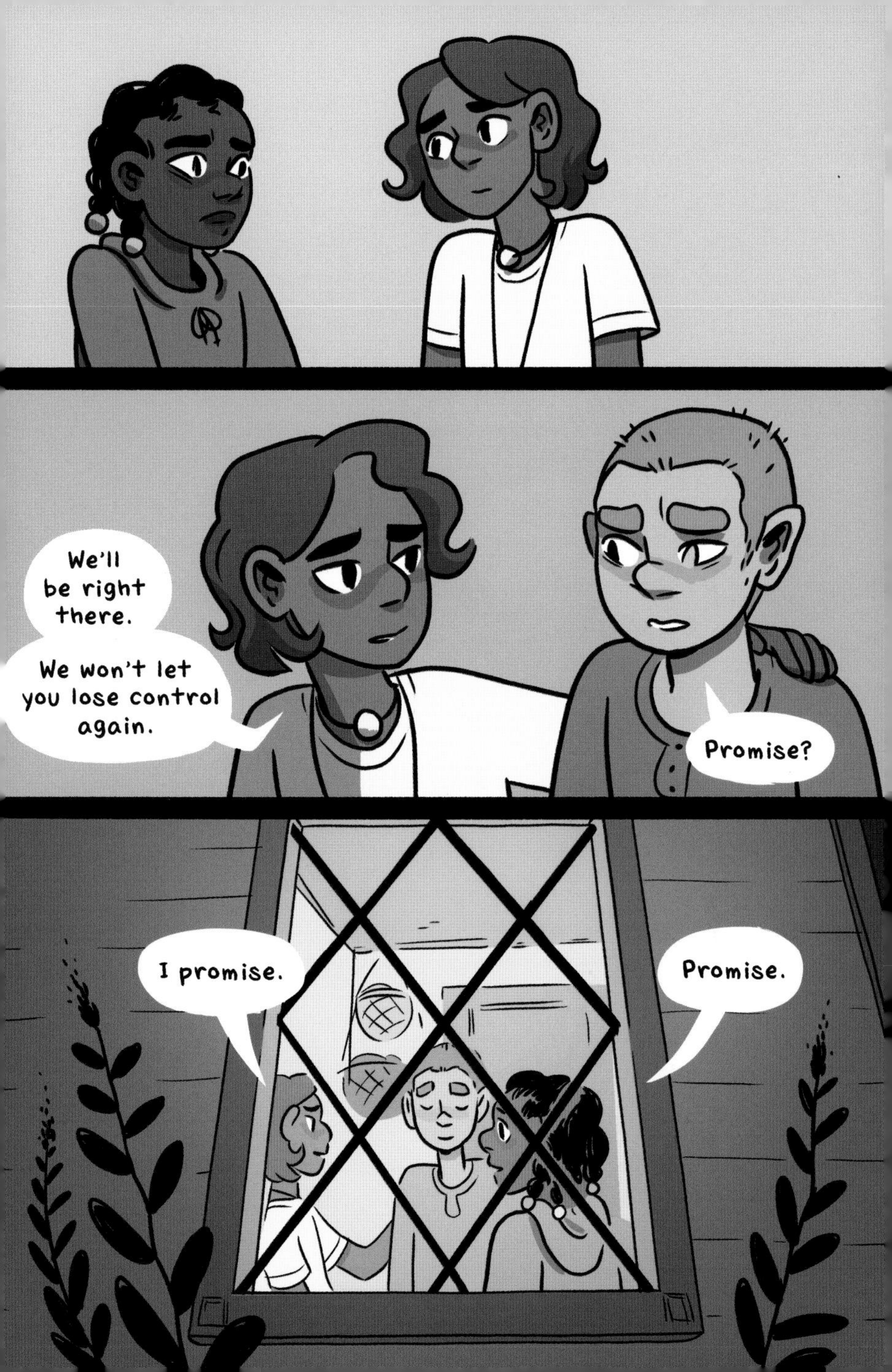
We'll be right there.
We won't let you lose control again.
Promise?
I promise.
Promise.

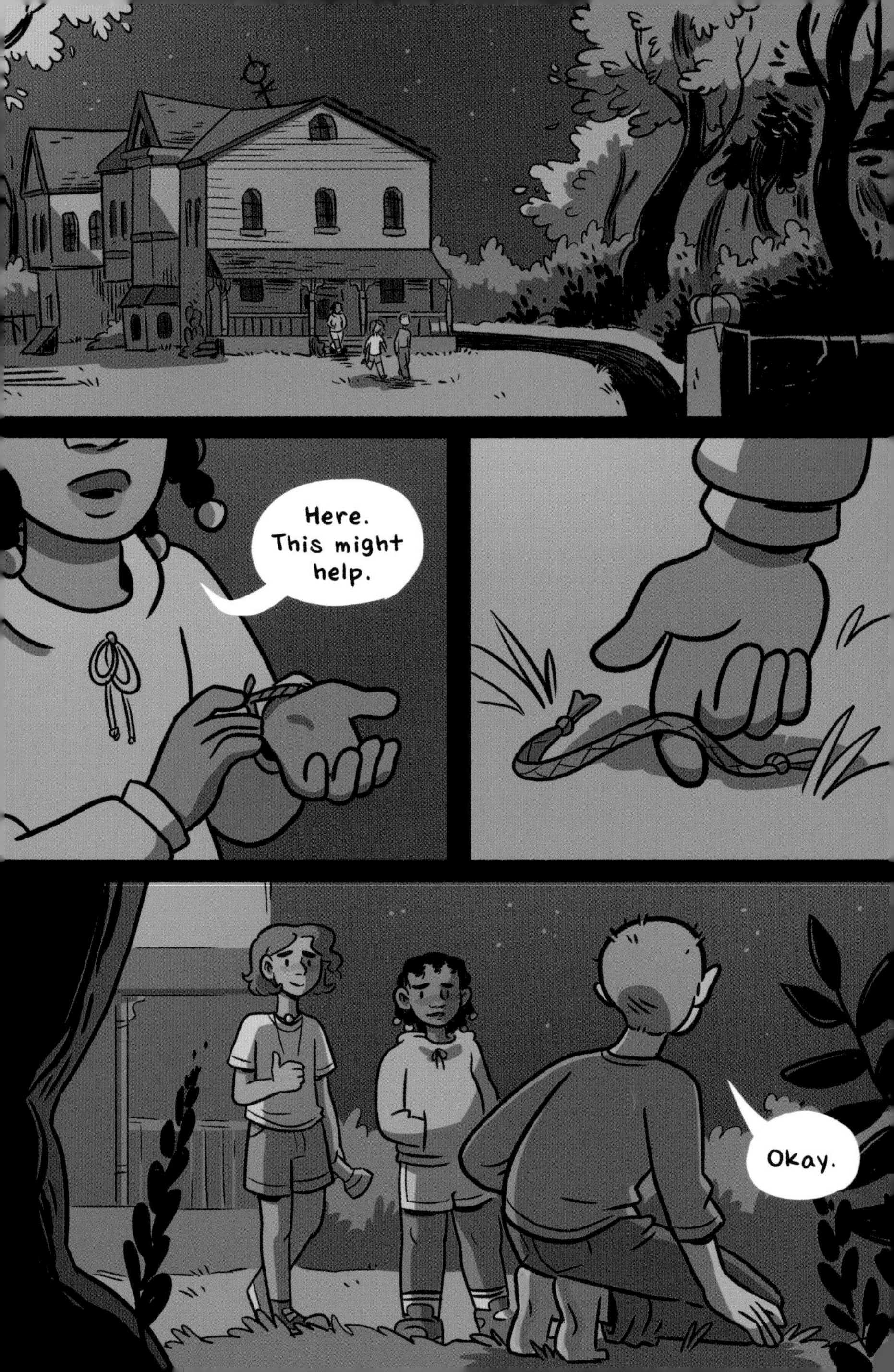
Here. This might help.
Okay.

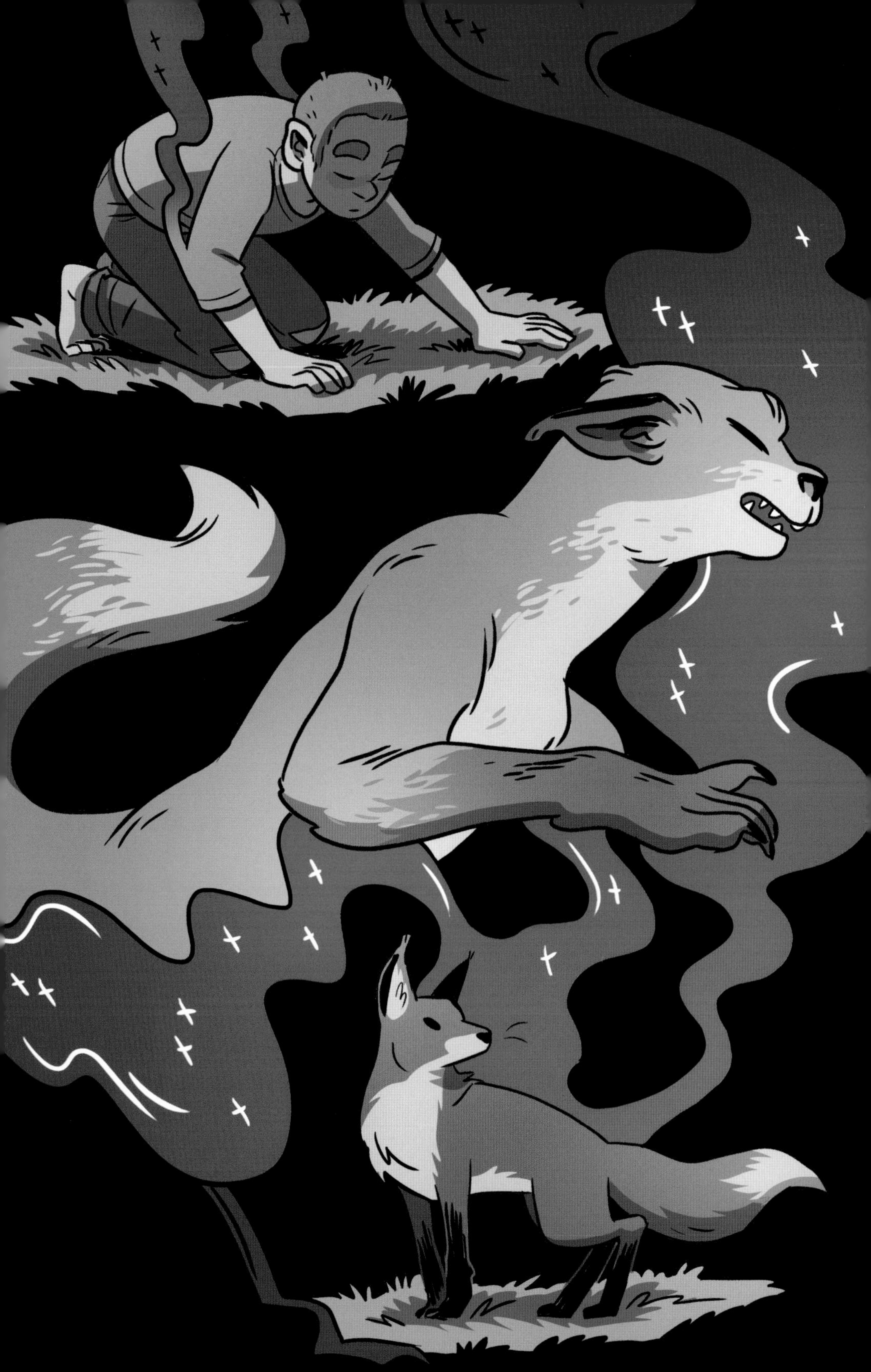

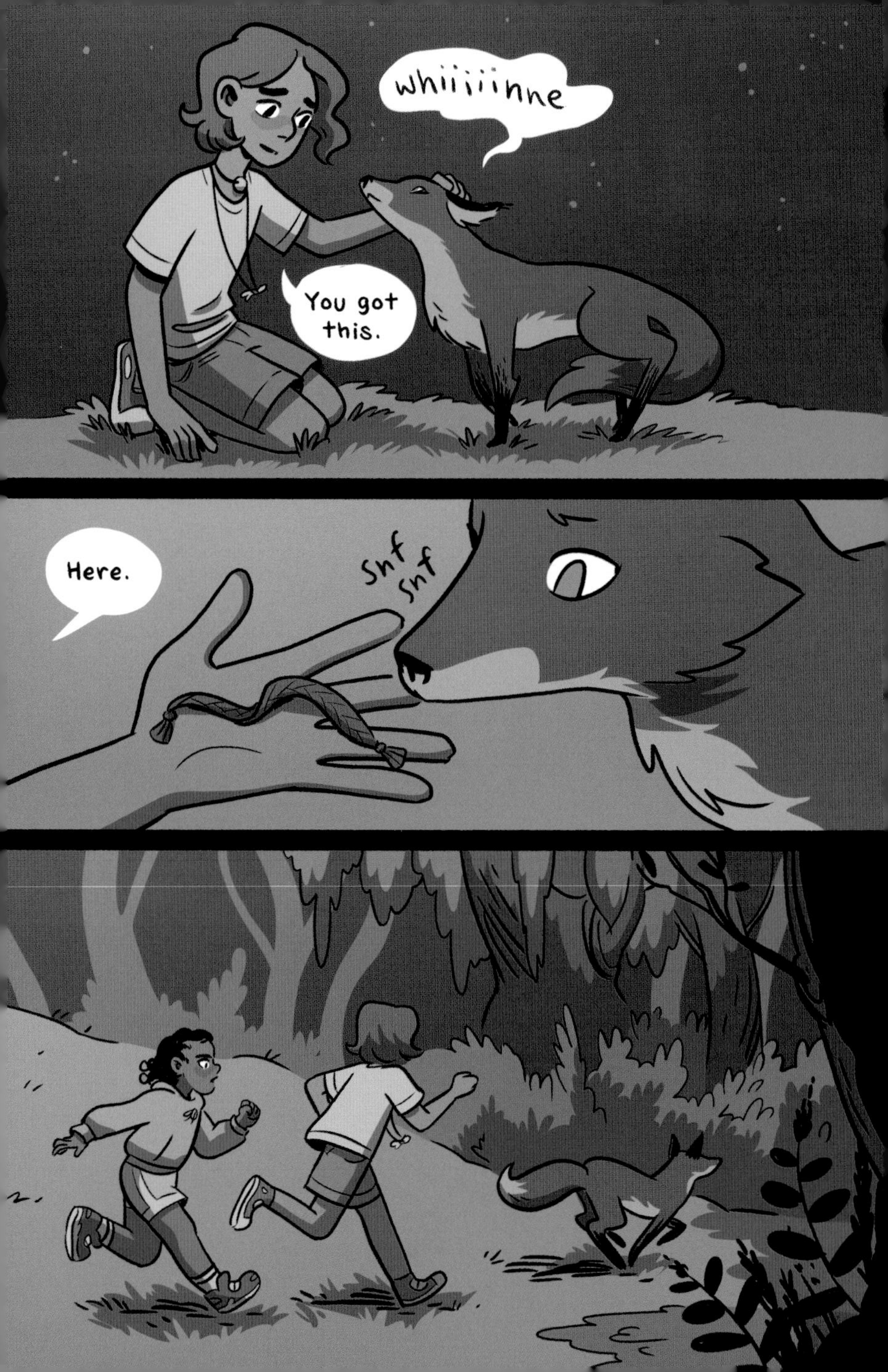
whiiiiinne
You got this.
Here.
snf snf

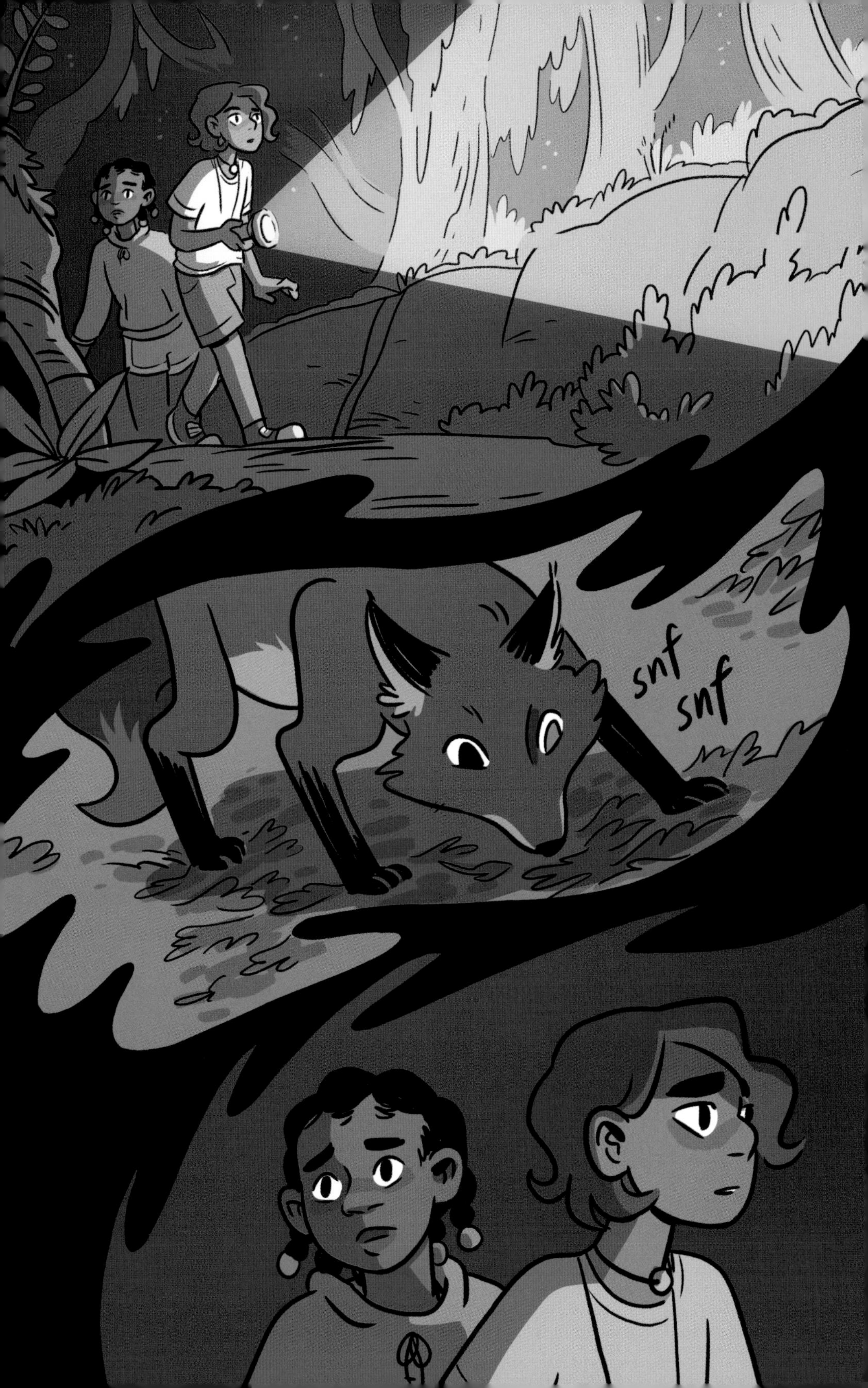
snf
snf

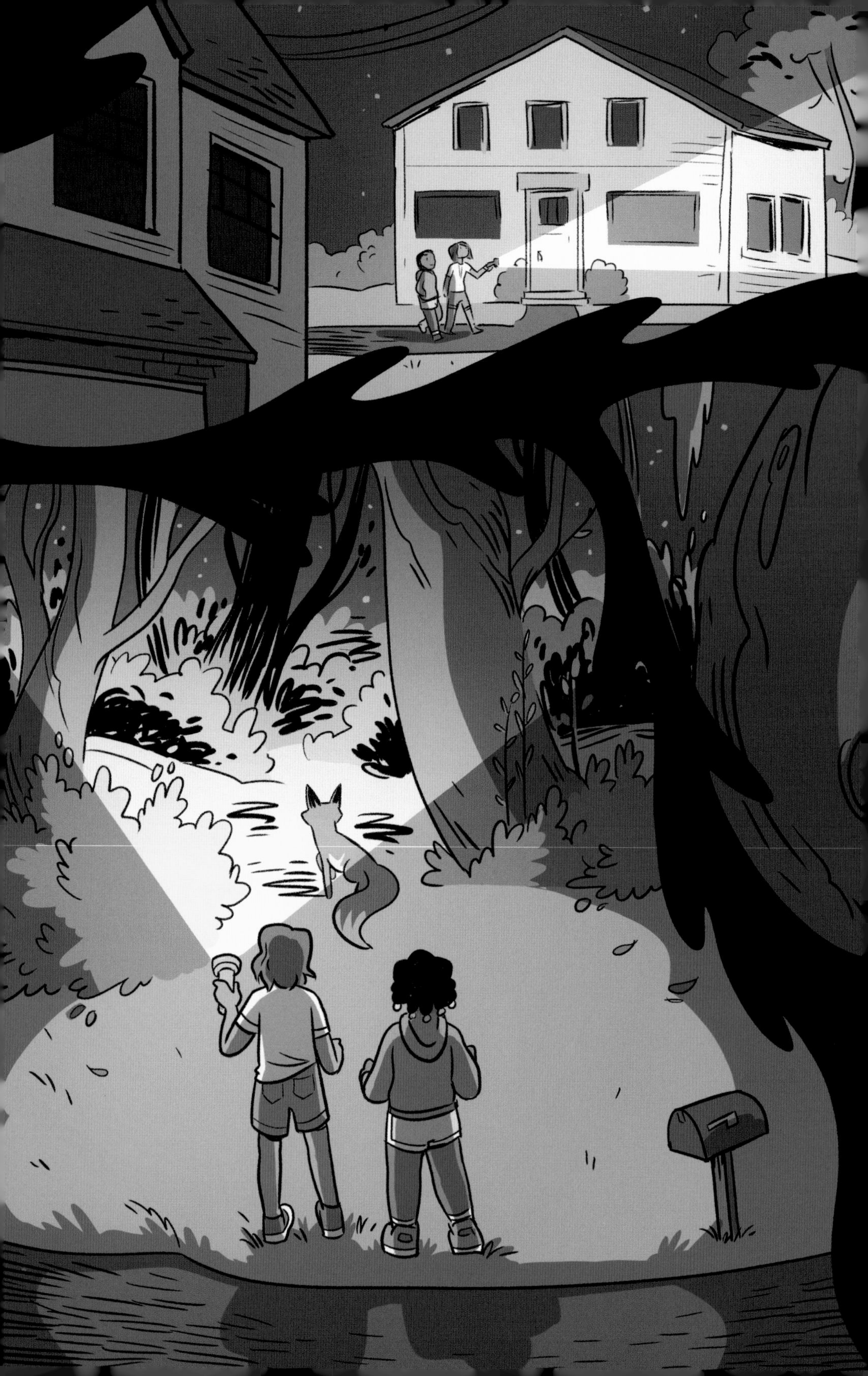

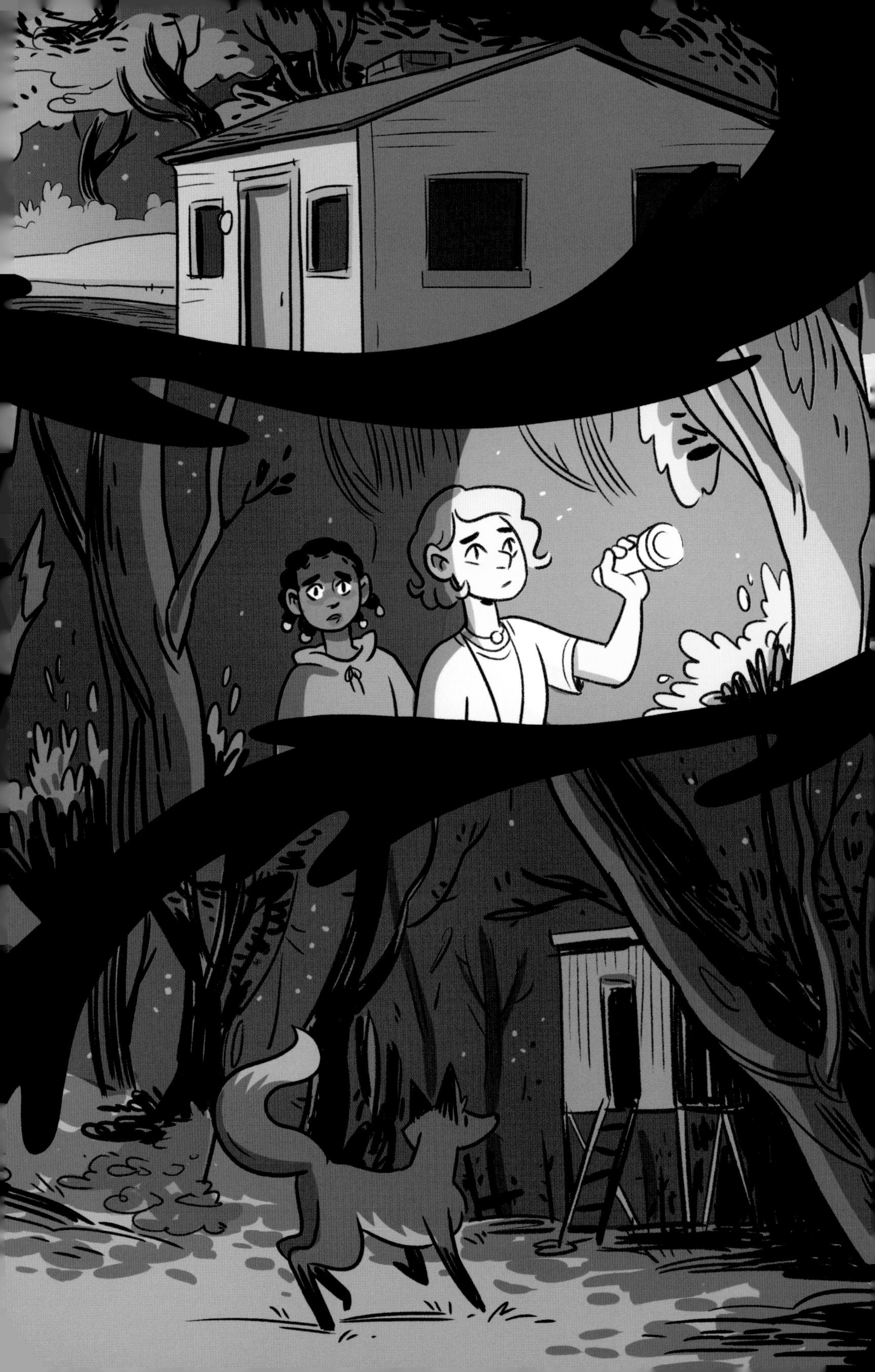

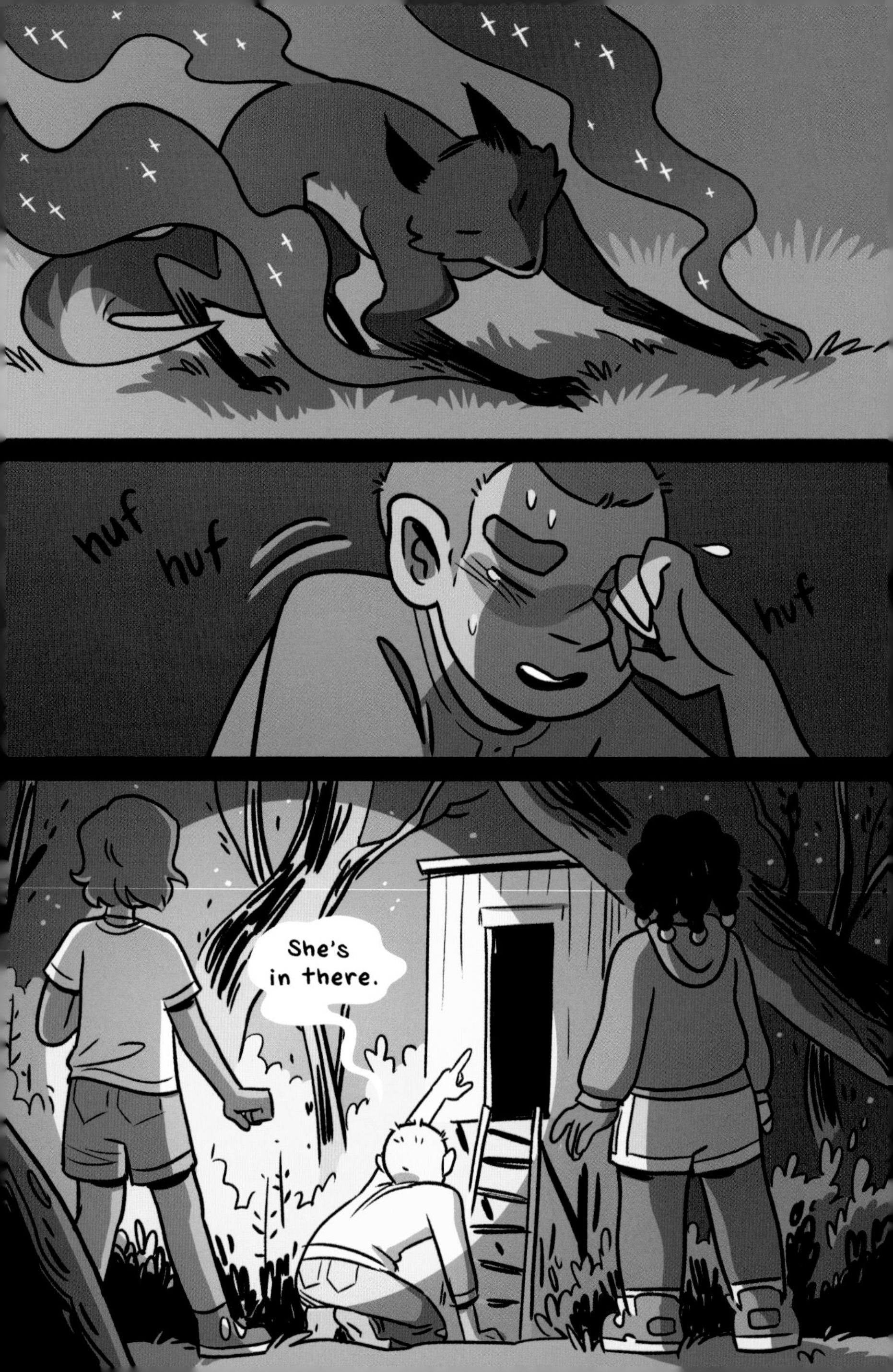
huf
huf
huf
She's in there.

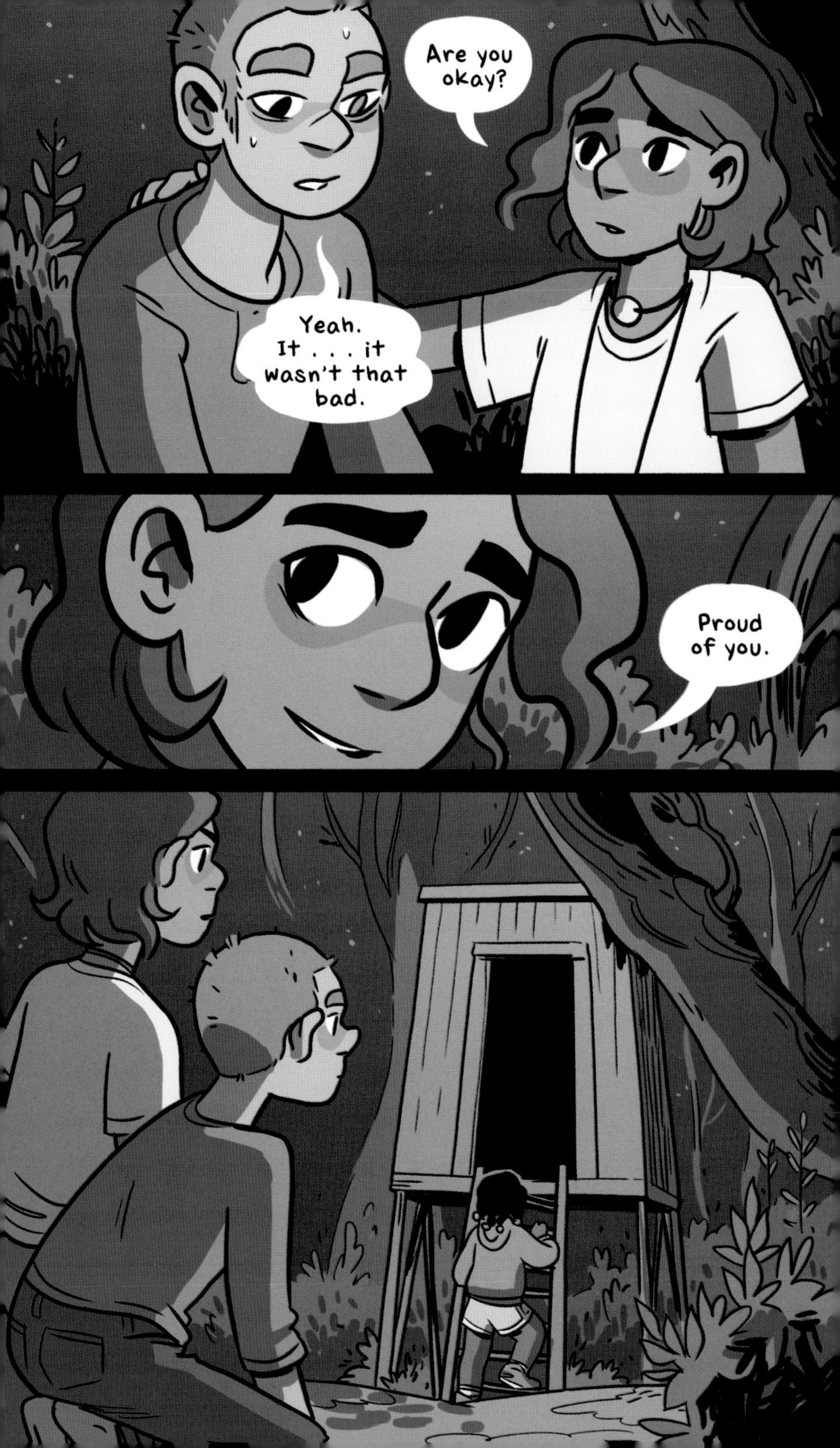
Are you okay?
Yeah. It . . . it wasn't that bad.
Proud of you.

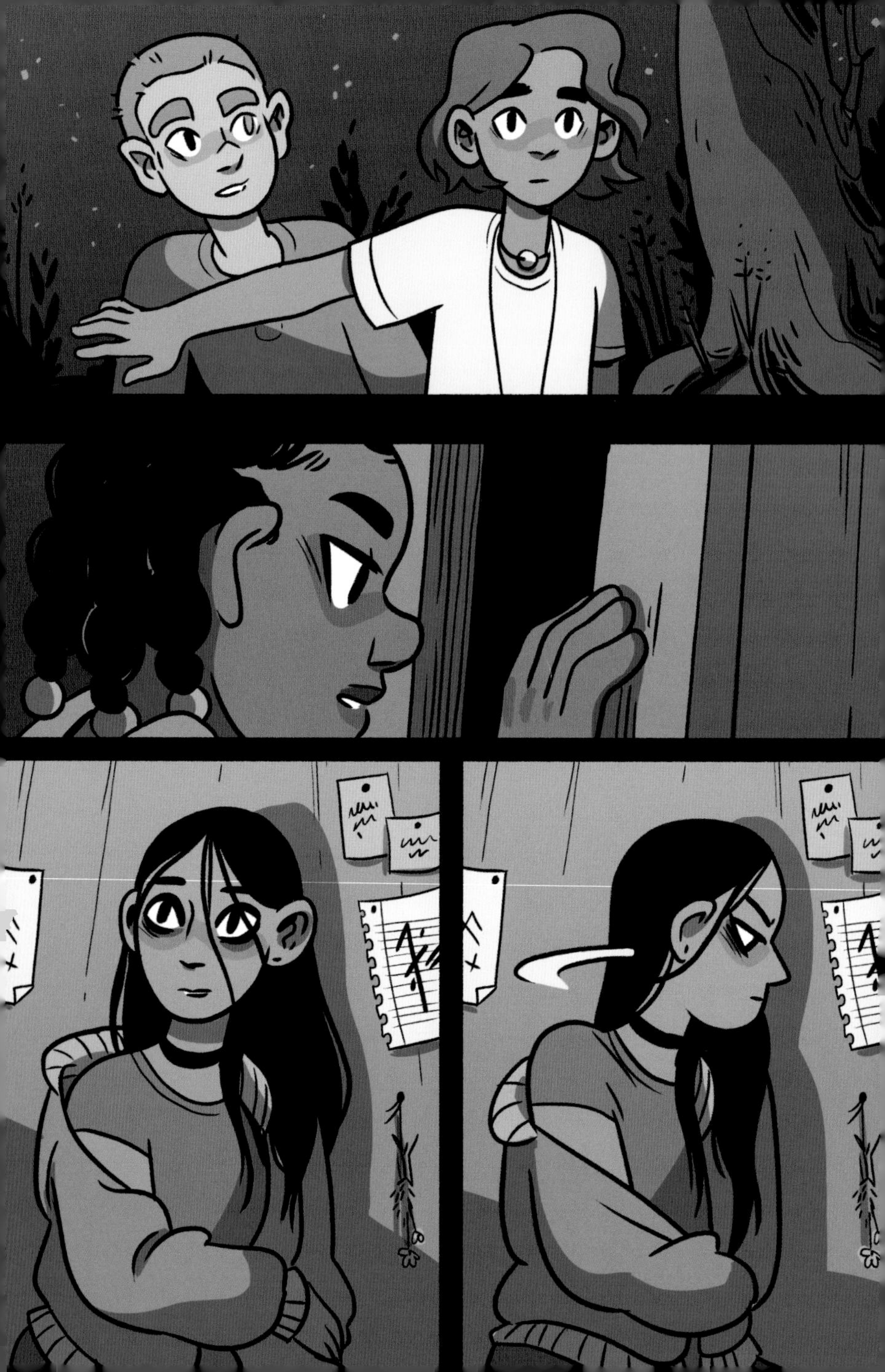

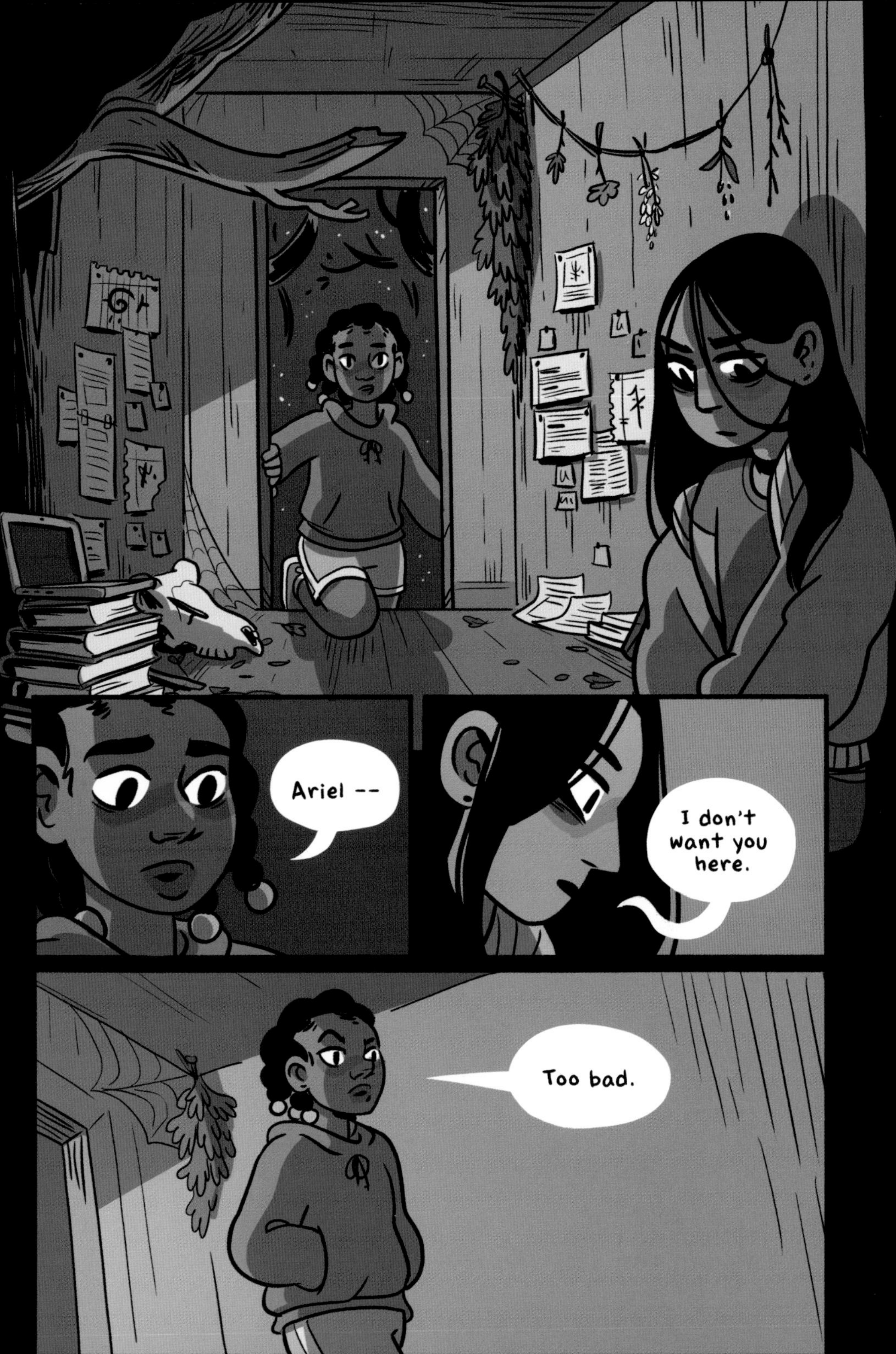
Ariel --
I don't want you here.
Too bad.

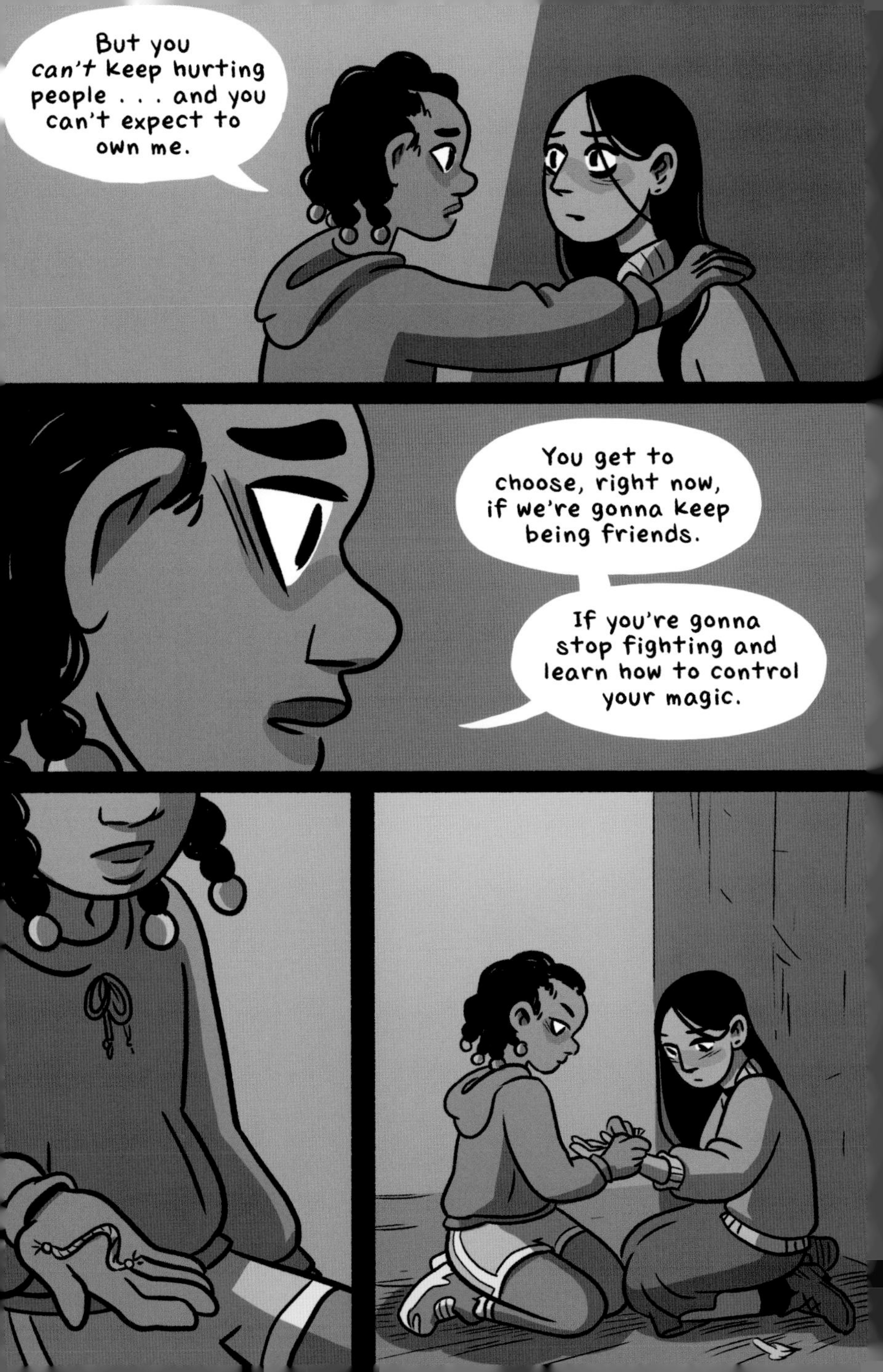
But you can't keep hurting people . . . and you can't expect to own me.
You get to choose, right now, if we're gonna keep being friends.
If you're gonna stop fighting and learn how to control your magic.

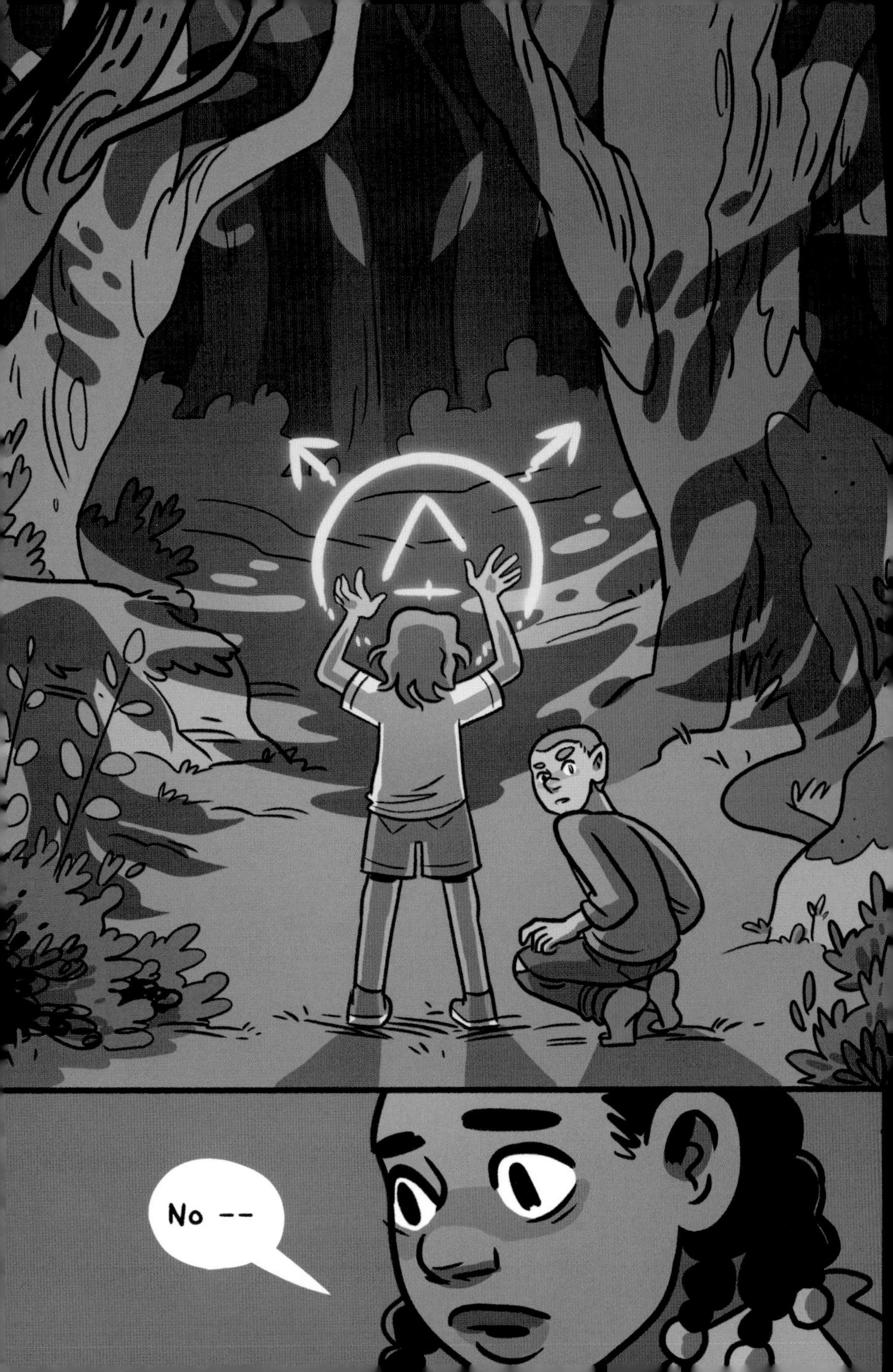
No --

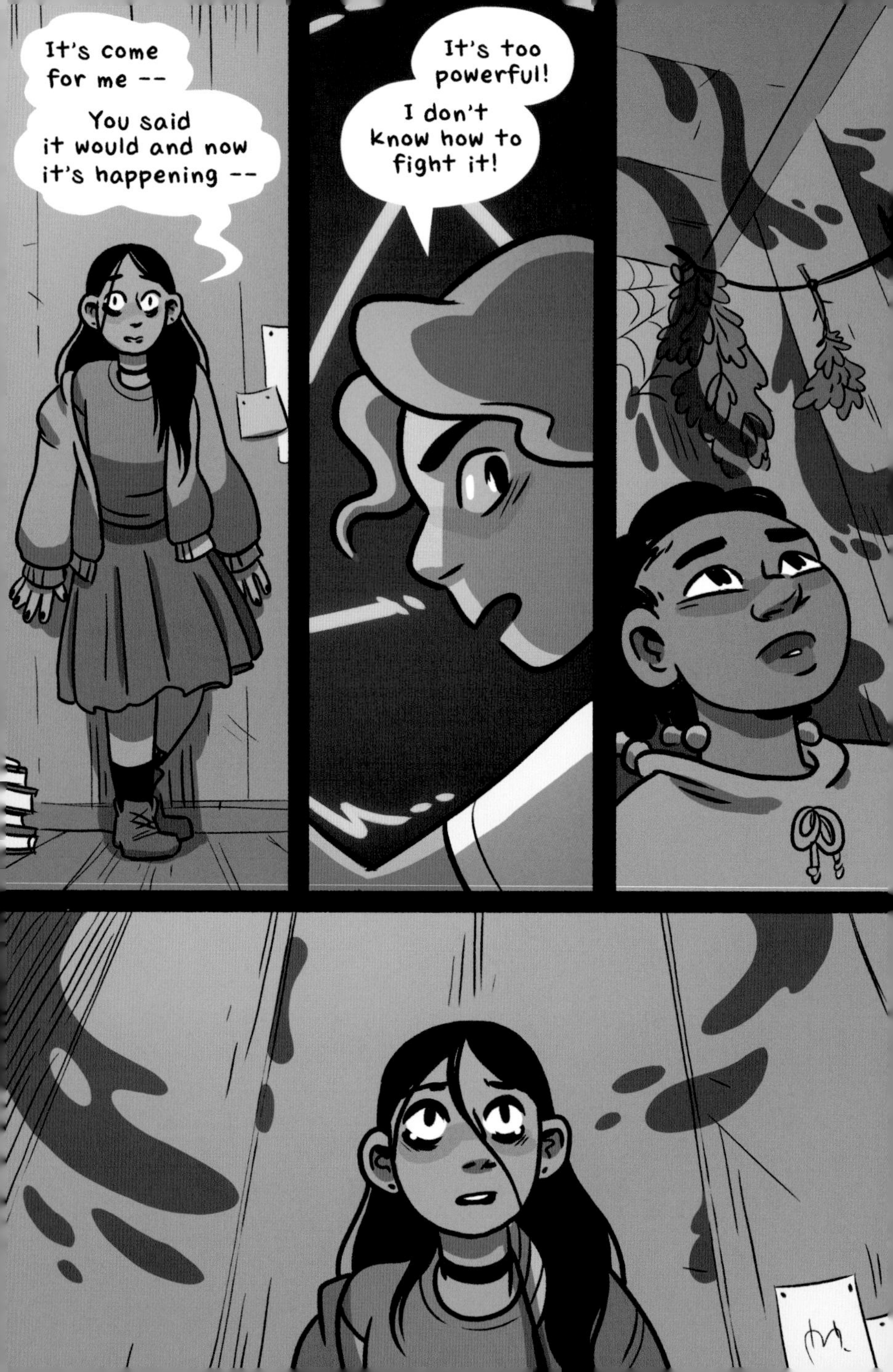
It's come for me --
You said it would and now it's happening --
It's too powerful!
I don't know how to fight it!

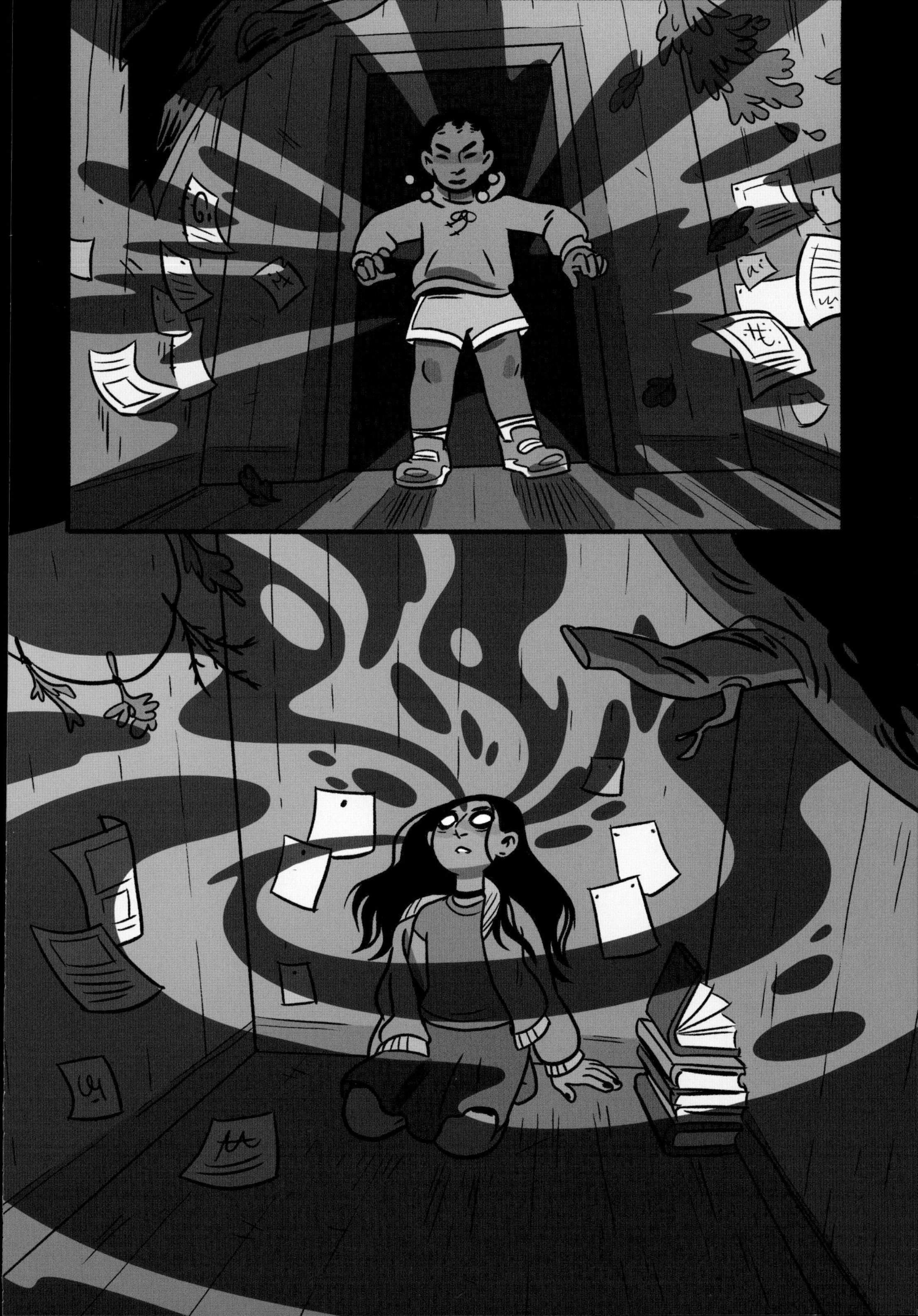

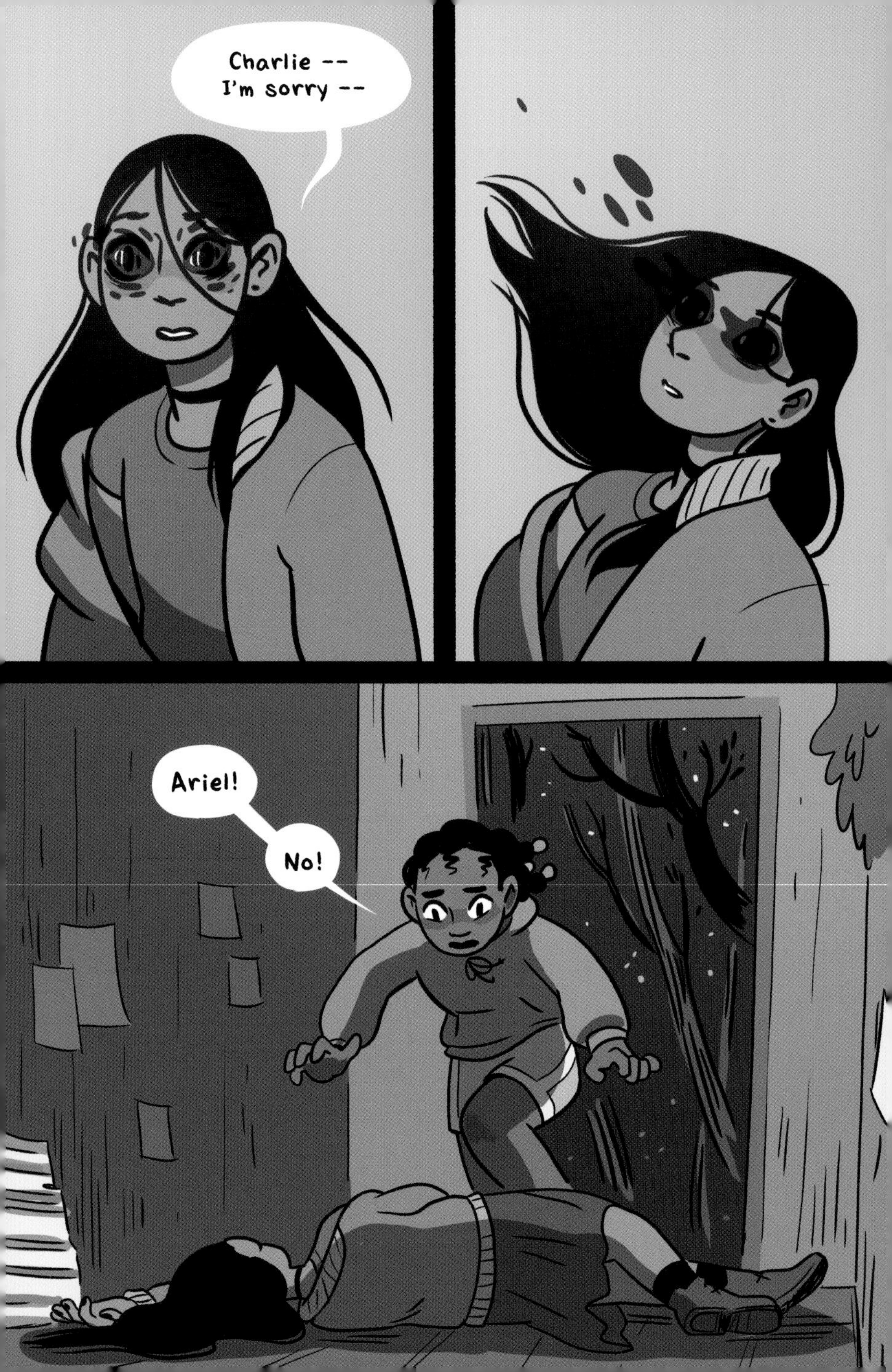
Charlie --
I'm sorry --
Ariel!
No!

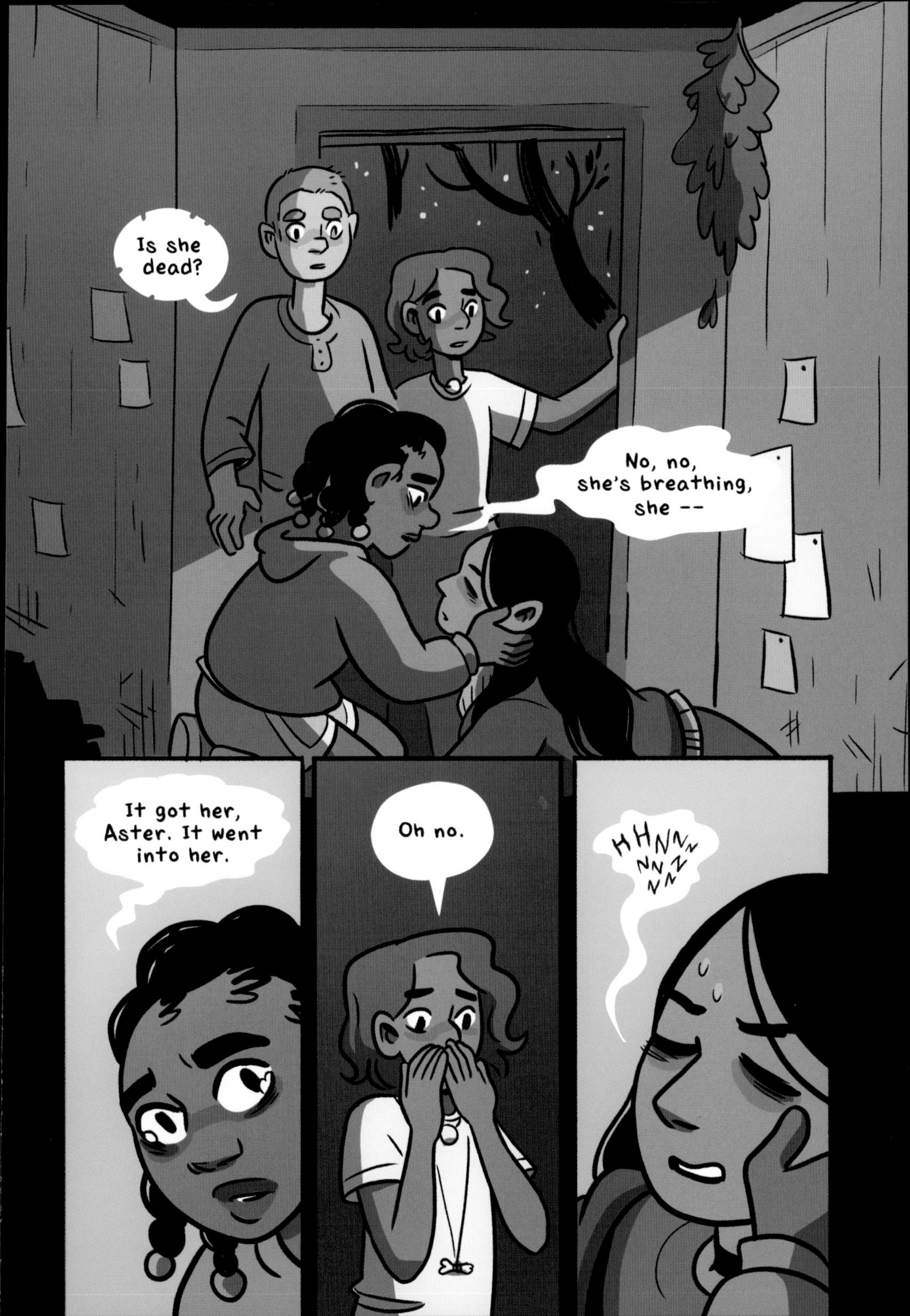
Is she dead?
No, no, she's breathing, she --
It got her, Aster. It went into her.
Oh no.
HHNNN NNZ NN

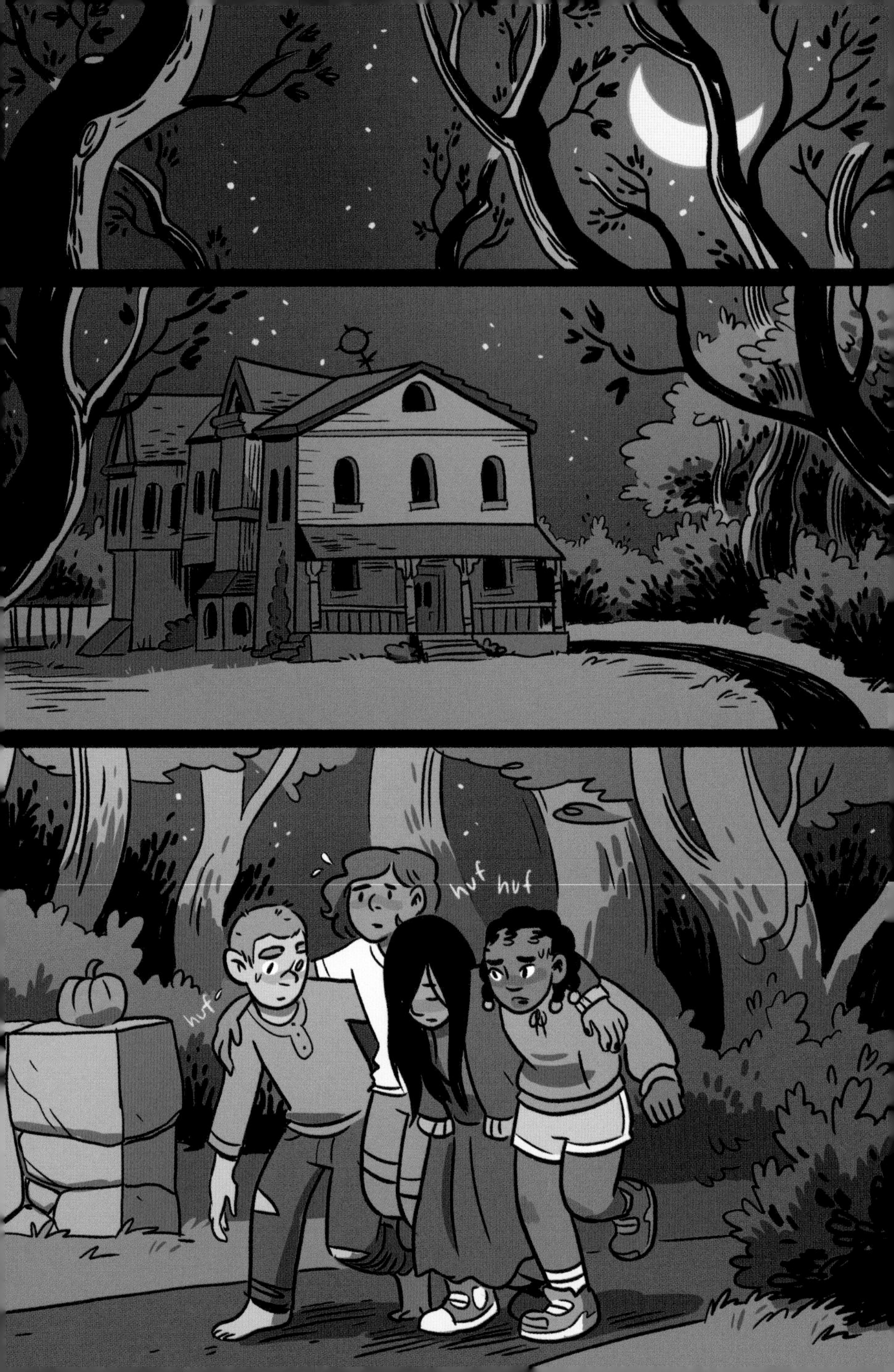
huf
huf huf

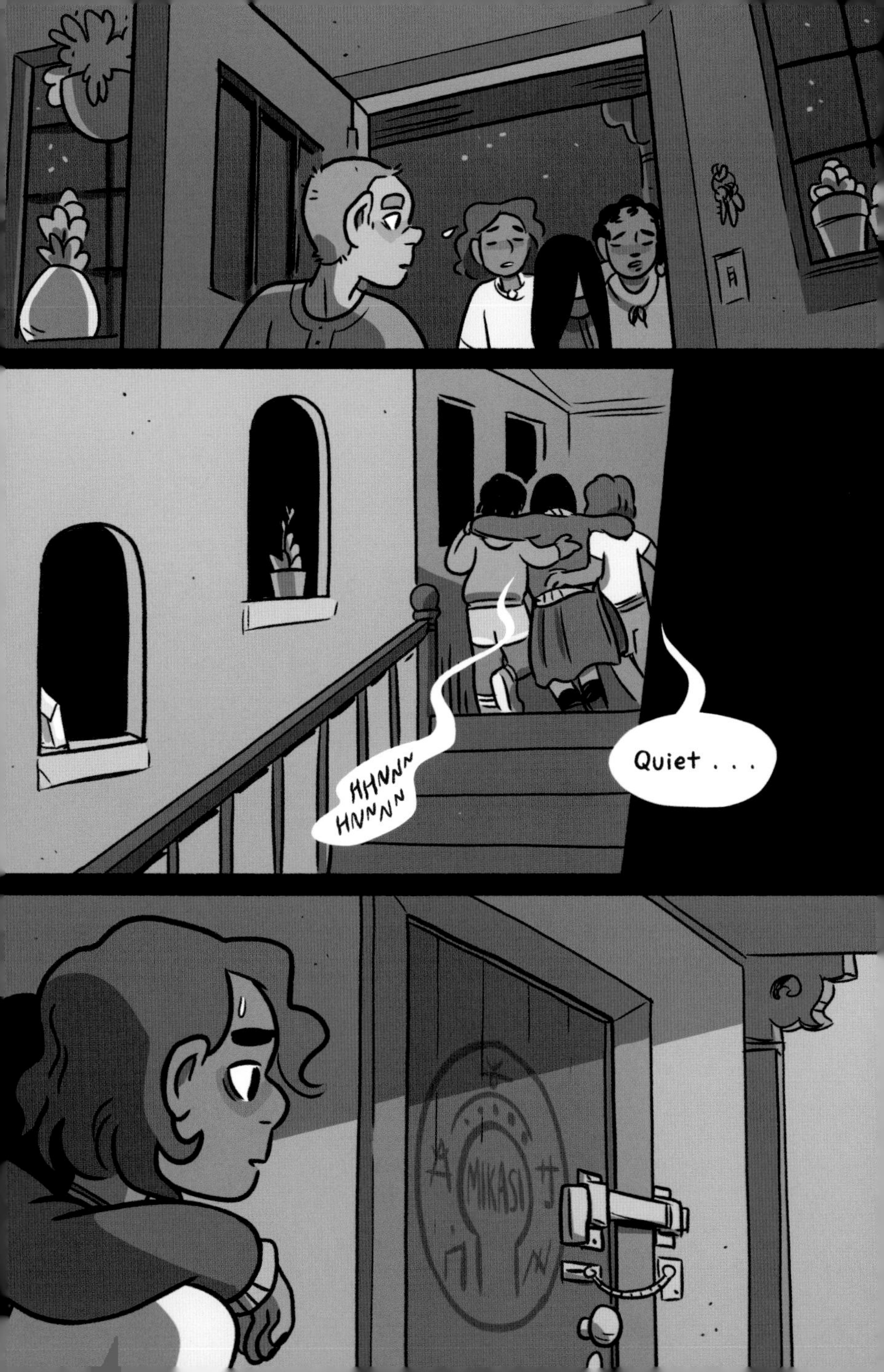
HHNNN
HNNNN
Quiet . . .
MIKASI

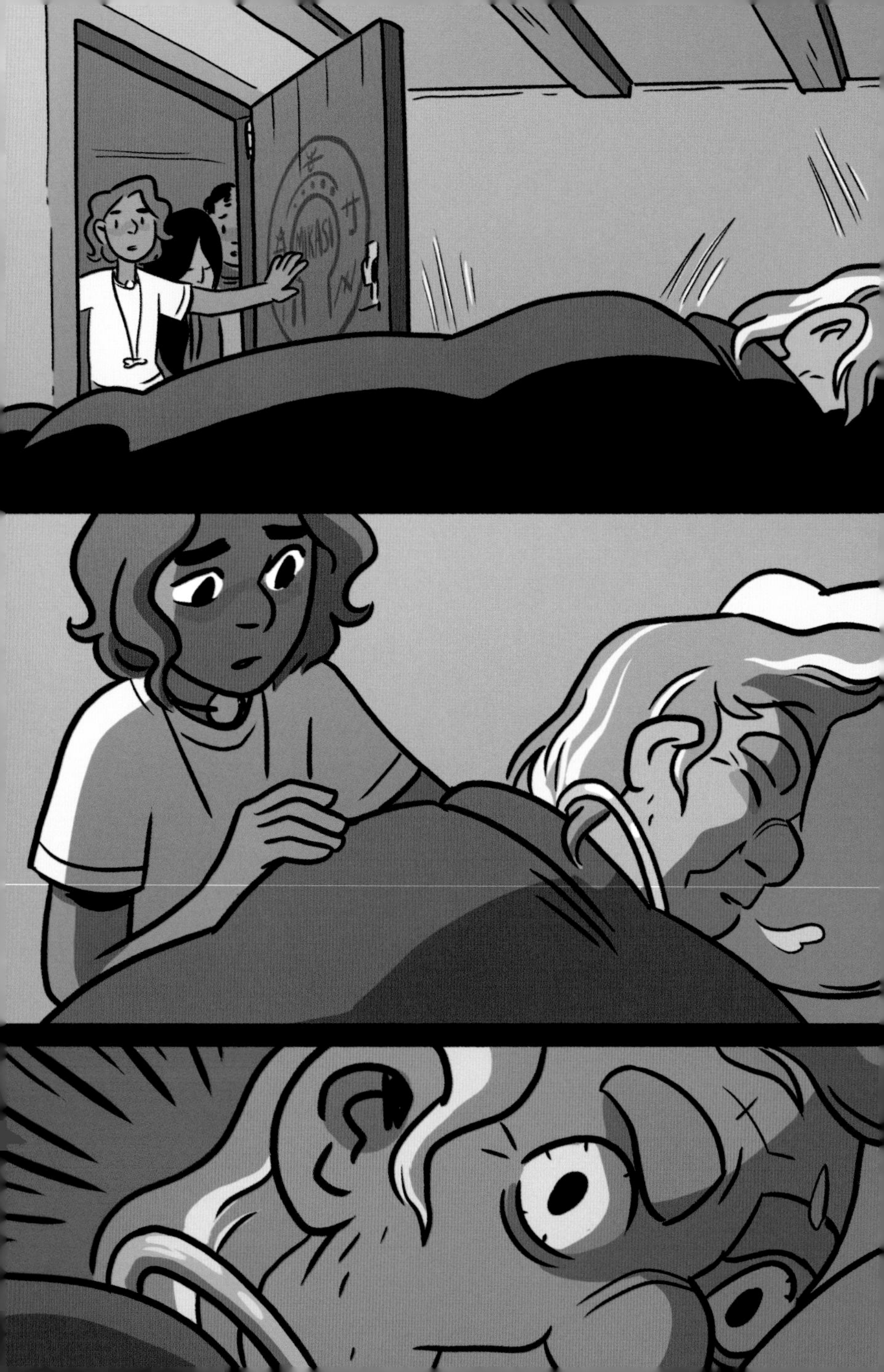
MIKASA

GRAA
Witches! Intruders!
I'll eat your disgusting hearts--
I recognize you...
The shifter with great talents, yes?
Have you let yourself be weakened?

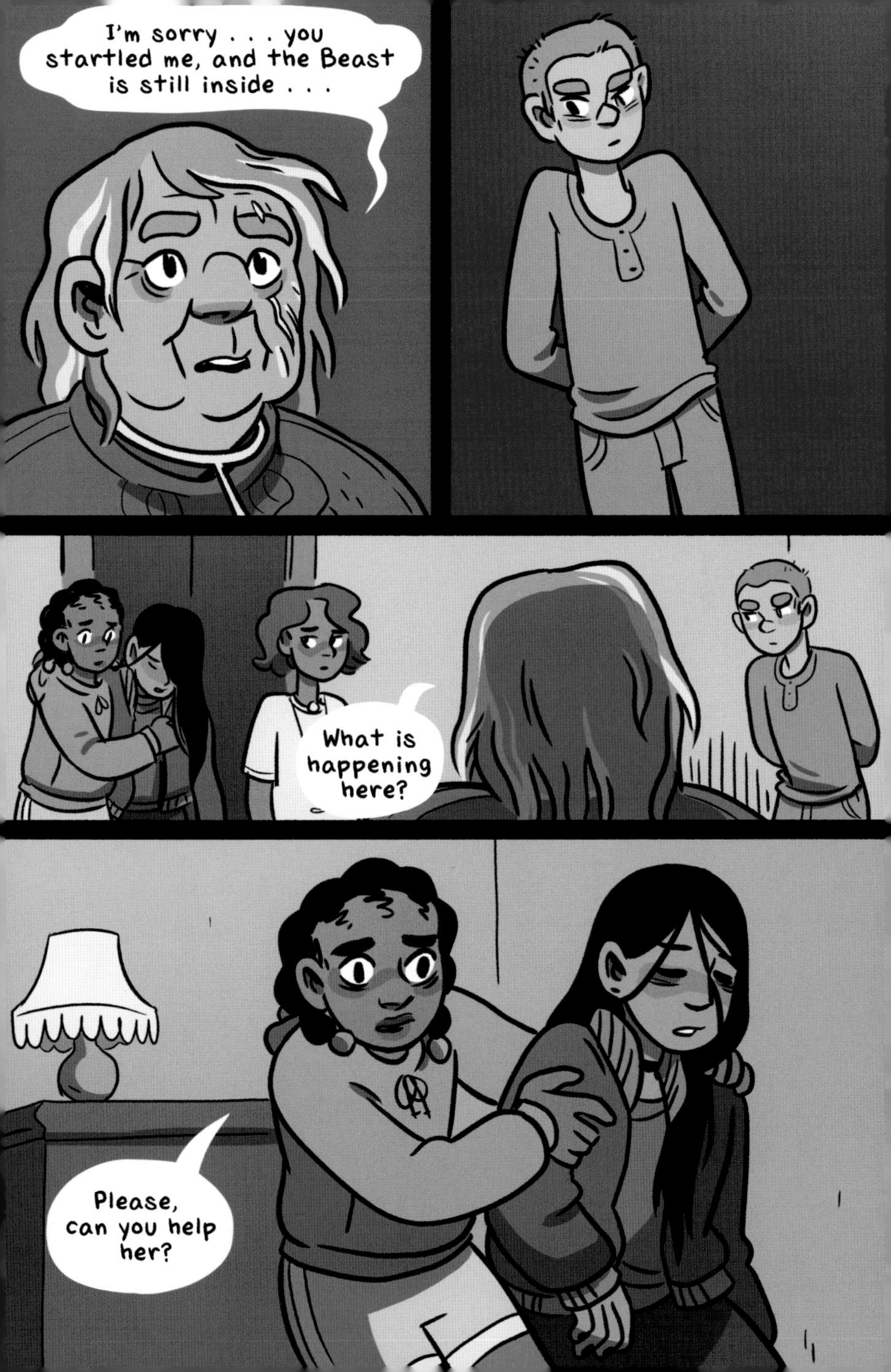
I'm sorry . . . you startled me, and the Beast is still inside . . .
What is happening here?
Please, can you help her?

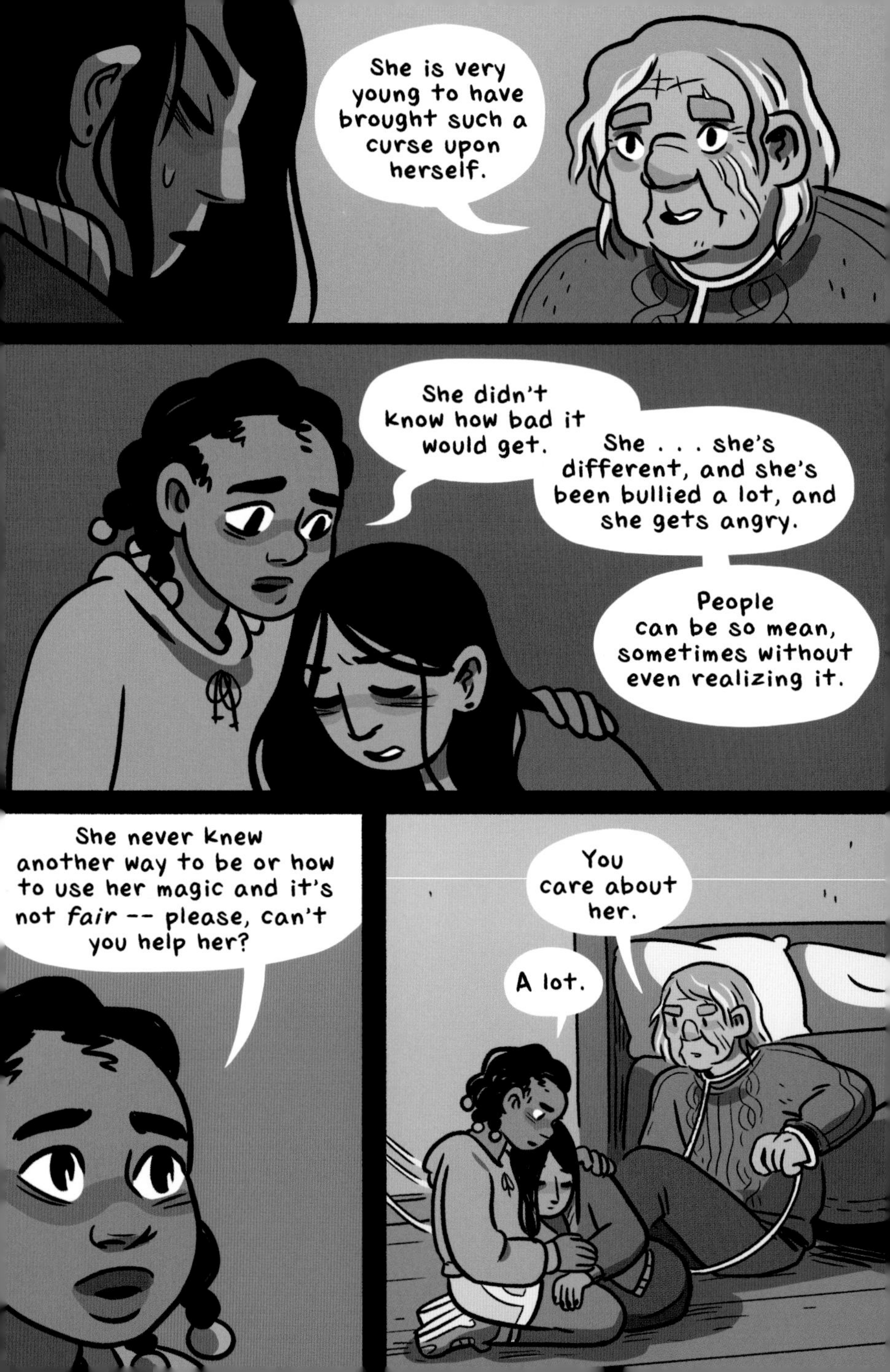
She is very young to have brought such a curse upon herself.
She didn't know how bad it would get.
She . . . she's different, and she's been bullied a lot, and she gets angry.
People can be so mean, sometimes without even realizing it.
She never knew another way to be or how to use her magic and it's not *fair* -- please, can't you help her?
You care about her.
A lot.

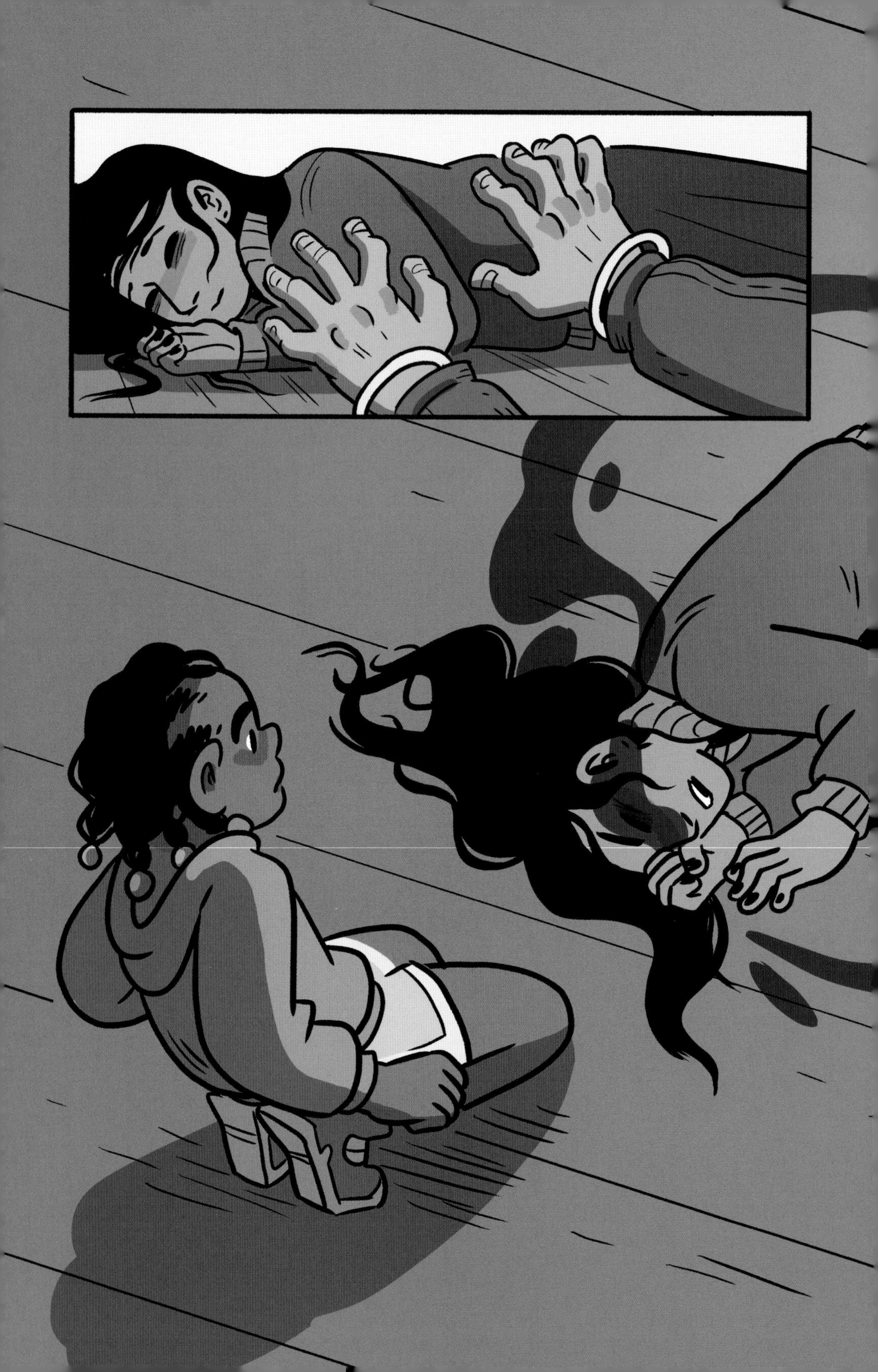

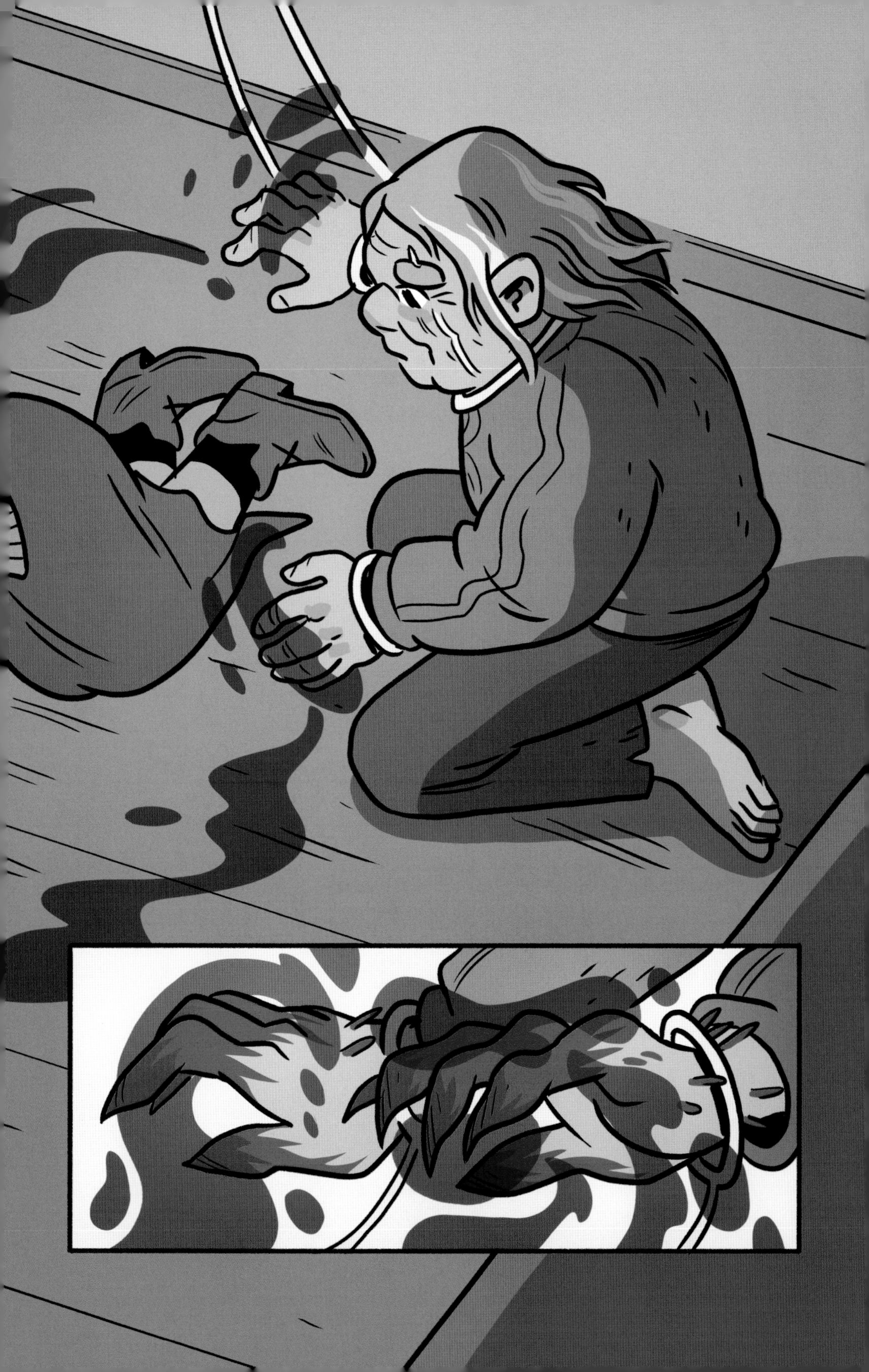

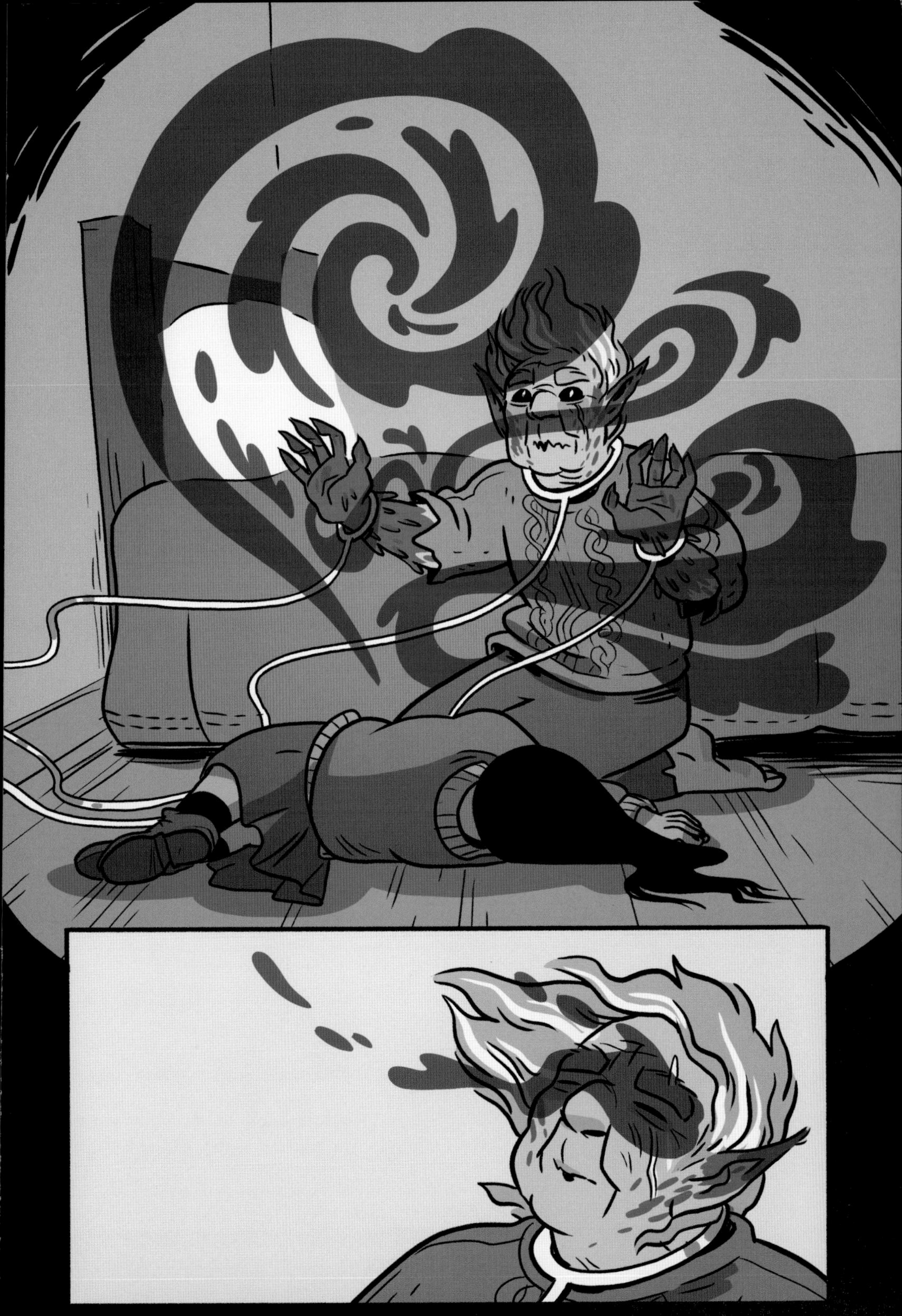

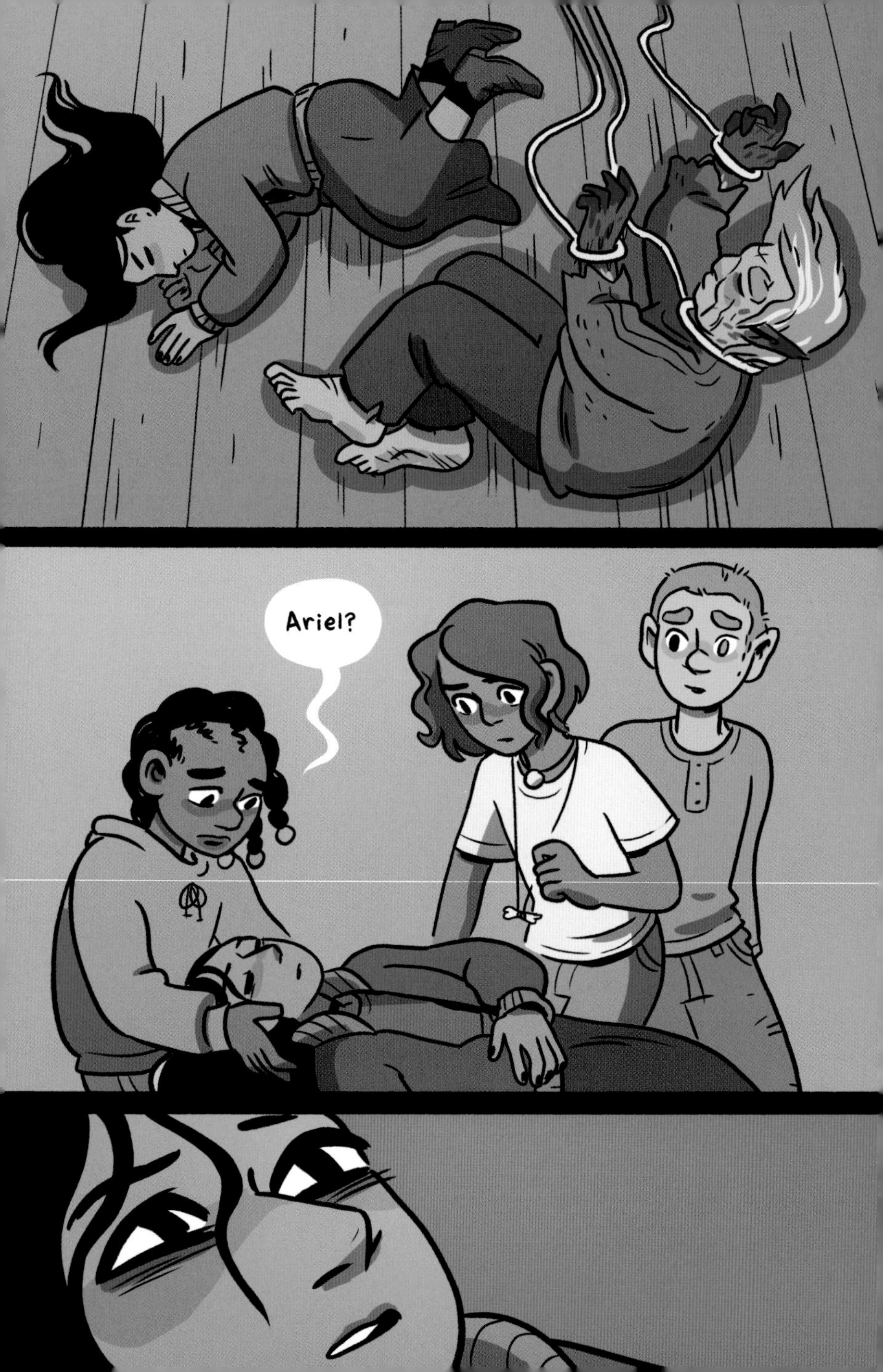
Ariel?

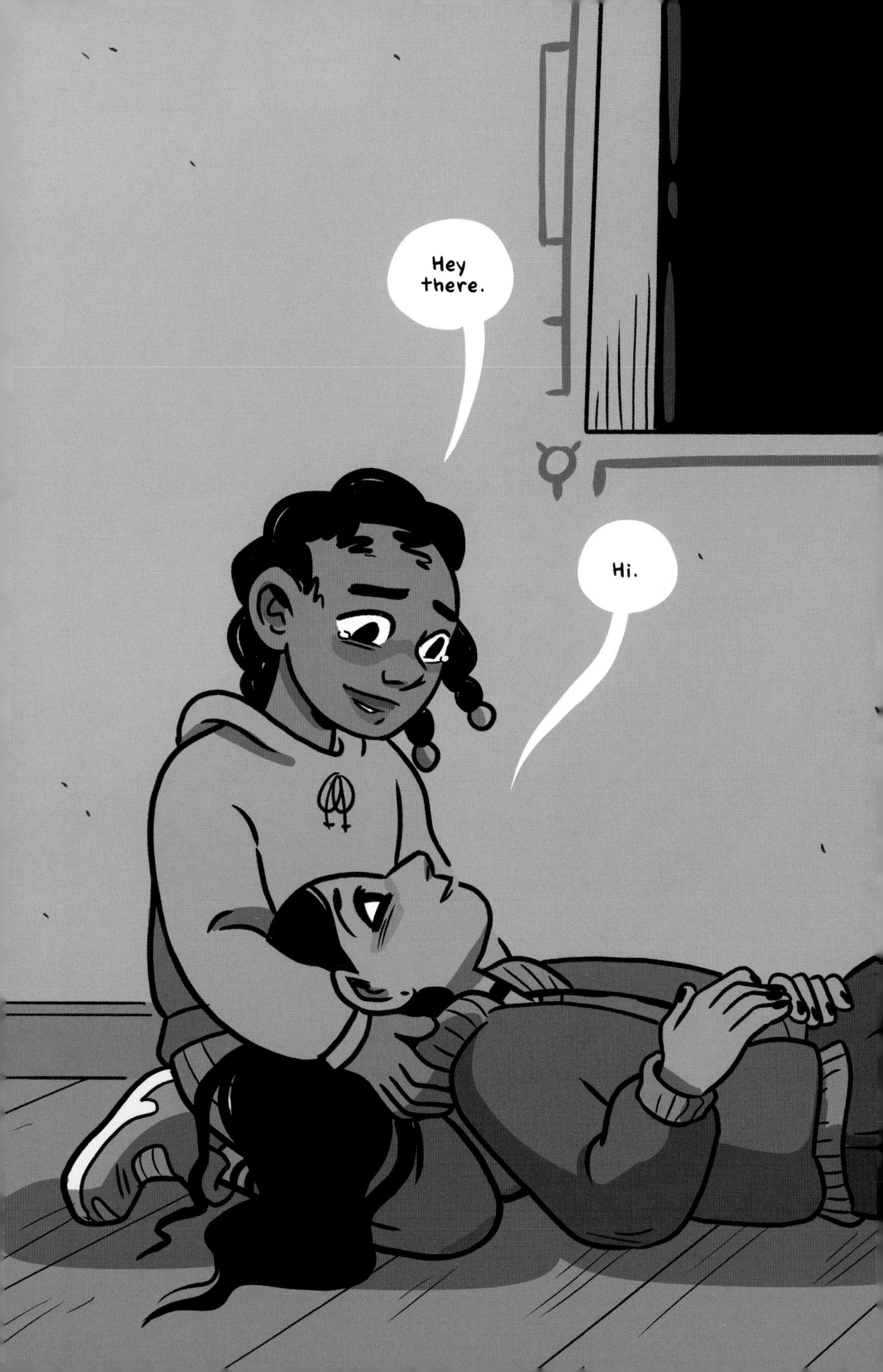
Hey there.
Hi.

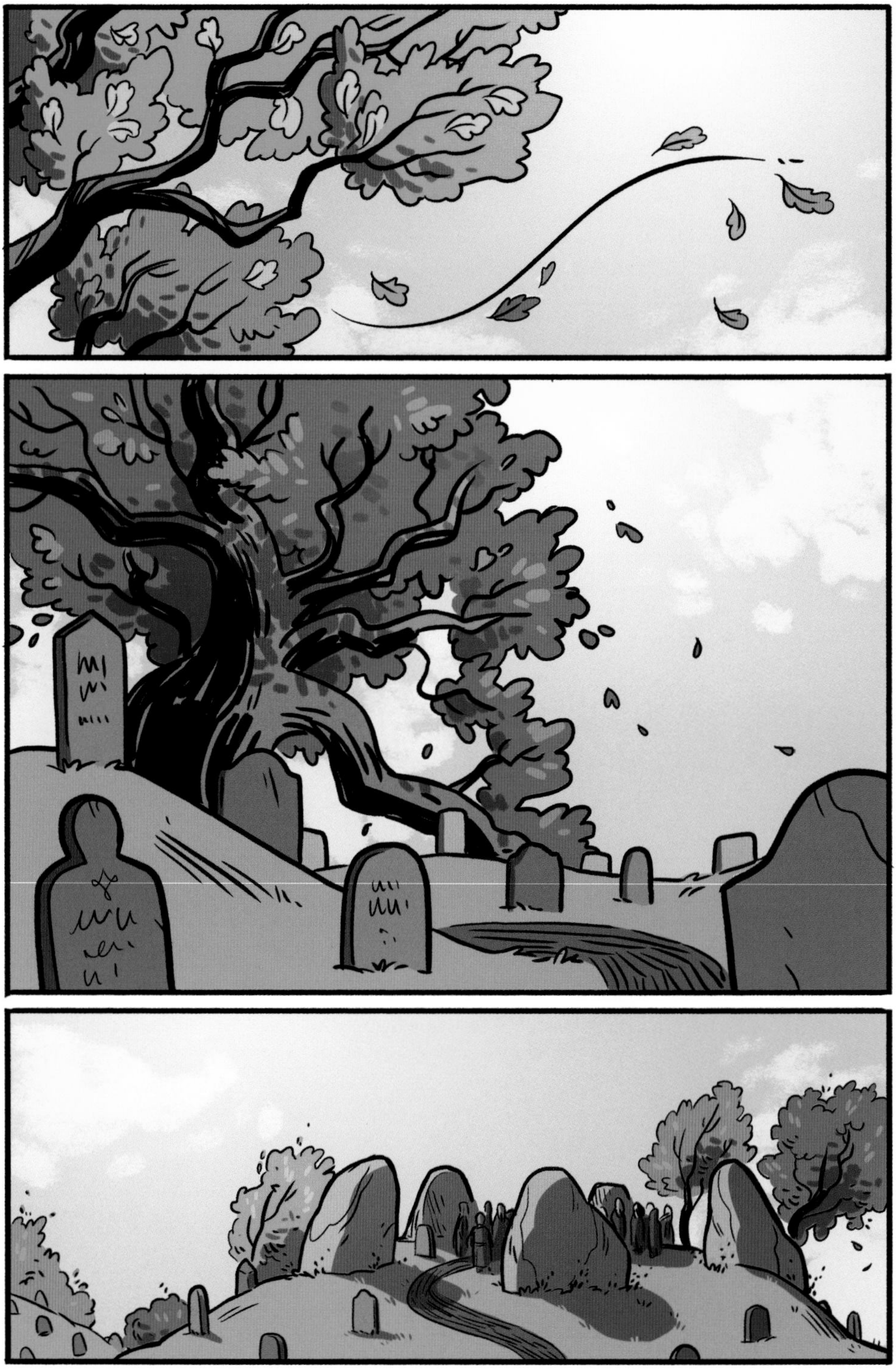

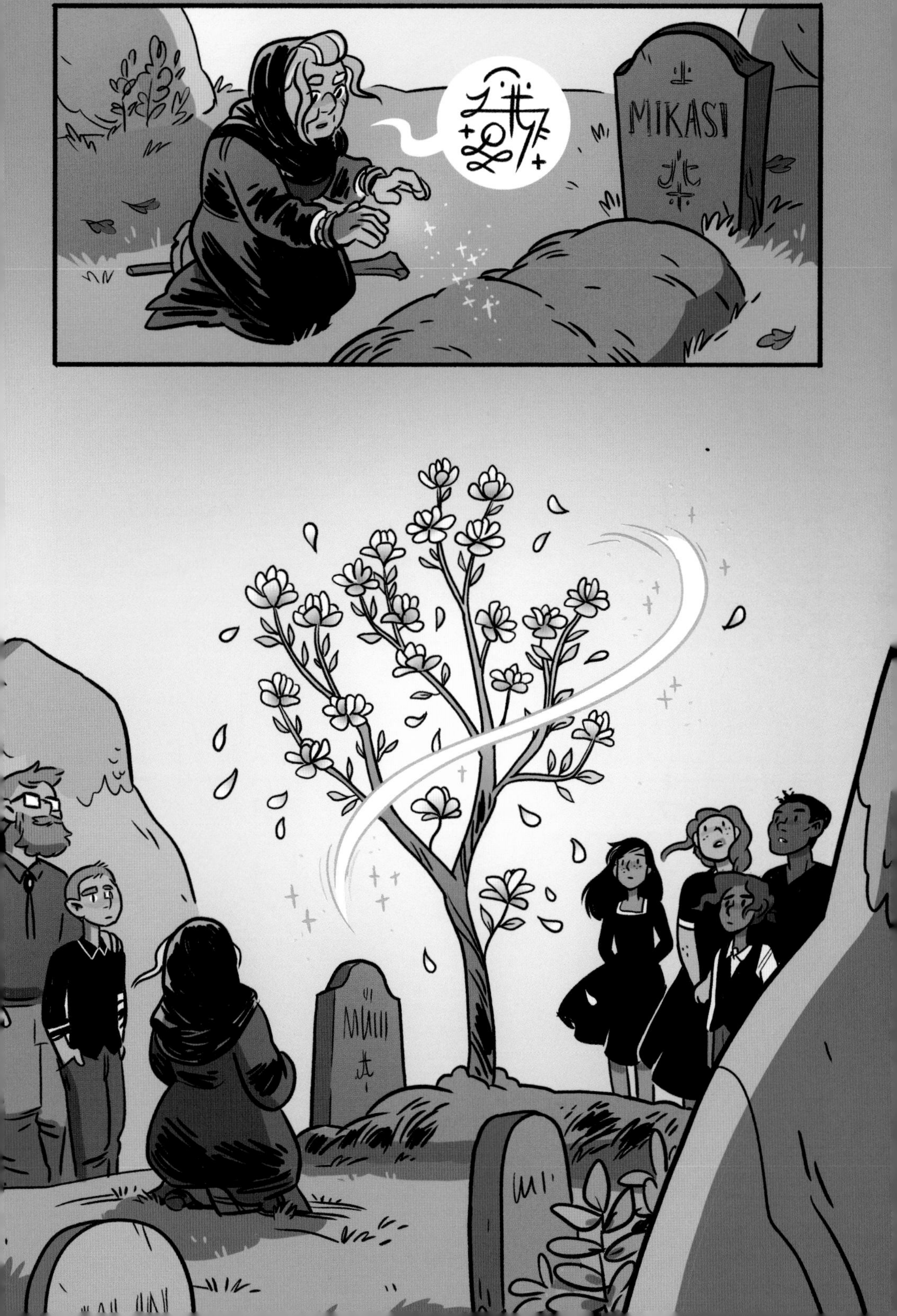
MIKASI

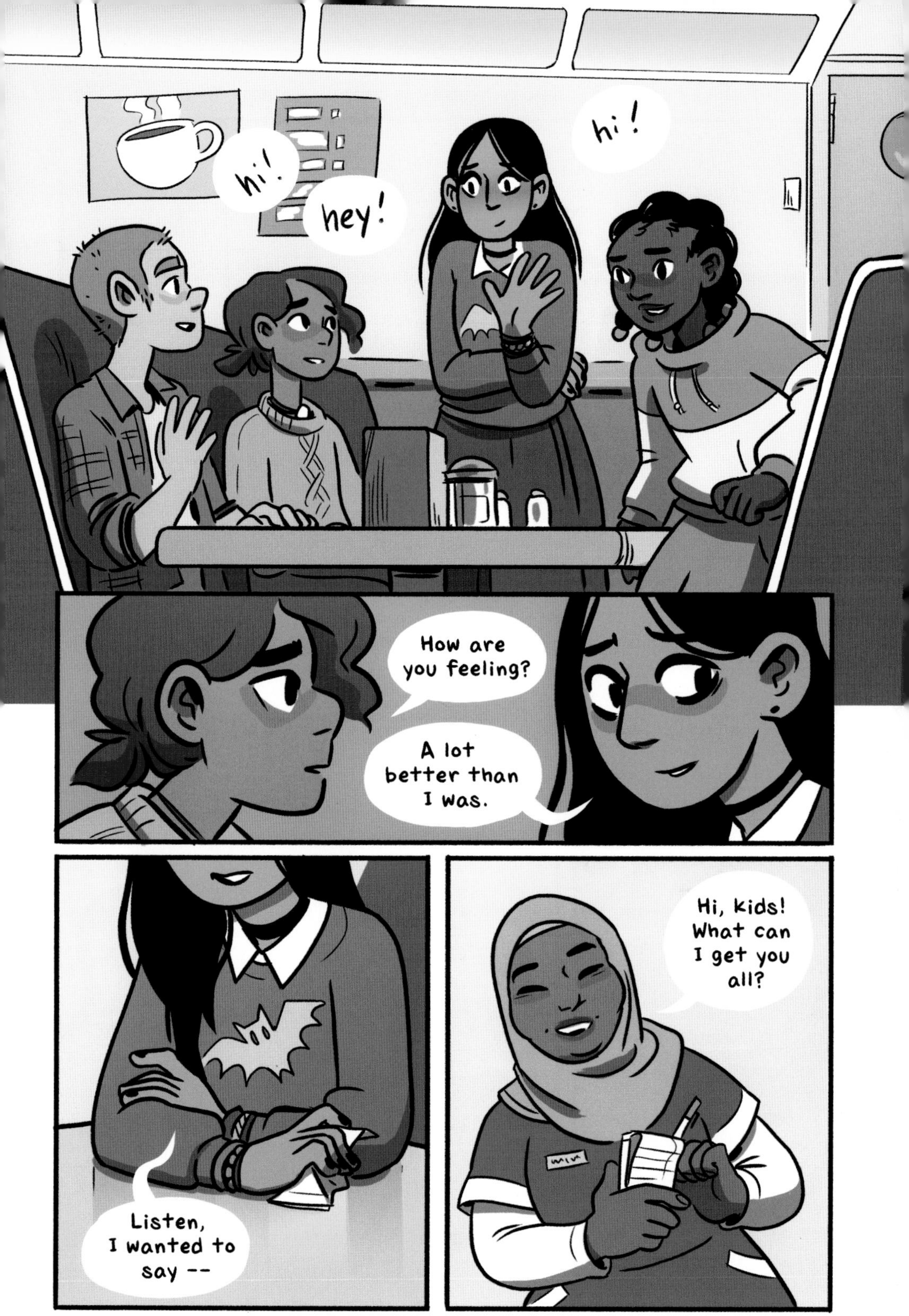
hi!
hey!
hi!
How are you feeling?
A lot better than I was.
Listen, I wanted to say --
Hi, kids! What can I get you all?

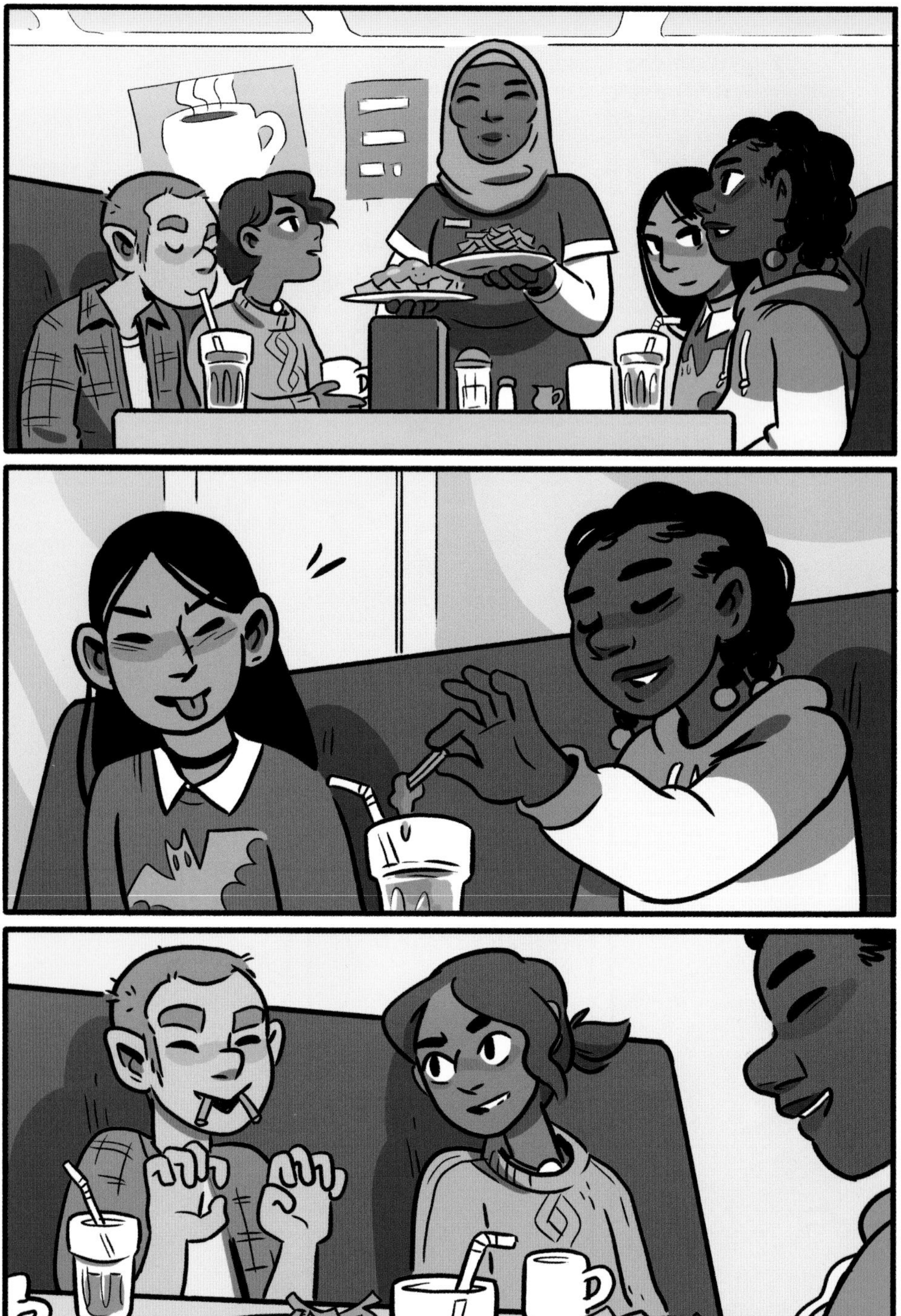

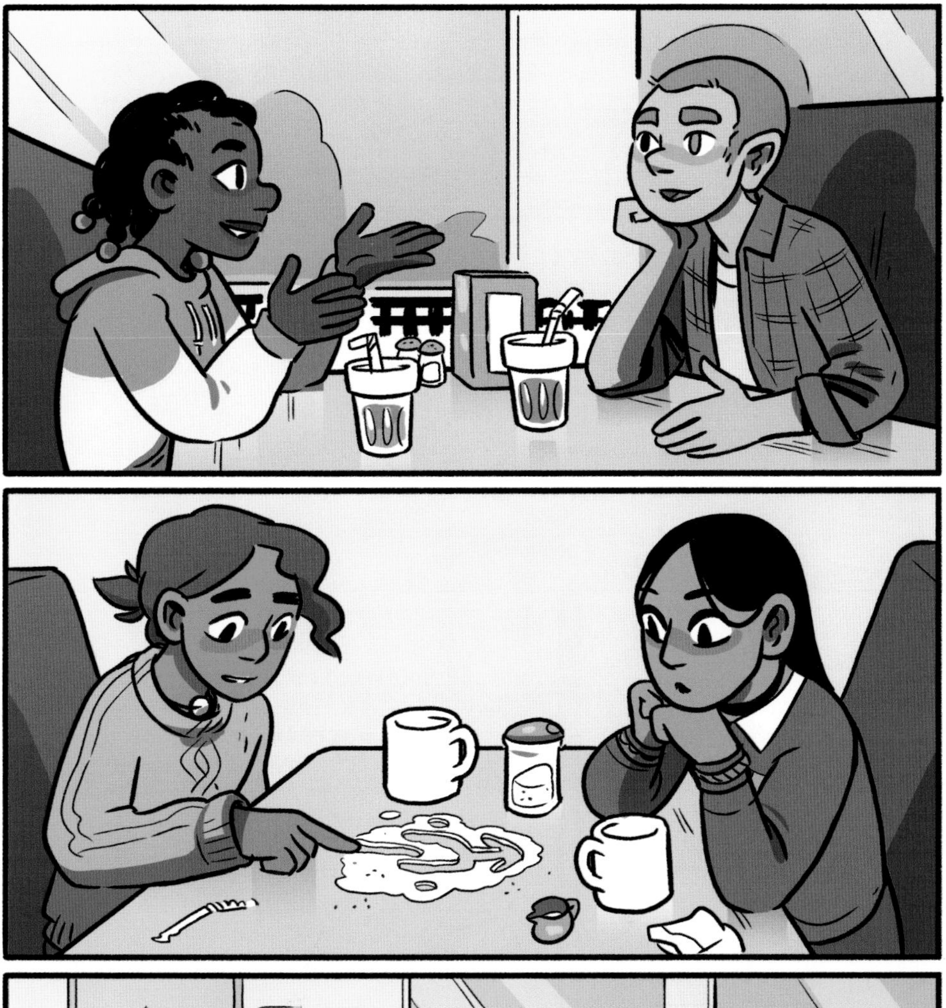

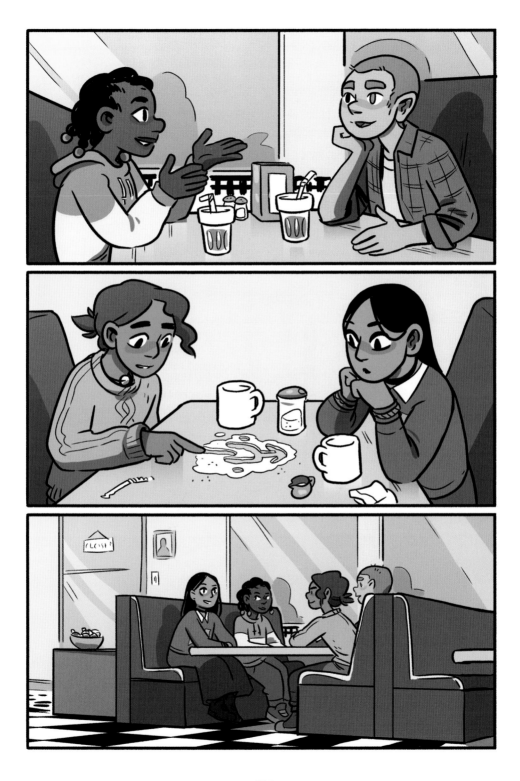

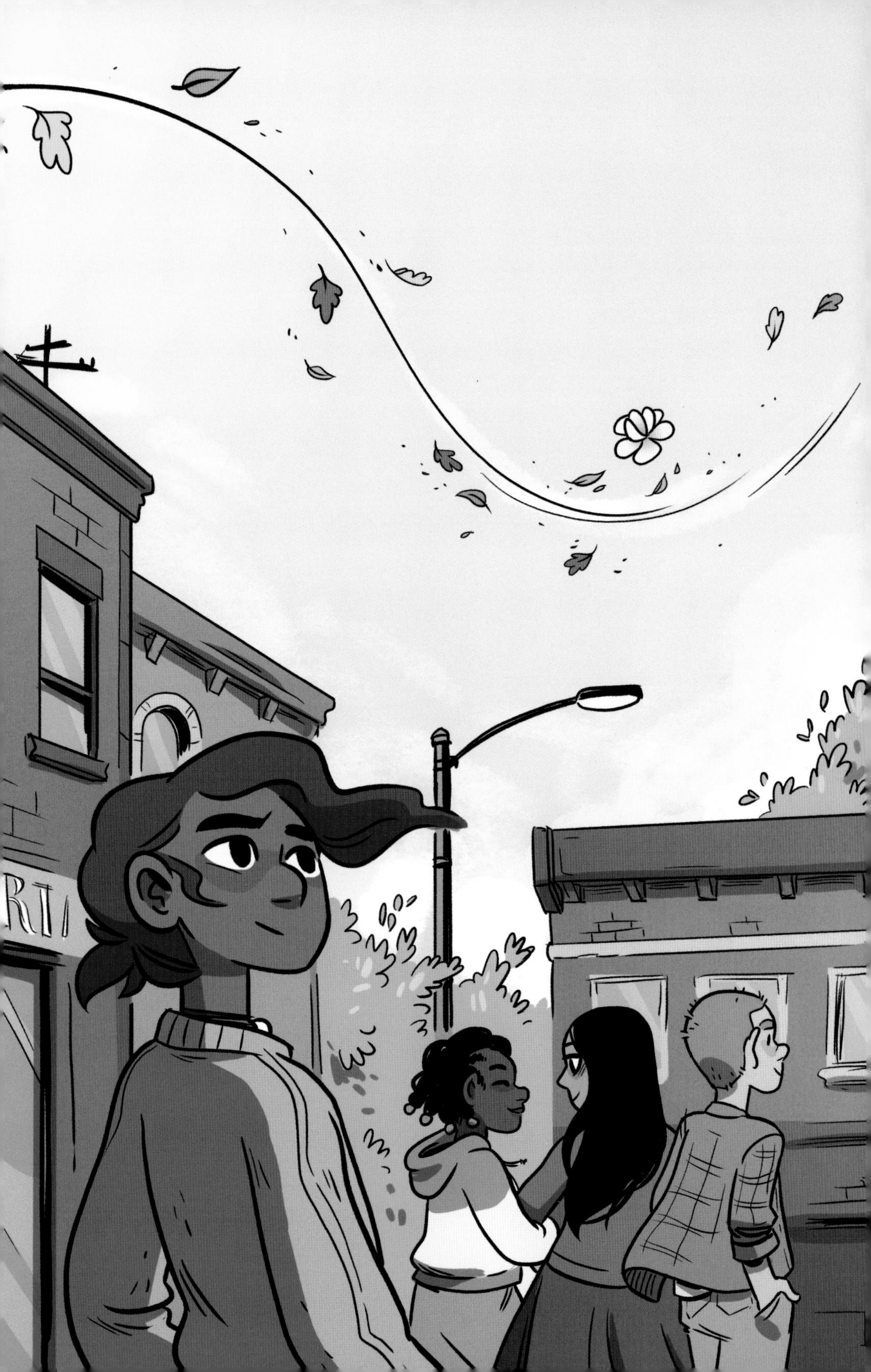

ACKNOWLEDGMENTS

Is the second one always easier, or did I just get lucky? This was one of those graphic novels that flowed so naturally from my first book, *The Witch Boy*, that the process of writing and drawing it was a joy.

I'd like to thank the kind and dedicated people who helped me make it. Jen Linnan, my agent, always responds to my rambling emails and tells me when she has dreams about my cats. Amanda Maciel, my editor, loves these characters at least as much as I do, and always makes time in our discussions to go off track and talk about our shared love of true crime. Phil Falco makes the book look beautiful with his wit and wisdom, and Niki Smith is an amazing artist who helped make the process of coloring this a breeze.

I drew this book with my evenings and weekends while working on the excellent animated show *Star vs. the Forces of Evil*. I really appreciate my coworkers at Disney for many, many coffee trips and our chats about art and comics and storytelling.

The support for *The Witch Boy* from teachers, parents, librarians, independent bookstores, and — most importantly — young readers has meant the world to me. I hope I can keep making books that you enjoy reading!

MOLLY KNOX OSTERTAG

is the author and illustrator of the acclaimed graphic novel *The Witch Boy* and the illustrator of several projects for older readers, including the webcomic Strong Female Protagonist and *Shattered Warrior* by Sharon Shinn. She grew up in the forests of upstate New York and graduated in 2014 from the School of Visual Arts, where she studied cartooning and illustration. She currently lives in Los Angeles with her girlfriend and several pets. You can find her online at mollyostertag.com.